CAPTURE ME

HELENA NEWBURY

FOSTER & BLACK

CAPTURE ME

A STORMFINCH SECURITY NOVEL

HELENA NEWBURY

NEW YORK TIMES BESTSELLING AUTHOR

For Nina

Cover by Mayhem Cover Creations
Main cover model image licensed from (and copyright remains with) Wander Aguiar
Photography

First Edition R4 October 2023

ISBN: 978-1-914526-25-1

PROLOGUE

I FELL for Tanya before I ever met her.

I fell for her before we talked, before the sweet whispers in *that* accent and the taunts that made me want to spank her ass and rip her goddamn clothes off all at the same time.

I fell for her before we fought, before I wrestled her to the ground and felt those soft curves against me, before I hogtied her and tossed her over my shoulder.

I fell for her when there was still eight hours and a thousand miles between us, when all I had to go on was one scowling, black and white photo.

Tanya was my mission. My target. My prisoner.

But long before I captured her, she captured me.

1

COLTON

I'D SPENT the last year building a life in the small town of Mount Mercy: a job I loved, buddies I could count on...true, I didn't have a woman I'd buy flowers for, as my momma used to say, but I'd had plenty of one-night stands with women from Koenig's Bar who got all hot for beards and tattoos, and damn well soaked their panties when I told them I had plenty of handcuffs and ropes and knew how to use them. And anyway, I had a *bear,* and a truck that ran...mostly. What else do you need?

I had everything squared away. And Tanya was about to upend it like a burglar tipping out a dresser drawer.

The day started out great. The air was so clear, I could look out over the mountains and see halfway across Colorado and it was warm, for September, the sun baking my bare arms. It wasn't even eight in the morning yet and I was about to turn in the prisoner I'd bounty-hunted. I figured that earned me a cup of coffee from the little café on Main Street.

Heads turned as I wrestled the guy out of my truck. Haywood Lyce was a mean SOB, a six-foot biker who'd stabbed his girlfriend and then skipped bail and fled to Vegas. But then they don't call me when it's an office nerd who's stolen a stapler. I got his arm up behind his back and marched him across the street towards the police station. Doctor Kitner was coming the other way. She's some sort of scientist from Hanagan's Hope, the tiny little community downriver of Mount Mercy. She's a timid mouse of a woman with gold-rimmed glasses: kind of adorable, if you like that type. She balked when she saw my prisoner. Or maybe it was me she balked at: with my beard, tattoos and band t-shirt with the sleeves torn off, I look like a biker, too.

"What are you lookin' at, bitch?" Lyce spat.

Doc Kitner flinched and stumbled back a step. And I saw red. I jerked Lyce to a stop and then hauled his arm up between his shoulder blades, just like I used to do with drunk soldiers when I was Military Police. "Apologize to the lady!"

Lyce scowled and then leered at her. I notched his arm higher, until his fingers brushed his hair. "Ow! *OW!* Jesus, okay, I'm sorry!"

With a respectful nod to the doctor, I marched him the rest of the way across the street, into the police station and into a waiting cell. "I didn't even do it!" he yelled as I slammed the door. "I didn't stab her!"

The officer on duty, an old guy named Earl, glanced up at me as he signed off on the paperwork. "You think he did it?"

After twenty hours sharing a truck with Lyce, I knew him well enough that I was pretty sure he *did* do it, and probably much more. But it didn't matter. "I don't care who's innocent and who's guilty," I told Earl. "I just bring 'em in."

I strolled out into the sunshine and grinned, already turning towards the café. But at that second, my phone rang. It was JD, the big Texan who leads Stormfinch Security, the private military outfit I work for. "Can you come in?" he asked. "A job just came up and it's right up your street."

Coffee would have to wait. "On my way, boss."

We call our place *The Factory,* because that's what it used to be. It was derelict when we bought it, with holes in the roof: I still remember sitting on crates for our first briefing. Now, there's a proper briefing room with a big, polished table and a big screen TV. JD was sitting at the head of the table, nursing a cup of coffee, but other than him it looked like I was the first to arrive. He nodded as I walked in. "Thanks for getting here so fast."

I gave him a solemn nod. Even if I'd been in the middle of a bounty-hunting job, I'd have dropped it in a heartbeat. Everything stops for Stormfinch. "Cody ready for the start of school?" I asked. Cody is JD's girlfriend's son and next week he'd be starting at the little school in Mount Mercy. We'd all helped rescue the kid in New York and we were all a little protective of him.

JD rubbed at his stubble and nodded. "After all he went through, a new school's not so scary. Plus, he'll be the cool kid from New York in a little town: that's gotta help." He grinned. Back when Stormfinch first started, he'd been solemn and sort of grumpy. But since Lorna and Cody had come into his life, he was happier, *lighter*. They'd changed him...or maybe changed him back, to how he was before he was widowed.

The others trooped in: Danny, the Brit, looking sharp as always in his suit, and with him his girlfriend—and JD's little sister—Erin. Next was Gabriel, our reformed thief, grinning as he showed a card trick to Bradan, one of the two Irish brothers. Then Cal, our huge sniper, in his plaid shirt, and Gina, our pilot, yawning and scowling as if this was altogether too early in the morning for her. Last of all was Kian, Bradan's brother, the guy who set up Stormfinch and who gets us our missions. "I'm heading out of town straight after this," he told us. "Got to go to Washington."

"Washington?" Bradan leaned forward. "You finally going to ask him?"

Him being the President. And the question being *could I have your blessing to marry your daughter?* Kian had been dating her for years and he'd been on the verge of asking for close to a year, now. To be fair to the guy, asking that question's a pretty big deal even when your girlfriend's father's *not* the most powerful man in the world.

Kian nodded. "Next week, he's taking us to a football game. His team is playing at home, in Arlington, Texas. I figure I'd ask him after the game...if Texas wins."

"Like *that's* in any doubt," rumbled JD, ever loyal to his home state.

"Can you get some pictures of the stadium for me, from inside?" asked Erin. She turned to Danny, grinning, in full geek-out mode. "The roof is so cool! It's huge, but they can close it completely when it gets too hot!"

Danny nodded patiently and kissed her forehead.

JD's phone beeped with a message and he stood up. "Alright, let's rock and roll. The guy who's going to brief us just arrived."

Erin kissed Danny goodbye and hurried off to another room, where she was working on our communication links. JD left and a moment later came back in with a guy in a gray suit. He was no more than thirty-five and with his blond curls, tan and easy smile, he looked like a surfer who'd thrown on a suit for a job interview. But I knew straight away he was a spook. The CIA does something to people: you can see it in their eyes. It's like it moves them out of the nice, warm little bubble we all live in so they can peer in at us from outside. That lets them see everything better, but it's a cold, lonely place to be.

"This is Casey Steward," JD told us. "From Langley. He's going to be our contact with the CIA on this one."

Danny frowned. "What happened to Roberta?" Roberta Geiss, a tough-but-fair woman in her sixties, had been our CIA contact since we started, and everyone liked her.

Steward winced. "Roberta was in a traffic accident yesterday. She's in the hospital. I'm her deputy, I'm filling in."

We all shook our heads and cursed. "I'll send some flowers from all of us," said Danny.

Steward hooked up a laptop to the big screen. "This is your target." He tapped a few keys and—

The photo was black and white and grainy: you could tell it was an old-fashioned, paper-and-ink photo that had been photocopied and scanned and printed out again about a billion times until all the subtlety in the grays had been washed away and it was brutally hard and contrasty, literally just *black* and *white*. But it didn't matter. It couldn't take away from what she was.

The most beautiful woman I'd ever seen.

Some women are girl-next-door beautiful. Pretty as hell but *attainable, believable.* She wasn't that. She was movie-star beautiful, launch-a-thousand-ships beautiful.

The first thing I saw were her eyes. Big and pale: I couldn't tell what color they were but...you know that dumb shit people say about falling into someone's eyes, getting lost in them? Suddenly, that didn't seem so dumb. I felt like I was back in Missouri, standing on my houseboat on the hottest day of the year, looking down at the cool surface of the lake and just wanting to fall forward, clothes and all, into those glittering depths. Her eyes were so heartbreakingly beautiful, they almost made me hesitate: she was like an oil painting I was afraid to touch in case you messed it up. But then I saw her brows, perfectly shaped, one of them arched in a look that was one part disapproving, two parts taunting: *well, what are you doing just standing there?* It was so rawly sexual, I swore I blushed and there's not a goddamn thing that can make *me* blush. The heat washed all the way down my body to my cock and I wanted to crawl right across the table to her.

Her cheekbones had a sculpted sharpness that had to be Eastern European. She'd have looked too sharp, too severe, like some evil dominatrix, if the sharpness hadn't been balanced by the softness of her hair. It was dark, I guessed dark brown, and it fell in tumbling waves down to her shoulders. Even in the lousy photo, it seemed to shine and move: I could *feel* how soft it must be.

And then, finally, I saw her lips. She was scowling, obviously unhappy with whoever was taking the photo, and her lips pouted sulkily in a way that made me forget to breathe. I stared at them, transfixed. I couldn't figure out if I wanted to pull her close and just kiss that scowl away, or...

Or gather her hair in my fist and guide those lips towards my aching cock. *Who the hell is this woman?!*

"Tanya Yesh—Yeshev—Yeshevsk—" JD was trying and failing to read the name at the bottom of the screen.

"*Yeshevskaya,*" said Steward effortlessly.

It was cold and hard, while at the same time elegant and delicate, like ice crystals. So much more exotic and sexy than my last name, *Stockburn,* which sounds like a wooden gatepost worn smooth with time. I found myself silently mouthing it: *Yesh-ev-skay-a.* Then I realized what I was doing and closed my mouth quick.

"She's GRU," Steward continued. "Russian intelligence. Two days ago, she killed this guy, Castor Barlow." He showed us another photo, this time a scene-of-crime photo. A guy in a suit lay slumped forward over his desk, a red flower blossoming across the paperwork. "He was a Wall Street stockbroker. A security camera caught her leaving his house, minutes after it happened." This picture showed Tanya hurrying across a street. She was in skinny jeans and a hooded top, her body lithe but mouthwateringly feminine, with lush, full breasts and flaring hips. She'd put her hood up to try to hide her face but the camera had caught her at just the right angle as she looked furtively to the side. It was definitely her.

The others muttered and cursed. The murder looked *nasty:* this woman wasn't to be taken lightly. I should have felt the same, but as I stared at the image, my eyes just kept moving back and forth between her eyes and her lips, like my brain was a skipping record.

"Why'd she kill him?" asked Gabriel.

"We don't know," Steward told him. "Neither do the GRU. She wasn't even meant to be *in* America. They claim she's gone rogue and they've disavowed her."

I was still staring at her photo. It was like I was floating off into a dream world where all that existed were those big, pale eyes and those soft, soft lips.

"Do we know where she is?" asked Bradan.

"An apartment in New York," said Steward. "Your job is to go in and capture her alive, then bring her to a safehouse in West Virginia where we can interrogate her." He looked at each of us in turn. "I can't express how careful you've got to be with this woman. She's one of the best the GRU ever had. Off-the-scale smart, utterly convincing in her lies. She can make you believe anything. She'll try to get inside your heads, turn you against each other...and she's not above using her body to get what she wants."

"Danny, don't get any ideas," warned Gabriel.

Danny put his hands up in protest. "I'm a changed man!"

Danny used to be notorious for seducing every woman we came across, until he fell for Erin, JD's little sister. Everyone laughed. Everyone except me. I was still sitting there, entranced. The news that this woman was some sort of evil seductress should have poured cold water on my attraction to her. But it didn't. It only made me more fascinated.

JD turned to me. "Colton, wrangling prisoners is your specialty. I want you to help plan the op and you'll be responsible for handling her."

I nodded, my chest filling with pride. The truth is, however close we've all become, I've always felt kind of like I don't belong on the team. Everyone else is former Special Forces but me? I'm just regular Army. This was my big chance to contribute and prove myself. And also a chance to royally fuck everything up. That thought finally cleared my head and I sat up straight. "Don't worry, boss. I got this."

It's a point of pride that I've brought in every single prisoner I've ever gone after. And no matter how gorgeous she was, Tanya Yeshevskaya would be no different.

We planned and rehearsed all morning. Kian headed off to Washington and we all wished him luck with the President. Then, around noon, it came time for the rest of us to leave. All the women showed up to say goodbye to their men and suddenly, everyone was hugging. It was like one of those diagrams from chemistry class: a whole bunch of stable particles made up of protons and neutrons clinging tightly together: JD and Lorna, Bradan and Stacey, Cal and Bethany, Gabriel and Olivia, Danny and Erin...and then, bouncing around the room like a couple of loose electrons, Gina and me, the only members of the team still single. Fortunately, Bethany had brought their huge German Shepherd, Rufus, so Gina and I ruffled his fur and told him what a *good good boy* he was until the hugs broke up.

I caught Erin as she moved away from Danny. "You had any luck with that toy you were working on?"

Erin pushed her glasses up her nose and dug in her shoulder bag. "I think I can make it smaller, but if you want to give it a test run, go ahead."

She passed me a package: she'd even gift-wrapped it. I broke into a big, wide grin and pulled her into an impromptu hug, delighted.

Then it was time to go. As I watched all the couples say their final goodbyes, I couldn't help but feel a little sad. *Must be nice to have someone.*

Colorado to New York was too far to go by chopper, so Gina had rented a small plane instead. As we flew east, the sun behind us turned the clouds in front to pink cotton candy and then to gold-edged mountains. We all knew each other well enough that we could just sit and experience it, without having to fill the quiet with small talk, and I loved that.

We crossed the line that separated day from night and it felt as if we were crossing into another country, one where only bad things could happen. I scowled at my reflection in the window: *don't be stupid.*

The cabin grew dark, with just Gina's instruments up front throwing out a dim green glow. Next to me, Bradan was dozing. Cal, who needed all the leg room he could get, was twisted in his seat, legs filling the aisle. Danny was reading on his phone, probably another of those huge, thick fantasy novels he and Erin read. I flipped on a little flashlight and carried on reading through Tanya's file, wanting to know everything there was to know about her. Her spy mission stuff was all redacted but that still left plenty of personal details and with every one, she became more fascinating. She spoke six languages: *six!* I barely spoke English. She was an expert chess player: I was more of a checkers guy. She was a trained dancer...and now I was imagining those full breasts in a leotard...

I caught my reflection in the glossy surface of the photo and frowned at myself. *Remember she's a bad guy.* Someone to be taken down, restrained and transported. The enemy.

I flipped the last page of the file, not really expecting to find anything. A photo slid out and fell. I grabbed it on instinct...and stared.

It had been taken with a long lens in some sort of café. The photographer had caught Tanya as she lifted her coffee cup to take a sip and for once, her expression was open and unguarded. She was gazing off to the side and there was a hint, just the tiniest hint, of a smile on her lips. I felt something lift, right in the center of my chest. But that wasn't what made me stare.

She was wearing a tight, turtleneck sweater. It was ribbed and the lines curved and stretched over the soft mounds of her breasts like contour lines on a map, making me growl low in my throat. But that wasn't what made me stare, either.

Unlike the others, this photo was in color. Her ribbed top was bottle green. Her eyes were the sort of freezing blue you only get high up in the clouds, out of reach of us dumb grunts on the ground. And her hair...

Her hair wasn't brown, it was *red.* Red like the sun just as it sinks below the horizon, melting copper and liquid fire. It gleamed and shone, the vivid color the perfect contrast to her milky skin. The combination was so damn sexual...suddenly, I was mentally stripping her of that sweater, imagining those full, soft breasts bare and in my hands, the tips of her red hair caressing the backs of my fingers as I squeezed and rubbed. And then I started thinking about what was under those skinny jeans: would the curls of hair between her milky thighs be that same vivid copper?

"You know how long you've been staring at that picture?" The voice was smooth as bourbon and warm with humor. *Gabriel.* I'd forgotten he was in the seat behind.

I felt my face heat and tried to brazen it out. "Just doing my homework." I swallowed. "One time, I was after this guy who'd skipped bail down in Aurora. Nobody could find him. But I'd done the research, found out he had a medical condition. Picked him up coming out of a pharmacy."

"Mm-hmm," murmured Gabriel. I could hear the grin in his voice.

I snapped the file closed, mad at myself. *What's wrong with me?* It didn't matter that she was a woman, or that she was gorgeous. She was going *down,* just like all the others.

An hour later, we were sitting in a darkened SUV across the street from Tanya's apartment building. It was just after midnight.

"Anyone else think it's weird that the CIA got *us to* do this?" muttered Cal. "They got their own people."

"He's got a point." Bradan's Irish accent was like a silver knife in the dark.

JD shook his head. He had binoculars up to his eyes, watching Tanya's window. "This is a good opportunity for us. Could open all sorts of doors."

I sympathized with Cal and Bradan: both of them had had bad experiences with the CIA. But I was automatically on JD's side: he was the best damn leader I'd ever seen and if he said it was okay, it was okay. I nodded firmly and Cal sighed, backed down and went to find a good sniper spot.

Moments later, the rest of us were stacked up against the wall outside her apartment building. "Let's be clear," JD told us. "The aim is to take her alive but if you have to, you put her down. I don't want anyone getting hurt." We all nodded and glanced at each other, our breathing shaky with adrenaline, and I felt my chest tighten. *Man,* I loved this team. I'd found my family.

Gabriel picked the lock. Bradan slipped inside and led the way upstairs, moving silently: the guy was one stealthy fucker. Four floors and we were outside Tanya's apartment. This lock took Gabriel a little longer, but then we were swarming inside, guns up, ready for anything. Just as we'd planned, the others fanned out and checked the other rooms one by one, while I headed straight through the living room for the bedroom. "Clear," I heard Bradan murmur from the kitchen. "Clear," from Danny in the guest room, "Clear" from JD in the bathroom.

My breathing went tight as I approached the bedroom door: she *had* to be in here.

I kicked open the door.

And suddenly, she was *real*.

She wasn't in the bed, like I'd expected. She was standing right in front of me, fully dressed, her head cocked curiously to one side. I froze in the doorway, panting, and just stared at that face I'd gazed at for so long. Those high, sharp cheekbones. Those soft, pouting lips. And those long waves of copper-red hair. *Jesus,* the photos didn't do her justice.

My eyes roamed down her body, over the creamy valley of cleavage revealed by her open leather jacket and the V-neck of her blue vest top, past her slender waist to the lush flare of her hips in her tight black jeans. My cock was rising in my pants: I felt like I'd walked off a damn cliff and was falling, flailing. Her perfume was in the air. Part of it was soft, sensual, and very, very feminine: I felt like someone was slowly trailing an orchid's delicate petals over my cheek. But there was another part, a tang that made me think of sharply sweet red berries. *What was I meant to be doing, again?*

I looked into her eyes and they were so cold it was like inhaling on a winter's day. That coldness should have made me run but it just drew me in deeper. She was the razor sharp blade I had to touch, the poison candy I had to taste. And as I gazed at her, I thought I saw the ice change, turning from frosted and impenetrable to clear. Beneath it was a scalding, desperate heat. I could feel myself leaning forward—

She looked away, breaking the spell, and I blinked, mad at myself. *Focus!* I had a job to do.

But now I'd seen her, that job seemed insane. Even in her heeled ankle boots, she was six inches shorter than me. *Her?* She's *the big threat?!* I glanced down at my combat gear, feeling ridiculous. I lowered the shotgun and took out a set of handcuffs.

She looked at them and raised one perfect eyebrow. "My safeword is *Cincinnati.*"

I froze again, utterly thrown. First there were the images she'd put in my mind: images of her naked and tied down and begging. Then there was her voice. God, it was incredible. Her Russian accent carved every word from a block of ice and then that sexy, gently mocking tone warmed each icy syllable until it was glossy and dripping. My cock was twitching and at the same time my face had gone skillet-hot: I felt like a goddamn teenager caught jerking off.

"Kneel down," I said, trying to take back control.

"*Oh.*" She glanced at my groin and her eyes went wide, innocent. "So *that's* what you want?"

I couldn't think, probably because all my blood was rushing south. "No! I—Kneel down!"

She pursed her lips, as controlled as I was flustered. "I think not." She took a step towards me.

"Make it easy on yourself," I told her desperately. "You got nowhere to run. Only way out of this room is through me."

"Shouldn't be a problem," she said sweetly. And she punched me in the face.

2

TANYA

Two Minutes Earlier

I STOOD IN THE BEDROOM, staring at the diagram I'd created on the wall. Scarlet threads drew connections between people, dates, and locations. And at the center of it all was a face. A man in his fifties with a broad, brutish face and a pointed, snow-white beard. *Maravić.*

The man who must die.

I looked between the diagram and my laptop screen, scowling. I'd been standing there close to an hour and I still couldn't figure it out. What was Maravić doing in America? Why had he killed that stockbroker? When I found the murder scene, I'd managed to raid the stockbroker's computer before the police arrived, but all I'd gotten was some computer code full of equations that I didn't have the math skill to decipher and a list of contacts. The only name I recognized was Konstantin Gulyev. I was meeting with him tomorrow to ask why the hell a stockbroker had been talking to a Russian mafia boss.

There was a sound behind me: distant and quiet, just a delicate metallic scraping, but it made me whip around, heart thumping, because I knew what it was. A lockpick working in a lock. Someone was trying to get into my apartment. *"Chyort!"* I whispered under my breath. *Damn!*

I brought up the feed from the camera in the hallway. Five men. From their boots and weapons, Americans. *CIA.* I grabbed my phone and dialed from memory. "I need to speak to Roberta Geiss," I told the voice at the other end. "Urgent!"

"I'm sorry, Director Geiss is in the hospital. She was in a car accident yesterday—"

I cursed and ended the call, a creeping dread soaking through me.

Footsteps from the hallway. They were inside, searching the apartment. I heard voices calling *clear, clear, clear.* And one set of footsteps, heavier than the rest, was heading straight towards the bedroom. I glanced around the room. I'd been trained not to acquire possessions: they only slow you down. There were no lover's letters, no framed photos, nothing I couldn't leave behind. The computer data I'd collected was already backed up to the cloud, so I could access it from anywhere. All I had to do was get out of there.

The door flew open, crashed against the wall and wilted, one hinge broken. And standing there was—

I froze, staring. I'd expected a man but—*Chyort!*—this was a *beast.*

He wore huge, black leather combat boots, his feet twice the size of mine. Black combat pants were stretched over calves and quads as thickly solid as tree trunks. My eyes crept up his body to where he narrowed to a midsection loaded with power. Then he began to flare out again, his muscled torso giving him an X shape, his chest like two huge whiskey barrels placed side by side. He was huge but lean, his body carved by hard physical work.

That's when I felt it, deep in the core of me, under all my layers of ice and rock where nothing should have been able to reach me. A tremor that completely unsettled me. A weakness.

The sleeves of his black combat shirt had been cut off—no, I could see the dangling threads, they'd been *torn off*, as if he'd grown tired of them constraining him. His shoulders were big, tan boulders and they brushed the edges of the door frame. His biceps were scarcely any smaller and they were covered with the dark ink of tattoos: from this distance, all I could make out was a leathery wing spread across one arm and what looked like a vine curled around the other. My eyes tracked down over forearms thickly corded with muscle. He was holding a shotgun with a barrel that looked big enough to swallow me whole, but in his huge hands, it looked like a toy.

My gaze locked on those hands. On the big, solid palms and the thickly powerful fingers, on the brutish knuckles. I suddenly felt...*small.*

Another of those tremors. It ran straight down to my groin, making me catch my breath. It was even more unsettling, the second time, and I silently cursed, furious at myself. *Weakness!*

He was tall enough that I had to tilt my head way back to see his face and from that angle the sheer, muscled size of him was overwhelming. I felt like I was an inch tall, clambering up a giant, sinking my hands into his soft, black beard for grip. I climbed *up, up, up...*

Oh God. He was gorgeous. Roughly, brutally gorgeous in a way I was completely unused to. Suddenly, the rich men I spent so much time with felt absurdly fragile and fake, pampered and coiffured like poodles at a dog show. This man wasn't a king, he was the barbarian who overthrew him.

He had a wide mouth, his hard upper lip curling a little as he scowled and his soft lower one pouting sexily. My gaze roved helplessly over that mouth, darting around like a deer in the forest seeking escape and finding none. I would have *no chance* against those lips. So big and strong, he'd just force me open and take what he wanted.

The thick black beard couldn't conceal the line of his jaw, hard and stubborn and magnificent. I could imagine him as some medieval village blacksmith, lifting his chin as he told the cruel tax collector that his people wouldn't pay. Or the Detroit assembly line worker, standing up for his friends against a merciless boss.

The eyes that scowled down at me from beneath dark, brooding brows were brown, but not a safe, chocolate brown. They were heated and raw, closer to amber. Somewhere, deep under the earth, there was a mine where men toiled with pickaxes and sledgehammers, their work illuminated by waterfalls of bright orange, molten rock. They'd extract gemstones formed by nature grinding its continents together, stones that were the concentrated essence of the earth, staggeringly hard and blazing with the heat of the planet. *That's where he must have gotten his eyes.*

I'd never seen a look of such determination, such single-minded intent. I was the enemy and he was going to take me down. But there was humanity there, too. He wasn't just some robot following orders. He believed he was doing the right thing and it was so long since I'd seen that sort of moral core in anyone that it almost broke my heart.

And then, as he stared down at me, his eyes narrowed and *burned,* the heat melting the hardness, overpowering it, consuming his resolve like a forest fire. The air between us turned scalding hot and as his gaze ran down my body it felt like my jacket, my vest top, my jeans, even my underwear disintegrated into ash, leaving me naked, skin throbbing. God, I was getting turned on. I'd gotten so used to faking it, the lipsticked gasps and little moans that feed men's egos, that I'd forgotten what real arousal felt like. This wasn't just on my glossy, icy surface, reflecting a man's desires back at him. This was deep inside, right where I lived, a sensation like a silk sheet fluttering and then twisting into a tight, tight rope. Was I *blushing?!*

The man leaned forward as if drawn by an invisible string, his lips parting, and I felt that tremor again. Only this time, I realized to my horror what it was.

It wasn't just weakness. It was a longing to be weak. To be helpless.

That's what finally snapped me out of my stupor. I swallowed and looked away. And with the spell broken, he glanced away, too, his face hardening. He'd only leaned an inch towards me but from the expression on his face, he was furious at even that loss of control. He squared his massive shoulders and straightened up, moving back from me. And I tried to ignore the traitorous tug of loss.

With a quick, shaky breath, I cinched everything down tight

inside and forced myself back to cold, hard efficiency. He lusted after me. I could use that to get his guard down. As he took a pair of handcuffs from his belt, I made my voice singsong and light. "My safe word is *Cincinnati*."

It worked better than I could have hoped. He went stock still, his face going crimson. I felt an unexpected rush of...*something* in my chest. *Chyort*, but he was *adorable* when he was embarrassed, like a big, clumsy bear.

"Kneel down," he growled.

Just two words but it was enough to get a taste of his voice and I immediately wanted more. I was used to spies and politicians, men whose words were polished blades wrapped in silk. But there was no trickery here, no games. He just said what he wanted, in a voice as rough and raw as moonshine, his low growl resonating right through me and turning my core to liquid. There was a twang of something deeply country in his voice, bold and unapologetic: he didn't give a shit what anyone thought of him and that made it even hotter.

It felt like I split in two. The external me knew just what to do to make him uncomfortable. I glanced between his legs and let my voice rise, innocent and shocked. "So *that's* what you want?"

But there was another me. An internal me. A me whose knees had gone shaky at that low growl, who longed to just sink to the polished wood floor and submit.

I pushed her viciously down inside.

"No! I—Kneel down!" snapped the man.

He was as distracted as he was going to get. "I think not," I told him, and started moving towards him.

"Make it easy on yourself," he insisted. "You got nowhere to run. Only way out of this room is through me."

"Shouldn't be a problem," I told him. One good punch to the face would send him crashing to the floor and, as he went down, I'd slip past him. The living room and hallway seemed to be clear behind him, the other men still in the other rooms, so in a few seconds I'd be out of the apartment and racing down the stairs to the street. He'd be left with a sore jaw and a bruised ego. I almost felt bad for him.

Almost. He was still the enemy.

I took one step forward, light and bouncy on my feet, and slammed my fist into his cheek as hard as I could. I started forward so I could slip through the doorway as he fell...

Except he didn't fall. His head turned a little, but his body barely moved. I bounced off him and staggered back, my arm aching: it had been like punching a warm granite statue.

He slowly turned his head to look at me and ran his hand over his cheek. *"Ow,"* he said darkly.

He wasn't just big, he was used to getting hit, able to take the punishment. My stomach dropped...but a tiny, secret part of me went fluttery, again. It wasn't often I met someone who could take me on. This man could actually *win,* if I wasn't careful, and that was a little bit thrilling. And he was so controlled: any other man would have spat insults at me but he just scowled and stretched his shoulders, readying himself.

"Let's try that again," he growled.

And he ran at me.

3

COLTON

I LOWERED my head and charged like a bull, each big stride shaking the room. I was raging at myself for letting my guard down. She'd cast a fucking spell on me. That long red hair, that accent and all that teasing...she'd gotten me so horny, I'd forgotten she was dangerous.

Now I had to get her under control. Quickly and quietly, so the neighbors didn't hear and call the cops. I'd grab her and ram her up against the wall, then flip her around and get the cuffs on her...

Except it didn't work out like that. As I grabbed her, she fell backwards, tumbling gracefully, and used my own momentum to launch me through the air. All two-hundred and seventy pounds of me crashed into the sliding, mirror-fronted doors of her closet. The mirrors shattered and came raining down in tinkling shards all around me. One of the doors came off its tracks and fell to the floor next to me with a *boom* so loud it made my ears ache. *Well, the neighbors sure heard* that.

I clambered to my feet and chased after her, catching her in the living room. I grabbed a handful of her leather jacket and hauled her back: she broke free, but it let me get in front of her and block her path again.

I was mad, now. This mission was my big chance and I was

screwing it up. I'd been wrong to let my guard down and I'd been wrong to get mad and charge at her. Well, now I'd do it right. She was about to learn what made me good at my job.

I bent my knees, getting my weight low, and slowly moved towards her.

4

TANYA

I WATCHED him stalk towards me, my breathing going tight. *Chyort,* that wasn't good. He was taking his time, this time: I wouldn't catch him out with a judo throw again. And from the way he moved, weight low and feet spread, he was a wrestler. That was just about the worst case scenario, for me. All he had to do was get close enough to grab me and his weight and power meant that he'd easily overpower me.

That tremor, again, deep inside. I blinked, incredulous that there was some tiny part of me that wanted that, that wanted to be pinned and...*mastered.* I buried the feeling deep, grabbed a book from the bookshelf and hurled it at him. Then another, and another. I knew they wouldn't hurt him, but all I needed was for him to flinch and duck, and then I could slip past him...

But he didn't flinch. He kept his eyes locked on me as he batted the books away with those huge hands. And the whole time, he was slowly advancing.

We met in the middle of the living room and began to move back and forth, me ducking and dodging, trying to find a path past him to the door, and him sidestepping, arms outstretched, blocking me. I made the mistake of venturing too close to one of those huge hands and he grabbed my wrist. In a split-second, he levered my arm up behind my back, making me gasp in pain. He walked me over to the wall and pushed me up against it face-first. His whole body was pressed to my back and I could feel the heat of him throbbing through my clothes. I caught my breath as I felt his hard cock, the base of it grinding against the top of my ass cheek, the tip of it right down—*God, he's that big?*

He put his mouth to my ear, his beard roughly scratchy in a way that unleashed a shower of silver sparks in my chest. Then he spoke in that growly, country voice and the sparks coalesced into heavy liquid silver that ran right down to my groin. "Are you gonna be a good girl?"

I swallowed, glad that he couldn't see my face. Then I planted my feet against the wall and pushed as hard as I could. He staggered backwards into the center of the room, fighting to keep his balance. There was a crash of glass: I guessed he'd just put his boot through the glass coffee table. He stayed on his feet but his grip on me loosened a little and that was all I needed. I whirled around and slipped out of my jacket, leaving him gripping it by the sleeve.

I dived for the door. He sidestepped and I crashed into a chest that felt like warm rock. I lashed out, desperate now, clawing at his face with my nails. His huge hands chased mine and then lunged, capturing one wrist. Then he did the same with the other and suddenly I was powerless, my hands grabbing at the air either side of my head.

I panted, my breathing shaky. I could see his tattoos better, now: it was definitely a wing, leathery like a bat's, on one arm, and what I'd thought was a vine was a tail wrapped around the other. It wasn't two tattoos, it was one really big one, some sort of monster that must cover his entire chest or back.

I glared up at him.

"Are you gonna behave?" he demanded.

In answer, I scraped my foot down the inside of his shin. It must have hurt, but his only response was a tightening of his mouth. Then he tugged me up against him. I gasped as my breasts pillowed against his chest. He wrapped his arms around me, pinning my arms to my sides. Then he hooked one leg around my legs so that I was completely wrapped up and powerless.

"*Now* are you gonna behave?" he asked.

I struggled, but I could barely move at all. And every time I shifted, I could feel the hardness of his cock rubbing against me, the heat of it soaking straight through the denim of my jeans and the thin cotton of my panties to radiate out through my groin. With any other man, I'd have worried about provoking him into taking advantage of the situation. But with him I knew, on a gut level, that he wouldn't do that. My whole job was sniffing out the corrupt and morally weak men, so I could tempt them into betraying their countries. That meant being able to spot the good ones, too. And this man, whoever he was, was one of those.

I stopped struggling.

At that moment, the other men arrived, led by an older guy with amazing, pale blue eyes. "What happened to *quiet?*" he asked in an accent that was pure, sun-baked Texan. He looked around the living room and the bedroom beyond and, for the first time, I took in the devastation: we'd completely wrecked the place.

"Sorry, boss," muttered the man holding me. "She got away from me. But I got her in hand, now."

Oh, do you? I scowled up at him and he glared back at me.

The Texan looked towards one of the other men, who was listening to a radio. "Gabriel, any sign of the cops?"

Gabriel shook his head. "Not yet, but we gotta figure the neighbors are calling them right now. We should get out of here."

The Texan nodded and keyed his radio. "Cal, we're securing the package now, be out in a minute."

The man holding me—I still didn't know his name—looked around on the floor. I looked, too, and spotted the handcuffs lying amongst the debris behind me. He must have dropped them during our fight.

Another man, younger, with green eyes, stepped forward. "It's alright, mate. I'll get 'em" His accent was British and he gave me what he must have thought was a charming grin as he picked up the cuffs.

Then he stepped up behind me to put them on. "Ease up on her," he told the man holding me. "I've got her."

"Careful," growled the man holding me. "She's a slippery little thing." But he reluctantly unwound his arms so the Brit could put the cuffs on.

I stayed passive and meek while the Brit gently pulled one arm behind me. I felt one cuff close on my wrist and ratchet tight. Then he reached for the other wrist.

I craned around and looked up at him over my shoulder, making my eyes go as big and scared as I could. "Please, that's too tight." I bit my lip for effect and forced tears into my eyes. "You're hurting me!"

The Brit looked horrified. He let go of my arms for a second...and that's all it took. I whirled around, using the handcuffs that dangled from one wrist like a whip, and managed to catch him on the side of the face. As he staggered sideways, I dived and forward-rolled, coming up next to the dining table. Then I grabbed the gun I kept taped to the underside and turned to fire.

5

COLTON

As soon as I saw the gun in her hands, I raised my shotgun on instinct. But as Tanya turned towards us, my finger froze on the trigger.

JD stared at me. *"SHOOT!"*

Tanya was bringing her gun up, about to fire. I dropped the shotgun and sprang at her, ramming my shoulder into her chest. There was a deafening boom next to my ear as the gun went off. Then I was riding her down to the floor. The gun sailed out of her hand and she *oof*ed as my full weight came down on top of her.

I looked over my shoulder, terrified. "Everybody okay?"

The team all looked at each other, everyone white-faced and shaky. For a second, it wasn't clear where the bullet went. Then we all registered that Gabriel had his hand clamped to the side of his head. He took it away and his fingers were bloody. The bullet had clipped the very top of his ear. A few inches to the right and he'd be dead.

JD marched over to me. "What was *that?*"

I swallowed and looked up at him, feeling ill. I had no answer.

"Next time I tell you to shoot," he snapped, "you *shoot!*"

I nodded quickly, chastened. He was mad at me and he had every right to be. But I could hear disappointment in his voice, too, and that was way, way worse.

And even worse than *that* was that, despite everything, part of me was thinking just how good Tanya's body felt under mine. I was full length on top of her, my legs were between hers and I had her wrists pinned to the floor above her head. Every time she breathed, her chest swelled and her breasts pushed up against me in a way that made my cock twitch.

She stared up at me, and those cold blue eyes seemed to flicker again. Weakening and showing me the heat beneath? Or tricking me, just like she had Danny?

I rolled her face-down and finished cuffing her wrists together, then hauled her to her feet. All of us gave a sigh of relief: *finally,* she was secure.

But she had one last weapon none of us had thought of. She took an enormous gulp of air—

I realized she was going to scream. A real long, shake-the-walls, bloodcurdling scream, one that would bring her neighbors running.

Before I even knew what I was doing, I hooked an arm around her waist, pulled her back against me and clamped my hand across her mouth. She screamed but I've got big hands and not much sound escaped. JD caught my eye and gave me a grudging nod: *well done.* That made me feel a little better. And it helped to distract from how amazing Tanya's lips felt against my palm.

As the scream ended, I put my mouth next to her ear and spoke, quiet but firm. "You try that again and I'll gag you, and you can stay silent for the entire journey. Understand?"

She huffed angrily against my palm and the sensation made me close my eyes for a second as I fought to keep myself under control. God, I was *dangerously* smitten with this woman.

When I opened my eyes, I looked across the room to a mirror on the wall. I could see her reflection glaring back at me. Her blue eyes were furious, sullen...but resigned. She understood.

I slowly lifted my palm from her lips and she didn't scream. I exchanged relieved looks with the rest of the team. Then I put my hands on her shoulders and turned her to face me. "I gotta search you," I told her.

She gave me a glare that could have frozen lava. Then she lifted her chin and stood there like a statue, waiting.

I could feel the tension in her body as I felt around her ankles and calves, then made my way up her thighs. She was expecting me to grope her. But even though her legs felt fucking amazing through those tight jeans, there was no way I was going to take advantage. I kept it clean and clinical, sweeping up over her hips and waist, where I found two nasty-looking knives hidden in her belt. I checked her back, then under her arms. My wrists brushed the sides of her breasts and I forced myself not to react but the soft, weighty feel of them burned itself into my mind. I checked along the length of her arms, then leaned in close to feel around her neck and under her hair. As I ran my fingers through the silky waves, we stared at each other, our faces six inches apart. She was still glaring at me but, beneath all the coldness, there was something else: a hint of confusion and surprise.

JD keyed his radio. "Cal, package is secure. We're coming out." He looked at Danny. "Get the car ready."

Danny nodded, rubbing his cheek: there was a red welt where Tanya had hit him with the handcuffs.

"I need to use the bathroom before we go," said Tanya.

"Hold it," I growled.

"I don't think I *can. Please?*" She looked around at us. "Or should I just pee myself in the car?"

"I wouldn't have a problem with that," Gabriel told her, glaring. He was holding a bandage to his injured ear.

Danny looked uncertain. "It's ninety minutes to the airfield. And it's a really nice SUV. Leather seats."

Gabriel listened to the police radio. "Cops are coming. Five minutes out."

JD sighed and nodded to me. "Take her, but be quick!"

I hauled her to the bathroom, cursing under my breath. I was sure this was another trick. Pushing her inside, I looked around and checked behind the toilet and in the cistern in case she'd stashed another weapon there. But there was nothing. The window didn't open and it was four little panes of glass, all too small to climb through. Plus, we were four floors up. "You got ten seconds," I told her, pushing her towards the toilet.

She jangled her cuffs. "Take these off for a minute."

"You'll manage."

"You expect me to get my jeans off with handcuffs on?"

"You want me to do it for you?"

Her eyes widened in what looked like genuine shock. Then they narrowed in anger, but as she pouted and glared, it almost looked theatrical. Like she was trying to cover up some other emotion.

She put her thumbs in the waistband of her jeans, preparing to wriggle them down. Then stopped, blinking at me. "Go!"

I crossed my arms. "I don't trust you alone."

Her cheeks flushed and for once, it felt genuine. "At least turn around," she choked.

I glanced around the bathroom. There was nowhere she could go. And despite all her tricks, I didn't want to humiliate her. I turned my back to her, keeping my ears peeled. I listened for footsteps coming towards me, in case she was planning to strangle me with the shower hose. But there was nothing. Not even the sound of peeing. "Hurry it up," I told her.

A few seconds later, I felt something on the back of my neck that made me frown. Was that...a draft?

I spun around just in time to see her feet disappearing through a hole.

What? I dived across the room but it was too late. I stared at the hole, aghast. The entire window, frame and all, was gone. I stuck my head through the hole. *Shit!* There was a fire escape outside and Tanya was sprinting along it. The window was lying out there and I could see now how the whole thing had been designed to pop silently out when pushed: her emergency escape route.

I tried to squeeze out after her, but my shoulders wouldn't fit. *Fuck!* I ran into the hall, past JD and the others. "She's gone!" I yelled.

"*Gone?!*"

I didn't have time to answer. I ran to the window in the living room, which looked out onto the same fire escape, opened it and climbed out. Then I made the mistake of looking at the ground.

Shit. My eyes did that thing where they crawled all the way down the brickwork to the alley below. I could *feel* the drop, feel the wind whistling past as I went headfirst towards the concrete, and it made my stomach flip. Invisible hands wanted to push me over the rail. I gripped the fire escape with both hands, the soles of my feet prickling, my head going light.

I have a small problem with heights. Back in the army, I had no issues running headlong into enemy fire but I was always the last one roping out of a chopper. I don't like high buildings, or rooftops, or *especially* fucking rope bridges, and this job has thrown all three at me. I'm not as bad as I was when we first started, but that's not saying a whole hell of a lot.

Right now, though, Tanya was getting away. And she was my responsibility. I took a deep breath and ran for the stairs, the whole fire escape shaking as I pounded along the metal walkway. I raced down the first flight of stairs, ran to the next...

And that's when it clicked that I couldn't see her ahead of me, or even down in the alley below. Could she be *that* far ahead?

Then I thought about how tricksy she was. And looked up.

Silhouetted against the moon, a female silhouette was silently climbing *up* the stairs above her apartment, heading for the roof. *Shit!*

I reversed course and chased after her, but she had a good head start. By the time I reached the roof, she was a good way across it, heading for the next building. *Shit!* I sprinted after her, trying not to feel the drop all around me, or think about how there wasn't even a parapet around the edge. If a stray gust of wind sent me staggering sideways, I'd go straight over and—*stop it! Stop thinking about it!*

I'm not built for speed and, normally, she would have easily outrun me. But her hands were still cuffed behind her and you can't run full speed, without using your arms, so I was slowly gaining on her. Then I saw what was ahead of us and my stomach tightened down to a cold, hard knot.

We were racing towards the edge of the roof and the dark gulf that separated us from the next building. She wasn't slowing down. She meant to jump. Except, with the handcuffs slowing her down, she didn't have nearly enough momentum. She wasn't going to make it.

"Stop!" But it sounded like an order, not a warning, and she ignored it. "Stop!" This time, it came out more worried, but she still didn't slow down. "It's too far!" I yelled desperately.

She looked back over her shoulder and her eyes were diamond-hard. Something had hold of her. Something so important to her that she was willing to risk the jump rather than be captured. *What the hell is this? Some loyalty-to-Mother-Russia bullshit?*

"*Stop!*" I yelled, begging, now, but she didn't even slow down. So I did the only thing I could do. Panting, gasping, I pushed my legs even harder and tried to close the gap between us.

The edge of the building rushed up to meet us. I growled in frustration, craned forward and just managed to hook her handcuff chain with my fingers. Then I hauled her back hard. She was light enough that she came right off her feet and slammed into my chest, sending us both to the floor, arms and legs tangling. But I still had all my momentum and it carried us forward, rolling over and over, straight towards the edge.

I clawed with my fingers but there was nothing to grip onto and the world was a tumbling, confusing mess. Tanya screamed, right in my ear, as she realized what was about to happen. On instinct, I wrapped my arms around her and hugged her close, as if that could protect her from a six-story fall.

We rolled and rolled, the concrete scraping my bare arms. I sensed the space opening up behind me, felt the wind on my back—

We stopped, hugging tight as lovers, both of us heaving for breath. I didn't dare look behind me. I didn't want to know how few inches of building there were left.

I pushed her hair back from her ear and grunted into it, getting the words out between pants. "Don't...ever...do...that...again."

I heard feet pounding across the rooftop and then the rest of the team were there, helping me to my feet. "Gotta go," JD told me. "Cops'll be here any minute." He keyed his radio. "Cal, meet us downstairs. Danny, start the car." He scowled at Tanya as I muscled her towards the fire escape. "The package is secure...again."

Tanya glared at him over her shoulder. "You call me *the package* one more time and I'll kick you in the balls, cowboy."

6

TANYA

I COULD HEAR sirens approaching as they bundled me into a huge, black SUV. We pulled away and before we were even a block away, red and blue lights were filling the street outside my apartment building. The men all sighed in relief.

I quickly thought through my options. Escape? They'd put me in the center of the middle row, so there was a big guy either side of me, two more up front and two more in the row behind. No way was I getting out of the car, especially not with my hands cuffed behind my back.

Could I tell them what was going on? No. They worked for the CIA and even if they weren't in on it, they had no reason to believe me.

And then I felt it. A heat bathing my skin, a gaze so intense it made me stiffen and catch my breath. I turned to my right.

The man I'd fought, the one who'd wrestled me into submission not once but three times, now, was sitting next to me. We locked eyes and, as I stared into that amber-brown fire, it was like I knew exactly what he was imagining.

His arm hooking around my waist, pulling me effortlessly along the seat and scooping me up onto his lap. One of those big hands forcing its way up under my vest top and bra to palm a breast, my nipple hardening against the palm. The other hand sliding down between my thighs, rubbing me through my jeans and panties. The soft scratchiness of his beard as he kisses his way along my throat—

I looked quickly away. God, why was I flushing like a schoolgirl? So he lusted after me. So what? That was a good thing. Lust made men easy to control.

But it wasn't his lust that had me flustered. It was my own response, that need to be weak that he brought out in me. When I thought of his big hands on my body, I could feel my resolve melting into liquid heat.

I didn't understand: why *him?* I'd never had this kind of deep, instinctual reaction to any man. Not Russian politicians with their soft voices and power plays, not Bratva bosses with their expensive suits and dark violence. Why would I have it with *him,* a rough, unsophisticated American?

And that wasn't even the most worrying part. I was staring stubbornly out of the window as if refusing to meet his eyes. But really I was looking at his reflection in the glass, watching him watching me. His gaze didn't focus on my breasts long enough for it to be simple lust. He was staring at my profile, drinking me in as if fascinated. And however much I wanted to deny it, that made some silly, teenage part of me *lift.* I'd forgotten that part of me even existed.

No one *likes* spies. We're hated, hunted, manipulated and, when we're no longer useful, abandoned. But he'd risked his life to save me, up on the roof.

I pushed the thought away. *Focus!*

I turned to face front, ignoring him, ignoring everything.

And quietly, behind my back, I began lightly scraping at the inside of my left wrist with my thumbnail. *There:* I could feel the ridge on my skin. I kept scratching, and a rectangle of skin-colored latex began to peel loose. Beneath it was a lockpick.

I just had to bide my time and then, when they relaxed...I'd strike.

7

COLTON

I SPENT the journey staring at the sharp lines of her cheekbones, at the perfect silken softness of her lips. It wasn't just that she was beautiful. She was smart and devious, an actress who could be scared and vulnerable one moment, fierce and vicious the next. Which of her faces were real? Were any of them?

I knew I should be watchful and cautious. I'd seen how dangerous she could be: fuck, thanks to me, she'd almost shot Gabriel. But instead, I was just...*hypnotized.*

The car slowed and I realized we were pulling up at the airfield. I shook myself, scowling. *Snap out of it!* I had a job to do and I'd already messed up twice. The second the car stopped, I hauled Tanya out and started walking her towards the waiting plane. It was only a short flight to West Virginia. Then we'd hand her over to the CIA and—

My steps slowed a little. *And then I won't see her again.* My stomach twisted at the thought. *Ever.*

Then I scowled even harder and picked up the pace again. *What the fuck's wrong with me? She's the enemy. She's a spy. Hell, she killed a guy.* She deserved everything that was coming to her.

Which is what, exactly? I hadn't thought too much about what would happen to her. Interrogation, I guessed. And then jail. Or maybe they'd do one of those exchanges with Moscow, one of ours for one of theirs, wasn't that how it worked, with spies? She'd go home to Russia...I guess they'd be mad at her for getting caught. She'd lose her job...

So? Since when did *I* care what happened to a prisoner? *I just bring 'em in,* remember?

We reached the plane. Gina opened the door for us, giving Tanya a curious look as she passed. Then Gabriel climbed aboard with his bandaged ear, and then Danny with the red welt on his cheek. "What happened to you guys?" asked Gina, incredulous.

Gabriel looked darkly at Tanya and shook his head: *don't ask.* Gina smirked.

The rest of the team took their seats. The plane was small and very, very basic, with only one row of seats on each side, so I sat Tanya directly across the aisle from me, her hands still cuffed behind her back. "What's the in-flight movie?" she asked as I fastened her seatbelt.

"The Eternal Sunshine of *sit quietly and do what the fuck you're told,*" I growled.

She rolled her eyes at me in a taunting, *you're no fun* way that made my cock swell. God, what was it about this woman?

Gina taxied and we took off, then turned south. "Settle in, people," she yelled over the drone of the engines. "It's about two hours to West Virginia."

The plane was too small to be pressurized so at this time in the morning it was cold, but we did our best to make ourselves comfortable. Danny and Gabriel demonstrated that military types can sleep anywhere by reclining their seats, closing their eyes and nodding off almost instantly. Cal —who we'd given the seat by the door because it had a little more leg room—started whittling a hunk of wood with his knife. Bradan put on headphones and started listening to something and JD started tapping out emails on his phone.

I probably should have done the same. I had plenty of music on my phone, or I could have finally given in and started one of the fantasy books that Erin and Danny kept badgering me to try or, hell, I could have scrolled through the numbers of some of the women I'd met in Koenig's bar and see if any of them were up late.

But instead, I looked at her.

I told myself it was because she needed watching, even handcuffed and surrounded by soldiers. But there was another reason.

It was like I knew I was in the presence of something rare, something special, something that'd soon be gone forever and I couldn't waste a second of the time I had left. I would have just sat there staring, but the others would have noticed and *she* would have noticed, so I wound up scanning the plane like a lighthouse, gazing out of the windows at the dark clouds rushing by beneath us until I figured I'd saved up enough time. Then I'd allow myself one quick glance across the aisle and in that second I'd eat her up, just devour her in big, hungry chunks, until all too soon I had to look away again. I'd look at Danny or Cal or out of the window, but all I saw was the memory of her face: the liquid glint of her eyes as she stared straight ahead at the seat in front, the silk cushion of her lower lip and that curtain of long, shining red hair....

"You don't have to fly so low," JD called to Gina. "For once, this is a legitimate flight."

"Force of habit," Gina told him. "Plus, it's good practice."

I looked out of the window and, for the first time, I stared long enough to let my eyes adjust to the gloom. *Fuck.* What I'd thought were dark clouds whipping past below us were actually the tops of trees. My stomach dropped and I looked away. Being at a hundred feet bothers me a lot more than being at thirty thousand feet: I guess the ground feels close enough that I can imagine falling.

An hour passed, then two. I figured we must be over West Virginia but I couldn't tell because it seemed to have gotten even darker, out there, the ground just featureless blackness beneath us. I sat there slowly scanning around. Tanya. The others. Window. Tanya. The others. Window. Tan—

She was gone.

My sleepy body jerked like someone had just touched me with a live wire. Her seat was empty and she was—*there,* halfway down the aisle, slipping silently between the snoring Danny and Gabriel.

I clawed at my seat belt release, jumped up and raced after her. By now, she was passing JD. His eyes lifted from his phone and he stared at her in shock. Then he jumped up to grab her, just in time to collide with me. We both cursed. Tanya was heading for the front of the plane: I figured she must be meaning to grab Gina and take the controls. The only person in her way now was Cal. *"Cal!"* I yelled desperately.

Cal came awake fast and stepped into the aisle. He was so tall, he had to duck his head to avoid the ceiling. He completely blocked her path and I gave a silent sigh of relief. We had her trapped.

But Tanya didn't even slow down. She stepped right up to Cal and punched him, hard and fast in the stomach. And Cal, who I've seen shrug off plenty of hits, just folded and staggered backwards towards Gina.

JD and I rushed forward. I wasn't *too* worried: even though I was hurt, Cal still made a pretty good barrier. We could still grab Tanya before she made it past him and got to Gina.

Except...she didn't head for Gina. She turned to the side, pulled on the big red emergency lever and the door hinged open. Tanya glanced over her shoulder at me, her expression unreadable.

Then she stepped out into the darkness and was gone.

8

COLTON

FOR A SECOND, I froze. Then I forced my way past JD and got to the door, Bracing myself against the sides, I stuck my head out and searched around. Was she clinging to the wing, or to a wheel?

No. Just darkness. She was gone. Someone reached inside my chest, grabbed hold of my heart and crushed it. *She's gone. She killed herself, so that she couldn't be interrogated.* I couldn't breathe.

And then, as I stared down at featureless black, a white circle appeared, spreading outwards like a smoke ring. I blinked as everything rearranged itself in my head. The featureless darkness below us was water: we must be flying over a lake. And the white circle was a splash.

I sucked in a huge lungful of air and strained my eyes, trying to find the center of the splash. I could barely make anything out but I could see movement. *She's alive!* As I got my perception dialed in, I realized how low we were, only about fifty feet above the water.

The splash dropped away behind us. That's when the relief started to fade and a sickening realization sank in. *She's getting away!*

While I'd been staring out of the door, I'd tuned out everything else. Now, I started to pay attention to what was happening around me and it was chaos. With the door open, the engines were deafening. Everyone was shouting over the top of them and Gina was shouting loudest of all, demanding to know what the hell was going on behind her. "She jumped!" I yelled.

"She *jumped?*" repeated Gina. "Where were you guys? There are *six* of you!"

We all looked at each other guiltily. "She was handcuffed," said Danny. "What happened to the handcuffs?"

Bradan, who'd been sitting at the back of the plane, picked up the handcuffs from Tanya's seat and held them up. *How did she get out of those?!*

I looked out of the door again, peering through the darkness behind us. *Shit!* The ripples where Tanya had hit the water were almost gone. "Circle around!" I yelled to Gina.

The plane banked and circled. The ripples faded completely and I stared at the exact spot of blackness that had been their center: if I looked away, I'd never find her again in the endless blackness. Finally, as Gina flew us over the spot again, I made out movement in the water: Tanya must be swimming to shore. "Land!" I yelled.

"It's not a helicopter, you idiot, I'll have to find an airstrip!" Gina yelled back.

"Lads?" Danny's voice sounded small, fractured. "We've got a bigger problem."

I reluctantly turned back to the cabin. Danny was hunched over Cal, who was lying on the floor. I frowned. *How hard did she punch him?*

Then Danny shone his flashlight and we saw the spreading red stain on Cal's abdomen. Tanya hadn't punched him. She'd stabbed him.

9

COLTON

GINA REACTED FIRST. She dug out a paper map and threw it at JD. "Find me a hospital!"

JD stared searching on the map with his flashlight. The rest of us crowded around Cal, who was sucking in slow, shaky breaths. I shone my flashlight on his face and my stomach knotted when I saw how pale he was. I shook my head, furious and worried. "I searched her before we put her in the car. What the fuck did she stab him with?"

We all looked at each other. Then Bradan suddenly bent and groped at his ankle. His shoulders slumped. "My knife is missing," he said sheepishly. "I was sitting behind her. When she got out of her cuffs, she must have reached back and taken it without me noticing."

"Got a hospital," said JD. "And an airfield, about twenty miles north."

The plane banked as Gina changed course. Through the open door, I watched the lake dropping away and my chest went tight. This was my fault. She was my responsibility.

I had to fix it.

"Wait!" I yelled. "Make one more pass over the lake! As low as you can!"

Gina looked at me over her shoulder, confused. Then she saw my expression and her eyes widened as she realized what I was planning. The plane began to circle around.

"You're going to *jump?*" asked Danny.

"She made it," I told him, grabbing my pack and strapping it on. "I can too." I sounded a lot more confident than I felt.

"You're not going after her on your own!" JD told me.

I turned to face him. "We don't have time to argue, boss. This is my mess. If I don't get after her right now, the trail'll be cold. Get Cal to the hospital, I'll run her down and bring her to you."

"Here we go," yelled Gina.

I ran over to the door and looked down. The moon had gone behind a cloud and I couldn't see anything: just blackness. *What the fuck are you doing, Colton? At least when Danny and Erin did this, it was by accident.*

I allowed myself two quick breaths. And then, before I could change my mind, I jumped.

10

COLTON

THERE WAS a second of *oh shit wait I actually did it?* And then the plane was gone and I was falling into stomach-churning nothingness. I couldn't even brace myself for hitting the water because I didn't know where the water was.

I kept falling, picking up speed, now, *plummeting. Shit. Shit!* Gina must have climbed. I'd jumped from way too high, the water would be like concrete when I hit it. *Shit, shit, shit—*

I hit the water boots first and went right under, plunging deep. I was so surprised, I just hung there in the blackness for a few seconds before I thought to kick for the surface. Then my face broke through into air and I gasped and panted. I could see the lights of the plane and it wasn't that high, after all, only fifty feet or so. But it had sure *felt* a lot higher. Whatever else Tanya was, she was brave as hell, to have jumped. Whatever mission she was on, she must really believe in it.

I looked around, still blinking the water out of my eyes. *Jesus,* it was dark. I couldn't see her. I couldn't even make out the edge of the lake, just a little of the water around me.

The drone of the plane's engines was still drowning out everything and I treaded water impatiently, waiting for the noise to fade. *Come on, come on...* I was getting madder and madder, the image of Cal's pale face seared into my mind. This was all my fault: I was the one they'd all trusted to keep her secure. If Cal died, that was on me.

The plane's engines finally faded and I listened. Nothing.

I closed my eyes and *really* listened, holding my breath. *There...*a tiny noise, almost just a rhythmic break in the silence. The sound of her swimming.

I zeroed in on it, turned to face that way and started swimming. I wasn't like her: she seemed to slip through the water with barely a sound, a goddamn mermaid. I was a paddle steamer, churning up the water with my arms and kicking at it with my boots. But I didn't have to be quiet. I just had to catch her.

As I swam, I stewed on how she'd gotten away from me. Was it because she was smarter and more devious than anyone I'd hunted before, so smart that she made me feel slow and stupid?

Or was it because I was sweet on her? My face burned in the darkness. Before I'd even met her, I'd been smitten with her. Borderline *obsessed* with her. And that had made me sloppy.

Well, no more. From now on, it was all business. I was going to catch her and bring her in, even if I had to hogtie her and carry her back to the team with her over my shoulder.

I swam on into the darkness. Every few minutes, I'd stop and tread water, checking I could still hear her ahead of me. It was September, but the water was still cold enough to make me shiver and I was getting tired now. It occurred to me that I had no idea how big this lake was. I started wracking my brains: what lakes were there, in West Virginia? I had no clue. If we'd landed ten miles from shore, we were both dead.

Finally, the noise ahead of me changed, the splashing getting louder. I could hear her wading, and then pushing through undergrowth. She was out.

I flung myself forward in the water, desperate to catch up before I lost her. A minute or so later, I felt the ground under me and staggered up a bank, mud sucking at my boots. Ahead of me, I could just make out thick forest. I hesitated. *What am I doing out here?* I was alone, with no backup, chasing a woman who'd already injured three of us. No one knew where I was. *I* didn't even know where I was. I looked down at myself. My clothes and pack were soaking wet and felt like they were made of lead. I was bone-tired from swimming, it was two in the morning and I was ready to drop.

But I wasn't coming back without her.

I heard a rustling, up ahead. I scowled...and set off after her.

11

TANYA

I COULD HEAR HIM COMING.

I was doing everything I could to move silently. I was stepping lightly, ducking under branches and dodging dry twigs that would snap underfoot. But I couldn't seem to throw him off: he was like an animal that had my scent. And *he* didn't need to be quiet. It sounded like a bulldozer coming through the forest behind me. He was just smashing things out of his way, going through them instead of dodging around them and that made him faster.

He was gaining on me. That made me panic and the more I panicked, the more I made mistakes and the easier I was to track. *Chyort!*

I glanced up at the moon as it broke through the clouds for a second. It was maybe a little after two in the morning. Tonight, at ten, I had a meeting set up with Konstantin Gulyev, the Russian Mafia boss, to find out how he knew the stockbroker murdered by Maravić. That was my only lead, my only chance of finding out what Maravić was doing, tracking him down and finally getting my revenge. I had to get back to New York, get to one of my safehouses and prepare, and then get to that meeting. But first, I had to lose the guy chasing me.

He was still gaining on me and I was getting tired. Between the swimming and the running, my legs ached, but I kept pushing myself on. *Surely he must slow down soon?* I was still getting over the fact he'd jumped from the plane to chase after me. What was it with him? I'd never known someone so obsessed.

Except...maybe me.

The realization threw me off guard and, for just a second, the memories I kept locked up deep slipped free. I thought of Lev. His laugh. How the wind ruffled his hair. The way he kissed me on the back of the neck, so softly I almost wondered if I was imagining it. The way, wherever in the world we were living, he would find the nearest used bookstore and begin filling the apartment with musty books—

I stumbled and almost fell. I recovered quickly and pushed the memories viciously down, locking them away. But I'd lost precious seconds. I cursed at myself and forced my legs into a desperate sprint, on and on until the lactic acid turned every stride into a burning agony. It still wasn't enough. I could hear him right behind me, his boots pounding the ground.

I felt him grab for me, felt the breeze as his fingers closed just shy of my hair, and the fear spurred me on, buying me another few seconds.

Then he growled and threw himself at me. The solid, muscled mass of him took me right off my feet, and we went crashing to the ground.

I rolled and sprang to my feet, panting, a thread of fear unfurling within me. God, the brute power of him...it had been like being hit by a truck.

He was getting to his feet, too, slower than me but so *big*...he spread his arms wide and hunched over a little, and it was like facing off against a gorilla.

He grabbed for me. Time seemed to slow down and I just stared at the hand as it came towards me: the palm that could cup the entire side of my face, the fingers, twice as thick as mine, that could so powerfully squeeze or knead or—

Fortunately, my reflexes took over and I swayed to the side. His hand closed on thin air and I snapped out of it, breathless and furious at myself. I couldn't afford to make a mistake with this man. He might be big and stupid but he was so strong that if he got hold of me just once, it would all be over.

A different sort of thread unfurled inside me. A gleaming silver one that looped right down to my groin, setting off another of those now-familiar tremors. That need to be weak. *What is this?!*

He advanced slowly, taking his time. I faked left, then dived right, rolling and coming up behind him. Before he could turn around, I kicked him in the back of the leg, hard enough that most men would have crumpled. He just grunted and scowled. God, he was made out of rock!

He shambled towards me again. I was running out of tricks. I'd lost the knife when I plunged into the lake. I grabbed a stone from the ground. It was roughly triangular with a good, sharp point...

My stomach tightened. The problem with hitting someone in the head is that it's not like in the movies. To knock him out, I'd probably have to fracture his skull. And if I left him lying out here with a skull fracture, there was a good chance he'd die. That shouldn't have bothered me, but it did.

He grabbed for me again. I ducked under his arm and swung with the stone, wincing, telling myself I had no choice—

His hand flashed up, shockingly quick, and grabbed my wrist. The stone stopped just short of his head. He pulled me towards him, dragging me off balance, and for a moment, our faces were less than an inch apart, our lips almost touching.

He glared down at me.

I glared up at him.

Then he shoved me backwards and I went sprawling on the ground. I tried to get up but he was already on top of me, slamming me back down. A knee pinned one of my thighs to the ground. Then his other knee trapped my other thigh.

I still had hold of the stone. I swung it in an arc but he grabbed my wrist again and pressed it down to the dirt. I clawed at his face with the one hand I still had free. He leaned back, dodging my nails.

Then his hand darted out and strong fingers closed around my wrist. I heaved against his grip, determined to win, or at least to defy him, and for a second we strained against one another. I thought I saw something cross his face, something like respect.

Then he *pushed.* His bicep bulged and I felt my muscles give out. He forced my wrist down to the ground and that was it, I was completely trapped.

I lay there staring up at him, my chest heaving. He'd pinned me spread-eagled, my legs apart and my wrists wide above my head. I instinctively braced myself for what would happen next.

But it didn't happen. He scowled down at me. "Why'd you stab Cal?"

I blinked. I could see the molten amber in those hard, brown eyes. He wanted me, but the lust was contained, an animal trapped behind thick steel bars. "So you wouldn't have time to come after me," I heard myself say.

His scowl deepened and I saw his shoulders tense. He was mad, but not at me. At himself, because I'd gotten free and hurt that guy. And instead of exploiting that guilt like I normally would, I said, "Your friend will be fine."

"Oh, you're sure of that?" he snarled.

"I went *up,* not *in.* I didn't hit anything vital. He'll bleed, but it won't kill him."

His eyes narrowed and then his shoulders fell in relief. He believed me. Maybe he could sense that I was telling the truth, for once. And weirdly, *I* felt relieved, too. It bothered me that he'd been beating himself up. *What's the matter with me?*

"You learn that in spy school?" he growled.

I mentally shook myself and got myself back under control. "Yes," I said coldly. "Very useful in interrogations. You make them think they're going to die and they'll tell you anything."

He stared into my eyes and I saw all the things I'd seen before, when a soldier meets a spy. He was appalled. Disgusted. And—

I quickly looked away, staring furiously off into the trees. *No. Screw you.* I didn't want his pity.

For a moment, we lay there in silence. I could feel him studying me but his gaze wasn't focused on my boobs, even though my vest top had a V neck that was stretched down a little, after all the struggling. His eyes seemed to be trapped on my face, tracing the line of my jaw, the shape of my lips.

There was an unexpected flutter in my chest, stupid and girlish, pink ribbons in the breeze. I scowled and studied a nearby tree stump in great detail, refusing to meet his eyes.

I thought I heard him sigh. Then he flipped me face-down and pulled my hands behind my back. "Handcuffs don't work so good on you," he mused. "Figure you had a handcuff key or something hidden on you, and maybe you still got it. So how about we go back to basics?"

I felt the bristly scratch of rope looping around one wrist and the rasp and jerk as knots formed and pulled tight. Then the other wrist, and suddenly my hands were snugly trapped behind my back. I pulled, testing the rope. God, he was *good* at that: I could barely move my hands at all, but it didn't feel like it was cutting off my circulation. "What are you, a boy scout?" I spat.

He didn't answer. I felt him get up, then he took hold of the rope that bound my wrists and hauled me up onto my feet, so fast and effortlessly that it made me gasp. I tottered and cursed. When I regained my balance and glared at him, I found him staring at me.

That lust again. God, his gaze was like a flame licking over my skin. With my arms behind my back, my chest was thrust out and, this time, he wasn't able to stop his eyes dipping to my breasts. That shouldn't have turned me on, but it did. Then he dragged his gaze back to my face, looking sweetly embarrassed.

"Now you can be a good girl and walk," he told me. "Or I can throw you over my shoulder and carry your ass. Which is it gonna be?"

He wouldn't really, right? He wouldn't just tie me and toss me over his shoulder like some sort of caveman. I stared up at him...

And realized that *yes,* he absolutely would. And *could.*

Another tremor ran down through my body and this time, at last,

I understood what it was about him, why he triggered this crazy, infuriating need.

He was strong enough to overpower me but he was man enough that he didn't need to take me by force. He'd wrestle me to the ground, pin me, tie me...but he wouldn't fuck me. Not unless I begged him to. And that made me melt completely.

A lock of my hair was hanging down in front of my face. I blew it out of the way. "Walk," I told him, trying to keep my voice level.

He gestured to a path and we set off.

12

COLTON

I STAYED two paces behind her. Far enough away that she couldn't mule-kick me but close enough that I could grab her if she tried to run. Between the trees and the clouds, almost no moonlight made it down to us and it was dark and disorienting as a funfair haunted house, with tree branches that came out of nowhere to hit you in the face and pools of blackness that you thought were just shadows until you stepped into the hole. She'd already shown how slippery she was: if she got away from me even for a second and hid, I'd have a hell of a job finding her. So I made sure I kept my eyes glued to her.

Which wasn't exactly a hardship. Her ass was a ripe, perfect peach. I remembered her jeans being pretty much skin tight even back at her apartment and now, soaking wet and glistening, they clung to every curve. It was impossible to walk behind her and not stare at that ass. Or think about bending her over the end of a bed, her pussy rising into view as her upper body sank down. My thumb, tracing down the line of her lips, feeling them moisten and part—

I tripped on a root that had no right to be there and stumbled for a few steps before I caught myself. Tanya looked back over her shoulder and smirked. "*Neuklyuzhiy gorilla.*"

I had no idea what the first word meant but apparently *gorilla* was the same in Russian. I gave her a glare but I was flushing. Did she know I'd been gawping at her? I studied her eyes. Yeah. Yeah, of course she knew. "Keep walking," I growled.

She faced the front and walked. But her steps suddenly lengthened: three quick strides and she was pulling away from me, fading into the darkness. I saw her body tense, ready to run—

I lunged forward, grabbed the rope that bound her wrists and jerked her back. She stumbled against me, her damp hair fragrant under my nose, that perfect ass bumping my groin. "Slow down." My tone told her that I knew what she'd been about to try.

She craned around and glared up at me, then tossed her hair back from her face, flouncing like a teenager caught trying to sneak out of the house. "*Chyort!* You want me to walk, you want me to not walk. Make up your mind!"

I stared into those frozen blue eyes. The perfect, warm curve of her ass was cozied up against my cock, which was helplessly swelling and lifting. I tried to take a deep, calming breath but all I got was her scent, that softness of flowers calming me and, underneath, the tang of berries tempting me in. I opened my mouth but all of the words in my brain had suddenly decided to fly away on vacation. So I just scowled instead.

She pouted, which only made my cock harder. "Do you even have a plan?"

"Of course I got a plan. Now walk. And stay with me, or I'll put a fucking leash on you."

She glared, but walked on at a nice, steady pace. And that gave me a chance to think.

What exactly *was* my plan? When I'd jumped from the plane, I hadn't had one. I'd just known that I couldn't lose her.

I frowned. *Couldn't lose her as a prisoner.* That's what I meant.

I tried my radio, without much hope. All I got was static: the others would have gone out of range within a minute of me jumping out of the plane. I checked my phone and cursed: it was dripping wet.

I'd have to let it dry out before I risked switching it on and even then, it might not work.

I looked down at myself. I was soaked through and, now that the adrenaline of the chase and the fight was wearing off, I was getting cold. We were lucky that it was September: in January, we'd both have frozen to death, running around in wet clothes. Even so, I was starting to shiver as the temperature dropped and the wet cloth pulled all the heat from my body.

I looked around at the darkened forest. I had no idea where we were. I wasn't even a hundred percent sure which state we were in, though I was guessing West Virginia.

I tried listening but there were no voices or music that might mean a campsite, no distant rumble of traffic that would lead us to a highway. This part of the US wasn't an empty wilderness, I knew we couldn't be *that* far from some sign of civilization but I had no idea which way to go to find it.

We walked in grim silence for a half hour but, eventually, I had to face facts. We were soaked, cold and exhausted. This was a big forest and, moving carefully in the darkness, we weren't going to reach the edge anytime soon. It was so dark that there was a real chance one of us would put a foot in a rabbit hole and twist their ankle or break something: especially Tanya, who wouldn't be able to use her hands to catch herself. There was only one thing for it.

"Stop," I told her. "We're going to have to camp. Get some rest and carry on when it's light."

She didn't protest. From the relief in her eyes, she was as tired as I was, even if she'd never admit it. I could hear rushing water somewhere close by and I followed the sound until we came out on a river bank. There was enough room to light a fire without setting the whole forest on fire and we could boil water from the river and drink it: it was as good a place as any. I looked downstream and cursed under my breath. Less than fifty feet away was a cliff and when I cautiously peeked over the edge, I saw the river arc down in a waterfall as high as a two story building. Vertigo made me go queasy and I quickly stepped back. *Good thing we stopped.* The cliff had been right in our path.

I had to figure out some way to secure Tanya while I got a fire going. Eventually, I untied her wrists, got her to wrap her arms around a massive oak tree and then retied her wrists so that she was left hugging it. As I collected wood, she scowled at me.

"Wish I had a camera," I told her. "You look like the world's grumpiest hippy."

"*Idi na hui!*" she snapped. "*Bol'shoy dolboyob!*"

"Oh, I'm a *dolboyob*, now?" I muttered, raking through the grass for twigs. She winced at my pronunciation. "Is that better or worse than a gorilla?"

She shook her head and rolled her eyes. I began building the fire.

"You're doing it wrong," she told me. "Not enough air will get under the sticks."

"I know what I'm doin'," I said firmly. Truth was, I didn't. I might have grown up in the country, but my idea of cooking outdoors involves a smoke pit and a rack of ribs, not trying to build a fun-size wigwam out of sticks with my sausage fingers. I messed with it for a few minutes and then glared at my sad, lopsided pyramid. *How does Cal do this? Fuck it, that'll do.*

I reached into the breast pocket of my combat shirt and slid out my cigarette case. I don't smoke, but it's the one thing I never leave home without. It's a flat steel box about the size of your hand, the corners rounded off so that it'll slip easily into a pocket. One side is carved with the Stars and Stripes. It kept my granddaddy's smokes dry when he was trudging through swamps in Vietnam, and then it kept the sand out of my dad's smokes when he was rolling into Iraq in a tank. When my dad died, he left it to me and when I went off to Basic Training as a wet-behind-the-ears nineteen year-old, I took it with me. I kept my Zippo lighter and some torn-up paper for kindling in it, for times like these. And...it was stupid, but the inside of the lid was just the right size for a photo, and there was even a metal lip that would hold it in place. I had this dumb ass idea that one day, I'd meet a girl: not just a casual fuck, a real, hits-you-right-in-the-chest special someone, like in the movies, and I'd put her photo in there and I'd be able to pop it open and look at it, wherever I was in the world.

I was just a kid, okay? Don't be too hard on me.

The case had kept my Zippo and kindling bone dry and I soon had a fire going. I threw on branches and when I could feel the heat blasting my face, I gradually started peeling off my soaking clothes, wringing them out and hanging them on trees close to the fire. First my black combat shirt with the sleeves torn off. Then my boots and socks and finally my pants. It was only as the clothes came off that I realized how cold I was, and how much worse the wet clothes had been making it. I crouched next to the fire in just my jockey shorts, feeling like a caveman, and let the heat soak into my chilled skin. *Damn,* that felt good. I wasn't sure I'd be able to get my clothes all the way dry, but I could at least get *me* dry and warm, and then I had some dry clothes in a waterproof bag in my pack. I've been caught in downpours enough times that I never go on an op without dry clothes.

Then I glanced up and saw Tanya, still hugging the tree. She was looking right at me but, as soon as I looked up, she looked away. A shiver ran down her body, her spine arching as sinuously as a cat's.

"Cold?" I asked.

"I'm fine," she said tightly. And shivered again.

I sighed, stood up and walked over to the tree. "Come on, come get warm."

She stared at me, her expression unreadable. "Worried about me?"

It shouldn't have been a difficult question. I always make sure my prisoners are okay. Even when they're a two-hundred pound gang enforcer with a shaved head and a full-face tattoo, I don't leave them sitting in the car in an Arizona heat wave while I take a leak, or take them on a six-hour road trip without a bottle of water and a bag of chips. But for some reason, I felt my face heating. "I got enough problems without you catching pneumonia," I growled, and untied her wrists.

She stepped back from the tree and rolled her stiff shoulders. Her breasts lifted under her soaked vest top and I couldn't stop myself staring. When I finally dragged my eyes away, she was looking at me. "What if I run?" she asked.

"I'll chase you."

She looked down at my groin. "In your underwear?"

"In my underwear."

She followed me over to the fire, coolly indifferent. But even she wasn't able to hide her relief when the wall of heat hit her. She crouched down and held her hands out, then started turning slow circles, roasting like a rotisserie chicken. But she was still shivering.

"You've gotta lose the clothes," I told her. "They're sucking all your body heat."

She raised one perfect eyebrow. "You expect me to strip off for you?"

"I'm just telling it like it is, princess. You want to stay cold, be my guest." *Princess? Where did that come from?* But she *was* like some sort of princess. She could be a Tsarina, with the graceful way she moved and that coldly sophisticated Russian accent.

She sat there shivering by the fire for another few minutes before she grudgingly pulled off her ankle boots and then stood and wriggled her soaking jeans over her ass. I watched, trying to keep my face impassive, as flaring hips appeared, then long, shapely legs. Right in the middle of the smooth perfection of her right thigh was a raised line four inches long. A scar from a knife. Rage boiled up in my chest alongside the lust. I wanted to kill whoever had hurt her.

As she struggled to pull the jeans over her feet, I got a flash of black, lace-edged panties and her lush, pale ass. Then she was crouching again and pulling the vest top over her head. Her breasts swayed, gorgeously full and soft. Her black bra matched her panties and that little touch of sophistication summed up everything about her: even out here in the backwoods, even soaking wet and with her hair all messy, she still had this...*mystique*. She was like one of those women who come knocking on the private investigator's door in old movies, all lipstick and come-to-bed eyes. You know she's trouble but you can't take your eyes off of her.

She crouched opposite me with the fire between us. The flames were up past our heads and they gave her a little privacy but it was a shifting, flickering curtain. One moment she'd be hidden from me and the next, the flames would curl to the side and I'd catch a glimpse of creamy-white cleavage or the smooth softness of her stomach. I wound up staring so hard at the fire that I saw bright flames even when I closed my eyes. But it was worth it, for those little glimpses.

She turned back and forth, warming her bare shoulders and arms. After a while, she started plucking at the bra, trying to hold the cups away from her skin. I glanced down at my bare chest. I was already pretty much dry. I'd never thought about it before, but bras must *suck* when they're wet. "Take it off," I thought out loud.

She narrowed her eyes, fingering the edge of her bra uncertainly.

"Or don't," I told her. "Up to you."

She thought about it for a moment. "Are you going to turn your back?"

"That didn't work out so well last time, did it? So no."

"*Chyort,*" I heard her mutter. The flames hid her for a moment. When they broke again, she was looking right at me, jaw set and cheeks a little flushed. "You first."

"Me first what?"

She nodded towards my groin. I looked down at my jockey shorts.

"Then it's fair," she said with a shrug.

I blinked. Was she...*shy?* No. No, no way. I remembered her back at her apartment, teasing and manipulative. This was just another trick to make me trust her, make me like her.

I already like her.

But so what if she wanted me to undress first? It'd feel good to be out of my wet shorts and *I* wasn't shy. I stood, slid my thumbs into the waistband of my jockey shorts—

Her eyes were locked on mine. My thumbs ran back and forth around my waist, stretching out the elastic. It was suddenly very quiet: all I could hear was my breathing. And all I could see were those cold blue eyes. Painfully cold. Burning cold. *Searingly* cold.

This was just a mission. Prisoner and guard. We got wet, now we had to get dry. Getting naked didn't mean a fucking thing. Right?

Right. I shoved my shorts down over my thighs and let them fall around my feet.

13

TANYA

I TRIED NOT TO REACT. I tried not to even look, to keep my cold gaze firmly on his eyes, but as soon as his shorts came down, my eyes dropped like a mountain climber whose rope has been cut. I skittered down onto his chest, rolled off the jutting slabs of his pecs and fell again, grabbing for grip on his washboard abs. Then dark curls of hair entered my vision. *Stop! Stop!* And then—

I was looking right at it. He was half hard and the shaft curved down between his thighs, weighty and *thick*. God, it was as big as the rest of him. I stared at the bulbous, plum-shaped head, imagining how it would swell, glossy and smooth. The tan skin of the shaft looked silky soft and I could almost feel how hot he'd be, throbbing inside me...

His cock twitched, as if reacting to my thoughts. My gaze darted away like a startled bird and found his eyes. And despite all his gruff authority, in that second he looked...*helpless*. Staring at me as hard as I was staring at him.

He hung his shorts matter-of-factly on a branch, then squatted down by the fire. His damp skin gleamed in the firelight, making him look like an immense statue cast in bronze: we were eye-to-eye but he just dwarfed me. Strip someone of their clothes and they normally look *less* powerful but this man was a beast set free. I stared at the huge, hard spheres of his shoulders, rising and falling as he breathed.

He turned away to get another log for the fire and, for the first time, I saw his naked back. I'd been right, the tattoos on his arms connected but I wasn't ready for *how* they connected. Across his back was a scene straight from a heavy metal album cover. A huge dragon was crouched, its wings and tail thrown back, its head lowered. It roared at the prey it was about to attack, a handful of tiny figures an inch high. The flickering firelight seemed to bring the dragon to life, the wings twitching, the scales gleaming. The tattoo was intimidating as hell: even in the roughest biker bar, people would shy away. But...

It's my job to notice little details. Just to the right of the cluster of people the dragon was snarling at, there was another tiny person, this one lying on the ground. And the cluster of people all had weapons in their hands.

The dragon wasn't attacking innocent people. It was protecting the weak.

He turned to face me and my eyes tracked down over the broad curves of his chest and the deep ridges of his abdominals. His groin was hidden in shadow but I could see his naked thighs...God, so thick, the muscles coiled as if he was ready to spring. He rested his elbows on his knees and I stared at his chiseled forearms and those brutish, powerful hands. The raw strength of him was overwhelming. *Strong enough to just pick me up...or pin me down.* The thought sank down through my body and detonated in my groin.

And before I could recover, he raised one of those brooding, dark brows. *I did my part...*

I swallowed. I'd almost forgotten that *I'd* have to get naked, too. I reached behind me to the clasp of my bra and found my hands were shaking. *What's the matter with me?* Letting a man see me naked had never bothered me before. Seduction is part of being a spy and it might surprise you how big a part. And not just the female spies, either. We like to think that only men would be dumb enough to let a spy slide into their bed but plenty of smart, savvy women have given up their country's secrets to a hot guy who whispers the right words.

And that's without even getting into all the other combinations of sexes. The truth is, we're all vulnerable. Everyone needs to be loved.

Everyone except me. I don't love. I don't need to be loved. And getting naked for someone is just a way for me to control them. Right?

I unhooked my bra and stripped it off my arms, laying it over a rock. I told myself that my breasts throbbed because of the heat of the fire, that my nipples tightened from the shock of the air. I tried to look at him...and couldn't. *What's wrong?!* What had happened to the strutting, vampish woman who'd let her dress fall to the floor in the Italian ambassador's office? Where was the woman who'd gasped and moaned and arched her back until the traitorous Russian general she was riding hissed the names of his co-conspirators?

Then I realized what was different. With those men, my body had been a weapon, perfumed and perfectly presented. I'd hoped it would work but if it didn't, I'd just have tried something else: blackmail, bribery, or stroking their ego. But tonight, with this man...it was *my* body. It was *me*. And for some reason, I wanted him to like me.

I took two quick breaths...and looked at him.

He was gazing at me, his eyes tracing a path from my face down to my breasts and back again. When some men look at you, it's like they're taking, stealing little slices of you so they can violate you in their mind when they're alone. But this man *gave*. His lust broke over me like a scalding wave, making every inch of skin sing and glow, making me feel more, not less. A tight little ball of hesitant, awkward pride throbbed in my chest. *What are you doing,* screamed a little voice inside me. *He's the enemy!*

I ignored it. And, breathing fast, I stood up.

Immediately, his eyes locked on that flimsy triangle of black material between my legs. I could feel that I had power over him, knew that this was the part where I should taunt and tease him, but...

But I wanted to feel that lust *there,* right where I lived. I was almost drunk on the idea. He needed to see me. But I needed him to see me even more.

I pushed my panties down my thighs and let them fall around my feet, then stepped out of them. I stood there breathing hard, feeling his eyes rake up my legs in slow motion and settle on my groin. It was dark: could he see?

His eyes widened and then narrowed, glittering. Heat crashed against the damp folds of my pussy lips and rippled outwards through my belly, then coalesced and sank down, becoming an aching void. *He can see.* Then, if I'd needed confirmation, I saw the shadows at his groin move and change, his cock rising and thickening. The ache became needy.

He leaned forward minutely. I watched his thighs tense, his weight shift onto the balls of his feet: he was about to stand, to march around the fire to me and—

The air went thick and heavy. Something was about to happen and I wanted it. It scared me, how much I wanted it.

Then I remembered Lev and the pain and guilt hit me right in the center of my chest, vicious and jagged. *How dare you!* Self-hate flooded out like dark blood and I remembered what I was.

I looked quickly away and knelt so that the flames hid me, then wrapped my arms around me to shield me more. And when I tentatively glanced at him again, he'd looked away, too. He'd sensed that he should avert his eyes. The big brute was a gentleman.

We sat silently for a few moments. Then he dug in his pack and pulled out a waterproof bag. He tossed it over to me and I caught it, confused, then looked inside. A dry shirt, pants and socks.

By now, the fire had dried my skin. I pulled on the dry clothes and had to stop myself letting out a moan of delight. They were comically big on me and there was no underwear, but just being warm and dry after so long cold and wet felt amazing. "Thank you," I muttered.

He just nodded. I waited for him to dress, too, but he didn't, he just crouched there keeping warm by the fire. It took me a while to realize that he was waiting for his wet clothes to dry. He'd only had one set of spare clothes and he'd given them to me. I swallowed, completely thrown. I knew how to deal with any kind of man...except one who was kind.

"You hungry?" he asked. "Got an MRE in my pack."

My training told me not to show any weakness to the enemy. But I hadn't eaten since that morning and after all the swimming and running, I was ravenous. I nodded.

He heated a foil sachet over the fire. By the time it was hot, his clothes had dried enough for him to put them back on and he dressed. We sat side-by-side on a log next to the fire and passed the ration sachet between us. Pasta, in a rich, creamy sauce. What the Americans call Mac N' Cheese, or at least, it was meant to be.

The man grimaced. "Are yours any better?"

"My what?"

"Rations. Russian ones. You're military, right? Or you were."

I poked at the pasta. It was suddenly very quiet, just the crackling of the fire and the soft gurgle of the river. I wasn't used to talking about myself. I've spun a thousand stories, told men I'm an archeologist or a tech executive or a politician's mistress but none of that would work, here. He knew I was a spy. My only choices were to say nothing or tell the truth.

"Yes," I told him. "Army. Then military intelligence." The truth felt strange, coming out of my mouth. I kept my eyes on the Mac N' Cheese. "The goulash is okay. Better than the pâté."

"You get *pâté?*" He rubbed at his beard. "That's some classy rations."

I felt my lips twist into a smile. "You haven't tasted it." Then I caught myself. *What am I doing?!* "I'm your prisoner, why are you being like this with me?" I demanded.

"Like what?"

"*Nice!*"

He just looked at me, those brown-and-amber eyes smoldering, and I knew why.

I felt bad because it wasn't him I was really angry with, it was me. This was the first conversation I'd had in years where I wasn't lying, or threatening, or trying to manipulate someone, and...it felt *weird.* Scary and uncomfortable and disturbing. Hot shame welled up inside me.

I'd been lying so long, I'd forgotten how to tell the truth.

I looked away and we fell into silence. I should have left it like that, just been his prisoner until it was time to escape. But I could feel him staring at me, huge and patient and infuriatingly *good*. I had a ridiculous, childish urge not to hurt his feelings.

"Sorry," I muttered, not meeting his eyes.

"What's it like?" he asked.

I turned to him. "The pâté?" I asked, breaking into a chuckle.

"Being a spy."

The chuckle died on my lips. "You already know that," I said sadly.

He shook his head.

I scrunched up my forehead. "You and your friends...you're CIA."

He shook his head again. "We were *hired* by the CIA. And one of my buddies *used* to be CIA. But not me."

I frowned again. "What are you? Delta? Green Berets? A SEAL?"

His sigh was sweet with humor but bitter with pain. "Nope. Just regular 'ol Army."

That bothers him. I stared at him, fascinated and a little shocked. I'd been caught not once but four times, now, by a regular Army grunt? But then there was nothing *regular* about him. He was *good* at this: at hunting someone down, at fighting them, at restraining them. The best I'd seen. I thought back to his question. "Solitary," I said at last. "Being a spy is solitary." *Solitary* was a euphemism. I really meant another word ending in *y* but I wasn't going to admit to that.

It didn't matter, though. His chest filled and his massive shoulders squared as if he knew damn well the word I meant and he didn't want me feeling that way. The amber in his eyes seemed to burn hotter, brighter, and I felt...*something*. Like a hug without him touching me, or when my grandmother tucked a blanket over me, or when I was lost in a crowd once and a policeman took my hand and helped me find my mother.

It took me a moment for me to identify the feeling because it had been so long since I'd felt it.

I felt...*protected.*

14

COLTON

SHE STARED AT ME AND, just for a second, those pale blue eyes lost their coldness and looked so innocent, I felt like someone had punched me in the chest. Then she looked away, into the fire. Her breathing had gone shaky, like each breath hurt. I narrowed my eyes and looked around for something to thump, the protective rage filling me. *Who did this to her?*

"You know my name," she said, struggling to keep her voice level, "but I don't know yours."

I just glared at her stubbornly, not willing to let her change the subject.

Her eyes pleaded with me to let it go.

Fine. "Colton," I told her. "Colton Stockburn."

It wasn't much of a name but she repeated it silently, nodding. Then she pulled her knees up to her chin, wrapped her arms around them and rested her chin on them, like she was a college kid at some sorority camp-out. Her voice went light and flirty, sugar-sweet but with a husky, Russian edge. "And how did you wind up catching spies for a private military group, *Colton Stockburn?*" She didn't so much say my name as wrap herself around each syllable and I felt my cock go instantly hard.

I stared at her, amazed by the transformation. I knew now this was an act, something she'd fooled hundreds of men with. But knowing that didn't stop it working. God, even in the oversized military gear and with her hair damp and tangled, she was beyond gorgeous. Her eyes sparkled like polished ice and her voice promised pleasures I couldn't even imagine. I was way, *way* out of my depth. Even Danny had fallen for her tricks and he was a fucking genius when it came to women. What chance did I have? I felt like I was clinging to a cliff edge, slowly losing my grip.

And then I remembered how she'd been before, when we'd shared the food. I'd seen the *real* Tanya. Even connected with her, a little. When I focused on that, it broke the spell because I knew how much better that real connection felt. It let me see her flirting for what it was and it was more than just a way of manipulating me: it was *armor.*

I nodded to myself, feeling a little proud. And when I looked into Tanya's eyes again, I could resist...just.

"Not a whole lot to tell," I said. "Army. Afghanistan, mostly. A lot of house-to-house. You kicked in a door, didn't know whether you were going to find a bunch of guys with guns, or a terrified woman. Or sometimes a terrified woman with a gun. Had to be ready to shoot or calm things down." I shrugged. "I guess someone thought I was good at it because they got me to cross-train as Military Police."

I glanced sideways at her. She was listening intently and, now that the focus was off her, the flirty armor seemed to be dropping away. "Sometimes, I was hauling drunk grunts out of bars. Sometimes, it was moving prisoners around the country. And sometimes..." I gave a long sigh. "Sometimes, I'd have to arrest someone who'd done some bad shit. I mean, war crimes level stuff. Executing civilians. Torture. Worse." I shook my head. "You see too much of that stuff, it gets in your head and won't come out, you know?"

Tanya met my eyes, the fake flirtiness gone completely, now. She knew.

"So anyway, I got out, came home, didn't know what to do with myself. Wound up bounty hunting. Then some Irishman came along and offered me a job doing this."

She studied me. "Out of all the things you could have chosen, you became a bounty hunter. You believe in justice." It wasn't a question.

I shrugged. "I don't know about that. I've just seen enough to know there's too many of them and not enough of us, so somebody better do something."

"Who's *them?*"

"Bad guys."

She blinked. "*Bad guys?* You still think there are bad guys and good guys?"

"You think that's dumb?"

She stared at me sadly for a moment. Then she turned away, gazing off into the trees. "No. I'm just envious."

What happened to this woman? I felt this *ache,* inside, as I studied her profile. It wasn't just that she was so damaged, it was that I could see glimpses of the person she used to be, before, and it was fucking heartbreaking. But I didn't know what to say, or how to help, if she'd even let me. I wished Gabriel was there, or Danny. Or Bethany, Bethany's good at talking to people. I felt like a big dumb animal trying to repair some intricate, multi-layered puzzle box, one that was loaded with razor blades and poison needles.

I sighed. "We better get some sleep. That means I gotta tie you up again."

She turned and looked at me, her expression revealing nothing. God*damn,* she was good at that, like a freaking sphinx. Then she held her wrists out submissively in front of her.

I got some rope and bound her wrists together. Then I tied her ankles, too. "Okay," I told her. "Lie down. By the fire, so you stay warm."

She obediently lay down on her side facing the fire. I lay down too, but with my back facing the fire so I could see her. I didn't want to block all the heat, so I stretched out so we were end-to-end, but with our heads overlapping. That left me looking into her eyes upside down. We probably looked like one of those romance book covers where the dude and the girl are lying on a bed. "Well, goodnight," I muttered, and closed my eyes.

I lay there listening to the crackle of the fire and her soft breathing. Then I heard a rustle of clothing. *She's trying to escape!* My eyes flew open and I tensed, ready to grab her—

She was just lying there, eyes open, staring back at me.

I closed my eyes again. Close to a minute went by. Then there was a soft crunch of grass as her body moved. I opened my eyes again—

I was staring straight into that cold blue again. She raised one eyebrow.

"This ain't working," I growled.

"Well, what do you suggest?" she asked coldly.

I sat up. "I need to keep hold of you while we sleep. To make sure you don't run away."

"So you expect me to...what? Let you spoon me? Like we are..."— she paused for effect—"*lovers?*"

I looked at the trees. The fire. Anywhere but her face. "It ain't like that," I said, and rubbed at my beard. "I just gotta make sure you don't escape."

"And to do this, you must lie snug against me so your *khuy*—your *cock,*" she clarified, "—is pressed up against my ass?"

She sounded as coldly imperious as a captured Tsarina, as if having me touch her would be the worst fate she could possibly imagine. I knew she was trying to make me squirm and it was working. "Yes," I grated.

"And if I say *no?*"

"Well, then I guess I'll think of something else," I told her. "Maybe tie us together or something."

She drew in a breath, then let it out with a sigh of resignation. "Fine. You may hold me."

I walked around behind her and lay down, then prepared to scooch closer. It should have been an easy enough job but suddenly, the blood was thundering in my ears. Even in the oversized clothes I'd given her, the silhouette of her body against the fire was enough to make me catch my breath. The curve where her body narrowed at the waist, the flare outwards to that ripe, perfect ass...

"Are you coming?" she asked without turning around. "Or are you going to lie there staring at me?" Her voice still slashed the air like a knife made of ice. But was that a tremor of excitement in her voice? Or was I imagining it?

She felt so small and fragile next to my big body, even though I knew how dangerous she was. I slid forward on the grass until my chest pressed up against her back. That left me on a weird diagonal so there was nothing else for it but to—

I shifted my lower body forward. Our bodies gradually kissed: ankles, calves, thighs...last of all, my cock touched the warm softness of her ass.

She reacted instantly. Her entire body tensed, her spine stiffening. I looked down at her face and saw her jaw tense. *How could you, you beast?* Then she gave a sort of *hmph* and glared straight ahead. Her breathing was definitely faster, now. Anger? Or something else?

I rested my head on the ground. That put my chin against the top of her head and suddenly, all I could smell was the orchid and berry scent of her. *Don't get hard,* I willed myself. *Don't get hard.*

I tentatively slid my arm around her waist. I went slow because I was paranoid I was going to misjudge it and accidentally touch her boobs. But the result was that what was meant to be a simple, businesslike touch became a stroke: I could feel the warmth of her throbbing through the thin army shirt, the smooth, feminine softness of her belly under my fingertips. And that sent blood surging exactly where I didn't want it. My cock rose and stiffened, nestling into the valley between her ass cheeks.

Tanya's breathing caught. I couldn't see her eyes, but I could feel she was staring straight ahead into the fire. Furious or turned on? *Both?*

I closed my eyes. And gradually, I felt her body relax.

I knew I wasn't going to be able to sleep. I never really sleep, when I'm transporting a prisoner. But I could rest my eyes and maybe doze.

She flexed slightly and the lush, soft cheeks of her ass rubbed my cock. *Nope. Not gonna sleep a wink.*

I closed my eyes.

And slept.

15

TANYA

I LAY there staring at the fire without seeing it. All of my attention was on the feel of him against me.

The press of his chest against my back, so wide that it made me feel tiny. I could feel that, if I scooched down just a little, my head would slide into the perfect cradle between his pecs. I didn't, of course.

The warmth of his thickly-muscled legs, their hardness pressing against my softness all the way from my hips down to my ankles. I could feel the brutal, unstoppable power of him: God, a man with muscles like that could fuck all night long, just *riding* you.

Most of all, I could feel his cock, the scalding length of it pressed between the cheeks of my ass. It was already weighty and thick enough that it set off that infuriating weakness every time he shifted position and it nudged against me. And he was only half hard.

Then there was his arm, locked like iron around my waist. His bicep was all of an inch away from caressing the side of my breast and the soft skin was aching and throbbing, crying out to be touched. God, his arm was so heavy, loaded with muscle. I felt like a doll, with it wrapped around me. If he wanted to roll me onto my back, all it would take would be a casual tug with that arm. Then I'd be panting up at the stars as he pulled my pants down and spread me wide—

I glared at the fire, hoping he couldn't see how red my cheeks were. I could feel I was wet, just from imagining...

The brutal weight of his body pinning me to the ground, my wrists in his hands, his lips forcing mine apart. His big hands squeezing my breasts, thumbs rubbing my nipples. His thick fingers opening me, discovering my wetness...

I crushed my thighs together, hoping he couldn't feel it. Inside, I'd gone trembly and flighty. My whole body was responding to him, the warm throb of him against my back resonating through me and dissolving all rational thought. My heart was racing and I felt like I was skittering on ice skates, arms flailing and out of control. A tiny, crazy part of me wanted to crane my head back and whisper to him. Three little words, that's all it would take to slice through the leash that restrained him.

I want you.

I scowled. *No!* All that mattered was tracking down Maravić. To do that, I had to get away from Colton. And to do *that,* I had to maintain my edge. As long as I kept things how they were, *I* had the power. It wasn't the first time I'd kept a man panting and desperate in order to control him: what my old instructor used to call *leading a man around by his cock.* I just wasn't used to doing it when I wanted him as much as he wanted me. If I was leading Colton around by his cock, he had me one growl, one look away from sinking to my knees.

If I was weak and fucked him, I'd lose that power I had over him and there'd be only one way to get it back. The only thing stronger than sex: love.

I knew how to do it, how to take that closeness we'd shared and twist it into a weapon. I'd make him believe I liked him, that we had a connection that went beyond lust.

Seduction is *easy*...fun, even. I'm good at it. Throwing out smiles and compliments, like tiny silver threads that loop around a man. You draw them slowly tight and he becomes your puppet. Then, as you come to understand a man, he hands you thicker threads, golden twine weighty with promise. You wrap it slowly around him: you love his work, you support his beliefs, you promise to one day give him the family he wants. And simultaneously, you snip away the threads connecting him to anyone else. *She* doesn't understand you, only *I* do. He doesn't even realize he's becoming your prisoner. Finally, when he trusts you completely, that's when he hands you the thick, black rope you can wind around his neck: the kinky stuff he likes to do in bed, the money he stole from the company, the traitorous plans he has to overthrow his government.

But when I imagined looping those threads around Colton, something went wrong. It felt awkward and slow, as if something was holding me back. As if I'd somehow gotten tangled in threads myself.

Ridiculous. I don't feel anything. For anyone. Not anymore.

Staring into the fire was hurting my eyes. I closed them and lay there silently, listening to his breathing. I wouldn't give in to temptation and fuck him. I wouldn't seduce him, either.

I'd escape. Working slowly and carefully, I'd untie the ropes and slip away. By the time he woke, I'd be miles away. All I had to do was wait until he was fast asleep.

As I lay there, I became aware of how exposed we were, out here in the forest. That primal part of my brain was kicking in, the one that reminds us that at night, we should be safely in a house or a car or a cave, not *out here* in the dark where there are predators and especially not just lying on the ground with our eyes closed, vulnerable. A cold unease crept out of the dark places between the trees, scuttled over the ground and threatened to sweep over me.

But as it reached me, it slammed up against something solid. A kind of forcefield thrown out by the huge, warm body that was pressed against my back. It didn't feel like anything bad could happen to me, when he was holding me like that. His arm around my waist was a shield, a warning to anyone that might hurt me: *she's mine.*

I was a prisoner, captured and bound. And I felt safer than I had done in years.

I inhaled the scent of his cologne, sharp like grapefruit and then sweet, like chocolate and vanilla. I felt my body relax.

And I slept.

16

TANYA

Somewhere above me, a bird twittered, annoyingly shrill. I grudgingly cracked one eye open and—

Chyort! The sky, which should have been inky black, was a rich, royal blue, lightening towards the east. *I fell asleep. How did I fall asleep?!*

Most worryingly, I was holding onto Colton's chiseled forearm, clutching it the way a child clutches a teddy bear, and I'd hitched his arm higher around me. His arm was now pressed against the underside of my breast in a way that made me swallow hard.

I lay there for a second, furious with myself, listening to his breathing. Thankfully, he still sounded like he was fast asleep. But I'd wasted the entire night and now it was almost dawn. Soon, the light would wake him. I had an hour, at most.

I'd been planning to spend hours on the ropes, teasing them gently apart with tiny movements. Now, I had to work a lot faster and somehow still pull it off without waking him. I slowly bent my elbows and eased my bound wrists up to my face so that I could use my teeth. At least with the sky lighter, I could see what I was doing.

Colton was good with rope. The knots were tight and didn't loosen easily. But he was a kind captor: he hadn't tied me so tight that the ropes cut off my circulation, which would have made my hands numb. I eventually managed to grip the crucial knot that secured everything in my teeth and then, with tiny back-and-forth movements of my wrists, I started to loosen it.

Behind me, Colton stirred in his sleep. I froze, the knot still in my mouth. He mumbled unintelligibly, then his arm pulled me tighter against him. I felt something fill in my chest, expanding until I could barely breathe. A wave of warmth flooded through me, right out to my fingertips. I couldn't help it, I just felt so...*protected.*

Stupid girl! I screamed at myself. *Get a hold of yourself!*

Colton started breathing deep and slow again. I focused on the rope—*only* on the rope—teasing the rest of the knots free. Above us, a worrying yellow and pink glow was starting to bleed into the blue. *Come on! Come on!*

At last, the final knot loosened and I slipped the loops of rope off my wrists. *Free!* But Colton's arm was still firmly around my waist. I lay there, burning precious minutes trying to work out the best way to sneak out. Eventually, I decided to roll onto my back and then slide out from under his arm. I wouldn't have to lift his arm as much and, hopefully, he wouldn't wake.

I took a deep breath and rolled. More and more sky came into view and then *he* came into view, immense and rugged and utterly gorgeous. I paused for a second, gathering myself, and then started to slide sideways—

His arm scooped under me and pulled me hard against him. My face pressed into the warm valley between his pecs. I tensed, about to fight my way out—

Then I realized that he hadn't woken. His breathing was still steady and deep and I felt his body relax against mine like a sleepy child who's found their favorite toy.

I tried to slow my panting. My breasts were squished up against the hard lines of his chest and, since I hadn't put my wet bra back on when I'd dressed, there were only two thin layers of cotton separating us. Each time he inhaled, his chest expanded against my breasts, gently squeezing them. I could feel my nipples waking and peaking, crackles of pleasure racing straight down to my groin.

Then he shifted slightly and the bulge of his cock slipped between my thighs. I swallowed hard. He had morning wood, more like morning *rock,* and the head of his cock was pressing right against my pussy. I hadn't put my wet panties back on, either, and I was pretty sure Colton had gone commando. His cock was so hard, it felt like it was going to rip straight through the thin army pants we wore and surge right up inside me—

I had to struggle not to pant, again. Colton wasn't the only one afflicted by morning hormones. My mind was racing but my body was still in a treacly, horny, fog. Part of me just wanted to mash myself against that big, hard body, rub my softness against him until he came awake, grabbed me and pounded me into the ground.

There was something else, too. When I'd first woken, my back had been deliciously warm but my front had been chilly. Now my front was pressed tight against him and my back was still glowing and protected by his arm around me and I felt so safe and snug...I didn't want to move. I gently craned my head back and looked up at him. In sleep, his face had lost its scowl. He looked peaceful, almost childlike. What would it be like, to feel so secure and carefree?

Then I closed my eyes, took a deep breath and told myself not to be so stupid. I rolled onto my stomach and slid...and this time, I managed to slip out from under his arm without him grabbing me again.

I lay there for a second panting, then quickly rolled over and started untying my ankles. The clouds were lighting up in shades of rose and gold and a line of viciously bright sunlight was slowly advancing across the clearing. I had to be gone before it hit Colton.

The last knot came free and I pulled the rope off my ankles, then climbed silently to my feet. I took one step away from him before the voice of my old instructor in my head pulled me up short.

You should kill him.

I balked and looked down at the sleeping Colton. *Yes,* technically, I should kill him. When he woke, he'd chase after me. He was *good,* at least as good at catching me as I was at escaping. If he caught me this time, I might not get away again. The sensible thing would be to grab his knife and slit his throat. It was...what did the Americans call it? A *no brainer.*

A wave of nausea rose in me and I shook myself, cursing what they'd made me into. *No.* I wasn't going to kill him.

But...I could slow him down a little.

I crouched down beside him for a moment and went to work. Then I crept to the edge of the clearing...and ran.

17

COLTON

I WAS DOWN at the bottom of a deep, warm ocean, slumbering peacefully in the soft sand a world away from my troubles. I was dreaming a dream where this big lunk had found a sinuous, red-haired beauty and they were happy together.

But something was tugging at me. At first, it was just a vague feeling, like a single, tiny fish nudging my sleepy form. But then there was another and another and soon a whole school of brightly-colored fish had hold of me and were towing me upwards. I grumbled and cursed and grudgingly opened my eyes as I broke the surface.

Blinding, pink and gold sunlight streaming down through the trees. The smell of wood smoke from the smoldering fire. And a space, right in front of me, where she should be.

My stomach dropped. *Wait. Don't panic. Maybe she's off in the trees, taking a leak.*

With her hands and feet tied?!

Then I saw the discarded rope. "Oh, *fuck,*" I said aloud. For a second, I didn't move. My thoughts were still tripping over fragments of my dream: seconds ago, I'd had my arm around her at a state fair, introducing her to butter on a stick. How could she be *gone?*

I growled and shoved the dream from my mind. My chest was still warm from her, so she could only have left seconds ago. There was still a chance.

I scrambled up, took my first step—

Something went horribly wrong. My front foot snapped to a stop and my back foot was pulled along with it. I went down face first and thumped into the ground so hard my teeth hurt. I lay there wheezing for a moment. I could feel her getting away but I couldn't move: all the air had been knocked out of me. I rolled onto my back and looked down. *What happened?*

She'd tied my boot laces together.

I finally managed to get a lungful of air, hissing it in through my gritted teeth and huffing it out through my nostrils like a bull. *Oh, so that's how it is?*

I untied my laces, got back on my feet and grabbed the rope, stuffing it into a pocket. I was panting with anger. She had a good head start, now, but I was in luck: the forest was quiet, with barely a whisper of wind. I listened.

There. I spun around towards the sound and listened again, making sure. *Yes!* Someone forcing their way through the trees, off to the west.

I plunged into the forest. *I have* never *lost a prisoner,* I raged. *I'm not about to start now.* My legs pumped, taking me up to a dead sprint. Fury was filling me, pouring energy into my muscles. It felt like a dark, expanding storm cloud, shot through with bright, crackling heat.

I'm coming, Tanya. And when I catch you...

18

TANYA

I'D LEARNED from last time, when he chased me after the lake. I'd run into the forest where it was thinnest, where I could run faster. And it helped that this time, I could see the low branches coming. I had a good lead on him and I figured I should have no problem pulling away from him.

The dawn light was streaming through the trees above, outlining every leaf and branch in a baby-pink glow. It would have made for a beautiful, romantic walk...but by now, Colton might be awake and romance probably wasn't what was on his mind. I tried to move faster, putting as much distance as possible between us.

Then I skidded to a stop. The ground under me suddenly wasn't lumpy and random, woven with tree roots. The dirt was smooth and hard-packed. A path, winding off through the woods. It was the first sign of civilization we'd seen since we swam ashore and it had to lead somewhere. Plus, I could move more quietly on a path. I turned onto it and ran, following it down a slope that became steeper and steeper, until my legs were almost running away from me. Then it rose again, crested a rise...

And suddenly, the trees thinned and ended and I was at the edge of a meadow of waving grass that reached past my ankles. The golden grass was littered with wildflowers and a few industrious bees had gotten an early morning start. But what made me stare was the mist. It rolled across the meadow just above the grass, lit up salmon and gold by the sunrise above, and it felt as if I was running across the tops of the clouds.

I was halfway across when I heard running footsteps behind me. I checked over my shoulder and what I saw made me twist around and stumble.

Colton was at the edge of the field. *How is that possible?* How had he even known which way I went? *He really* is *good at tracking people down!*

I forced my legs to move faster. Maybe if I could make it across the meadow and into the trees on the far side, I could lose him. But when I checked again, he was closer. His big, bulky form was *hurtling* towards me. How could someone so big move so fast?

Then I saw his face. He was *furious,* and the anger was driving him. He was thundering towards me like a steam train with its boiler fully stoked. *Chyort!*

My lungs were straining, now, my thighs and quads burning. I tried to focus on running but I could hear him behind me, each footstep seeming to shake the ground. I was a squirrel, chased by an angry bear. *Prey.*

And just for a second, a wisp of silver twisted down through my body and tugged at something dark and secret, sending heat spreading through my groin. A tiny part of me *wanted* him to catch me.

Then I came to my senses and *ran.* I ran so fast my feet barely brushed the ground, so fast it didn't feel as much like running as falling, plunging forwards at the very edge of control, one slip away from disaster. And still I could hear him, grunting and panting behind me, close and getting closer. I pushed on, pumping my arms and clawing at the air, eyes locked on the forest ahead of me.

His fingers brushed my shoulder and I flinched away and managed to push myself just a little faster. *Come on!* He touched me again and I strained and *pushed,* my legs screaming. Then his fingers closed around my shoulder and, this time, I had nothing more to give. I was smaller, maybe theoretically I was faster, but he'd beaten me with sheer power.

He wrenched and I went down hard, tumbling into the thankfully soft grass. I'd been going so fast that I bounced and rolled over twice before I came to a stop.

He had so much momentum that it took him a few seconds to stumble to a stop. By the time he marched over to me, I was on my feet, shaky from the tumble I'd taken.

We stared at each other. He was at least as exhausted from the run as I was, that huge chest heaving and sweat pouring down his forehead. But the panting and red face only made him more intimidating. He stabbed a finger at me and then pointed to his feet. *Come here.*

I shook my head, not bothering to speak. I figured I should save my air.

He roared, a sound that shook the forest, and ran at me. I jumped back a few steps, panicked, dodging his hands as he grabbed for me. God, the amber in those big brown eyes was *on fire,* glowing like the core of the earth. His gaze kept flicking down to my breasts and it clicked that *my* chest was heaving a lot, too, and I wasn't wearing a bra. He was mad *and* horny. And maybe mad that he was horny. What really troubled me was that every ounce of heat he glared at me seemed to ripple down my body and coalesce in my groin.

"You tied my *laces?*" he growled, and grabbed for me.

I dodged. "See?" I hissed. "I know a few knots, too."

"I oughta put you over my knee, just for that."

"Promises, promises," I panted. Then flushed. *Chyort! Where did that come from?!*

He ran at me and I scurried backwards, praying there wasn't a rogue tree root or stone behind me. He was so overwhelmingly *big!* The rising sun was behind him, edging him in fire and trapping me in his huge, cold shadow. I frantically looked around for a weapon, a hiding place, some clever trick...but there was nothing, just him and me.

He surged forward again and his hand closed on my wrist. My judo training took over: I ducked, twisted and pulled and he flipped and crashed down on his back. But he was up again in a second, looking even madder. *Why is he so angry?* It wasn't personal.

And then I saw something in his eyes I hadn't noticed before. It had been lost beneath all that heat. *Hurt.* He was hurt that I'd run. He'd thought that we'd made a connection.

My instinct was to mock him, to laugh at his weakness. With any other man, I would have done. But with Colton...the words turned to ash on my tongue.

That cruelty people like me have, it's a defense mechanism, something taught to us in training as a way to distance ourselves. We learn that emotions—real emotions—are a weakness, something to be eliminated. We learn that we're better, because we don't feel them. But there was something about Colton that let me see the truth. Not feeling things isn't brave, it's cowardly. And being hurt, when someone betrays you, isn't weak, it's normal. Especially because he was right. We *had* made a connection.

He came at me again and I had to dive and roll on the ground to get clear. I scrambled up, flustered and shaken. *It doesn't matter that you hurt him,* a little voice inside me said. *There's nothing real here. Nothing he feels for you* can *be real. He can never know the real you. If he did, he'd hate you.*

I knew what I was. A fake person, an expendable plastic doll that knew how to fuck but not how to cuddle. Who knew how to kill but not how to have a friend. The self-loathing boiled up inside and with it, the guilt. The only real thing in my life had been Lev. And the only thing that mattered was killing Maravić. To do that, I had to get away.

I centered myself and found my balance. And when Colton ran at me again, I took two running steps towards him, grabbed his arms and boosted myself up into the air, swinging myself up onto his shoulders. Then I scissored my thighs around his throat and clung on.

At first, he just swatted angrily at me. Then he began to move, leaning left and right and stumbling around, trying to throw me off.

But I was gripping with my thighs like a cowboy on a bronco. And now I started to squeeze.

His face began to turn red. He twisted and shook, snorting like a bull, his face contorted with fury. He began to hammer on my legs with his fists but the angle was too awkward: he didn't have any power. When he started to stagger, I knew the world must be getting dim for him and I watched his face carefully: I wanted to make him pass out, not die.

His legs buckled and he fell. I twisted around at the last second so that I didn't wind up underneath him.

We hit the ground and...

I swallowed. We'd landed with him on his back and me facing him, my thighs scissored around his throat and his gorgeous face glaring up at me from between my legs. I was pretty much sitting on his face and the feeling made me go trembly. And I couldn't *afford* to go trembly because he was still thrashing and kicking, tipping this way and that, trying to throw me off. The sheer size and strength of him was terrifying: if I made one mistake, if I loosened my hold at all, he'd overpower me in a heartbeat. *Focus!*

But it was hard. His lips were less than an inch from my groin and every time he panted for air, the hot little blast went straight through the thin fabric of my pants and soaked into my pussy. "Don't fight it," I said, trying to keep my voice level. "Go to sleep."

His face was beet red, now, and he was angrier than I'd ever seen him. I locked my ankles together and squeezed harder. "It's alright," I whispered. "Just sleep."

His eyelids fluttered and he trembled. His thrashing became weaker. I began to relax.

Rule one: *never* relax.

He suddenly *heaved* and rolled us over. Now *I* was on my back and he was on top, his head still between my legs. I desperately squeezed and the hardness of his chin ground against the soft lips of my pussy. Silver-edged pleasure earthquaked out from the contact and I had to fight to keep my mind clear. "Go to sleep!" I grunted through gritted teeth. "*Please* go to sleep!"

Maybe he shook his head in answer. Maybe he was just thrashing around. But the result was that his lips rubbed back and forth across my pussy and it was impossible not to arch my spine and bite my lip. And then, suddenly, one big hand came up and grabbed hold of my left knee.

I squeezed desperately, even though that meant drawing him harder against me. His lips ground against the sensitive bud of my clit. *Oh Jesus.*

His other hand came up and grabbed my right knee. I drew in a shaky breath, panicked, and then—

He *pushed.*

No no no no no! I clamped my legs hard together. But the massive, tan globes of his biceps bunched and I felt my legs begin to open. *Oh, God, he's strong!* I groaned and strained but it felt like there was a tow truck attached to each thigh, hauling them outwards. My legs shook...and began to weaken. I felt space open up between my thighs and his neck. *No no no!*

He drew in a long, long breath, sucking in all the air he'd been missing, and I felt tiny as I saw that huge chest fill. Then he pushed again and my legs opened more. I gave it everything I had and, for a moment, I managed to resist. Then my muscles gave in and he spread my trembling thighs wide.

Right at my core, underneath all the layers of ice, I felt that tremor again.

He lifted his head from between my legs and glared at me. His color was gradually returning to normal but his face was like thunder.

He got his left leg on top of mine and pressed, pinning it there. Then he did the same with my right leg. Then, very slowly and deliberately, he moved up my body, hunkering down over me.

He grabbed my left wrist and forced it down to the ground above my head. Then my right. Now I was spread-eagled, shaking and panting under him. He spoke and that rough, moonshine accent washed over me like liquid sunshine. "You do that to all your men?"

"Only the lucky ones," I panted.

He shook his head slowly. "Someone oughta teach you some manners."

I fought back a rogue urge to snap, '*Well why don't you, then?*'

His eyes raked down the length of my body and I went liquid inside. Then they came back up to my face and I caught my breath as I stared into burning, boiling amber. "I told you what would happen if you misbehaved."

The words soaked into me and sank all the way down, scalding and heavy, exploding like a depth charge in my groin. Did he mean when he said he'd spank me?! I swallowed and stared up at him, my breathing shaky.

He stared down at me and *God,* the lust in his eyes...

Then he flipped me over onto my stomach and pulled my arms behind me. I felt my wrists being bound with rope. My ankles were pulled together and they were bound, too. *What's he going to do?*

He stood me up, ducked and pushed his shoulder into my hips and—

I yelped as he stood and I was hoisted into the air like I weighed nothing. My upper body flopped down onto his back, my lower body hanging down his front. "W—*Wait!*"

He paid no attention. One big arm hugged my legs to his chest, preventing me from moving. And he started to walk, with me hanging like a ragdoll over his shoulder.

I panted and struggled. My breasts were pillowed against his muscled back and all I could see was the ground and the firm curves of his ass. My hair hung down around my face and I had to splutter it away from my lips. "You can't—I'm not going all the way back like this!"

"Yeah, you are."

"No I'm not!"

"Doesn't appear you've got a whole lot of say in the matter."

With every step, my body rose and fell against him, my nipples dragging over the hard contours of his muscles. His shoulder ground against the crease of my hips, a spot where I've always been sensitive, and whenever he shuffled sideways to go around a rock or a tree, that warm, solid muscle would roll against my clit, just for a second, and I'd bite my lip and silently arch my back. It became a maddening drumbeat of pleasure, rolling through my body. I huffed and blew my hair away from my lips, my face turning red. I had to let it out, but there was no way I was going to let him know what he was doing to me.

So I cursed him, in Russian and French and Italian, and then in English for good measure. It helped me vent the pleasure but Colton seemed to ignore it completely. He just kept walking, an unstoppable machine.

19

COLTON

WHEN WE FINALLY GOT BACK TO the clearing where we'd spent the night, I stooped and gently rolled her off my shoulder onto the grass. She was gasping and her face was flushed. Angry, I guess. She tossed her hair out of her eyes and glared up at me.

I was mad, too. But if I was honest, it was mainly myself I was mad at. I should have tied her tighter, or just stayed awake all night to keep an eye on her. She'd very nearly gotten away, all because I let my guard down. The night before, sharing food with her, I'd felt like there was...

What? A connection? I felt my ears go hot. *Idiot.* She'd duped me, that's what had happened. She'd pretended to be vulnerable and I'd fallen for it. Well, that wouldn't happen again.

I opened my mouth, but when I looked down into those cold blue eyes, my words had a multi-word pile-up in my head. *Jesus,* she was beautiful. So many different sorts of beautiful: right now she was *angry* beautiful, and last night she'd been *sad* beautiful and...I sighed. I'd had to hide the effect the walk back to camp had had on me. The entire way, I'd felt those soft breasts bouncing against my back, and that perfect ass had been *right there*, lush and firm and so damn spankable.

I took a deep breath and started over. "We got a fair way to go," I told her. "Could be miles before we hit a road. I don't wanna have to carry you all that way, but I will if I have to. What do you say, are you gonna do as you're told?"

"You're cranky," she muttered.

"Well someone got me outta bed and made me sprint a half mile before I'd had my coffee. Walk? Or be carried?"

"Walk," she said in a small voice.

I nodded. Then I got a stick and dug down in the remains of the fire until I found the parts that were still smoldering, and threw on some twigs to get it going again.

"I thought we were leaving?" she said, sounding confused.

"We are." I felt my stomach rumble. "But not without breakfast." As the flames began to rise again, I set some water heating in a can, and dug out the instant coffee from the ration pack. "I got cookies and crackers," I told her, showing her the packets. "Which do you want?"

She blinked at me for a second in genuine surprise, like she hadn't expected me to feed her again. She studied my face. "Which do *you* want?"

I shrugged. "I don't care."

She frowned. "Yes you do. You have a terrible poker face." She paused and I felt like a mouse in a maze being peered at by a scientist. "You want...the...*cookies!*" she said, grinning. "You have a sweet tooth."

My ears went hot again. *How did she do that?* I turned away and poked the fire. "When we find the others," I muttered, "I'm gonna lock you in a room with Gabriel and the two of you can mind-read each other."

"It suits you," she said. "Just a big *plyushevyy mishka.*"

"What's a *plyushevyy mishka?*" I asked.

She shook her head, still smirking, and I rolled my eyes. Even flat on her back, tied up, she still managed to get under my skin. "Fine," I grumped. "I'll have the damn cookies."

I brewed the coffee. Then I frowned at her. "I'm gonna tie your hands in front of you so you can eat. But if you throw hot coffee in my face, you're going over my shoulder again the whole rest of the way."

Her eyes glittered. "I thought we were escalating to spankings?"

I stared at her. Those icy blue eyes were teasing but I couldn't see what was beneath that. Was she trying to embarrass me, to get me off balance? Tempt me over the edge into grabbing her and kissing her? Or goad me into actually spanking her? Was it possible it was all three?

I leaned close. "Keep on teasing," I growled. "See what happens."

She raised one perfect eyebrow in challenge.

This is dangerous. If I let my gaze drop to that pouting lower lip for just a second, I really was just going to snap and kiss her. But I wasn't going to look away and...*lose.* I *glowered.*

She raised her chin, Tsarina-haughty, and I felt my cock twitch. My mind started playing a highlight reel of all the ways I'd been fantasizing about fucking her. I could feel her nipples raking my palms, hear her cry my name in *that* accent as I plunged deep into that gorgeous, pale body.

She must have read it in my face because she drew in her breath...and the ice in her eyes fractured and melted. But seeing her melt, seeing her *undone* like that, sent a ripple of energy straight to my cock. My eyes went to her lips—

Both of us dropped our gaze at the same second. *Draw,* I decided.

The sun was fully up, now, bathing the clearing in golden light, but the morning mist still curled around the trees. I untied Tanya's wrists and tied them again in front of her. Then we shared the coffee, passing the metal tin between us.

I glanced up at the sun and sighed: I'd planned on being back in Mount Mercy by now. "Hope Atlas is okay," I muttered.

"Who's Atlas?" asked Tanya.

"My bear."

Tanya wrinkled her nose, then shook her head. "I do not know this breed of dog."

"No, he's an actual bear."

"A bear? Like..."—she bared her teeth and raised her hands—"*Grrr?*"

I faltered because her bear impersonation was just about the cutest fucking thing I'd ever seen. "Yeah," I said at last. "A bear cub. I rescued him last year."

"He'll get big," warned Tanya.

"So everyone keeps telling me."

We devoured the crackers and cookies. I was starving. *As soon as we get back to the team, I'm gonna find a diner and get myself some pancakes.*

I glanced up and saw her watching me eat the cookies. She was smiling but it wasn't one of her infuriating smirks. This was more like the smile you do when you see an animal do something funny. Like she thought I was cute.

I thought back to how she'd figured out I had a sweet tooth. "Why does everything have to be a mind game, with you?" I asked.

"Because that's how you win," she said flatly. "Know people better than they know themselves. Figure out their strengths." She looked meaningfully at the cookie packet. "And weaknesses."

"And you do that with everybody you meet. Figuring 'em out so you can use 'em." I sipped some coffee. "Doesn't seem like you'd make many friends."

"People like me can't have friends."

"Yeah, you said. It's...*solitary.*"

She looked away.

"What about other spies? Your own side? Are *they* friends?"

Her head jerked round and she looked at me in shock, like I'd slipped a knife through a gap in her armor. She suddenly looked smaller, more fragile.

I leaned forward and gave her a questioning look. *What?* She had a friend? Or she used to?

She gave a little shake of her head and put her hand out for the coffee tin.

I sighed and passed it to her. And figured I might as well try to get an answer on something that had been bothering me from the start, "Why'd you kill the stockbroker?"

She dipped her head, saying nothing.

What am I doing, I wondered. I'd never cared before why a

prisoner did it. Was I hoping it'd be self defense? Some other reason that made it okay, that made her...*good? What happened to 'I just bring 'em in?'* But I needed to know. I made my voice as gentle as I could. "Tanya?"

She looked at me. Bit her lip.

I leaned closer.

She sprang at me, knocking me flat on my back, and grabbed the handgun from my belt.

20

COLTON

THE WORLD FLIPPED and all I could see was sky. Even as I fell backwards, my stomach was sinking. I'd fallen for her tricks again, let my guard slip because I thought she was sad and vulnerable. I was a fucking idiot.

I hit the ground with Tanya on top of me. All of the air *oof*ed out of me and by the time I reached for her, she was already kneeling, out of reach. My handgun was in her bound hands and she was working the safety. I winced, waiting for the shot.

She brought the gun up and fired twice at something behind me. I twisted around awkwardly on the ground, craning my neck, and saw a guy in military gear fall to the ground at the edge of the clearing. *Oh Jesus.* Had the rest of the team shown up and she'd just killed one of them? I checked his face: no one I recognized. Then there was a rattle of gunfire from the trees and bullets hissed over my head. Tanya ducked and fired again.

"Who the *fuck* are these guys? What's going on?" I panted.

"They're here for me." She got awkwardly to her feet, her bound ankles making it difficult. She glanced down at me for a second. "Trust me, if you want to live. Get my back."

I looked at the dead guy. She'd saved my life.

I scrambled to my feet, grabbed my shotgun and pressed my back against hers. Shadows were moving through the trees. "Two my side," I called. My shotgun boomed and I cut down one guy as he ran towards us.

"Left!" Tanya said urgently, and turned that way, firing again. I kept watching my way, ducking as another guy fired from the trees. He tried to creep around to the side but I tracked him through the trees and fired. He went down and then it was quiet.

"Okay," I demanded. "Start talking, who were—"

A voice cut through the stillness. It wasn't loud, but it had an authority that came with age: it *carried*. His English was good, each word polished smooth but hard and cold, like wood that's been left outside for years. His accent was strong and I couldn't place it: it reminded me of Russian but it wasn't Russian. It was like a strand of rusted barbed wire cinched painfully tight around those polished-wood words, snagging and scraping them. He spoke slowly and as the wire caught and scratched on the syllables, it made the hair on the back of my neck stand up. "*Why are you hunting me?*" he asked.

Tanya went instantly rigid, a deer who's heard a wolf. Even her breathing stopped. I twisted around to look and saw her turning pale. My stomach flipped: it was the first time I'd ever seen her scared.

I strained my eyes, looking into the mist, but I couldn't see a damn thing. *Where is he?* I couldn't home in on his voice because of the sound of the river echoing off the trees.

Tanya's throat bobbed as she swallowed. She took two quick breaths and then managed to yell, "For what you did to Lev!" Her voice was shaky with anger and fear, almost a sob.

I stared at her, worried. *What's going on?* But it was like she'd forgotten I was even there.

The voice came again, indifferent and faintly mocking. "*I don't even remember a 'Lev'.*"

Tanya's lips pulled back over her teeth and she screamed in wordless rage. She snapped the handgun up and fired into the trees, again and again, even keeping going for a couple of clicks after the magazine ran empty. Her arm fell to her side and she stared into the darkness, panting.

There was no warning. He came out of nowhere, *big,* as tall as me and leanly muscled, dressed in black military gear with body armor protecting his front and back. He was in his fifties, with close-cropped hair and a short beard that were both pure white. He was on Tanya in a heartbeat, grabbing her by the neck and hoisting her into the air.

I did something I've never done before. I froze.

It was the way he picked her up. I've seen plenty of awful shit in warzones. But even when two guys are trying to kill each other hand to hand, they make eye contact: they acknowledge the other person is human. But this guy...he picked up Tanya the way a bad-tempered parent grabs a kid's toy they've found on the stairs. It was the most unsettling thing I'd ever seen.

Then his hand started to crush her throat and that snapped me into action. I was still holding my shotgun but I didn't dare fire with Tanya so close to him. *Shit!*

Tanya was trying to claw at him with her bound hands but he was big enough that he could just hold her there, arm outstretched, and she couldn't reach him. Her face turned purple.

Protective fury boiled up inside me. "*Hey!*" I hollered to get his attention, and then I went to work on him, angrier than I've ever been. I slammed a fist into his kidneys, then slugged him in the face. *That's what you get if you touch her!* I was already stepping forward, ready to hit him again as he staggered backwards.

Except...he *didn't* stagger backwards. He'd barely flinched when I hit him in the side and the punch to the face just made him scowl. And now I was way too close to him, and off balance.

He lifted one leg, planted a boot on my chest and shoved me backwards, and I went sprawling on the ground. By the time I sat up and got my eyes on him again, he'd thrown Tanya aside and was marching towards me.

I struggled up onto my elbows, panting, and looked towards Tanya. She was lying on her back, struggling to breathe. I turned back to the guy and he was almost on me. *Shit.* I'd dropped my shotgun, too, it was on the ground behind him. I scrambled to my feet just as the man pulled out a slender, wicked-looking knife. The two of us faced off.

I heard Tanya give a raspy groan of horror. *"Don't! He'll kill you!"*

The guy stabbed with the knife and I had to jump back, panting. *Don't? Don't what? Don't fight him? What choice have I got?*

Tanya rolled onto her stomach and clutched at the grass, trying to lever herself upwards, but she was still struggling to breathe and her wrists and ankles were still bound. She locked eyes with me and croaked one word. *"Run!"*

I stared at her. *Run? Run and leave her?!* I turned back to the guy. *No fucking way!*

He advanced again, passing the knife from one hand to the other and crouching low. I started to get a sick feeling in the pit of my stomach. There was something about the way he moved, quick but not showy. *Efficient,* like a surgeon or a butcher. The knife flashed through the air and I had to twist and dodge. *Fuck, he's good with that thing.* It flicked out again, so close I felt the breeze on my face, and I knew why Tanya had tried to get me to run. If we were both unarmed, I could take him. But with a knife in his hand, this guy was going to kill me.

The knife darted again. *Jesus,* he was good. The knife moved almost too quickly to follow and if I lost track of it even once and dodged the wrong way, it was going to be buried in my guts.

He forced me back and back. My foot suddenly skittered down a slope and I slithered into freezing, knee-deep water. *Shit!* He'd backed me into the river. Now I had a new problem: if I tripped on something under the surface or my foot slid on a smooth rock, I'd go down and it would all be over.

He climbed down into the river too and circled around, forcing me downstream with quick stabs and slashes of the knife. He was making me dodge around to wear me out, and it was working: I was panting and wheezing but he wasn't even breathing hard. Any time now, I was going to make a mistake and that's all it would take.

Then it got worse. The sound of the river became a low roar

behind me. I risked a glance and cursed. He was herding me towards the waterfall.

I got that sick feeling again. Tanya had been right.

He came at me again, getting so close that the knife slashed a burning line across my forearm: I didn't dare look but I felt my arm turning wet. I could feel open space behind me. Water foamed around my knees and the current almost dragged me off my feet. I was at the edge of the waterfall. There was nowhere left to go.

And then I heard Tanya's voice, still weak, from the river bank. *"Get down!"*

There's a trust you get, when you've been working with a bunch of people long enough. When they tell you to do something, you just do it, no questions or second-guessing. I had it with my buddies in the Army. I have it with the Stormfinch guys. I shouldn't have had it with Tanya. I didn't know her, hadn't worked with her, and she was the enemy.

But I had that same instinctive reaction. I threw myself full-length in the water.

A shotgun boomed and the guy went stumbling past me and over the waterfall.

21

TANYA

I KNEW Maravić wouldn't be dead. I'd hit him in the back and his body armor had easily stopped the blast. I'd just been lucky that the force of it had sent him over the edge.

My hands and feet were still bound so I'd had to crawl all the way over to the fight on my hands and knees, Colton's shotgun dangling from a strap around my neck. Now I raised my hands to Colton. "Cut me free!"

He hesitated, but only for a second. He waded over to the bank, pulled out a knife and sawed through the rope binding my wrists, then did the one binding my ankles. I jumped into the river, splashed to the edge of the waterfall and looked down.

Maravić had landed in the river, twenty feet below. He was already crawling to shore, dazed and bloodied but alive. I was white-faced and panting at the thought of going down there. Maravić triggered the same primal terror in me that a wolf triggers in a deer.

But he killed Lev.

I grimly checked the shotgun, then slung it on my back and readied myself to jump.

Colton grabbed me around the waist from behind and hauled me backwards. "What the fuck are you doing?" he asked, incredulous.

I didn't look at him, my eyes locked on Maravić. "Let go of me." My voice was still croaky and rough from being choked.

"You can't jump down there," Colton told me, "you'll be killed!"

I tried to pry his arms open, desperate, now. "*He* made it!"

"Even if you land okay, he's going to have the drop on you!"

I twisted and glared at him. I knew he was right but that didn't matter. "*He can't get away!*"

Colton frowned, trying to understand. "He said you were hunting him. Why? Who is he?"

I was almost hysterical, now. I could see Maravić moving towards the trees. If I lost sight of him... "*Please,*" I begged. "This is the closest I've been in two years!"

I tried to heave his arms apart but he had them locked like iron bands around my waist. One arm was injured and gripping me must have hurt like hell but he *would not let me go.*

"Please," I sobbed. My eyes had filled with tears. "Please, Colton!"

He pulled me even closer, my back against his chest, and pressed his cheek against mine. That low, country rumble vibrated through me. "I don't know what the fuck's going on here. But I know if I let you go down there, he'll kill you. And I ain't letting that happen."

I screamed. I screamed in raw anger and frustration, because after two years I'd finally found him and now he was getting away. I screamed for Lev, for the vengeance that he'd been denied. But mainly, I screamed at myself, for not finding a way, for not sacrificing myself. For being alive.

Maravić heard the scream, stopped at the edge of the trees and looked up at me. His mouth twisted, sneering at me for being so weak.

Then he strode into the forest and was gone.

I went limp and, when Colton felt that, he hauled me gently over to the river bank, then lifted me up onto dry ground and sat us down with him holding me from behind.

And for the first time in a very long time, I cried.

22

TANYA

BEING a spy is about being alone.

At first, it's because you love people. You start to distance yourself from your family and friends because you're worried for their safety, should your enemies come looking for you.

Then, as the job consumes you, you disconnect yourself even more, out of loyalty. Loving people makes you *weak*.

When you sever the last few connections, it's out of shame: you can't stand to be close to anyone because you don't want them knowing what you've done.

Eventually, you're like a comet, tumbling through the dark of space, completely alone and frozen solid. That's how it should be because, when you're completely independent and armored with ice, nothing can hurt you.

In my case, though, I got lucky. And unlucky.

There was another spy, alone in the dark, just as frozen and alone as me. Just as damaged and ashamed, just as good at hiding their emotions. His name was Lev. We worked together, fought together, patched up each other's wounds. And, after two years of circling each other, trying to remember how to trust again, we let ourselves fall for each other, even though such things were forbidden. Our two comets fused into one: a tough, icy shell on the outside but in the very center, a shared molten core that no one could see. For the first time, I knew what it was to be in love. To have someone in your life you *need.*

Then, after just two years together, I found out what it was like to lose them. Lev was ripped away from me, leaving my vulnerable center open and exposed to the darkness. I had no one I could tell, no shoulder to cry on. Utterly alone, I very nearly gave up.

And then, in the center of my pain, I found one thing worth living for. *Vengeance.*

I took my heartbreak and forged it into a new shell, even harder than before. Love was a weakness, one I couldn't afford ever again.

23

TANYA

THE TEARS in my eyes were coursing down my cheeks like I was a pathetic, bawling child but there was no noise, just a silent quaking. I sat there, broken and open, my back against Colton's broad chest. He didn't say anything, didn't ask questions. He kept his arms around my waist, but it wasn't to imprison me, anymore. He just held me. I needed it, and I hated that I needed it.

I felt...*lost.* I'd spent the last two years preparing to come face-to-face with Maravić again and I'd thought there were only two ways it could end. I'd kill him or, more likely, he'd kill me. I was okay with that. At least I'd die knowing I'd done my best to avenge Lev.

I'd never planned for *this,* for some big, stubborn American to get in the way and try to...*save* me. Unless I could get away from him, he'd hand me over to the CIA and they'd kill me. I'd die knowing Maravić was still out there.

It took a while for me to get myself under control. Then I sniffed, wiped my face, and shakily got to my feet. I gave Colton a warning look: *that didn't happen.* And he nodded.

He led the way back to our camp and dressed the wound Maravić had given him. Then he hunkered down by one of the men we'd killed and searched the body. "No ID," he said. He rolled up the man's sleeve, then moved aside so that I could see. A Marine Corps tattoo. *American.* So Maravić was hiring American mercenaries, now.

Colton stood. "You gotta tell me what's going on. Who was that guy? Why's he after you? Why did he say *you* were after *him?*"

I took a deep breath, wincing as my bruised throat opened. He deserved to know. I'd be dead, if it wasn't for him.

And then, just as I went to speak, I realized something. Maravić had tracked us down in the middle of rural West Virginia. Even *we* didn't know where we were. How could he possibly have found us?

The only people who knew I'd jumped out of the plane were the people on it: Colton's team. And the only people they'd have told were the ones they worked for: the CIA. That confirmed what I'd already suspected: Maravić was working with someone at the CIA.

I was pretty sure I could trust Colton. Maybe the rest of his team were decent people, too. But anything I told him was going to get back to the CIA sooner or later. And it got worse. Even if Colton believed my story, he still had to bring me in, and after all this time we'd spent together, the CIA would ask him a lot of questions. If they even suspected he knew anything, they'd torture him to get it out of him, then kill him. Just as they'd kill me.

I wanted to tell him. But the less he knew, the safer he was. I shook my head.

Colton glared at me from beneath knitted brows. But it wasn't anger in those brown and amber eyes, it was hurt, and that made me feel even worse.

He took hold of my shoulders and spun me around, then pulled my hands behind my back. "Fine," he growled. "Have it your way." And he started to tie my wrists again.

"I saved your life," I protested.

"I saved *your* life," he snapped back. "But if you can't trust me, I can't trust you." The rope cinched tight. "Let's get out of here. If that guy finds a way back up the cliff, I don't want to be here."

He kicked dirt over the fire, packed up his gear and we set off into the forest.

24

COLTON

I TOOK her back to the path she'd been following when she'd tried to escape: I figured it must lead *somewhere*. This time, though, we turned the other way because that put us a little further from the white-haired, scary dude.

We walked for close to an hour, with Tanya in front so that I could keep an eye on her. For a little while there, we'd almost felt like a team. But she still wouldn't tell me what was going on so we were back to prisoner and guard. That bothered me more than it should.

The path seemed to be getting a little wider and sometimes, right at the edge of my hearing, I thought I could hear traffic in the distance. Maybe we were getting closer to civilization. Maybe, in a few hours, I could hand Tanya off to the CIA. Then I was going to find a donut shop and buy myself some fucking donuts, and a cup of coffee the size of my head. That was another reason I was grouchy, I hadn't had my morning cup: even the one I'd tried to share with Tanya had mostly wound up on the ground when she dived on me. *I'm gonna get a maple glazed and a strawberry cream—*

"*Freeze!*"

The voice came from off to our left. I whirled and cursed when I saw a guy less than ten feet away, stepping out from behind a tree.

Not one of the military types we ran into before: he was in camouflage pants and cap but he was wearing a bright orange bib. A hunter. He had his rifle leveled right at us.

Tanya reacted first. *"Oh thank God!"* I stared because suddenly, she was from Kansas. Her accent was *perfect,* soft and sweet and as American as root beer floats. "I was hiking, he kidnapped me!" She ran towards the hunter, holding up her bound wrists. "He was going to—He was going to—" Her eyes glistened with tears. *How did she do that?!* "He s—said he was going to—"

The hunter snarled in protective fury and the rifle shifted to point right at my chest. *"Get your hands up!"*

"Now *wait!*" I put my hands in the air, still trying to catch up. "She's not—She's a *Russian spy!*"

I winced as I heard myself say it, but it was too late. The guy gave me a disgusted look. *You expect me to believe that?*

"I swear it's true," I said. "She's my prisoner, I'm taking her to—" I winced and bit it back.

"To *who?*" the guy demanded.

"The CIA," I said, knowing how it would sound.

The hunter shook his head. "Drop your weapons. Real slow."

I sighed and slowly took off my shotgun and handgun and put them both on the ground. "I know how it looks. But I'm transporting this woman."

The man snorted. "On your own?!"

"I work for a private security company—"

"Bullshit!" snapped the man. And with my tattoos and beard, I couldn't blame him.

Tanya had sidled over to the man and grabbed onto his arm. "I think he's a biker," she told him. "He said he was going to have me first and then..." She blinked away fresh tears. "Give me to the whole gang."

The hunter's face turned crimson. *Ah hell.* Tanya was completely convincing. And I *did* look and sound like a biker.

"You're going to jail," the hunter told me. His eyes flicked to Tanya. "You know how to use a gun?"

"I—I *think* so," said Tanya, her eyes huge. God, she was *jaw-droppingly* good at this. "My brother taught me once."

"Don't give her a gun," I said quickly.

"Shut up," the hunter told me. Then, to Tanya, "I got a pistol on my belt. Take it and point it at this guy while I tie him up."

"Do *not* give her that gun!" I pleaded. "*Please!*"

"Quit your yappin'" the guy told me. Tanya slid the pistol out of its holster. "Good," he told her. "Now—"

She smacked him across the back of the head with the pistol and he crumpled to the ground. Before I could take a step, Tanya had the pistol pointed at me. I cursed.

She found a knife on the hunter's belt and quickly sawed through the rope binding her wrists, keeping one eye on me the whole time. Then she searched him and took his phone.

"That accent..." I said, shaking my head in wonder. "Is it just Kansas, or can you do anywhere?"

"I do a particularly good New Jersey," she said calmly in her normal, Russian accent. She stood up. "Goodbye, Colton."

In another few seconds, I'd lose her forever. "That all you gonna say?"

She blinked as if that caught her off guard, then sighed. "Good luck," she said at last.

I knew I wasn't Danny, or Gabriel, when it came to understanding women. I wasn't what people call sensitive. Fuck, most of the time I had no idea *what* was going on in women's heads. But I knew I'd better get this right, or she was gone. So I stared into those cold blue eyes, scrunched up my brow and *thought,* sorting through everything I'd seen in the last few days.

How sure was I? Sure enough?

I took a long, slow breath.

And then I started walking towards her.

She balked, panicked. "Stop!"

"No," I growled, taking another step.

"*Stop!* I'll shoot you!"

My heart was bouncing off my ribs and my stomach was churning like a washing machine but I kept walking.

"Colton, *stop!*" She was panting, now. "*Please* stop!" It was almost a sob.

I took the final step and wrapped my big hands around her smaller ones. I didn't try to take the gun from her, just lifted it so that the muzzle pressed into my forehead.

"Now you can shoot me," I growled. "But you're gonna have to kill me."

Those icy blue eyes *blazed.* Her jaw set and the gun trembled. I felt my stomach flip.

Then her eyes changed. It was like watching the surface of a frozen lake on a hot day, the rock-solid ice slowly turning to wetness. She closed her eyes, threw back her head and unleashed a long stream of Russian curses at the sky.

I gently pried the gun from her fingers and she didn't resist. She suddenly looked so small, so vulnerable, that I just wanted to put my arms around her and pull her to my chest.

A sound made me glance up. The hunter had woken just in time to catch the tail end of the cursing and he was shaking his head in disbelief. "She really *is* a Russian spy?"

I nodded.

He tentatively investigated the back of his head with his fingers. "She had me totally—" He touched where she'd hit him and winced. But he still gazed at Tanya in wonder. I knew how he felt: he was trying to figure out how he could feel angry and betrayed and at the same time be just utterly bewitched by this woman.

I knew because I felt the same way.

I sighed and looked around, planning my next move. It was no good just getting to a road: I couldn't exactly hitch, with Tanya in tow. A taxi was out for the same reason. And I had no idea how far away the team was or how long they'd take to get to me, so I didn't want to just hole up in some little town and have the white-haired guy show up again. We needed to get out of the area and that meant transport.

"Is there a town near here?" I asked the hunter. "Some place big enough that I can rent a car?" I passed him his gun and phone.

The hunter rubbed at his chin, thinking, then pointed. "Follow that path up to the top of the ridge. Take you maybe three hours? It ain't all that far but it's uphill the whole way."

Great. I thanked him and we set off.

25

TANYA

THE PATH PLUNGED into the forest and as the trees grew thicker, the canopy closed above us, leaving us in cool green darkness. Here and there, the sun found weak spots where it could punch through the foliage and it formed golden pillars of light that trapped lazily circling dust motes. It was hauntingly beautiful, the sort of place couples would walk hand-in-hand.

I marched stiffly, silently, keeping a good pace but not getting too far ahead. I didn't want Colton to have any reason to make me turn around. Maybe I could make it all the way to the town without having to look him in the eye.

What happened? One quick squeeze of the trigger, that's all it would have taken. I'd done it plenty of times before. But with him...

In the old American gangster movies I'd watched growing up, the criminals called it *taking him out*. I'd always thought it was a strange euphemism but now, thinking about Colton, feeling him plodding along behind me...it didn't. I'd have taken him out of this world. Removed him from existence. And Colton wasn't like the others I'd killed. They were like cold hunks of gritty stone and all they did was cast shadows around them. A net negative. I didn't feel bad about killing them.

They were like me.

But Colton was like a campfire that threw out heat and light. If I'd taken him out of this world, the world would be a colder, darker place.

I tried to pretend that that was the only reason, that it would be *wrong.* As if I still had that childish notion of right and wrong. But it wasn't.

I hadn't pulled the trigger because he was huge and strong and made me feel tiny and weak. Because he was gorgeous and felt like warm rock. Because I wanted to be the princess to his beast, to have him just throw me down and fucking *ravish* me. Because he was *good,* in a way I hadn't seen in years. And gorgeous and adorable at the same time, and brave in a way I wasn't: brave enough to trust someone.

I hadn't pulled the trigger because...I had feelings for him.

I glared at the ground, my cheeks heating. *This isn't me.* I'd never allow something like this to happen. But he'd blindsided me because he was so utterly different to Lev, to *any* spy. He wasn't devious and tricksy, he was big and straightforward and wore his heart on his sleeve. I'd been utterly unprepared for that. I'd ignored those feelings, pushed them down inside me out of anger and guilt: I had no right to feel those things anymore.

And then I'd tried to kill him and those feelings had boiled up inside me. My layers of ice had cracked wide open, right in front of him, exposing my weak, helpless core.

That's why I couldn't look into his eyes. I had no idea how I was going to control myself, if I did.

The path tilted gradually upward. As the going got tougher and tougher, both of us began to breathe hard. My legs were already aching but I pressed on.

"Hey," he called from behind me.

I didn't stop.

"Hey, wait up."

I pretended I hadn't heard him, delaying the inevitable for as long as possible.

"*Hey!*" This time, there was a warning in his voice. That edge of authority that told me he'd throw me over his shoulder again if I disobeyed. I stopped, but didn't look back.

His footsteps grew louder behind me: I could feel the solid, muscled mass of him through the ground, hear the twigs cracking under his boots. Then his breathing, deep and slow, only a foot or so behind me. He was waiting for me to turn around.

I didn't.

He gave a grunt of disapproval and walked around in front of me. I quickly found a tree to study. *This should be easy,* I thought furiously. I'd looked men in the eyes countless times and pretended I had feelings for them. Why couldn't I do the opposite?

I could feel his eyes on me, the heat of his gaze baking one side of my face, willing me to look at him. My heart started to pound but I stubbornly refused to look.

He sighed and swung his pack off his back, then crouched in front of me. "We've still got a long way to go. Figure it wouldn't hurt for you to carry some of the load. Might slow you down a little."

He emptied things out of his pack and pulled out a second, smaller backpack. He filled it with the clothes I'd stripped off after the lake, a bottle of water and a few other odds and ends. He passed it to me and I pulled it on. For all he talked about putting me to work, the pack was only about half full. He'd kept all the heavy stuff for himself and the gesture made my chest ache.

He stood, towering over me, and started adjusting the straps, making sure the pack was comfortable for me. *Like I'm a child,* I thought savagely, desperately trying to be angry. I realized I was staring at his hands as he worked the straps and buckles, fixated on those strong, thick fingers. *Stop it,* I told myself.

Then something started to happen. His hands slowed on the straps. Then they stopped completely, his palms resting on my shoulders, the heat of them throbbing through my thin shirt. Time became thick and syrupy slow. I could hear him breathing, quick and shallow, and I could feel his gaze, furnace-hot, on my lips. My own angry breathing faltered.

Very slowly, his hands lifted from my shoulders. They began to rotate as if...

As if he was about to cup my cheeks and kiss me.

I set my jaw and made my face like ice. I stared off into the distance so hard I thought my eyes might water.

His hands paused...and then fell to his sides and he turned away. I'd won. But it didn't feel like victory.

We set off again and the trail got steadily steeper. My thighs started to burn from the constant uphill grade. The sun was high in the sky, and I was glad we were in the shade.

After another half hour, the going got so steep that Colton called a halt again. This time, he came to stand in front of me and just *waited* until I looked at him. I kept my eyes stubbornly fixed on a tree root.

His finger and thumb gripped my chin and lifted my head to look at him. I panicked, trying to find something that wasn't him, but he was so *big*, filling my vision—

My eyes met his and suddenly I was falling, *plummeting,* into rich, deep brown and glowing, smoldering amber. I swallowed and my breathing went shaky.

"I'm gonna free your hands so you can climb," he told me. "You run off again and this time, I *will* take you over my knee."

Just the sight of him unleashed all the feelings. They rushed into my brain and locked it solid: it sparked and smoked, a computer infected with a virus. Then he said the part about taking me over his knee and my brain just melted into a pool of molten metal. My cheeks went scarlet and all I could manage was a single, tight nod.

He untied my hands and we began to climb, picking our way carefully up the trail, clinging onto rocks and roots, crawling on all fours when we had to. I stared at the rocks without really seeing them, moving on autopilot. On the outside, I was silent and calm but on the inside, I was a hurricane. *What am I going to do?*

I could hear Colton climbing behind me and I started to breathe faster, my chest going tight. Something I couldn't control was trying to tear me loose from the rocks, spin me around and just hurl me against his wide, muscled chest.

It's impossible, I thought furiously. We were on opposite sides.

You could tell him the truth, a rogue part of me whispered.

And then what? Even if he believed me, he still had a job to do. He still had to hand me over to the CIA. Or was I going to ask him to betray his country? And I'd be putting his life in danger. There was no happy ending where we ran off into the sunset together. There never was, for people like me.

A sudden stab of pain in my chest. Pain was good. Pain, I understood. I focused on it.

A man like Colton deserved better than me. He deserved someone real, not a weapon made of lipstick and lies. He was a good man, a soldier. I couldn't drag him into my world.

I thought of Lev, and the pain grew razor-sharp and brutal. I pressed my mind against it, letting it slash deep. I needed the clarity. *People like me are meant to be alone.* I'd forgotten that once, and look what happened.

I felt my face twist in agony and then I snarled and threw myself forward, climbing as fast as I could. The trees gave way to rocks and thin scrub and the full force of the sun hit us, but I let the heat drive me on, panting and sweating. I swarmed up the rocks, going in a straight line instead of following the easier, winding path.

"Jesus," muttered Colton behind me. "Slow down!"

I went even faster, ignoring the scrapes on my palms and the burn in my muscles. I was climbing almost vertically, now, anything to get away from the tempting, wonderful, impossible fantasy that was behind me.

"Tanya!"

I gritted my teeth and hauled myself up onto a boulder, then jumped and caught a ledge above me, pulled and—

My hand slipped free and I dropped sickeningly. My feet couldn't find the boulder below me and I dangled from one hand, legs kicking, raw fear gripping me.

I heard Colton curse and scramble up the rocks behind me. He couldn't reach me from below so he hauled himself up onto the ledge, lay full-length, grabbed my hand and pulled me up beside him. We lay there panting. "What's with you?" Colton demanded, his voice tight with panic. "You almost—"

I stared up into his eyes. The scare had shattered all my carefully-constructed self control. He still had hold of my hand and the heat of him throbbed up my arm and exploded in my chest. All the unfamiliar emotions slipped free and surged up inside, turning into words. "I—"

Then I saw what was behind him and stopped.

It wasn't just a ledge we'd climbed onto: we'd reached the top. I'd been climbing so fast, I hadn't realized how close we were getting. We were lying on a rocky plateau and I could see the town in the distance. But closer, no more than ten feet away, was something else, something far more important. A patch of waist-high weeds.

I focused on Colton again. Looked down at our joined hands... and let go. "I'm fine," I told him.

He frowned at me. He knew. He knew I'd been about to say... something. But I just stared coldly back at him, brazening it out. A cool breeze was blowing across the top of the plateau and I let it bathe my body and cool my cheeks. I pushed the emotions down inside me, where they belonged.

I'd been saved, just as I was about to do something stupid. Everything was different, now.

Because now, I had a plan.

26

COLTON

I HELD her gaze for a moment longer, stubbornly unwilling to let her go. I'd seen what was in her eyes. She'd been about to say something else. I knew it.

She stared back at me, imperious and icy.

I felt all my certainty crumble away. Had I just misread it? Had she just been shaken after nearly falling? Or had the entire thing, the silent sulking, the slip, me catching her, been just a performance designed to put me off guard again? Did she know how close I'd come to kissing her, when I'd been putting the backpack on her and she was staring off over my shoulder, perfect and haughty and her lips all pouty?

Did she feel it, too? I frowned at her, determined.

She cocked her head innocently to one side. *What?*

I sighed and dropped my gaze. Then I looked towards the town and realized something: this close to civilization, I might have a phone signal.

I pulled out my phone, turned it on and held my breath...then exhaled when one bar appeared on the display. My phone started filling up with missed messages but I ignored them and just called JD. He answered after three rings. "Colton!"

"How's Cal?" I asked immediately.

"He's fine. It looked worse than it was. She didn't hit anything vital."

I sighed in relief. Tanya arched one eyebrow: *see?*

"Where are you?" asked JD.

"The ass-end of nowhere, boss. But I got our friend with me."

"You found her?!" His mouth moved away from the phone. *"He found her!"* he told the others, and I heard a cheer. Then he came back on the line. "Good work," he told me, and there was something in his voice that made my chest fill with pride. There wasn't a better leader in the world than JD.

I told him I was going to figure out transport and then I'd rendezvous with him, then ended the call because I didn't have much battery left. I took a deep breath. I hadn't realized how much Cal's stabbing had been weighing on me. Now, everything was going to be okay. We'd hike into town, rent a car, drive to where the rest of the team was holed up, take Tanya to the CIA and...

And then I'd never see her again. I wasn't ready for the way that made my stomach lurch.

I pushed the thought away. I had a job to do. I started to get to my feet—

"Can we rest for a second?" asked Tanya. "Drink some water?"

I looked at her in surprise. It was rare for her to admit *any* kind of weakness. But she was right, we could use some water after that brutal climb. "Good plan." I sat down and pulled a bottle of water from my pack, draining almost half of it in one go, and she did the same. And of course, once I'd sat down and got comfortable, I didn't want to move again. My legs were aching and we'd been on the go since dawn. I stifled a yawn. "I could use a cup of coffee right about now," I muttered.

Tanya glanced at me, started to speak...then changed her mind.

"What?" I asked.

She shook her head. "It was a stupid idea."

I still couldn't get over that accent, each syllable carved out of ice with a scalpel, each word glossily smooth and heavy with sultry mystique, melting into my mind and numbing my brain. "*What?*"

She sighed and waved at a bunch of weeds. "I was going to say I could make you some nettle tea."

"*Nettle* tea?" The only tea I knew was the stuff Danny, the Brit, drank. He'd made me a cup once and I'd taken it politely, tasted it once and then poured it away when he wasn't looking.

"Very refreshing," she told me.

I felt my brow furrow. "Doesn't it sting your throat?"

She laughed and it was amazing, musical and natural. She leaned forward, hugging her knees and for a second it was like whatever was weighing her down had lifted. "No, it doesn't sting." She shook her head and her smile died. "But we would need to make a fire. It's a waste of time."

I blinked. Just for a moment, I saw two sides of her, fighting it out. One was the cold, ruthlessly efficient spy I knew. The other was lighter, more innocent...and she wanted to do something nice for me.

I *was* tired. I really could use something hot and refreshing. And I wasn't ready to say goodbye to her just yet.

"We're not in *that* much of a hurry," I heard myself say.

She snapped her head round to look at me, almost like she was trying to catch me by surprise, to make sure I meant it. She pressed her lips together hard and there was a need in her eyes that broke my heart: that same need we all have, the need to be close to someone, to feel something...except she looked so completely unused to it.

Then she nodded quickly, smiled and stood. "You build a fire," she said. She marched over to the patch of nettles—

"Wait!" I called.

She looked around, confused.

"You're just going to grab them with your bare hands?" I asked.

She blinked. "How else would I grab them?"

"You'll get stung!"

She looked at me as if I was insane. "It's only nettle stings." And she reached out again.

I don't know what it was that bothered me more, the fact that she was going to hurt herself or the fact she didn't care. But I marched over to her, grabbed her shoulders and pulled her away from the nettles. Then I pulled my shirt down over my hand and grabbed a big fistful of nettles. "There. What do we do with them?"

She just stared at me for a second, open-mouthed. Then she shook her head to herself as if I was crazy...but her face had softened. She sighed, made a big show of slipping *her* shirt sleeve over her hand and took the nettles.

I built a fire while she fussed around with twisting and breaking the nettles so that they'd fit into my metal mess tin. It took me longer than it should to get the fire lit because I kept stopping to watch her. She was in outsize military gear, she had dirt on her cheeks from scrambling up rocks and her ankle boots were still soaked and muddy from when she'd climbed out of the lake. But she'd never looked more beautiful. She'd pulled her hair back to keep it out of the way, exposing new, secret areas of soft, milky skin at the back of her jaw and just beneath her ear. The sun made her tightly-pulled back hair gleam and, as she knelt and leaned forward, I could see the outline of her breasts push out the front of her borrowed military shirt.

I finally got the fire lit, Tanya filled up the tin with water and we set it boiling.

"This is like something Cal would make," I said.

"The one I stabbed?" She said it as easily as you'd say, "The one in a hat?"

"Yeah. He's good at all this stuff. Where'd *you* learn it?"

"The academy."

"Spy school?" I said it as a joke. But when she glanced up at me, her eyes were sad.

"Yes," she said tightly. Then, "It's ready, now."

I wrapped my hand in my shirt sleeve again and lifted the hot tin off the fire, peering uncertainly at the contents. I glanced at Tanya and she nodded, enthusiastically: *go on!*

I blew on it and gingerly sipped, then drank some more.

"Good?" asked Tanya.

It wasn't good. It was terrible, like someone had boiled celery for a week. But she looked so childishly hopeful and proud... *"Mmm!"* I told her. "Refreshing."

She grinned in delight and that made it worth it. I drank half, then offered her the tin. She shook her head. "I never got the taste for it. You have it."

I smiled like I was grateful and finished the whole thing. *That* was a taste that was staying with me forever. "Thanks," I said, and she smiled shyly.

I looked around. The view was incredible, up here. I could see for miles across the forest. There was the lake we'd jumped into and the river we'd camped by. *We walked that far?!* The sun was warm on our bodies and the breeze kept it from getting too hot. We had a fire and I was with a beautiful woman. We didn't have to get going *right* now. It wouldn't hurt to just enjoy the moment.

I sat back, leaning against my pack. I hadn't realized how exhausted I was. Not just muscle-tired but sleepy-tired. But then I'd been up most of the night and I'd only had a few gulps of coffee that morning. I was pretty sure nettle tea didn't have any caffeine in it: maybe the god awful taste was meant to keep you awake.

I leaned back and back. My pack was unbelievably soft...

I blinked and snapped my eyes wide for a second. I'd nearly dozed off. *Why am I so tired?* Already, my eyelids were descending like huge, heavy roller doors.

Tanya crawled closer, watching me carefully, and I suddenly realized what was going on. I tried to make my mouth work. "Oh, you b—"

She put a finger to my lips. *"Shh,* my *plyushevyy mishka."* She smiled as if I was sweet. "Sleep, now."

I slept.

27

TANYA

I smiled down at Colton. So big, so intimidating...but sometimes, he really was just a big *plyushevyy mishka*. A big teddy bear.

I opened my hand and looked down at the little nub of gold in my palm. The top of my ring, which I'd unscrewed as I made the tea to reveal a tiny chamber filled with white powder. It hadn't been hard to tip it into the tea. A very old-school move. But sometimes, the old tricks are the best.

I should have felt victorious: I was finally free of him. But as I knelt beside him, I felt an ache deep in my chest.

I stood, kicked dirt over the campfire and pulled on the backpack he'd given me. The ache became a *pull. This is it.* I'd never see him again.

I was careful not to look over my shoulder as I walked away. I wasn't sure what I'd do if I did.

Getting to New York wasn't difficult. After hiking into town, I skulked in a parking lot near a car with New York plates and, when the owner approached, I burst into loud, messy tears. He was perfect, a married guy in his forties, old enough that he felt protective of me, young enough that he still thought he might have a chance of fucking me. When I told him how my boyfriend had dumped me during a camping trip, he offered to take me back to New York with him. I rewarded him with gentle flirting and left him with a fake email address on a street that wasn't mine.

Ten minutes later, I retrieved a key taped inside an air conditioning vent and let myself into my safehouse, a little apartment in Queens. It was modest compared to the one Colton and his friends had caught me at, but it had the advantage that no one knew about it, not even my Russian intelligence bosses.

I stripped off as I walked to the bathroom, groaning in relief as I pulled off my soaked, ruined ankle boots and filthy clothes. I groaned even louder when the shower's hot spray blasted my body. I scrubbed myself and washed my hair, then wrapped myself in a soft towel and sat in front of the mirror while I applied make-up.

I thought that once the borrowed clothes were gone and I was clean and fresh, *he'd* be gone, the memories washed down the drain along with the dirt. But when I saw my bare shoulders, I remembered his hands there, when he'd nearly kissed me. When I went to apply eye shadow and saw the faint, red rings on my wrists where the ropes had been, I thought of that sudden weakness that had washed through me when he'd pinned me down. I glanced down at my stomach and felt the ghost of his arm there, when he'd held me during the night.

Stupid. I stood and pulled open a drawer of clothes. It was Konstantin, so I went sexy but classic: I'd studied enough photos of his girlfriend that I knew what he liked. I wasn't planning on sleeping with him to get what I needed, but it's always good to have options.

I pulled on a dark green garter belt with gold clips, and black stockings. Then a matching dark green bra and panties with gold embroidery, a dark gray, stretchy pencil skirt that hugged my ass and a black blouse with two buttons left open at the neck.

I pulled on some calfskin knee boots and dabbed on a little scent. Then I carefully emptied the rest of the clothes from the drawer, swung up the fake bottom and loaded up with basics: money, a new passport, a phone, a gun. I threw them all into the backpack Colton had given me, and I was done.

I refilled the drawer and then hesitated, staring at the neat stacks of clothes. I buy clothes the way I buy a silencer for a gun, or a lockpick: *this* dress will work on *this* man and it's short enough to run in, when he's dead, *these* pants are boring enough that no one will look at me when I sneak into this office to plant this bug. I wondered what it must be like to buy clothes on a whim. I couldn't imagine going into a clothes store with friends, buying clothes together for a girls' night out. But then, I couldn't imagine having friends.

I slammed the drawer shut and went to meet Konstantin.

28

COLTON

I was asleep, but it wasn't a comforting, peaceful sleep. This was like being wrapped in a scratchy, too-hot, suffocating blanket. I fought my way up and out—

And immediately regretted it. Someone was playing a drum solo using my head as the bass, hi-hat *and* snare. I opened my eyes and grimaced. If I was just waking up, why was there dazzling sunshine? Why was I *outside?!*

Then I remembered and struggled up to sitting. Whatever she'd given me had left my head swimming and my vision blurry, but I could see that she'd gone. And the sun was well across the sky: she'd probably been gone a few hours.

I crashed back onto my backpack, panting. I was weak as a newborn foal and I was *furious,* mainly with myself. I'd fallen for her tricks again.

I was an idiot. But maybe not as dumb as she thought.

I rooted around in the bottom of my pack and finally pulled out the little gadget that Erin had made for me. I held my breath as the screen came to life. I had to squint to get my blurry eyes to focus but then I saw a pulsating white arrow with a number showing distance.

She was already a few hundred miles north, probably heading back to New York.

The tracker had been too bulky to plant on her body. But it had slipped into the bottom of the backpack I'd given her no problem. And as I hoped, she'd taken it with her.

I pushed myself up to standing. The pounding in my head got ten times worse. When I pulled on my pack, it felt like it weighed a thousand tons and my legs almost gave way. But I managed to get one foot in front of the other and began stumbling down the path towards town.

Tanya Yeshevskaya, I'm coming for you.

29

TANYA

I DOUBLE-CHECKED the address Konstantin had given me, then looked up at the hotel, puzzled. I was in Manhattan, which made sense. The hotel looked ridiculously, extravagantly expensive, which made sense.

What didn't make sense was the plastic tape stretched across the doors. *No Entry. Closed by order of the New York State Department of Health.*

I went around back, picked the lock on one of the employee entrances and crept inside. The place really was lavish. Spotless, thick red carpets that swallowed up my footsteps. Glass chandeliers the size of small cars overhead. I walked the halls for a few minutes but there was no one there: no guests, no staff, not even a cleaner or a security guard. What made it doubly eerie was that everyone seemed to have left in a hurry. The ballroom was set up for a wedding reception: one table held a pyramid of champagne flutes three feet high, another an enormous, four-tier wedding cake. It was like everyone had walked out mid-shift. *What happened here?* I slipped the backpack off my shoulders and stashed it under a table. I wanted to look confident and in control, not like a woman on the run.

A convoy of black Mercedes pulled up outside. I peeked out of a window and saw bodyguards in suits checking the area. Then one of them opened a door and nodded to the man inside and—

I've met many leaders, even heads of state. But not all of them were *powerful*. Some were nothing more than puppets: amicable, empty vessels that the public would vote for, manipulated by someone behind the curtain. Some only won elections because their competitor was caught in a scandal, or only ascended to the throne because their father was killed.

Konstantin? You could *feel* the power radiating from him as he climbed from the car. A family walking down the street towards him suddenly stopped and turned the other way, the mother clutching her children close. A cop on his beat stiffened and then deliberately looked away, not making eye contact.

People forget that the devil isn't just evil, he's *tempting*. Konstanin's cheekbones and perfect, aristocratic nose had been shaped by fallen angels and that full lower lip was pure sin. There was something regal about him: in another age, there'd have been marble statues capturing those features, stamps that showed off that hard jaw. Instead, there were gossip sites full of photos of him in tuxedos and about a million nice respectable New York women who fantasized about what Konstantin Gulyev might do to them.

He smoothed the lapels of his suit. Through the thin fabric of his tailored shirt, I could just make out the shadows of his Bratva tattoos. He turned and offered his hand to someone still inside the car.

Christina. Konstantin's long-time girlfriend, gorgeous and glamorous. There were all sorts of rumors about where New York's most notorious criminal had found his lover. Some say she was a high class call girl. Others an exiled princess. Then there are the *really* outlandish ones, the ones about her being some geeky FBI agent who impersonated the real Christina and switched places with her. But I pay no attention to ludicrous conspiracy theories.

Konstantin took Christina's hand and headed for the front door of the hotel. When he reached the warning tape, he just snapped it: rules were things other people followed.

I pulled back from the window and turned to check my face in a mirror. And that's when I saw Colton standing behind me.

30

COLTON

SHE WHIRLED AROUND and the look of disbelief on her face was so satisfying, it almost made my pounding head worth it. I smiled smugly.

A noise from the hallway caught her attention. "You can't be here!" she hissed. "The man I'm meeting—"

"...is Konstantin Gulyev. I know you think I'm a fucking hillbilly but I'm good with faces. I recognize the head of the Russian mafia."

"He's not expecting an American! He'll kill you!" I could see genuine panic in her eyes. Was she...worried about me?

Footsteps, right outside the door.

Tanya gave a sigh of despair. "Play along, if you want to live!"

She flung an arm around my waist, grabbed hold of my t-shirt and kissed me.

Suddenly, I was falling, tumbling into warm, sweet femininity. My eyes fluttered closed and I think I growled as our lips pressed harder. It wasn't like any kiss I'd ever had: not the soft, sweet kiss at the end of a first date, not the frantic, lipstick-smearing kiss of lovers up against a wall. This was a goddamn magic spell. It drew me in, made me crave more and more. My hands found her cheeks and I kissed her deeper, my lips forcing her open. Her tongue flicked over mine, darkly taunting, and I growled and drew her harder against me, seeking her out and fucking *owning* her. Her silky hair was brushing against the tips of my fingers and I was lost in the softly feminine scent of her. My heart was pounding: God, I was addicted. *Maybe there's a drug in her lipstick. Isn't that a thing spies do?* If it was, I didn't care. I just wanted to keep kissing her forever.

"Who the fuck is this?" The Russian-accented voice was deep, cold and intimidating as hell. Any other time, it would have made me jerk to attention. But I was too deep.

Tanya took control, breaking the kiss and gently pushing me back. "No one," she said. Her voice sounded a little shaky. "This is Gregori. He's just muscle."

I opened my eyes and straightened up, forcing my hands to let go of her. I turned and saw Konstantin glaring straight at us: I gave him a respectful nod. Behind him was a woman I assumed was his girlfriend. She was smirking as if we were cute.

I was dimly aware that my headache had gone. I put my hands behind my back and tried to look like a Russian thug. I was glad now that I'd stopped on the way to New York and grabbed a shower and some civilian clothes: dark jeans and a t-shirt.

"What's the deal with this place?" asked Tanya, waving her hand at the hotel.

Konstantin started to stroll around the ballroom, running his hand over the marble columns, glancing up at the chandelier. "Is owned by rival, doesn't want to sell to me." His English was fractured with a heavy Russian accent. "Last night, scientist from department of health says he find deadly mold. Staff and guests evacuated. Hotel shut down. Owner losing a quarter-million a day. Will soon sell." A smile touched his lips and he wagged a finger in the air. "Scientist no longer owes me gambling debt." The smile faded. "Now tell me, why should I help a spy? Even a Russian one?"

"The Russian government hasn't interfered with your...*business* in America," Tanya told him, walking closer. "That could change. But I can make sure they stay off your back."

Konstantin thought for a moment. "What do you want to know?"

"You were contacted by a New York stockbroker, Castor Barlow, a week ago. Why?"

Konstantin scowled. "He said he was working on some huge deal for someone. Offered to let me buy in."

"Did you do it?" Tanya asked.

Konstantin snorted. "No. He was crazy, or a con man. Told me I could ten-times my money in a few days. I told him to fuck off." He sighed. "Anything else?"

Tanya silently shook her head, her brow furrowed in thought.

Konstantin and his entourage moved towards the door. Tanya and I looked at each other, waiting.

Konstantin's girlfriend was the last one through the door. She looked back over her shoulder at us, grinning.

The door closed.

I pulled out the gun that was tucked in the back of my pants. Tanya pulled out the one that was tucked in the back of her skirt. We got them pointed at each other at the same instant.

"I'm taking you in," I growled.

"You are a *stubborn fool!*" she snapped. "You could have been killed! Just let me go!"

"Put your gun down," I told her.

"Put *your* gun down!"

"You're not going to kill me," I growled.

"Why? Because I kissed you? What are you, a child?" Her face was flushed. "I was acting!"

"Didn't feel like acting," I told her. My eyes were locked on hers. "If you'd wanted me dead, you'd have let Konstantin kill me."

She stared into my eyes. "You're not going to kill me either."

I couldn't argue with that. I thought for a second. "I could shoot you in the leg."

"I could shoot *you* in the leg!"

We stared at each other, panting. Then both of us cursed and tossed our guns down. We began to circle, ready to fight. "Fine," I told her. "You asked for it. I'm not going to go easy on you."

She cocked one eyebrow. "Who says I want you to go easy on me?"

I felt my face heat. She just couldn't stop teasing...

I ran at her and tried to grab her waist. She twirled and kicked and I got a flash of stocking-clad leg as her boot swept towards my head. I ducked under it, rolled, and hit a table, which tilted. There was a huge, sticky *whump*. I ignored it and ran at her again.

She danced backwards across the wooden floor, nimble even in her high-heeled boots. I grabbed for her once, twice, and she ducked under my hands, landing quick little punches on my torso. But I was so fired up, I barely felt them. I grabbed again and managed to snag one of her wrists. I spun her around and yanked her hard against me, pulling her arm across her body to trap her there. The perfect curves of her ass grazed my cock and I could feel I was rock hard in my pants. I growled and grabbed for her other wrist.

She elbowed me in the stomach and I folded. She whirled me around, trying to break my grip on her wrist. But I wouldn't let go and the two of us staggered into another table, which tipped. There was a sound like an avalanche made of glass.

I hauled hard on her arm and she shot towards me and piled into my chest, her breasts soft against my pecs. She tried to punch me in the side of the head but I grabbed her other hand and held it in my fist, trapping her.

We glared at each other from six inches apart, chests heaving.

And then we lunged at each other and kissed.

31

TANYA

IT HAPPENED SO FAST. His lips were on mine, forcing them apart, crushing them under his. All of the lust I'd stoked with my teasing and taunting was unleashed, thrumming down through my body in earthquake waves that shook every thought from my mind. *Chyort!*

We broke apart and stood there panting, staring at each other. For the first time, I took in the scene around us. We'd *destroyed* the hotel ballroom. A table was flipped over and the huge wedding cake was now a firework splat of crumbs and icing eight feet long on the floor. We'd knocked over the pyramid of champagne flutes, too, covering half the floor in a glittering carpet of glass shards. I knew we'd done it in the fight, but it felt like it had been the kiss, that the magnitude of it had blown the room apart.

What just happened?!

I gulped and the cynical, hard part of me, the one that had kept me alive since Lev, took over. *He kissed me!* That's what had happened. The big idiot had lunged forward and kissed me. It showed he was unable to control himself, which meant I could control him easily. I started to make new plans to escape...

But as fast as I shored up the ice walls around me, they crumbled and collapsed, melted by a heat inside. I knew the truth.

I'd lunged forward, too. And when we'd kissed, it had unleashed everything *I'd* been feeling, too. All my lust for the tanned, muscled hardness of him. All my empty, aching needs.

He'd felt it all. Now he was staring at me, panting and scowling. I knew my expression was exactly the same. We were teetering on the brink: start the fight again, or...?

My eyes flicked down over his body. The black combat gear was gone and he was in a plain white tee and dark jeans. That gorgeous, wide chest, like two whiskey barrels, stretched out the white cotton into two snowy mountains. I felt so *small*. A sound slipped out of me before I could stop it, a little sigh of longing.

And that sigh made *him* react. His hand tightened where it gripped mine. His eyes narrowed and the deep brown flared into molten amber. He growled low in his chest, the sound of an animal slipping its chain.

And suddenly, we were kissing again.

Our lips met and I could feel the control I'd been viciously gripping for so long slipping through my fingers. All my training, all my pain was screaming at me to cling on, but he used his grip on my hand to pull me towards him, my soft body draped down the length of his hard one and my control was *going, going...*

Gone. I gave a little mewl of need and tilted my head back further as he kissed down into me. Each press of his lips sent a ripple of pleasure all the way to my toes and it felt light and pink, a teenager being kissed by the boy she has a crush on. It bypassed all my layers of cynicism and ice and soaked straight to my secret, molten core. It felt so good, I wanted to cry.

He finally let go of my hands. *I'm not his prisoner anymore.*

Something tightened, deep in my chest.

Yes I am.

He used both hands to grab my waist and lifted me so that he could kiss me deeper. The heels of my boots left the floor and he pulled my body to his, so close I could feel each breath he took. He kissed me again and again, hotter and hungrier each time, and the light, pink pleasure began to go richer, darker, scarlet. I welcomed him in, *wanting* him to possess me, and that only made him kiss me harder.

We started to move and with him lifting and supporting me, it was like we were dance partners, blindly spiraling around the ballroom floor. I could hear his boots crunching through the broken glass and the sensation of being lifted, almost carried, my toes only just brushing the ground, made me go heady. It sunk in that my hands were free and I grabbed hold of him, wrapping my arms around him and exploring his shoulders and back, smoothing my palms over the delicious, hard warmth of him.

I was kissing him as hard, as hungrily, as he was kissing me. And with each kiss, I could feel all my rules and common sense evaporating. It was like I was inhaling him, drinking huge lungfuls of Colton, getting drunk on him...

He broke the kiss and we stared at each other. My lips ached from how hard we'd been kissing. "The rooms are all empty, upstairs," I heard myself say.

His eyes gleamed. He slid his hands down to my ass and then I was being lifted into the air. He swung me *up* and then *in,* so that my legs went either side of his body. My breasts pillowed against his chest and I went weak as my groin kissed up against the hot, hard bulge of his cock. I wrapped my arms around his neck—God, it was like hanging onto an ox, he was so wonderfully big—and locked my legs around his waist.

He marched out of the ballroom and into the lobby, then up the stairs to the guest rooms. The logical, rational part of me was thinking that we should have stopped at reception to grab a room key. *Or does he plan to just break down a door?* But the logical, rational part of me was having a hard time concentrating because with every step, I bounced into the air and then came down, my nipples stroking against the muscles of his chest and my pussy mashing against his cock. From the way his breath tightened when he took an especially firm step, he was enjoying it as much as me.

Luckily, the cleaning staff had been midway through their shift when the hotel was evacuated. A cleaning cart was in the hall and several doors were open. He marched into one and kicked the door closed behind us.

The room was huge, with a king-size bed and thick, purple drapes that were open to let the light flood in. The cleaners must have just been doing the finishing touches when they left because the bed was photo-perfect, with crisp white sheets and a chocolate on each pillow.

Colton walked us into the center of the room, then looked around, scowling. He was so turned on, so *ready,* that his muscles were like rocks under my fingers and his breathing was as fast and fierce as a bull ready to charge. I realized he was trying to figure out how to get my clothes off when he was using both hands to carry me. "Just put me down for a minute," I said breathlessly.

His scowl deepened and he met my eyes. "I don't *wanna* put you down," he growled.

I gulped. The amber heat in those brown eyes, like rocks being melted at the very core of the earth. He'd wanted me for days and now he had me, he wasn't letting even a half-inch of air open up between our bodies.

He glanced at the wall, grunted in approval, and walked us over there. I gasped at the shock of the cold plaster through the thin fabric of my blouse. He pressed me there, using his thighs to wedge me firmly against the wall. That pushed my legs open a little further, and the bulge of his cock rubbed against my pussy. I could feel my lips flowering open a little from the way my thighs were spread apart and my panties were soaked.

Now his hands were free and he ran them up my sides, making me tremble as his palms just skimmed the sides of my breasts. He captured my head between his hands, his fingertips brushing through my hair, and kissed me again, long and deep. My lips opened under him and I moaned as his tongue found mine and danced with it.

He ran one hand down my body and began to stroke my thigh, sliding his fingers up under my skirt. He reached the top of my stockings and stopped in shock, then continued over naked skin. His thumb bumped up against one of the silky straps of my garter belt and then his fingers found the lacy edge of my panties. I felt his cock twitch. I'd completely forgotten about the fancy underwear.

He broke the kiss for a second. "What the hell are you wearing under there?" he panted.

I smirked. "Why don't you take these clothes off me and find out?" I was trying to find my way back to being *me*: cold and calm, teasing him like I'd tease a cat with a ball of string. But my voice didn't sound like my own: the words came out in a hot rush that told him I was desperate for him.

He stared into my eyes and I felt his cock twitch again. Then he looked down at my legs and used both hands to push my skirt slowly up my thighs. I heard his breathing tighten as my pale upper thighs came into view, bisected by the dark green garter straps with their gold clips. He didn't stop, pushing the skirt right up to my hips, revealing the silky green panties. His eyes locked on the thin panel of fabric that covered my groin and I ground my ass against the wall: it felt like his stare was lasering the material away.

Without words, he unbuttoned my blouse, his big fingers clumsy with lust. Two buttons were already undone and in the space of a few breaths he'd popped the rest and flung the two halves wide. The feel of his cock against me had me panting and he stared at my pale cleavage, rising and falling in its green bra. I swore I felt his cock swell even harder. "You wear all this for Konstantin?" he snapped.

I nodded.

His scowl deepened. "So you could seduce him?"

"If I had to."

His face became thunderous: he didn't like that idea *at all*. I stared at him, amazed. I'd had lots of men want me. I'd never had anyone want to protect me, want to guard my virtue like he was some noble knight and I was...

Like I was someone who mattered.

Deep, *deep* in my chest, where Lev had lived, for a while, I felt something lift and pull, and I had to press my lips together hard to stop it showing on my face.

Luckily, at that moment he looked down, trying to figure out how my skirt unfastened. He found the button and zipper and the thing went loose on my hips, only his body holding it in place. He took a step back, still carrying me, so my back was clear of the wall, and used one big paw to brush my blouse back over one shoulder and then the other and tug it loose until it fluttered to the floor. For the first time since we'd entered the room, he set me down on my feet and my unfastened skirt slipped down my legs and puddled around my feet.

I tottered a little in my heeled boots, my legs shaky, and he put his hands on my shoulders to steady me, his thumbs toying with the straps of my bra. For long seconds, his eyes just scanned up and down over my body, taking in all the crazy silk and lace and finery. It was weird, I'd worn fancy underwear a thousand times before, but I'd always thought of it as a weapon, something to cut through a man's defenses. When it worked—and it always worked—I felt satisfied, like I would if a lockpick worked. I'd never felt pleased or proud because it had never been real.

Colton's eyes finally made it back up to my face. "Goddamn. It's like Christmas."

And I swallowed and said nothing. I couldn't, I was pressing my lips together very, *very* hard because suddenly, it *was* real.

Colton moved closer, then hesitated. He rubbed his beard, glanced at the door. "You're not my prisoner, right now," he said at last, his voice strained with lust.

I understood what he was saying and it sent a big, warm swell of emotion through my chest. He was making sure that I wasn't doing this because I thought I had to. He wanted to make sure he wasn't taking advantage of me. He really *was* a good guy. I nodded and saw the relief on his face. But deep inside, I could feel that tremor again, stronger than ever. That need to feel weak, to be overpowered. Part of me *wanted* to be his prisoner.

His hands closed on my waist and I was lifted into the air again and tossed onto the bed, bouncing to a stop with my legs open and my hair everywhere. A ball of energy took flight in my chest and started to thump back and forth inside me in a gradually building drumbeat. Colton climbed onto the bed, his hulking form filling my vision. He stared down at me as he stripped the white t-shirt over his head.

Chyort! He seemed even bigger, topless, and a pulse of dark heat shot down to my groin as I took in the sheer power of him. Shoulders that looked like they could carry tree trunks—or carry *me*. That huge, curving chest that gave him all the strength he needed to pin someone down. Biceps like smooth caramel melons that could throw me effortlessly around, *pull* and *press* and *spread* me exactly how he wanted. Below that, the hard ridges of his abdominals, leading my eyes down like a flight of steps to the bulge of his cock under the tight denim of his jeans. The *real* source of his power. I remembered the size of him, from when we'd stripped off by the campfire, and my groin tightened.

He put a knee between my legs and hunkered down over me. I felt my heart rev like a race car and the energy thumped inside me faster and faster, each impact soaking me with heat. He leaned down and brushed my cheek with a knuckle and the tenderness set off an unexpected flurry of silver stars that made my chest ache.

He leaned down to kiss me.

On impulse, I twisted my face away and he got my cheek.

He frowned at me, confused, and moved in again. This time, I put my hand on his face and pushed him away, going melty at how good his lips felt against my palm. He moved back, and I kept pushing. On instinct, he grabbed my wrist.

I stopped dead and let my arm go limp, my heart pounding.

He looked at me.

I looked at him.

Slowly, experimentally, he pushed my wrist towards the bed. A wave of heat rippled down to my groin, so strong my whole body flexed. I slid my other wrist up above my head so that as his hand came down, it caught both of them, pinning them down to the pillow. I was captured.

Realization dawned on his face and I felt my cheeks go hot,

embarrassed in a way I'd never been, before. I'd never shared this part of me.

But Colton didn't look shocked or appalled. His eyes glowed like hot coals hit by a rush of air. "So *that's* how it is," he murmured.

I swallowed and nodded.

I could see him re-running all my teasing in his mind. "I guess your safeword really *is* Cincinnati," he said, staring into my eyes.

The ball of energy sped up, becoming a blur as it thumped back and forth.

He leaned forward, pressing my wrists down harder. "Better be careful what you wish for, princess," he told me, his voice thick with lust.

I tried pushing upwards with my wrists, just to see if I could free myself. His hand didn't move at all. I pushed harder, then as hard as I could, but I might as well have been trying to lift a truck. I was helpless.

The now-familiar tremor ran through my core again but this time it was ten times stronger, a vibration that turned my center to liquid heat and sent hairline cracks through the walls of ice around me.

He reached down and grabbed the waistband of my panties, dragging them midway down my thighs. He looked down the length of my body at what he'd just revealed. "Well, ain't *that* just the prettiest thing in the world?" he murmured, and that rough moonshine voice soaked into my brain like blazing summer sunshine and unleashed a rush of pride that took me off guard.

He couldn't get my panties down any further with his hand while he was still gripping my wrists, so he hooked them with the toe of his boot instead and shoved them down my legs, over my boots and off. He put both knees between mine and then pushed outward. I swallowed as my legs began to open. I tried to resist, tensing my thighs and then straining, but it was like trying to hold back the tide. I opened wide and felt the cool air of the room against my sopping folds.

I panted, my eyes already on the bulge in his jeans. But instead of opening his pants, he slid his hand slowly down over my bare stomach, down between my spread thighs. His palm pressed against my pubis and then his fingers began to stroke my lips. My eyes went wide. I hadn't expected *this*. None of the men I'd been with since Lev had cared about my pleasure.

His fingers went to work, surprisingly skilled and gentle. He knew just the rhythm to use and just the right pressure, sending twisting streamers of pleasure up through my body. I arched my back and bit my lip.

He rubbed faster and the heels of my boots dug hard into the bed. The pleasure was feeding that ball of energy that slammed back and forth inside me, making me grind my ass against the sheets and pant with need.

He suddenly slid a finger up inside me and I bucked and writhed. God, his fingers were so *big,* and deliciously knobbly and strong. He began to fuck me with it, dragging it slowly back against my silken walls and then slamming it deep. I caught my breath as a steady strum of pleasure started to throb through me but I was off balance, too. I'd wanted him to pin me down, be rough with me, but I hadn't thought he'd focus on making me *come*. That was alien to me, scary: no man ever saw me come, not for real. "Just fuck me!" I begged.

"No," he said, and that one word echoed around the room. "You wanted this. Now you're going to come for me."

I stared up at him, astonished...and then the tremor in my core hit me again, harder than ever. I really *wasn't* in control.

The finger inside me moved faster. I stared down at his hand, watching it grind and move against me. My vision tracked up over his wrist and the thick length of his veined forearm. Up over the hard swell of his bicep and the huge, rounded bulk of his shoulder to his chest and torso. Only his finger was inside me but I could feel the entire brute power of him connected to it and that made me go heady.

He hooked his finger, found that secret spot and circled. My head went back and my boot heels danced on the bed. The pleasure swelled and surged up through me, filling me. "Oh God," I panted. I was going to come, at the hands of this big, gorgeous brute, and there was nothing I could do to stop it. The thought was scary...and darkly exciting. "*Chyort! B'lyad, b'lyad!*"

He didn't understand what I was saying but he could understand the noises I was making. He started brushing his thumb lightly over my clit in unpredictable little swipes, each one carrying me higher. "*God!*" I panted.

He leaned down until his lips almost brushed my ear. "Come for me, Tanya."

His country accent was exactly the rough friction I needed to send me over the edge. The pleasure spiked and exploded, stealing my breath and making every muscle tense. The orgasm rolled through me in long, shuddering waves and I felt myself spasm and flutter around his finger. Then I flopped on the bed, panting and red-faced. *What did I just do,* I wondered. I never let my guard down like that with anyone, never exposed myself, never let them see me...*vulnerable*. But with him, I had.

And it felt really, really good.

Colton was kneeling over me, my wrists still held in one hand. He reached down and started to unfasten his belt.

The ball of energy inside me, which had barely slowed, sped up again, ricocheting around inside me. I watched as Colton's belt buckle opened and he started to pop the button on his jeans—

"Fuck," he said suddenly.

"What?"

"I don't bring condoms on missions. I'm not *Danny!*"

"In my purse,' I said quickly. "Side compartment."

One-handed, he retrieved my purse from the floor, dug in it and retrieved a condom. He shoved his jeans down his thighs and—*God,* his cock reared up, hanging over me, hypnotic. He was even bigger than I remembered, and a pulse of dark heat throbbed down to my groin.

He looked at my near-naked body and then down at his cock. He stroked himself and I stared at the rock-hard shaft and satiny-smooth head. *Chyort!*

Then he looked at the condom and scowled. "You really *were* ready to sleep with Konstantin."

I nodded dumbly and his scowl deepened. This was about more than him protecting my virtue. He was jealous.

I wasn't ready for the way that made my stomach flip-flop. Not even Lev had wanted to keep me for himself. Spies are pragmatic. Colton was anything but. Old-fashioned and possessive and...

...and I realized I liked that. I'd just forgotten what it felt like, to have someone feel that way about me.

Colton kept his eyes locked on mine as he savagely ripped open the condom packet. *This is mine, now.* He rolled the condom down his cock, then positioned himself. *And so are you.*

He rammed himself into me and I drew in a strangled gasp as he stretched me, *filled* me. God, the size of him: I was just a gossamer sheet of pleasure wrapped tightly around him, feeling every vein. My feet came up off the bed, kicking in the air.

He leaned down low over me, bringing his face to within inches of mine, staring into my eyes. He wanted to make sure he wasn't hurting me but there was only tight, silken pleasure. I panted up at him...and he pushed with his hips and sank deeper.

I groaned, rolling my hips and rubbing my inner thighs against his muscled legs, delighting in the rugged hardness of him. He growled, withdrew a little and then surged forward again, pressing me down into the bed. My toes danced inside my boots as I felt him go deeper, *deeper*...and then his balls kissed my body and I knew he was hilted inside me.

He stretched out, settling himself on top of me. The weight of him pinned me completely, and that sent another tremor shooting through my core. I'd been so focused on how good he felt inside me, I'd almost forgotten he was holding my wrists. But now I began pushing upwards, not just with my wrists but with my whole body, fighting him.

He didn't move *at all.* His grip on my wrists was like iron and my body was like a toy beneath his. I was powerless, and the feeling of that unlocked something in my chest.

His hard ass rose and as his cock moved within me, pink pleasure flooded out from every sensitive inch he touched, light and intoxicating as champagne bubbles. Then, just as the gorgeous head was about to leave me, he slammed back into me and the pleasure compressed, becoming darker and hotter.

I arched my back and rolled my head on the pillow in ecstasy... and saw movement out of the corner of my eye. There was a huge, gilt-framed mirror across the room and I could see us fucking: my pale body stretched out beneath Colton's big, brutish one, the light gleaming on the hard contours of his back as he thrust into me. I could see my legs, wantonly spread and softly kicking, still in knee boots and thigh-highs, and glimpses of the dark green garter belt and bra against my paleness. There was something about the combination of all my over-the-top finery and Colton fucking me like some big, tattooed beast that sent a ripple of dark heat down to my groin.

Colton's thrusts sped up and I groaned as the pleasure tightened. The ball of energy slamming inside me was white-hot, now, *desperate.* God, he was so deliciously, roughly *big.* The bed was king size but I could still feel it moving under the power of his strokes and his pecs and abs were gloriously hard against the softness of my body. Each time he entered me it was tight, satiny perfection and on the end of each thrust, the base of his cock ground against my clit and added a sparkling, silver edge to the pleasure. My mind was whirling, drunk on raw sensation. I was used to being active during sex, being a moaning, sighing actress, lying to the man about how great he was as I rode him. *I* fucked *them.* I'd forgotten what it was like to lie there and *be* fucked.

He leaned back for a moment and gazed down at me, eyes hooded with lust. Then he suddenly shoved his free hand beneath my back. "I've gotta see them again," he told me. "Been thinking about them ever since the campfire."

He undid the clasp of my bra and it came loose around my chest. He pulled the cups off my breasts and I drew in my breath as the cool air bathed my breasts. Colton's eyes ate me up. "God*damn,* you're beautiful," he breathed, and a pulse of...*something* went straight to the center of my chest. He was so honest about what he felt. He sounded like a teenager talking to his girl as they made out after prom. He was the complete opposite of all the men I knew, with their games and tricks. The complete opposite of *me*.

Then his mouth descended on my breast and I lost the ability to think. His mouth opened wide to engulf me, sucking the soft flesh while his tongue lashed across my nipple. At the same time, he started thrusting again, his cock plunging deep as his tongue twirled and teased and coaxed my nipple into aching hardness.

The pleasure doubled, trebled. The energy slamming in my chest screamed to escape, an orgasm, close now. My legs kicked up in the air either side of his body, then scissored inward until the heels of my boots were on his ass, urging him on. He started to build the pace, his cock pounding me, his big body crushing me into the bed in just the right way.

I pushed against the hands holding my wrists. I twisted, I *struggled.* Not because I wanted to escape but because the more I tried and the more it didn't work, the more powerless I felt.

And the more powerless I felt, the more I could *just...let...go.*

I could feel the climax thundering towards me, now, and I let out something like a sob as the pleasure took over and the last shreds of control slipped through my fingers.

Colton's thrusts became a blur. The climax swelled and shook, about to burst. Then he teased my hardened nipple with his teeth and that tipped me over the edge.

My heels pressed on his ass, grinding him into me as I felt him shoot in long, hot streams inside me. I cried out long and hard and then his lips came down on mine and I was yelling into his kiss, panting and cursing as the orgasm picked me up and carried me, a doll in a hurricane. We rode the pleasure for long minutes, our bodies so tight together it felt like we'd become one.

Then slowly, very slowly, like a leaf drifting lazily down to the earth, I came back to myself. I opened my eyes and stared straight into that heated amber brown.

We stared at each other. *What happens now?*

I realized that he'd released my wrists. I lifted them experimentally, not used to being free.

Then I wrapped my arms around his back and pulled him close, and we lay that way until we fell asleep.

32

TANYA

HE SLEPT with both eyes shut.

No good spy ever relaxes completely, not even in sleep. If you're sleeping in someone's arms, they're probably someone who would kill you if you mumbled something in your sleep that revealed who you really were. Alone, in your safehouse, isn't any more restful. No safehouse is truly safe. You know that at any moment, someone could kick down your door and drag you off for interrogation, or worse. So we sleep with one eye open. Maybe not literally, but we doze in the shallows of sleep, never sinking into the dark, warm depths where real peace lies. That's why we can sleep in trees, or on narrow ledges. We never sleep deeply enough to fall off.

Colton, though, lay sprawled on his back, one arm flung casually out over his head, snoring softly without a care in the world. The other arm was extended towards me as if reaching for me. When I woke, he'd been spooning me, that arm clasped tightly around my waist, possessive and protective. Now, I was sitting on the bed, my knees drawn up to my chin, watching him.

He was so utterly, utterly different to me. He still believed in things like loyalty and right and wrong, and I adored him for that. His feelings were as clear and easy to read as his tattoos: no games, no tricks. He was *simple,* and that didn't mean I thought he was dumb. He was simple in the way a bulldozer is simple. Huge and strong and uncomplicated, with one clear purpose in life. I wished *I* was that simple. And the attraction...God, the attraction was like nothing else, that hard, brute maleness, the way he scowled at me with those scalding brown eyes...

But it was impossible. I couldn't have a normal, honest relationship with him, or anyone. With Lev, it had been different. Lev had been like me and we'd forgiven each other's flaws. We knew that neither of us was real.

Colton *was* real. Warmly, honestly, roughly real. And he deserved someone real. Someone who laughed because something was funny, not as a way to manipulate someone. Someone who could love him.

He came sleepily awake, groaning and yawning and then opening his eyes, scowling grumpily. Then he saw me and his cock rose and hardened. God, he was so wonderfully primal, like a caveman.

We looked at each other, unsure what came next. Then I leaned down to the floor and grabbed his gun. He sucked in his breath and tensed, ready to grapple me—

I held the gun out to him in a sign of peace. He sighed in relief and took it, then nodded to me. We weren't enemies anymore.

"I want to help you," he said. "But you've gotta start leveling with me about what's going on."

His phone rang. He checked the screen, grimaced and looked meaningfully at me. It must be his team, wondering where the hell he was. He tossed the phone on the bed, letting the call go to voicemail. His own sign of peace.

I gazed at him, debating. Then I nodded. "Okay. But let's go to the diner across the street. You're going to need some coffee."

33

COLTON

WHEN WE REACHED the diner and I smelled food, I realized I was *ferociously* hungry. I'd been on the go for over thirty-six hours with only a few rations to sustain me and I'd eaten nothing at all since yesterday morning. "Do you have pancakes?" I asked the waitress.

"Best pancakes in the city. You want pancakes with maple syrup and whipped cream, pancakes with maple syrup and bacon or pancakes with maple syrup, bananas and nuts?"

"One of each," I said seriously. "And coffee," I added, remembering what Tanya had said. "Like, a *vat* of coffee."

The pancakes really *were* the best in the city, crispy on the outside and fluffy inside, drowning in maple syrup and topped with salty bacon and sweet fruit. I worked my way through three platefuls and felt better. Tanya, who'd just finished a modest bowl of oatmeal, smirked at me from under her long, dark lashes as if I was cute. "What?" I asked.

She shook her head. "Nothing." She sighed and picked up her coffee cup. "Okay, listen. It's the nineties. There's a war going on in Bosnia, right in the heart of Europe. It's *bad,* Colton. The worst things people can do to each other. Rape. Mass graves. Ethnic cleansing." She leaned forward. "But there was this one guy who was worse than the rest. His name was Jadranko Maravić. Serbian Special Forces. He was responsible for some of the worst atrocities and he wasn't some guy sitting in an office a hundred miles away issuing orders. He was right there with his men, leading by example. He liked to kill in especially brutal ways and he always finished his victims off with a knife. The locals were terrified of him. They called him *The Devil's Wolf*. Not just because he was vicious, but because he'd do all of his higher-ups' dirty work, no matter what. Nothing was beyond him." She bit her lip and looked away, then summoned the strength to look me in the eye. "Pregnant women. Children," she said quietly.

The anger had been building inside me as she spoke, like storm clouds rolling out to cover the sky. But in the last few words it got darker, the muscles in my arms tensing, my knuckles going white on my coffee cup. I'd run into guys like that, when I was Military Police. Men who used the horrors of war as a smokescreen for their sickness. I'd already done the math in my head. "He was a soldier in the nineties," I growled. "That white-haired guy in the forest: that was him."

She nodded. "After the war, the UN tried to put him on trial but he escaped. Started selling his services as a mercenary around the world: when some warlord in Africa wanted a group run off their land, they'd call The Devil's Wolf and he'd do exactly what he did in Bosnia. People used him when they wanted to send a message, or when the crime had to be especially cruel." She sighed and stopped, then seemed to have trouble starting again. "Two years ago, someone —we suspect the Chinese—paid him to get information out of a Russian weapons researcher. So he kidnapped her fourteen year-old daughter, took her to a remote hunting lodge and sent the mother photos as he tortured her, to force her to give up the secrets he wanted. We managed to backtrace one of the photos and my partner and I were sent in to rescue the child. We thought we knew what we were getting into, but…"

She dropped her eyes to the table and didn't speak for a moment. When she managed to carry on, the words almost choked her. "We fought him and…it was like we were *nothing*, like we were just toys for him to play with. He cut my leg open, so I couldn't run—"—she touched her thigh—"you've seen the scar. Then, as I lay there bleeding to death, he killed my partner, Lev, right in front of me. And then he killed the child. *Just for fun.* He would have killed me, but the police arrived and he had to run." She looked up into my eyes. "Lev died in my arms. He'd been my partner for four years. My lover for two."

The rage had built into towering, black clouds shot through with white-hot lightning, filling my chest and making it difficult to breathe. I wanted to destroy this guy for hurting her. But there was something else underneath, a creeping, cold certainty I'd felt before. There's a reason Military Police exist and it's more than just the Army wanting to clean up its own messes. The military trains people to be lethal and cunning and when one of those people goes bad, they're more dangerous than any normal criminal. The police can't handle them and there has to be someone who can put them away.

This guy had killed people for thirty years, on every continent. Someone had to stop him. *We* had to stop him. The two of us.

"You've been hunting him ever since," I said.

She nodded stiffly. "I finally tracked him to the US. But my bosses at the GRU wouldn't let me go after him, too afraid I'd cause some international incident. So I had to go rogue." She crossed her arms defensively over her chest and suddenly she looked small, vulnerable. "I don't have anything to go back to, after this," she told me. "If I ever go back to Russia they'll probably arrest me. But I don't care." She met my eyes. "I just want him dead."

I suddenly understood a whole hell of a lot. I understood why she'd been ready to throw her life away, jumping over that waterfall to go after Maravić, and why she'd broken down when I stopped her. I understood why she was so coldly determined, why she hid behind flirting and teasing. Maybe I'm not Gabriel, but I'm not a complete fucking idiot. I know a broken heart when I see one. I reached out and put my big hand over her small one, to let her know she wasn't alone.

She looked down at it and...she didn't flinch or pull her hand away but I could see the fear in her face. The guilt. *She thinks she's cheating on him.* What did that mean for us?

I felt the heat go to my face and hoped she couldn't see. *Us?* Jesus, we'd slept together and I was already planning the wedding?

But I *did* want there to be an *us*. I looked into those frozen sky eyes and I wanted it so bad it made my chest ache. The realization made me feel dumb but, at the same time, the resolve settled into place inside me, unyielding as stone. I wanted there to be an *us*. Despite the fact we were meant to be enemies. Despite the fact I was meant to be bringing her in. Despite her broken heart.

And I can be real stubborn, when I want something.

"How does the stockbroker figure into all this?" I asked. "Why'd you kill him?"

"I didn't. Maravić did. I followed him to the stockbroker's house. Got inside just in time to see him stab the stockbroker to death."

"Why not just tell the CIA that?"

Tanya looked me right in the eye. "Because the CIA is behind all this."

I felt my jaw drop. "*What?*"

Tanya leaned forward. "After I saw the stockbroker killed, I called an old contact of mine at the CIA, Roberta Geiss, to warn them about Maravić."

"You know *Roberta?*"

"She worked in your Russia station for a while. Good woman. I tell her about Maravić and one day later, you and your friends kick down my door. And when I try to contact Roberta, they tell me she's been in a car accident."

I sat there staring. My stomach felt like it had fallen right through the floor of the diner.

"Roberta passed on my warning to the CIA," said Tanya. "And someone there tried to kill her, and sent you to arrest me, to shut me down. They're the ones paying Maravić, that's why he's in the US!"

I shook my head. I felt like a limpet trying to cling to a rock while the tide tried to drag it away. "No..."

"How do you think Maravić found us in the forest?" asked Tanya.

I went quiet. I hadn't thought of that.

"Who knew where we were?" asked Tanya quietly.

I thought for a moment. The only people who'd known we'd jumped out of the plane had been the rest of the team. I looked at Tanya, feeling ill.

"Your friends must have called the CIA, to give them an update," said Tanya. "And the CIA told Maravić where to find me. *Maravić is working for someone at the CIA!* Who sent you and your team on this mission?"

"A guy called Casey Steward," I growled. "Cal and Bradan tried to warn us. They said it was weird that the CIA would use a private security team. Guess now we know why: Steward was using us to clean up his mess without the rest of the CIA finding out."

"If I'd let you take me in," said Tanya, "This Steward guy would have killed me."

I squeezed her hand, furious. "That's not happening now." I picked up my coffee mug and drank, thinking. I was *pissed.* I was remembering how eagerly I'd jumped at this mission, how excited I'd been at the chance to prove myself. I don't like being played for a fool and Steward had played all of us. The only way to save Tanya was to expose him and clear her name. "Let me take you to my team," I said at last.

She shook her head. "Your team think I'm the bad guy."

"I can explain it to them."

"We don't have any evidence. It's just my word against Steward's. They won't believe you."

I shook my head. The team were good guys. They'd believe me... right? But she'd crossed her arms and was glaring at me stubbornly: no way was I going to convince her. I rubbed my beard. "Okay, so what *do* we do?"

"*We* don't do anything," she said. "You go back to your friends and tell them I escaped. I'll go find some evidence to clear my name and hopefully track down Maravić at the same time."

My stomach lurched. Maravić had nearly killed her, last time. "I'm not leaving you on your own!"

She cocked her head to one side and looked at me sadly. "Colton, I'm a spy. I'm *always* on my own."

I scowled. "Not anymore."

She stared at me. "You have *orders!*" As if on cue, my phone rang again: JD, worried about me. She waved her hand at it. "If they find out you helped me, you'll get in trouble."

My chest tightened. The last thing I wanted was to mess things up with the team. Those guys were the best thing to happen to me in a long time. But I couldn't leave her on her own, either. I turned my phone off and slammed it down on the table. "I'll deal with it. What's our next move?"

She stared at me, incredulous. Then I saw that frozen blue in her eyes soften. "I think the stockbroker was working for Steward, too. He had some big stock market deal going on, except he got greedy and tried to make some money on the side by cutting in people like Konstantin. Steward found out and sent Maravić to kill him. But you don't hire someone like Maravić just to kill a guy. Any low-rent thug can do that. So Maravić must *already* have been on Steward's payroll, he's doing something else for him, something bigger. If we can find out what the stockbroker was working on, maybe we can figure out their plan."

"How do we do *that?*"

"I pulled some data off the stockbroker's computer and stored it in the cloud." She pulled out her phone and typed in a web address that was nothing but numbers, followed by a long username and password that were just as random.

"You can just remember stuff like that?" I asked, awed.

She blinked, like, *can't everyone?* Then she thought about it for a moment. "It's one of the skills they look for, when they recruit us." The screen filled with text. "Look: it's some sort of computer code, but I have no idea what it does. It's full of equations. You any good at math?"

I thought for a while, then drained the last of my coffee. "No," I told her. "But I know someone who is."

34

TANYA

I SHIELDED my eyes from the sun and looked up at the skyscraper, amazed. It was a beautiful old art deco building, with stone balconies and gargoyles. And here, in the heart of Manhattan, each apartment must be worth millions. "Who are we visiting, a hedge fund manager?"

"A mathematician. She's one of this group of hackers who help us out, sometimes. And I got to know her boyfriend a little, last time I was in New York. He's an FBI agent."

An elevator whisked us up...and *up*. I realized Colton had pushed the button for the penthouse. *Who is this woman?*

The door was opened by a big, broad-shouldered guy in a suit. He had that sharp-eyed, always-watching look of an FBI agent but his tie was just askew enough that I wanted to straighten it for him, and his hair was tousled, as if he'd just gotten up. Or just gotten out of bed for some other reason. He shook my hand. "Sam," he told me. "But everybody just calls me Calahan."

The apartment was huge and beautiful, with polished wood floors and massive windows letting in lots of natural light, and there was a gorgeous scent in the air, like peaches and cream. One wall was covered in chalkboards, the huge green kind you get in colleges, where you can roll them down like a roller towel to get to unused space. They were filled with equations. But why were they mounted so low? You'd have to stoop to write near the bottom. In fact—I looked around—*everything* was too low, even the sink and oven in the kitchen.

"They're here," Calahan called.

"Just a minute," called a female voice. "I'm just— Okay."

A beautiful, dark-haired woman shot out of a doorway in a wheelchair. She took her hands off the wheels to resume frantically toweling her wet hair, then grabbed them again just in time to stop herself crashing into us. She looked Colton up and down. "I've only ever seen you on a screen. You're bigger, in real life." Then she looked meaningfully at me. "And this is...?"

"Tanya," I told her, and showed her a big white box. "We brought pastries!" The pastries had been my idea. I'd had to stop Colton from 'testing' them in the elevator.

Colton nodded solemnly to Yolanda. "Thanks for doing this."

"We don't turn down someone in need," Yolanda told him, and straightened her shoulders, proudly. "That's not the Sisters of Invidia way."

Calahan stared at her. "Not the—Since when did you three have a *moral code?* You just want a new math puzzle!"

Yolanda flushed, sheepish. "Let me see these equations."

I pointed Yolanda to where I'd stashed the stockbroker's files in the cloud and she downloaded them. For the first few minutes, she sat at her computer, her eyes flicking over her towering wall of monitors. "It's an algorithm," she said slowly. "Looks like it's designed to tap into some stream of data, looking for a certain pattern..."

She went quiet. And very, very still. With one hand, she was twisting her long, black hair around her fingers. But then even that stopped and she was like a statue.

We waited. And waited. I looked at Calahan, who was making

coffee. I saw now that the kitchen counters were on a ratchet system, so they could be at his height or Yolanda's. "Is she okay?" I asked.

Calahan nodded. "She does this," he said knowingly. He looked across at Yolanda and as soon as his gaze touched her, he got this look in his eyes, a look that made my throat close up. He looked at her as if she was the only thing in the world. Like he'd kill anyone who tried to hurt her. Even with Lev, our feelings had always been...ordered, like a river that was deep and powerful but that flowed quietly. Calahan and Yolanda, that was lightning and volcanoes. I wondered what it must be like, to have someone feel that way about you.

Then I saw Colton's reflection in one of the huge windows and...*Chyort.* Something expanded inside me, a bubble of warm, giddy starlight. He was looking at me in exactly the same way.

What do I do now?

Yolanda suddenly exploded out from behind her computer and tore across the room so fast I had to leap out of the way. She skidded to a stop in front of a chalkboard, grabbed hold of it and hauled it down to reveal fresh, empty space. She lifted one hand in the air and caught a piece of chalk tossed to her by Calahan. Then she was writing.

It was as if, the whole time she'd been sitting silently, she'd been coiling up like a clockwork spring and now all the energy was being released. The chalk moved so fast, it didn't squeak and scrape on the board, it went *tak tak tak,* like a machine gun. She filled up one board, then shot across to the next and filled that up, too. She wheeled back and forth neatening things and then finally pushed herself back and looked up at the boards, drained and breathless. Calahan handed her a mug of coffee and she nodded to him gratefully. She glugged down half the coffee, then turned to us. "I think it's for trading stocks. You said you got it from a stockbroker's computer, right? But it's...weird. Backwards."

Calahan dragged some chairs into the middle of the room and we arranged ourselves in a circle. Calahan passed out coffee, then sat in a chair next to Yolanda and slipped his arm around her.

Colton opened up the box of pastries we'd brought and we passed it round. "Backwards?"

"It tracks the price of one particular stock—I haven't figured out which one, yet—waiting until everyone sells it and the price is rock-bottom—"

"And then it snaps it up for a bargain price?" asked Calahan.

"No," said Yolanda, taking a Danish. "That's just it, it *sells,* which would push the price even lower. And it does it millions of times. Whoever runs this thing is going to lose billions. It makes no sense." She bit her lip and started twirling her hair around her finger again. Her big, green eyes stared right at me, but I got the impression she wasn't really seeing me, anymore. "Unless..." she mumbled, "...they're not *trying* to make money..."

She suddenly shot over to one of the chalkboards and searched through her equations until she found a particular one. She circled a value. "Would someone please tell me the exchange rate from Euros to dollars?" she asked in a strangled voice.

Colton pulled out his phone and tapped at it. "A Euro buys you a dollar and eight cents."

Yolanda turned to us. All the blood had drained from her face. "It's not selling stocks," she said. "It's for the currency markets, it's selling the US dollar!" She waved her hand at the chalkboard. "This thing isn't designed to make money. It's designed to crash the dollar!"

"*What?*" I asked.

She wheeled herself back to us. "This thing's designed to kick in on a certain date, when there's a panic in the market. Something will happen to make the dollar plummet in value. Everyone'll sell like crazy, but eventually people will calm down and the price will stop dropping. That's when this algorithm kicks in and sells hundreds of millions of dollars, starting a fresh panic. More people sell and the value falls even more. And just when things begin to calm down, the algorithm does it again. It's like pouring gasoline on a fire, each time it's about to die out. And it keeps going until..." Her voice cracked. "Until the dollar's worth zero."

"*What?* What happens then?" asked Colton.

"The FBI sent me on a training course on this stuff once," said Calahan. "Disaster planning: earthquakes, cyberattacks...one of the scenarios was the dollar collapsing." His face was grim. "Other countries would panic and call in all our debts. And we have *a lot* of debts. The banking system collapses, so no one's getting paid, or getting welfare, or a pension. Businesses collapse because they can't afford raw materials, farmers can't even grow food because they can't buy fertilizer or fuel for their tractors. The power would go out, then government services would shut down: police, fire, hospitals. After that, it's basically anarchy."

"You said it waited for panic in the market," said Colton. "Something has to make everyone panic and sell the dollar in the first place, right?"

Yolanda nodded. "Yes. Something has to start the house burning. And it's happening in exactly three days, five hours and sixteen minutes. That's when the algorithm's set to kick in."

Colton looked at me. "That must be what Maravić is for. He's going to do something to cause a panic, to set this whole thing off."

I frowned. It made sense but... "How's a mercenary going to do that?"

"Blow up an oil pipeline?" said Calahan. "That could cost the economy *billions.*"

"I got another question," said Colton. "Who's doing this?" There was a worried silence and he looked from face to face. "Who'd want to destroy our economy? We're talking about countries, right? I mean, this is full-on global politics, act-of-war shit. *China? North Korea?*" He looked at me. "Russia?"

My stomach flipped. *Chyort, could* it be us?

"All I know is, we're way, *way* over our heads," Colton told me. "You've got to let me take you to the rest of the team."

"They'll hand me over to the CIA!" I told him. "To this Casey Steward guy who hired the team, and then I'm *dead!*"

"No. Not once we explain." Colton pointed to the chalkboards. "We know what's going on, now. I can talk to them. We'll figure something out." He sighed and his voice became gentle. "Look, I trusted you. Now you gotta trust me."

When his voice went gentle like that, it made something deep in my chest flutter. I scowled and pouted to cover myself, and thought about what he'd said. It had been a long time since I'd put my faith in anyone. But Colton had been nothing but straight with me since this whole thing started. And we needed to stop this thing. If the dollar collapsed, how many Americans would die because they couldn't get medical care, or couldn't find food? Thousands? Maybe millions? I'm no one's idea of a hero but even I couldn't let that happen.

I sighed. "Fine. Take me to them."

35

COLTON

AFTER TANYA and I had jumped out, Gina had landed the plane in West Virginia and the team had been holed up there ever since, waiting to hear from me. JD said they could fly up to a small airfield west of New York and we arranged to meet at a nearby bar later that day.

The team was waiting for us in the parking lot and they swarmed around our rental car as we pulled up. Everybody looked relieved to see us, but not as relieved as I was to see Cal up and walking around. He lifted his shirt to show me the dressing on his wound. "Won't be winning any races for a while but the docs say I'm gonna be fine."

"Sorry," said Tanya. "Nothing personal."

Cal gave her a baleful stare. "Mm-hmm." Gabriel, who still had a bandage around his ear, didn't look impressed, either.

JD looked surprised when he saw that Tanya wasn't in cuffs. "You got her under control?"

It was weird: it bothered me that he talked *about* her and not *to* her when she was standing right there. But then that's what we'd all done back at her apartment when she was just a prisoner, a *package*. I kept forgetting that they hadn't spent all the time with her I had. "It's all good," I told him. "Listen, boss, a lot's happened. We can't just hand her over to the CIA. Let us fill you in."

JD glared at Tanya. "How about *you* fill me in? She can wait there." He nodded towards the bar.

Tanya rolled her eyes but nodded to me: *it's okay.* She went inside, accompanied by Bradan, Cal and Gabriel. I watched her go, unable to look away until she disappeared through the door.

JD went with them, then came back out to the parking lot carrying three long-neck beers. He handed one to Danny and one to me, then clinked. "Good to have you back, buddy," he told me. "We were worried about you."

I let out a long sigh I hadn't realized I'd been holding and sat my ass down on the hood of the car. It had been a *long* two days away from them and it felt fucking fantastic to not be on my own, anymore, to not be having to make all the decisions and take all the responsibility I'm not cut out to run around solo. The beer was cold, foaming nectar and I chugged a third of the bottle before I lowered it again. *Man, I needed that.*

"So what's going on?" asked JD gently. "Where have you been? Why weren't you answering your phone? Why can't we hand Yeshevskaya over?"

I started at the beginning and told them everything. They listened intently, nodding. But as I went on, they began to glance at each other, looking more and more worried. When I finished, they gave each other a look I recognized. It was the same look they'd all given each other when we'd found my bear cub in a cage and, blissfully unaware of Chinese medicine, I'd asked why someone would smuggle a bear. The look said, *are you going to tell him, or shall I?*

"*What?!*" I demanded, worried and exasperated.

JD put a hand on my shoulder. "Colton, buddy," he said softly. "She played you."

"No, boss!" I frowned, puzzled. *Weren't they listening?* "It's all real, they're going to crash the dollar!"

Danny looked like a parent forced to explain that Santa Claus isn't real. "Do you remember what Steward said in the briefing? She's a born liar. She gets in your head. She's..." He gestured towards the bar. "She's a female Gabriel."

It hurt that they didn't believe me. I tried to stay calm but I could feel myself scowling. "I'd know if she was lying!"

"Colton, she's a *spy,*" said JD gently. "Manipulating people is what she *does.*"

I was getting mad, now. "It's not like that! We're—I got to know her, out there, and—"

"Wait," said Danny, his face changing. "Did you sleep with her?!"

"I—" I swallowed, feeling my face going hot.

"Jesus," muttered Danny. "And people used to say *I* couldn't keep it in my pants."

"Look...okay, it happened," I said. "But we trust each other, now. That's why she's not in cuffs."

The horror on their faces changed to pity, and that was worse. "Colton, mate..." said Danny. "Listen to what you're saying. She slept with you and now you trust her. That's why she did it."

"I—No!" I spat.

"You said she was ready to sleep with Konstantin, just to get some information," JD reminded me.

"That was—With us it was *different!* She—" I bit it back. I'd nearly said *she really likes me!* Jesus, I sounded like a lovestruck teenager. My stomach lurched like I'd just tipped over the hill on a rollercoaster. What if they were right? What if everything I'd thought I'd seen in her eyes had been an illusion?

I fought back stubbornly. "You're wrong about her," I told them. "She doesn't—"—I thought back to how she'd got Danny to take off her cuffs, and how she'd fooled the hunter—"Okay, she lies. But she's not lying about what's going on!" I thought desperately. "What about the algorithm, from the stockbroker's computer?"

"Yeshevskaya *said* she got it from the stockbroker's computer," said Danny. "It's probably just a prop, a get-out-of-jail-free card she pulls out whenever she gets caught: 'Look, there's this huge, world-ending conspiracy going on and *only I can help you stop it!*'"

"What about Maravić finding us in the forest?" I demanded. "How the hell did he know where we were, unless the CIA told him?"

"You have no idea who those guys in the forest really were or why they were hunting her," said JD. "That whole story about Maravić could just be a line she spun you. Maybe someone planted a tracker on her, maybe someone followed our plane and saw her jump. You said two of the guys were American: for all we know, the NSA or some other agency is after her, and you killed two of *theirs!*"

Oh God. I swallowed and went quiet. I hadn't thought of that. The shock of it, that I might have helped kill two of our own people, knocked me right out of the warm certainty I'd been living in and into a cold, black void. "But...but—"

Danny sat down next to me on the hood of the car. "Mate, what's more likely: that our boss at the CIA is conspiring with a Serbian war criminal and China to destroy our country...or that a Russian spy who's desperate to escape is lying?"

That was the final straw. I felt hot shame flood my body. *Fuck. They're right.*

JD's voice softened. "Colton, it's okay. There's no shame in getting duped, not when she's that good. This is what spies do. Hell, it's happened to me."

It was a beautiful day and the sun was beating down on us. But suddenly, I couldn't feel its warmth at all. I looked towards the bar and it took me a while to get any words out. "What happens now?" I asked.

"I already called Steward and he's coming with some guys to collect her," said JD. "Should be here in less than an hour."

"Maybe it's best if you don't see her again," said Danny gently. "We can handle her until Steward gets here."

I glowered at the cracked concrete of the parking lot until I could speak again. "No," I managed at last. "I want to talk to her before she goes."

I felt JD and Danny exchange looks. "Are you sure that's a good idea?" asked JD.

But I was already up and marching towards the bar. They hurried along behind me.

The bar's dim lighting wasn't quite dim enough to hide the peeling wallpaper and cracked vinyl seats. This early in the afternoon, it was deserted, just a few hardcore drinkers huddled at the bar. Tanya was sitting in a booth, wedged between Bradan and the wall with Gabriel and Cal glowering at her from the other side of the booth. "Can we get a minute alone?" I asked.

The guys hesitated. Then I guess JD must have given them the nod from behind me because they mutely stood up and shuffled out. I sidled over to the booth where Tanya sat but my eyes dropped to the threadbare carpet. I couldn't look at her.

"What happened out there?" asked Tanya. When I didn't answer, her voice became pained. "Okay, I've got a pretty good idea."

I drew in a long breath and prepared myself. I was going to tell her that I knew how she'd played me and how it wasn't right. How maybe shit like this was normal for her and her friends and everyone else in this fucking spy game but it wasn't normal for *me*. How I knew I was just a big dumb idiot but I'd actually felt something for her: damnit, it was *real* for me. How she'd led me away from the *team,* from everything that was important to me, from my best friends in the world, and thank God I'd realized in time and—

I looked at her and everything changed. I could see pain in those frozen-sky eyes and not the old, familiar pain she'd been carrying for years, the *Lev* pain. This was something fresh and raw, so raw her eyes were shining.

She knew what had happened, out there. She knew that I'd believed them and not her and—

Oh shit.

It hurt because for once, she *had* been telling the truth.

I drew in one last angry breath and *scowled* at her, willing her to drop her gaze, praying I was wrong because hating her would be so much simpler. But she just stared back at me, open and vulnerable, and I felt my scowl crumble and fade. And *that* started a chain reaction in her: it was like layer after layer of ice was breaking and I was falling steadily through them. She pressed her lips tight together, as if trying to control herself—

She really *did* like me.

"Fuck," I plopped down on the bench seat beside her, suddenly exhausted. "It's real, isn't it?"

She didn't ask if I meant the conspiracy, or what we had together, or both. She just nodded sadly.

"Fuck. Fuck, fuck, fuck." I rubbed at the back of my neck. I'd been in the bar all of two minutes and somehow, everything had flipped on its head.

Something cool touched my back, between my shoulder blades, and I jerked. I looked up to see Tanya awkwardly rubbing my back, her mouth twisted in doubt: *am I doing this right?*

She could dance with an ambassador, seduce a prime minister, but when it came to showing actual affection for someone she cared about, she was clunky and uncertain. My chest ached and a hot surge of protective welled up inside me. I hated this whole spy game for what it had done to her.

I looked towards the door, towards my five buddies outside.

What the hell do I do now?

36

TANYA

COLTON SAT IN BROODING SILENCE. He was a huge ox of a man but in that moment, he looked helpless. Lost. Broken. And I cursed myself for ever having come into his life and messed everything up.

At last, he spoke. "Tell me you're being straight with me," he said quietly. He didn't look at me. His eyes were on the door, on his friends outside. "Tell me you're telling the truth and the whole country's going to hell if we don't stop this thing." He turned to me. "Because if you're lying to me, if you make me go against those guys and it's all a trick, so help me God, I'll kill you."

I swallowed. "I'm being straight with you."

I waited for him to ask whether what we had was real, too. I was ready to tell him *yes,* it was. But he didn't ask. Maybe he didn't dare.

He bowed his head and closed his eyes. Sucked in a long breath. Then his shoulders squared and all his strength and size seemed to return. "Alright then," he said to himself.

He'd committed to it. He was going to let me go. I should have been punching the air but all I could think about was how much trouble he was going to be in. *Since when did I care about anyone else?* "I can hit you with something, knock you out," I offered. "You can say I jumped you. Let me go see if the window in the bathroom is big enough for me to get through..." I motioned for him to let me out of the booth.

But he just sat there, blocking my way. "That ain't gonna work. JD's not dumb, he'll have Bradan or Cal or someone watching the back of the bar. And Steward's on his way here, with another bunch of guys. You won't even make it out of town." He sighed. "Not on your own."

I froze. *Chyort!* He wasn't just talking about letting me go. I shook my head. "No. Colton, no. No!"

"I've seen Maravić in action," he said. Those amber-brown eyes burned into mine. "You go up against him alone, he'll kill you. I'm not letting that happen."

"I'm a fugitive! I'm a *foreign spy!* If you go with me, you'll be a traitor. They'll arrest you. They could *shoot* you!"

His jaw set and I moaned under my breath because I knew what that look meant. He'd dug his heels in and nothing was going to change his mind. "Better grab your backpack," he told me.

Chyort! I grabbed the backpack and followed him to the door.

The one he called JD was right outside. He blinked when he saw me standing close behind Colton. "Everything okay?" he asked, his eyes flicking between Colton and me.

"Sorry, boss," Colton told him. "But I need you to step out of the way."

JD's face fell. "Colton, buddy," he pleaded. "Come on now, don't do something stupid." He raised his voice towards the end to get the others' attention. They came running over: the British one, the Irish one, and the one whose ear I'd shot. The really tall one appeared from behind the bar. He *had* been watching the back.

Colton stepped forward. JD stood his ground, his hands up defensively.

"Don't make me do it, boss," Colton said softly. "Get out of the way."

"Colton, *please,*" pleaded JD.

Colton grabbed his shotgun and leveled it at JD. The rest of the team cursed and scrambled for their own guns.

"Colt, what the fuck are you doing, mate?" yelled Danny. "Put it down!"

"I'm sorry," muttered Colton. "You know I am. But I can't let Steward take her."

JD's eyes went to me. "She's using you," he told Colton.

Colton gestured with his shotgun: *move.*

JD sighed...and stepped aside. Colton led me towards our rental car.

"Colton, just *think*," called Gabriel. "Think about what you're doing!"

"You drive," Colton told me, his voice tight with emotion. He threw me the keys and kept his shotgun leveled at JD while I jumped in and started the car.

"Colton, *please*," said JD desperately. "Please, buddy, just listen to me. It's *me.*" He looked at the rest of the team. "It's *us!*"

Colton and JD gazed at each other and God, the sadness in both of their eyes. My foot twitched on the gas pedal. I could just floor it, drive away and force him to stay here with his friends...

But Colton was right. I needed him.

"If you go," grated JD, "we'll have to come after you. You know that."

Colton looked around at all of them. "You do what you gotta do." He turned, pointed his shotgun at the team's rented SUV and fired once, shredding the front tire. Then he climbed in beside me and we raced away.

37

JD

I WATCHED their car disappear into the distance, my chest tight. What if she killed him? Shoved a knife into his neck as soon as they'd got out of town? The thought of something happening to Colton made me want to throw up. *This is all my fault.* Colton had a good heart and that made him easy pickings for someone like Yeshevskaya. I should never have tasked him with dealing with her, should never have let him jump out of the plane to go after her.

Then, just as I thought my day couldn't get any worse, Danny patted my arm and pointed across the parking lot. A snow white BMW was pulling up with Casey Steward at the wheel and right behind it was an SUV full of CIA heavies. *Oh great.*

Steward jumped out and marched towards us. We all put our guns away. Steward spread his arms wide, asking without words *what the hell is happening here?*

So I explained. And when he lost it and started yelling, I stood there and soaked up the full force of his anger. I didn't care what he did to me. I just wanted to get Colton back.

When he finally finished ranting, Steward pulled out his phone. "We'll have to put out an all-agencies bulletin," he told me. "And send out teams." He didn't have to say what sort of teams.

"Look, our guy's been duped," I said. "Give us a chance to bring him in before you start issuing kill orders. We know him. We can do it quietly."

Steward glared at me, still seething. Then he sighed and rubbed the bridge of his nose. "Twenty-four hours," he told me.

"Thank you," I said sincerely. I marched over to Danny and the others and pointed to the SUV. "Let's get that tire changed. We've got to figure out where she's taking him and find someplace quiet so we can stop them without anyone getting hurt."

Danny and Gabriel got to work. But Cal crossed his arms and scowled at me. "We're going to help them catch him?" he asked. "*Colton?*"

Bradan hadn't moved, either. "Ain't right," he agreed.

"Look," I told them, exasperated, "this isn't Colton's fault. That witch has got her claws into him so deep he can't think straight. But either we bring him in in cuffs, or Steward brings him in in a body bag."

Bradan and Cal looked at each other, then reluctantly nodded and started helping. I began working the jack, throwing worried glances in the direction Colton had disappeared. *Please, Colton, be okay.*

38

COLTON

Tanya drove fast. Not Danny-fast but way faster than I ever did. Within minutes, we'd left the bar far behind and were blasting down open roads, heading north. It was still a beautiful day, with a gloriously blue sky above, but over towards New York, clouds the color of wet concrete had formed and they were slowly spreading across the world, soaking the warmth and color from everything. *What the fuck am I going to do?*

"Pull over," I mumbled.

Tanya glanced across at me, then nodded. "Good idea. We'd better swap cars."

She pulled off the road and into a picnic ground attached to a nature reserve. The place was deserted, wooden picnic tables sitting empty, sandwich crusts and a lost squirt gun the only evidence of all the families who'd stopped there for lunch. There was just one car in the parking lot, a beat-up convertible sports car.

Tanya headed straight to the sports car and started hotwiring it. I stumbled over to the trees and leaned hard against one, the scratchy bark digging into my palm. My legs were suddenly shaky. I'd just run out on my *family.*

A white car flashed past on the road and my chest went heart-attack tight because I thought for a second it was a cop car. Jesus Christ, I was a fugitive, now. People were looking for us, watching surveillance cameras, putting up posters. This must be what it felt like for the guys I bounty hunted.

And somewhere, just a few miles back, the team would be scrambling to come after me. A bunch of people who were the best at what they did, who knew me. Suddenly *I* was their mission. *How did this all go so wrong?* Two days ago, we were all laughing and joking back in Mount Mercy.

An engine revved. Tanya had gotten the car started and she waved me over: *hurry!*

I ran over and climbed in, and we roared out of the parking lot. As we rejoined the road, Tanya glanced at me. "You okay?" she muttered. It was quick and awkward, but I could hear the genuine concern in her voice. She was trying.

"Peachy," I growled. Then I took a deep breath and pushed the sick worry down inside. The only way to get out of this was to clear Tanya's name and that meant exposing Steward and the whole conspiracy. "We got any leads?" I asked.

Tanya drummed her fingers on the steering wheel, thinking. "Maravić is the key to all this," she mused. Even now, stressed out of my mind, her Russian accent was like an immaculately-carved ice sculpture, so coldly brutal and yet sensuously smooth that I just wanted to close my eyes and let it caress my mind. "If we can find out what Steward's hired him to do, we can expose the whole thing. But to do that, we need to find him."

A light went on in my head. I'd been feeling pretty useless since Yolanda deciphered the algorithm: international conspiracies are way above my pay grade. But *finding* someone? That was exactly what I was good at. I narrowed my eyes, stared at the road ahead and *thought,* getting inside Maravić's head.

"He's using American mercenaries," I said at last. "And we killed two of them in the forest."

Tanya glanced at me and wrinkled her forehead. "So?"

"So he's going to need to replace them. And mercs talk, that's how they hear about jobs. We can probably find someone who knows someone who was hired and get a lead. We just need to ask around in the same places Maravić went to do his hiring. He killed the stockbroker in New York so we should start there. And in New York, there's only really one bar where mercs hang out."

Tanya stared at me, surprised and impressed, and I wasn't ready for the warm glow that spread through my chest. It charged me up like a goddamn battery...and made me do something dumb. I knew that I needed to be like her, all cool and professional, that I shouldn't mention what happened at the hotel, that I should just give her space and wait. But that wasn't me. I was crazy about her and I needed her to know that. My mouth opened all on its own and before I could stop myself, I was speaking. "Look—"

Her face fell. That's how good at reading people she was, she knew just from the tone of my voice what I was about to say.

"Colton," she said quietly. Her lips pressed tight together. "I like you. Much more than I should."

More than she should? What the hell did that mean? I realized she must have been trained to never develop feelings for anyone, and my chest ached for her.

"But I'm not someone who can...be *involved* with someone." Tanya's voice was normally so light and confident, but now her words were heavy, clumsy lumps of ice.

"You quit the GRU," I reminded her. "You don't have to do what they tell you anymore."

"It's not my *job*," she told me, her voice strained. "It's what I *am*. That's why they picked me. Do you know what they told us, in our first week at the academy? That our training would separate the mice from the spiders and the scorpions. They only wanted the ones with hard shells, with nothing but poison inside. That's me."

"I don't believe that," I told her firmly.

She looked across at me. "You are a good man, Colton. And you deserve a good woman."

I leaned closer. "I've found a good woman."

She shook her head viciously. "I'm barely a person. I'm a painted mannequin, I know how to lie and fuck and kill. Jesus, if you knew some of what I've done..."

"I don't care what you've done."

"People like me aren't—We aren't trained to love. We're trained *not to*. We can't be with someone." Her voice cracked. "Even one of our own kind."

Aw shit. I knew she was thinking of Lev. I tried to figure out what to say but before I could—

"From now on," she said, her voice shaking but firm, "we need to be a team. Just a team."

She held out her hand for me to grip but I just glared at it. I didn't want to be *just a team*.

Her eyes swam. Begging me.

I sighed and gripped her hand hard.

And we drove on towards New York.

39

TANYA

I CURSED SILENTLY and tightened my grip on the steering wheel. He was a good guy, and he deserved better than me: what did the Americans always say? *A wife and children and a white picket fence.* I'd never understood why they thought a fence was so important. But he did deserve a wife, some sweet thing who didn't have blood on her hands, who knew how to love and *be* loved.

The bar was on the far side of the city and we had to go slowly, avoiding toll roads because they were full of cameras, and changing cars frequently. The next car we stole had a bag of fresh laundry in the back seat, and we took a stretchy, bottle-green dress for me and a fresh t-shirt for Colton: he grunted in approval at the name of some metal band I'd never heard of, and immediately ripped the sleeves off. When we switched cars again, I watched, bemused, as he counted off some bills and left them on the seat to cover the clothes.

We weren't as lucky with food. We didn't dare go into any gas stations to buy road snacks so, aside from a half pack of gum we found in one of the cars, we didn't eat at all. By the time we reached the bar, the sun was going down and we were exhausted, grumpy and starving.

It was an area I'd never been to before, and I wasn't sure I'd be able to find it again if I wasn't with Colton. The street lights didn't work, a lot of the buildings were abandoned and the alleys looked like dark, gaping mouths. As we climbed out of the car, I looked up and saw the gray clouds that stretched right across the sky. We were in for a massive storm. *Great.*

Colton led me towards a squat, red brick building that looked like it had been there at least a hundred years. "What's this place called?" I asked.

"Butchers."

The guy standing watch outside the double doors frowned as we approached. He was almost as big as Colton, and his tattooed arms bulged beneath the sleeves of his t-shirt. He did a complicated fist-bump-handshake with Colton but shook his head apologetically at me. "Former military only. Sorry, rules are rules."

"I *am* former military," I told him. "Just not American."

He looked doubtfully at my dress. "Got any ID?" he asked. "Or some ink?"

I was too tired for this. I snatched the knife from his belt, then grabbed his wrist and pulled it behind his back and up between his shoulder blades. I held the point of the knife a finger's width from his eyeball. He froze. "I suggest you take my word for it," I hissed. He nodded minutely and I let him go.

Inside, men—and a smattering of women—sat at long, sturdy-looking wooden tables, some of them eating and all of them drinking. They all had the hardened, *ready* look of military service. I saw Marines and Army tattoos and there were several guys and one woman who I pegged as former Special Forces straight away.

"The guy at the door knew you," I said.

Colton nodded. "I bounty hunt. Some of the guys they send me after are former military. And if they run off to the East Coast, sooner or later they wind up here, looking for work, so it's a good place to check." He led me through the crowd. "'Bout a hundred years ago, this used to be the biggest butchers in the city. That's where the tables are from."

I looked closer as we passed a table. The surface was a complex pattern of thousands of tiny grooves, made by butchers bringing their cleavers down.

"The story I heard is, there was a group of mercenaries who'd made their money and wanted out. They were looking for a place to turn into a bar. Some folk call soldiers butchers...I guess they had a dry sense of humor."

There was a pool table and a TV, but most people were just talking. I saw two guys who'd just arrived, heavy packs still on their shoulders, being back-slapped and hugged by people they knew. Colton had been right, everyone was talking about work: I heard place names I recognized from the Middle East, Eastern Europe and a whole slew of African nations. *Two weeks close protection, three months guarding an oil field* and always the question, *how much are they paying?* It felt close-knit and safe, despite how intimidating some of the men looked.

I took a look at the food. There wasn't a menu, just a guy ladling out chili from a steaming pot. Pretty basic...but comfortingly familiar, if you'd spent a lot of time in mess halls.

Colton started asking if anyone had been approached by a white-haired Serbian guy. Between his intimidating size and his low, no-bullshit country growl, everyone listened politely. But no one had heard anything.

Then one guy, sprawled in the corner with his feet up on a table, overheard us and said, "I heard about that guy."

We looked up. The man was tall and his arms had the veiny, pumped-up look of a bodybuilder. His blond hair was shaved on the sides and stood straight up on top a full inch, like the bristled head of a broom. He was shelling pistachio nuts and crunching on them noisily. "My friend's working for him right now, bru." he said in a lazy South African drawl.

We walked over to him. "What's the job?" asked Colton.

The man gave us a big, white-toothed grin. "Nothing's free, my friend." He was younger than Colton, late twenties. He looked at me. Then, he threw a nut into the air, caught it in his mouth and crunched it down, not bothering to close his mouth. His eyes never left me for a second and I shuddered inside. "Is she yours?" he asked Colton.

"I'm *mine,*" I snapped before Colton could answer. I had a pretty good idea where this was going.

Colton's expression darkened. He stepped closer to the man, looming over him. But the guy didn't look intimidated at all. "It's *important,*" he growled.

"Well then, you'll be willing to do a deal, bru." said the guy calmly. He raised his voice, showing off to his friends. "Your girl comes into the back room with me and gets my cock up her, and I'll tell you everything I know."

Before I could react, Colton grabbed him by the collar and lifted him out of his seat. Immediately, four more guys rose to their feet around us. Asshole or not, the guy had friends and they had knives on their belts and probably guns under their shirts. I grabbed Colton's arm. "*Wait!*" I told him. I hauled him away but it was like trying to lead an uncooperative rhino: he kept stopping and glaring at the guy. I'd never seen him so mad.

When we were a safe distance away, I let out a sigh of relief. Colton scowled. "Why'd you stop me?" he demanded.

"His friends would have killed you!" I shook my head. "I'll just do it."

"The hell you will!"

I frowned at him, genuinely confused. "It's just sex."

To my surprise, that made him even madder. He stepped closer and he seemed to grow, his muscles swelling with rage. But it didn't feel like the anger was directed at me. "You're *not doing that!*"

I stared. "I'm a spy, Colton. It's part of what I do."

He loomed even closer, so close I could feel the heat from his body. "Not anymore, it's not!"

This was more than jealousy. He thought that I should be able to choose, that I should only fuck someone because I wanted to, not because my mission demanded it. I felt my forehead wrinkle in amazement. *Ridiculous. He wants to make me into some fairy-tale princess in an ivory tower—*

And then there was a wrenching disconnection, deep in my soul as I realized it *wasn't* ridiculous. It just seemed ridiculous to me because I'd had so many years of being a spy. All he wanted was for me to be allowed to be *a normal woman.*

He wanted to rescue me. As if I deserved to be rescued.

My chest went fluttery and light. *Stupid!* I screamed at myself. *You stupid, weak girl!* I should rage at Colton, tell him he was being a naive, romantic oaf, but—

But I couldn't. Because deep inside, there was a traitorous part of me that *wanted* to be rescued. That wanted to deserve it.

"Okay—" My voice quavered and I frowned and started over, furious at myself. "Okay then. What *do* we do?"

Colton marched back to the South African guy. "Let's go," he said. "You and me. Downstairs." People at the tables around us turned to look and Colton glanced around at them. "Or you can show everyone here that *you don't have any balls!*"

For the first time, the South African guy looked thrown. Then he stood up and I drew in my breath: he was taller than I'd thought, slightly taller than Colton. He leaned forward to snarl in Colton's face. "I'll take you apart!" Then he pushed past us, heading for a set of stairs.

"What's downstairs?" I asked. But Colton just grabbed my hand and followed the South African guy. Word spread fast and *everyone* started moving downstairs, eager to watch. *Watch what?*

We emerged into a stone cellar. Crates of beer and cleaning equipment lined one wall but most of the room was given over to a full-sized boxing ring. *Chyort!* The room filled up quickly: the whole bar seemed to have heard what was happening. Everyone was eying up Colton and the South African and money was changing hands.

I put my lips to Colton's ear. "Are you sure this is a good idea?" Colton was huge, but the South African was younger, slightly taller and he had a cruelty in his eyes I didn't like at all. I felt a flutter of panic in my chest, the same one I used to get when Lev was sent on a solo mission.

Colton looked at me. "This is what I do," he said simply. Then he climbed into the ring. The South African gave me an unpleasant leer and joined him.

The betting going on around me rose to fever pitch. I tried to get a feel for who the odds favored, but it seemed to be evenly split. *Not a good sign.* The South African was stripping off his shirt. His torso bulged with hard muscle: he obviously pumped a lot of iron and probably hit the steroids, too. He bounced on the canvas and raised his arms to the crowd, getting them baying and hooting. In the opposite corner, Colton stood still and quiet. I waited for someone to appear and tell the fighters the rules. Then I realized there weren't any. *Oh God...*

Someone honked on an airhorn and the fight began. The South African sprang forward, jumped and launched a vicious spin-kick at Colton's head—

Colton raised his hand almost lazily, grabbed the man's ankle and used it like a handle to slam him into the canvas with a *boom* so loud it hurt my ears. The crowd went utterly silent.

It sank in that all the times I'd fought Colton, he'd been trying to restrain me, not hurt me. Now I was seeing him unleashed and the sheer, brute power of the man was overwhelming.

He lifted the South African from the canvas and got him in a headlock, then did something with his arm that made him screech in pain. "Tell us what we want to know," Colton growled. *"Bru."*

I pushed my way through the crowd and got ringside just in time to hear the response. "I don't know what the job is but your Serbian's got money and he takes care of his men. My friend says he's got a big screen TV in their place with the whole NFL package!"

"Where's this *place,* where are they working out of?" demanded Colton.

"Right here in New York! My friend wouldn't say where but he sent me a photo of where he eats dinner. He likes the waitress there!" He fumbled his phone out of his pants and showed us a photo of a pretty, blonde-haired waitress in a retro-style pink uniform.

Colton made him send the photo to us, then a photo of the friend who worked for Maravić, so we could identify him. "One more thing," said Colton. "Apologize."

The South African wailed in pain. "Sorry, man, sorry!"

"To *her.*"

The South African looked up at me, panting and sweating in agony. "Sorry!" he pleaded.

Colton released him and he collapsed to the canvas, wheezing and moaning. I stared at Colton, awestruck. The whole crowd was staring at him. He wasn't even breathing hard.

Colton offered me his hand and I took it. Together, we walked up the stairs and out of the bar. My mind was spinning: now that he was out of danger, I had time to re-run how angry he'd gotten, when I'd said using my body was something I did. *Not anymore, it's not,* he'd said. Protecting me, even though we weren't together.

His hand felt so good, wrapped around mine. I wanted him. Oh, God, I wanted him so much, I wanted to just throw my arms around him and tell him I'd been wrong, wanted the sweet, warm dream of the two of us together instead of the cold reality of what I was. But I couldn't give in. I deserved to be alone and he deserved better. I'd already hurt him once. I had to be firm, or I'd hurt him again.

But there was one thing I *could* do. "Colton?" I mumbled as we got into the car.

Those brown and amber eyes burned at me from beneath his dark brows.

"Thank you."

He nodded and we sped away.

There weren't *that* many diners in New York where the waitresses wore retro-style pink uniforms and by looking at the decor in the background, I found it on our third try. The place was in Manhattan, which wasn't good. "Too many cameras," muttered Colton, glancing suspiciously up at the surveillance cameras perched on the corners of buildings.

He was right, his team would be looking for us and by now they'd have called in the help of The Sisters of Invidia to comb through surveillance footage using facial recognition. But even so, I felt a smile tug at my lips. When he frowned and peered upwards through the windshield like that, he looked exactly like a grumpy bear peering up at a songbird who'd disturbed his sleep. Then I caught myself and shook my head. *What's wrong with me?*

We had no idea if the South African's friend had already eaten, but it was the only lead we had so we walked in and hoped we'd get lucky. I spotted the blonde waitress straight away, down at the other end of the diner, but no sign of the guy. We hadn't eaten since that morning and we were ravenous, so we ordered: buttermilk fried chicken burgers with mustard mayonnaise and towering piles of crispy, seasoned fries. The burger took two hands to hold and my fingers got slathered with warm, dripping mayonnaise and melted cheese, but it was the best thing I'd ever tasted. I ate the entire thing and felt better. I was trying to find a delicate way to lick my fingers when I saw a reflection I recognized in the glass window in front of me and checked over my shoulder to be sure. "It's him!" I whispered to Colton.

The mercenary was sitting at the other end of the diner, flirting with the blonde waitress. We ordered dessert while we waited: I was too full to eat but Colton happily worked his way through a slice of blueberry pie. When it looked like the guy was finishing up, we quickly paid and waited outside for him. It had started to rain, that heavy, gray New York rain that soaks your clothes in seconds. We stood shivering, blinking water from our eyes, until the guy emerged. But was he going to meet up with Maravić, or just heading home for the night?

He walked off down the block and we tailed him. Fortunately, the hammering rain meant he had his head down and his hood up, so he wasn't checking behind him. He turned down a backstreet, walked past a beat-up brown van and disappeared into a run-down car bodyshop.

Colton dropped to a crouch and crept forward, readying his shotgun. But I put a hand on his shoulder. "*Wait,*" I whispered.

He turned to me. I slicked my soaked hair back from my eyes. "If Maravić is in there, don't get into a fight with him. Shoot him or run but *don't* get close. He'll kill you." I could hear the fear in my voice and that was good, because it would make him take the warning seriously, but bad because I could see the protective fury sparking in his eyes. He hated Maravić for making me live in fear and anger for so long.

"*Promise me*, Colton," I insisted.

He was silent for a long time, then gave me a grudging nod. We moved on, my heart thumping. The thought of something happening to him was terrifying. And the fact it terrified me was scarier still: I'd forgotten how weak caring makes you.

We slunk past the old brown van that was parked outside and crept up to the door. When we inched it open, we could hear voices deeper inside.

No lights were on and with the sky dark outside it was difficult to make anything out. But as my eyes adjusted to the gloom I gradually realized we were in an extension, really just a big shed tacked onto the main building for extra storage. The walls and roof were sheets of corrugated iron and rickety shelves were packed with cans of auto paint, oil, and jerry cans of fuel. In the middle of the room sat an old Honda with its hood lifted, spider webs stretched across its gaping maw. The car must have been sitting there since the place went out of business, years ago.

An open roller door led into the main garage and we crept through. There was an open area with three more cars, but it was dark and silent. The voices were coming from an office. We moved closer, hiding behind an SUV that had been stripped of most of its bodywork. I froze when I heard Maravić's voice. "Everyone has passports? Good. Wait: which way did you come in? The back way? Did you lock the door?"

Footsteps. We pressed ourselves close to the car as the guy we'd followed stalked past us, sighing in irritation, and went to the door we'd entered by. There was a rattle of chains and the sound of a padlock snapping closed. *Chyort!* How were we going to get out?

The man returned to the others. We peeked cautiously over the hood of the SUV...

There were six men, all with the lean, muscled build of mercenaries. They were standing in the garage's office, which had windows that looked out over the main room. I could see the big-screen TV the guy at Butcher's had told us about. And standing at the front of the office, briefing his men, was Maravić.

It felt like someone had plunged my heart into ice water. The visceral fear of what he could do to me spread inward, making me want to shut down, wrap myself in a fetal position and hide. But as the fear reached the center, it hit that jagged, ruined place where Lev used to live, and anger exploded outwards, pushing the fear back. My hand went to my gun. He hadn't seen us. For the first time in two years, I had a clear, easy shot. I could kill him, right now. I could avenge Lev. I could stop living in fear.

But this wasn't just about me, anymore. Colton was in trouble, now, too, and killing Maravić wouldn't clear his name. We needed evidence. I slowly uncurled my fingers from my gun.

Maravić was showing the men something on a laptop screen but we were too far away to make it out. I saw something that looked like pipes. *Maybe Calahan was right? Are they planning to sabotage an oil pipeline?* Colton gently patted my shoulder and pointed at something. I looked and my chest went tight. Seven assault rifles were laid out on a table. *Why do they need guns?*

"I've secured the van," Maravić told them. "It's outside. Steward's going to meet with the guy in charge tomorrow at two in DC. If he gets the final go-ahead, he'll call me with the location of the goods and we'll go pick them up, then head to the target to prepare. We'll pick up our friends from New Jersey on the way."

The beat-up van was part of the plan? That made no sense, why rely on something so old? The plan to crash the dollar would cost billions of dollars so whoever was behind this wasn't short of money.

And *what* were they going to do? What were the goods? Who were these friends from New Jersey?

I had to get closer. I had to see what was on that screen.

Maravić had turned to look at it, pointing out something to his men, and they were all facing away from me. I started to crouch-walk out from behind the SUV.

A hand grabbed my shoulder. I turned to see Colton viciously shaking his head at me.

I nodded insistently and threw off his hand. We had to get some hard facts: a name, a location, *something*. I hurried across the room and pressed myself against the wall beneath the window. Then I slowly straightened up until just my eyes peeked over the windowsill. Maravić's body was blocking the screen. I'd have to shuffle sideways a little. I started to move and then some instinct made me stop and look down.

A wrench was lying on the floor right beside my left foot. If I'd shuffled into it, it would have scraped on the concrete and alerted Maravić, like I was some idiot heroine in a movie. I let out a silent sigh of relief. Then I very carefully stepped over the wrench and lifted my gaze to the window—

Maravić had turned around and was staring right at me.

I turned and bolted, racing back around the SUV and ducking behind it. I'd barely got my head down when a bullet hit the fender. I could hear Maravić and his men pouring out of the office and grabbing their guns.

Colton and I shrank down behind the car but then the whole room went blindingly bright as someone switched the lights on. Bullets shattered the windows of the SUV and I felt scratchy pebbles of safety glass going down my neck. Colton fired his shotgun over the hood but then shook his head at me, worried. We were outnumbered seven to two and pinned down. It was only a matter of time.

After the next burst of gunfire, Maravić's ugly, barbed-wire accent filled the air. Each word seemed designed to puncture my defenses and taint me with poison. "I remember you now, Tanya Yeshevskaya. I remember sticking a knife into your thigh. I planned to throw you down and fuck you in the snow while the life drained out of you. Perhaps I'll still have that pleasure."

I felt Colton's muscles go hard with rage. Before I could stop him, he'd popped up above the car's hood and fired another shot at Maravić. I grabbed him by his t-shirt and barely got him down again before a burst of gunfire cut through the air.

"I remember the man you were with, as well," called Maravić.

I froze, squeezing my eyes shut. I wanted to press my hands over my ears like a child. *Shut up! Shut up! You're not worthy of speaking of him!*

"Were you in love?" asked Maravić. "I think you were. I remember the look on your face when I pushed the knife into his heart. Did you watch him die? Do you remember the sound as he drowned in his own blood?"

I screamed, half-stood and fired, trying to see through a film of tears. Now it was Colton who had to wrestle *me* back down. He pushed me to the floor beneath him as bullets hammered the SUV, his body covering mine.

"Is *this* one in love with you, too?" Maravić asked. Then, for Colton's benefit, "I hope you got your cock wet, before she gets you killed."

Colton shoved his shotgun under the car and fired at foot level and I fired too, but Maravić just laughed. And then both of our guns clicked empty.

The gunfire from Maravić's men stopped. There was silence and then the sound of a single pair of boots walking towards the SUV, patient and unhurried.

I knew what would happen now. Maravić would kill me, up close and personal, pushing his knife into my heart. But first, he'd kill Colton and make me watch. Colton was already getting to his feet and dropping into a fighting stance, riled up and protective. Exactly how Maravić wanted him.

I grabbed Colton around the waist. *"No!"* I begged. "No, *please!* Please, Colton!" But he didn't move.

I heard Maravić laugh.

I pressed my lips to Colton's ear and squeezed his waist, molding myself to him. *"Please! I don't want to lose you!"*

Maravić stepped into view.

There was no more time. If I wanted to save him, we had to go, *now*. I grabbed his hand and bolted towards the shed. My arm went taut and I prayed.

For an instant, Colton stood his ground. Then he let me tow him. I staggered on, slumping in relief.

But I'd only bought us a few seconds. The shed was just one room, with the car in the middle. The only door out was chained and padlocked and there were no windows.

I pulled Colton behind the old Honda. I could already see Maravić casually strolling towards us, and his men following behind him.

A siren wailed in the distance. "Cops," muttered one of the mercenaries. Someone must have reported the gunfire.

"Get our stuff," Maravić grunted. Then he picked up one of the jerry cans of fuel and upended it, sloshing gasoline across the floor. He hurled the can into the room and it bounced and came to a stop on its side only a few feet from us, spewing a lake of gasoline across the concrete. *Chyort!*

Maravić snapped open a lighter and tossed it onto the floor. A wavefront of neon blue shot outwards, blooming into orange and red, and suddenly the whole floor was on fire. Maravić stepped back from the doorway. "You can burn to death instead, you Russian whore," he said. Then he hauled down the metal roller door, sealing us inside.

40

COLTON

I LOOKED at Tanya in panic. *Fuck.* Almost the entire floor was already covered in gasoline and we had to dodge back against the wall so our clothes didn't catch on fire. The heat was already building: we were in a metal box with no windows and already, the air was like an oven. But the real problem was the air. The flames were eating up all the oxygen and in another few seconds there wouldn't be enough to breathe.

I grabbed Tanya around the waist and lifted her onto the roof of the old car. The flames had spread under and around it but, for now, they hadn't scaled the sides and the roof was a dark, cool little island. Then I found a shrinking path between the flames and ran to the door, hoping I could break the chain. But it was brand new, the links thicker than my fingers, and the padlock was good quality. I looked around frantically for a crowbar but all the tools were in the main garage. *Fuck.*

I ran to the roller door and heaved on the handle. Maravić and his goons might be on the other side waiting for us, but I'd take that over burning to death. But the door didn't budge: Maravić must have locked it from the other side.

I spun around and looked at the room. The flames had spread to cover the entire floor. Worse, they were climbing the shelves. Cans of paint were blistering and popping their lids, plastic bottles of antifreeze and brake fluid were melting and as all of it burned, it belched a thick, black chemical cocktail. I started to cough and once I started, I couldn't stop.

I tried to run back to the car, but there was no path anymore. I had to run through the flames and if my clothes hadn't been soaking wet from the rain, I would have had no chance. As it was, I scrambled up onto the roof with Tanya slapping out flames on my calves and thighs. My eyes were streaming from the smoke, now, but I could see her looking at me, terrified. *What do we do?*

I shook my head. I had no answer.

The heat was so intense I could feel my exposed skin being scorched. The flames were rising up to the ceiling and were climbing the sides of the car, the paint bubbling and peeling. The car's roof had become a small raft in a sea of orange. We collapsed on our sides, coughing, and stared at each other. *Fuck.* I'd thought about dying, in an abstract kinda way, but I'd never figured it would be like this. Not separated from the team. What really hurt was that the truth would never come out. JD and the others would forever think I was a traitor.

Tanya's hand found mine and squeezed, and I squeezed back. I was separated from the team, but I wasn't on my own.

I breathed in and got only smoke. I could feel the hair in my nostrils being singed. *This is it.*

My lungs filled with filthy, oily smoke and I wheezed and rolled over onto my stomach, choking, still holding Tanya's hand. Through tearing eyes, I stared down into the flames—

And that's when I saw it. Just for a second, as the flames flickered. Textured metal, and a name. C. SEW.

My oxygen-starved brain stared at it blankly. *Who is C. Sew?*

The flames flickered a little more. Some guy with two middle names. *N. Y. C. Sew.* The guy who owned the garage, maybe. But why had he engraved his name on the floor?

I closed my eyes, my muscles going limp. But some part of my brain kept working on the puzzle. *N. Y. C. Sew. N. Y. C. Sew...*

N.Y.C. Sewer.

My eyes opened wide and I stared down at it. This shed had been built illegally to extend the garage. The floor was part of the alley. And in the middle of the alley was a manhole cover.

I tried to rouse Tanya but she'd passed out. I looked down at the manhole cover, trying to get my brain to work.

A manhole in your garage was a pretty useful thing to have. If the owner had been the sort of guy to build an illegal extension, he was probably the sort who'd pour oil and paint down there, instead of disposing of it properly. Which meant he'd need a hook, to lift the cover. I searched the walls, the floor...and finally saw it hanging from the ceiling above my head.

I grabbed the hook, then leaned out over the flames. It was like putting my face an inch from the coals of a barbecue. Sweat was pouring off me and sizzling as it dripped into the fire, like I was the pig at a hog roast. I gritted my teeth and tried to thread the hook into the hole in the manhole cover. But between the flames, the smoke and the tears in my eyes, I could barely see. *Come on!* I glanced at Tanya. She barely seemed to be breathing. *Come on!* The hook bounced off the hole again. And now I had a new problem: the flames were heating the metal and it was starting to burn my hands. *Come on!*

The hook slipped into the hole. I heaved and lifted and a circle of darkness appeared below us.

I clambered to my knees and hauled Tanya up and over my shoulder. Then I winced and jumped down into the flames. They danced around my legs: by now, my clothes had dried out and I saw the fabric starting to catch. *Where's the ladder? Where's the ladder?!*

I found it and started to climb down into the darkness but my pants were alight now, flames spreading and climbing. I went down the ladder as fast as I could, but when I was still six feet from the water below, I felt my legs start to erupt in pain and I cursed, prayed and let go.

I plunged into icy, neck-deep water. Tanya jerked awake, spluttered and grabbed me around the neck. The air was foul and

God knows what we were swimming in but after the choking fumes and the heat of the garage, it felt like bathing in a Swiss mountain stream.

The water was flowing fast because of the rain and we let the current carry us through the darkness until we could breathe again. Then we caught hold of a ladder and climbed back up to the surface.

I inched the manhole cover up cautiously, in case we were emerging in the middle of a street. But it was some sort of pedestrianized area, calm and quiet. I lifted the cover and shoved it aside, then slithered out and helped Tanya out.

Then we just lay there, letting the cooling rain hammer down on our bodies, not caring at all that passers-by were staring at us. We were too exhausted and too glad to be alive. I offered up a little prayer of thanks to C. Sew, Esquire.

When the rain had washed away the worst of the sewer and some life had started to creep back into my muscles, I rolled over and scooched back against a low wall, pulling Tanya with me. I had no idea where in Manhattan we were, but it was some sort of paved area, with lots of greenery. My legs hurt and I figured I had some burns, and I wasn't sure I was ever going to get the chemical taste of the smoke out of my mouth. But all that mattered was that she was okay. I'd saved her. And she'd saved me, stopping me going up against Maravić. It stung my ego, but I was no match for him when he had a knife.

Tanya slumped against me. "We still don't know," she said, sounding utterly defeated.

I put my arm around her and stroked her hair. Even in the middle of all this, the feel of her against me and the sound of her accent was enough to lift me inside. God, I needed this woman. But she was determined to stay isolated, to keep torturing herself. And I had no idea how to break through to her.

I forced myself to focus. She was right. We'd used up our only lead. Maravić would have cleared the garage out by now so if we went back, there'd be nothing. And we still didn't know what he was planning. What were the pipes? Why did he need *guns*?

I sighed and looked around. Where the hell were we, anyway? It wasn't Central Park and I couldn't think of anywhere else in Manhattan where there was this much open space.

Then I peered through the driving rain and saw the shape of the emptiness in front of me: an immense square, surrounded by a parapet. I twisted around and saw the matching square behind me. And my stomach sank as realization hit. There *shouldn't* be this much open space in Manhattan.

It only existed because two massive buildings no longer stood here.

I knew where we were. And my stomach lurched because, suddenly, I knew what Maravić was planning.

I got to my feet, hauling Tanya up with me, and pointed through the rain to the parapets inscribed with thousands of names.

"When 9/11 happened," I said, "the stock market lost one point four *trillion.*"

Her jaw went slack and she turned sheet-white.

We'd been missing the obvious. What would give the economy that sudden, sharp plunge that the algorithm would turn into a tailspin? What would require someone like Maravić? What would need *guns?*

A terrorist attack on American soil.

41

TANYA

WE WITHDREW to an alley and stood shivering in the darkness, trying to stay out of the thousand little waterfalls of rainwater spilling down from the buildings around us. Between the sewer and the rain, our clothes were soaked through and there was enough of a breeze blowing that we were freezing. It was a low point. "What now?" grumbled Colton.

I thought hard. "Maravić said that your CIA boss, Steward, was meeting the person in charge tomorrow at two, in Washington DC. If we go to DC, find Steward and follow him, we can find out which country's behind this."

Colton stared at me, incredulous. "This guy's trying to catch us and you want to go right to his *home?*"

I shrugged. "It's the one place he won't think to look."

He cursed under his breath and scowled at the ground. "It's a dumb-ass idea," he said. Then, after a while. "I'm only saying *yes* because I ain't got a better one."

We stole a car and headed out of the city. At a truck stop, we stripped out of our stinking, wet clothes and had hot showers. Finally, I was able to wash my hair and feel clean again. The only problem came when it was time to put on new clothes. I'd put Colton in charge of buying us something to wear and he showed up wearing gray sweatpants and a red sweatshirt that said 'Bad Truckin' Attitude.' But the wad of clothes he held out to me was *pink*. And why did my sweatshirt have a cartoon rabbit on it? *Wait, that's not a sweatshirt.*

"*Pajamas?!*" I moaned in horror.

"It's a truck stop," he said apologetically. "There's not a whole lot of choice in women's clothes."

I held them up and stared at the lettering on the front. "Sleepy Bunny," I read, deadpan.

Colton gave a snort of laughter, but wisely turned away and pretended to be coughing. I glared at him, but it was either the pajamas or travel to DC in a towel. *Chyort!* I went back into the shower stall and pulled on the pajamas, then winced when I saw myself in the mirror. *If the rest of the GRU could see me now...*

I stomped out to the parking lot, feeling Colton smiling as he fell in beside me. It was a long drive to DC and he took the first shift driving while I curled up in the passenger seat. I didn't think I'd be able to sleep but it had been a long day. And the pajamas were soft and cozy. I was used to sleeping naked, or in lingerie. I hadn't worn pajamas since I was a child and I'd forgotten how comforting they were...

I jerked awake. I could feel I was in a moving car and immediately assumed I'd been kidnapped. I grabbed my gun and pointed it at—

I blinked at Colton and slowly lowered my gun, remembering. I was safe, or as safe as life ever got for me. And—my stomach flipped with the strangeness of it—I *wasn't alone*. Even though I'd pushed him away, Colton was still helping me, protecting me. I trusted him enough that I'd fallen fast asleep right next to him. And now he was glancing across at me like—

I frowned at him. *What?* I looked down at myself. I certainly didn't look sexy. After the fire and the rain, my make up had been a ruined mess and I'd scrubbed the remains of it from my face in the truck stop shower. My hair was still damp and I was wearing pink *Sleepy Bunny* pajamas. I frowned. I was used to wearing either black military gear and sturdy boots to sneak into an airbase, or plunging necklines and lots of lip gloss to seduce an ambassador. I never looked like *this,* like some woman lounging on the couch watching Netflix. And yet Colton kept glancing my way, smiling, as if I was—

I narrowed my eyes. As if I was adorable.

"Watch the road," I told him gruffly. And tried to ignore the unfamiliar warmth that was spreading through my chest.

Around three in the morning, we pulled over and I got behind the wheel. Since the passenger seat really wasn't big enough for him to sleep in, Colton stretched out on the back seat. After a few miles, I realized that he was lying down but wasn't closing his eyes. He'd pulled out a metal...*something* and was gazing at it. "What are you looking at?" I asked.

He stretched forward and showed me an antique cigarette case: I remembered him having it in the woods, now. "My dad used to carry this thing. My granddaddy before him. Both of them served. Neither of *them* ever disobeyed orders or went AWOL." He sighed and shook his head. "If you'd told me a few days ago I'd go against JD, go against the *team,* I'd have called you crazy."

I wondered what it must be like, to have that feeling of loyalty to something. I was used to allegiances shifting like the wind. "We're doing the right thing," I told him gently. "This CIA guy, Steward: he's the traitor, not you."

"I know," he said quietly. He flipped the cigarette case over and I saw the Stars and Stripes engraved on one side. He rubbed his thumb across the lines of it. "Just...I swore an oath, y'know?"

I met his eyes in the rear view mirror. "If we don't stop this thing," I told him firmly, "in twenty-four hours, there might not *be* a United States."

He grudgingly lay down and fell into a fitful sleep, mumbling to himself and twitching. Without really thinking about what I was doing, I reached behind me with one hand and put it on his sleeping shoulder and, after a few minutes, he seemed to relax and sleep soundly. I smiled. Then I caught myself and jerked my hand back. *What am I doing?* I'd never been like that with Lev. I'd loved him but I'd never been tender: it just wasn't in either of our natures. Colton brought out a side of me I wasn't used to. I hadn't even known it existed.

I glanced at him in the rear view mirror. My eyes tracked down from that gorgeous face, peaceful now in sleep. Then to his bicep, the swell of it pushing out the fabric of his sweatshirt, and his forearm, deliciously thick and weighty, reassuringly solid. His arm was across his chest and I knew that if I gently slowed and pulled off the road, I could slip into the back seat without him even waking. I could burrow under that arm and let it slip around my waist, put my head on the warm curve of his pec and just lie there, snug and protected.

I snapped my eyes back to the road and shook my head, silently cursing myself in Russian. *Weak, selfish suka!* Lev was *dead.* I didn't deserve Colton, or anyone. I couldn't give in to these feelings. I shouldn't even be having them.

The road's white center line went blurry. *See?* This is what happened when I let someone past all the ice.

I savagely blinked my tears away and drove on into the night.

I woke Colton by waving a cup of coffee from a drive-thru under his nose. He frowned, grunted, then sat up and rubbed his eyes with his fists. I kept my face expressionless but, inside, I was melting. *Chyort,* but he really was just a big teddy bear! I pressed the coffee cup into one of his hands and a bacon, egg and cheese muffin wrapped in greasy paper into the other, then climbed into the back seat next to him and closed the door so that we could talk while we ate.

Colton looked around, blinking. When he'd fallen asleep, we'd been on the highway. Now we were in the heart of a city. "Where *are* we?"

"DC." I sipped my coffee and nodded to a beautiful old townhouse a few doors down the street. "That's Steward's house. I got his address from his credit card company, via a hacker friend of mine back home. We'll tail him from here and follow him until he goes to this meet at 2pm. Then we'll know which country's behind this."

We finished the food and moved into the front seats to wait. At just before eight, a black SUV pulled up outside Steward's house and a couple of guys whose posture screamed *former military* knocked on his door. Steward came out and—

I leaned forward in my seat. "What's that he's carrying?"

"A suit," shrugged Colton.

"No..." I strained my eyes, trying to see the detail through the plastic garment bag. "It's a tuxedo!"

Steward and his entourage climbed into the SUV and it drove off. Colton followed at a distance. "Maybe he's going to an event tonight, straight from work," he said.

"Maybe," I muttered, worried. I already had my phone out and was frantically searching through lists of DC social events. After a few minutes, I cursed. "Got it. There's a party today, 1pm to 4pm, some kind of charity fundraiser. Lots of DC power players seem to go...and there's a picture of Steward there from last year."

"So he's meeting someone at the party." Colton slowed the car and pulled over by the side of the road, letting Steward disappear off into the distance. There was no point tailing him now. "Shit!" Colton thumped the dashboard. "His contact could be anyone at that party. We'll have no idea who he speaks to!"

I chewed my lip thoughtfully. "Not unless we're there, too."

Colton stared at me. "*Hell* no! I'm not sneaking into some rich guy's party in a tux! That's *your* department! You sneak, I hit people!"

"Can't do it on my own. Easier to follow someone with two. Plus, if I'm on my own in a cocktail dress, every male guest will be trying to hit on me." I was joking about the last part, but I saw Colton's eyes flare with possessive rage and that made warmth unexpectedly flood my chest and sink down to my groin. I quickly looked away.

"Have you forgotten that Steward is searching the entire fucking country for us?" asked Colton. "He'll recognize you. He'll recognize *me!*"

I'd gotten myself under control, now, and I turned back to him. "Colton, by the time I'm finished with you, your own mother wouldn't recognize you."

~

The rest of the morning was busy.

We needed a base, so we checked into a hotel, paying cash. Then we hit a shopping mall, first for some actual clothes for me, then for a cocktail dress, a tuxedo, fresh burner phones, make up, a hair trimmer, shaving cream, a razor, ammunition and a few other essentials. Back at the hotel, I had a long, hot shower, then wrapped myself in a towel. I passed Colton the bag of shaving supplies. He ran his hand mournfully through his beard and threw me puppy-dog eyes.

"Sorry," I told him. "You have to."

He grumbled and went into the bathroom, closing the door. I heard him showering, then the electric hair trimmer started to buzz.

I was laying out my makeup when the door opened again. I looked up and—

Wow.

The curse had been lifted: my gorgeous beast had turned into a gorgeous prince.

Without the beard he looked younger, gentler, and less intimidating. His full lower lip was more exposed, now, and it pouted like a rock star's. My eyes kept being drawn to it, and to the exposed skin on his cheeks and throat. What would it be like to be kissed by him, now?

He ran a hand over his cheek. "Feels weird. How'd I look?"

"You look good," I told him.

His mouth opened as if he was going to return the compliment, but then his eyes narrowed with lust and his gaze dropped, sliding slowly up my bare legs to where the towel finished, only a few inches below my groin, then flicking up to trace the curves of my damp cleavage before finally finding my face. His eyes said what his voice couldn't, and I felt myself flush.

"We should get dressed," I said, my voice strained.

He nodded. We looked at each other, both of us naked except for our towels. We were alone, in a hotel room, and for the first time in what felt like days, we weren't in danger. I felt the mood shift.

If I stripped off in front of him, I knew what would happen. And I wanted it, so bad it was an ache. But if we had sex again and then I pushed him away again, it was going to hurt him even more. I couldn't do that.

But what *was* I going to do? He'd seen me naked already, not to mention pinned me down on the bed, spread me and fucked me. I couldn't pretend to be a shy virgin now and run off to the bathroom to change.

I slowly turned my back to him. *There,* I told myself. *This will be fine.*

Then I heard the soft thump of his towel hitting the ground and, suddenly, it was like all my other senses had been dialed up to eleven. I was hyper-aware of his breathing, of the faint scent of him in the air, of the steam that wound around us like mist, bathing our bodies. I could visualize every naked inch of him, could see the water droplets beaded on the warm, caramel slabs of his pecs.

I hadn't heard him turn around, so I knew he was still looking right at me.

I loosened the towel and let it drop to the floor. The room was utterly silent, as if he was holding his breath. And I felt myself go lightheaded and spacey, as if *I* was holding my breath, too. I looked down at the floor and saw our shadows, thrown by the sunlight coming through the window to our left. We were like two characters in a shadow play, my silhouette soft and feminine, my breasts jutting out in front of me, his huge and muscled, a beast waiting to pounce. As I watched, the shadow of his cock slowly rose and lengthened until it was pointing straight towards me.

I looked around for the panties I'd bought and saw them on the floor. There was no way to grab them without...

I bent over, feeling almost drunk. I heard his intake of breath, felt his eyes climbing all the way up my legs to my pussy. I could hear the blood pounding in my ears, my whole body vibrating with each beat of my heart. I had to really focus to hook each foot into my panties and then slide them up my legs, very aware that they were a thong, and really didn't cover much at all.

I straightened up and pulled on the strapless bra. My hands were shaking so hard I could barely fasten the clasp. Then I pulled the cocktail dress up my body and stepped into my heels.

I glanced down at our shadows. As mine stopped moving, his finally, reluctantly, came to life. I saw him pull on his jockey shorts, then his pants, then his shirt and jacket and finally his shoes. *There. It's safe now.*

I lifted my hair and stepped backwards, towards him. "Do me up, please?" I didn't like how my voice quavered.

I heard him move closer and felt the warmth of his breath on the back of my neck. And suddenly, it wasn't safe at all.

He pulled the zipper slowly up, its metal rasp the only sound in the room. His fingers brushed my naked back and I had to close my eyes and focus on slowing my breathing: my whole body was crying out for his touch and I knew that all it would take was one soft moan from me and he'd whip me around and kiss me. When the zipper reached the top, I knew I should be relieved. But when he stepped back, it was like a physical loss.

I took a deep breath, sat down at the dressing table, and started doing my makeup with careful precision. It took a while and the ritual of it calmed me, just as a soldier is calmed by carefully loading his gun. The tension in the room eased, but only a little. I could feel it in the air between us, a storm on the edge of breaking.

When I was finished, I slipped in the contact lenses I'd bought, then secured my hair in the hair net and pulled on the wig.

"I'm still worried Steward will recognize you," said Colton from behind me.

I smiled to myself. Then, in one movement, I stood and turned around. "Recognize *who*, sweetie?" I asked.

Colton had been looking at my back the whole time I'd been getting ready so he got the full effect all at once. He gaped at me, genuinely bewildered. "How—How...?" He cocked his head and stared. *"How did you do that?"*

I'd used a few old spy tricks, contouring my face differently so that my cheekbones were less prominent, using lip liner to widen my mouth a little and adding colored contact lenses to make my eyes deep green. But the main change was my hair. The wig was a mass of honey-blonde ringlets that spilled down over my shoulders and caught the light whenever I tossed them. And I was going to be doing that *a lot*. I gave a light, musical giggle and shimmied my shoulders. "It ain't nothin'," I told him. The accent took it to the next level: it was rich with Alabama sunshine, sweet as iced tea and just a little naive. The sort of rich, East Coast men who'd be at the party would hear it and patronize the hell out of me, which was just what I wanted. If I was prey, I couldn't possibly be a threat.

"It's..." Colton shook his head. "I don't—" And then he glanced down and he stopped speaking altogether. I'd almost forgotten the *other* reason Steward wouldn't recognize me: the dress. It was a scarlet, stretchy tube that hugged my hips and ass. It was long enough to be acceptable at this sort of party...*just*. But it had a scoop neck that revealed a bountiful amount of soft, milky cleavage.

Sometimes, the least sophisticated tricks are the best. I still remembered my old instructor, Ms. Sobolevsky, lecturing us at the academy. *For a man to see through your disguise, he first has to be looking at your face.*

Colton finally dragged his eyes up to mine. "You're incredible," he said.

For a second, I just smiled, proud of my tradecraft. But he held my gaze, and the words started to take on new meaning. The amber in his eyes flared and *burned*. There was lust there: he liked me like this, with the honey-blonde hair. He wanted to fuck Rachel—as I was calling this identity—wanted to throw her on the bed, drag the dress up over her hips and see those honey-blonde curls bounce as he fucked her. But there was something else there, too. A need that went beyond lust, that burned straight through my Rachel disguise, and then all the layers of ice and flirting that made up Tanya, the spy, and cut right to my vulnerable core. To the authentic me, to the woman that he'd seen damp-haired and without makeup, in ridiculous pink pajamas.

The tension in the room changed again. We'd been on the edge of grabbing each other and fucking. Suddenly, we were on the edge of something far more dangerous.

My chest ached with how much I wanted it. I allowed the traitorous, selfish thought to creep in. *I don't want to be alone anymore.* But then came the stab of guilt. Lev's face as he lay in my arms.

I shook my head. *I can't.* And then I tore my gaze from his and grabbed the two halves of his bow tie. Taking quick little breaths, I criss-crossed the fabric, knotted and pulled. I was suddenly having trouble seeing, but I'd fastened enough bow ties for enough men that I could do it almost by feel.

I felt Colton's eyes burning down at me the whole time. But as I finished and tugged the bow tight, he finally sighed and nodded to himself.

I stepped back and forced my voice to be level. "Okay," I said. "Let's go crash a party."

42

COLTON

WE WERE HUNKERED down in our stolen car, watching from across the street. "Good luck getting in *there*," I muttered.

The party was in a beautiful old three story corner townhouse, right in the heart of DC. And with so many rich folk on the guest list, security was tight. Three big guys with earpieces stood at the door, checking each guest's invitation carefully before letting them in.

Tanya cursed under her breath. "Drive around the block," she told me. "Let's see if there's another way in."

I pulled away from the curb and started circling. While Tanya gazed up at the buildings, I had time to think about what had happened at the hotel. *Fuck,* when she'd stripped off right in front of me, those gorgeous soft breasts hanging down as she bent to put on her panties. I wanted her more than I'd ever wanted any woman: I only had to touch her and I was a pawing, panting animal, unable to think straight. But it went beyond sex, now, had done for a while. When I looked into her eyes I could see what this life had done to her. I wanted her to have all the shit I took for granted: having friends, a real life...hell, even just having a proper home. I wanted her to be able to feel again. Okay, *love* again, if you really had to hang a name on it.

But losing her man, Lev, had really destroyed her, just like losing his wife and kid had destroyed JD. JD had had Lorna to bring him back to life and show him he could have a second chance. Lorna was clever and subtle and female: women understand this stuff. How the hell was *I* meant to help her? I was a big, dumb bear trying to help a bird with a broken wing. I couldn't even call Danny for advice like I normally would because he was trying to hunt my ass down, along with the rest of the team.

I stole a glance at her while she was looking up at the buildings. God, I needed her. I felt a tug in my chest every fucking time I looked at her. But we couldn't be more different and it made me wonder whether we could ever make it work. She spun webs of lies out of nothing and always knew the right words to get someone to do what she wanted, while I just kind of scowled and muttered what I really felt. She was quick where I was lumbering and the way she tricked and betrayed and used people made me feel ridiculously naive, with my loyalty to the flag and to the team. Like this plan to infiltrate the party in disguise: she was great at all that stuff, but what could *I* bring to the table?

Tanya sighed. "No way into the house, not without alerting all the security. But it looks like the neighbors are out. If we can break into their house, I think we can get in that way."

I had to stop myself from punching the air. *Alright!* I didn't know how to sweet talk and lie but breaking a window or busting open a door, *that* I could do. "Once we're in, how do we get to the party house?"

She pointed up at the third floor. The houses both had stone balconies and they almost touched. "We can jump across," she said, smiling.

The rising excitement in my chest turned to cold, sick dread. *Oh shit.*

∾

Five minutes later, we were standing on the balcony of the neighbor's house. I knew I shouldn't look down, but the drop drew me in like a car crash on the highway. I peeked over the edge...

Shit. How come everything always looked so much higher, from up top? The sidewalk was just far enough away for me to imagine the screaming, flailing fall while being just close enough that I could see the texture of the concrete where my head would split.

I pulled back, glowering and panting. Hating the fear, hating myself.

Tanya, oblivious, had marched to the end of the balcony and looked over. "It's easy," she said, and started to take her shoes off.

I reluctantly joined her and saw with a lurch of my stomach that the balconies *didn't* almost touch. From down on the ground, the gap had looked like nothing at all but it was about four feet. I shook my head, feeling my feet go light, as if I was already falling. "That's not —" I mumbled. "We can't—"

She frowned at me, confused. "It's fine." Holding her shoes in her hand, she climbed up onto the balcony's stone handrail. Then, before I could stop her, she bent her knees and jumped.

My heart nearly stopped and my stomach plunged down to the ground below. Tanya landed lightly on the handrail of the other balcony, swayed a few times, then got her balance and jumped down onto the balcony itself. She turned and beamed at me.

I leaned against the handrail, my heart slamming against my ribs. I could feel sweat beading my forehead and running down between my shoulder blades, and it wasn't over: the sight of her jumping was running on loop in my mind, like the aftershocks of an earthquake. *Fuck.*

"Colton?" asked Tanya.

I didn't answer, determined not to let her see. "I'm coming!" I snapped, and tried to lift a foot to step up onto the handrail. But I could see the drop through the cutouts in the stonework and my legs and groin went cold and floaty, like I was plummeting through the air. This wasn't like racing around on the roof of her apartment building, or jumping from the plane. Back then, I hadn't had a chance to think about it. This time, I'd been thinking about it the whole time we were breaking into the neighbor's house and climbing upstairs, and the dread had built until it was huge and I was tiny.

"We need to go! Someone's going to see us up here!" Tanya told me.

"I know! Just—" *Fuck, fuck, fuck.*

"Colton?" she asked, her voice worried, now.

The humiliation burned up through me like lava and sent my face crimson. "I have a problem with heights," I spat, scowling at the floor.

I waited for her to start laughing. But there was just silence and, after a few seconds, I risked looking at her. Her eyes were big with shock and concern. "I didn't know," she said softly. "I'm sorry."

I scowled at her suspiciously, then gradually relaxed. The humiliation faded a little.

"You can do this," she told me firmly. "You can *easily* make that jump. Come on, I'll talk you through it. Climb up onto the handrail."

Her words cut through the fear in a way my own internal pleading couldn't. I let the smooth, beautiful ice of her accent sink into my mind and the cold logic numb me. All I had to do was listen. I took two more panting breaths, then cursed and lifted one foot onto the weathered stone and then the other. I wobbled sickeningly and the fancy dress shoes had no grip at all, but I was up.

"Good. Now look at the other handrail. You're going to push with your legs and *jump,* okay?" Her voice was awkward but heartfelt. "Come on, I'll count you down. *Ah-Deen!*"

I took a deep breath.

"*Dvah!*"

I tensed my legs.

"*Tree!*"

I sprang, with all my terror powering me. I landed hard on the other balcony, skated in my dress shoes and fell flat on my ass. But I was across.

Tanya ran over to me, put her arms around me and hoisted me to my feet.

"Thanks," I mumbled.

She smiled at me. Then, as if on impulse, she darted forward and kissed my cheek. I put my hand on the spot. "What was that for?" I asked.

"Being brave," she told me.

Someone had left a window open so we didn't even have to break in. We climbed through into a bedroom, then crept out into the hallway. From downstairs, we could hear laughter and the clink of glasses. We were in, but we still had to stay stealthy until we got downstairs: guests probably weren't meant to be up here and we didn't want some security guy asking to see our invite. We skulked along the hallway, looking for the stairs.

"Rats," muttered Tanya.

"What?"

"For me, it's rats." We found the stairs and started to creep down them. "I'm on an op in Armenia...I'm in a cellar and I hear a sound, like chewing, right by my ear. I look around and there is a rat, *here*—" She put a hand an inch from her nose. "I screamed. Blew the entire op. A month of surveillance, wasted."

I felt a little better. And that tug in my chest grew even stronger.

We reached the second floor. But just as we were about to start down the next flight of stairs, a security guy came out of a door behind us. "Hey!"

Tanya pushed me up against the wall and pressed her lips to my ear. "Kiss me and put your hand up my dress," she whispered.

All of the million reasons why that was a terrible idea, given how we felt about each other, filled my mind. But I could hear the security guy marching toward us and then she closed her eyes, tilted her head back and pushed her breasts against me and *oh fuck it.*

I grabbed her waist and kissed her hard, and as soon as our lips touched I was falling into deep feminine mystery and Russian magic. The softness of her lips as I crushed them under mine, the little moans that vibrated through me. *Is she just acting?* Because I sure wasn't. And then the tip of her tongue found mine and I growled and pulled her harder against me, my cock rising against her thigh. I put my hand on the smooth perfection of her leg and slid it up under her dress, smoothing my palm over her hip, her ass...God, I'd forgotten she was wearing a thong. I squeezed her ass hard and she groaned and writhed against me, her breasts caressing my chest.

Someone tapped me hard on the shoulder. I reluctantly broke the kiss and looked around, scowling, my hand still up Tanya's dress. It took me a few seconds to focus on what the person was saying.

"...supposed to be up here," said the security guy.

I'd completely forgotten about him. I slowly withdrew my hand from Tanya's dress, glaring like a grizzly deprived of its meal.

"Sorry," said Tanya in her *Rachel-from-Alabama* voice. "We were trying to find a bedroom."

The guy flushed. Then his eyes went to her cleavage and he flushed harder. "Downstairs, please," he managed.

Tanya grabbed my hand and we hurried down the stairs. I was still reeling from the kiss. I could still taste her on my lips, still feel the warm press of her against my body, But Tanya acted like nothing had happened. *Can she really just shrug it off like that?*

She glanced back at me, paused, and, for a split-second, I saw it in her eyes. *No, she can't.* We stared at each other longingly. My chest ached...

Then she broke my gaze and continued down the stairs, the giggly, flirty Rachel mask back in place.

A moment later, we joined the crowd on the first floor. Tanya plucked two champagne flutes from a passing waiter's tray and that was it: we were in.

I looked around in wonder. I'd never been in a place like this. It was old-money grand, with big windows that flooded each room with natural light, oil paintings on the walls and statues everywhere. I kept worrying I was going to knock over a vase worth half a million dollars. And the people were just as alien to me: young, beautiful women in a rainbow of brightly-colored dresses and silver-haired men who wore their tuxedos as naturally as I wore a uniform. The air buzzed with talk of elections, scandals and corporate takeovers. This was the ultra-rich and powerful, relaxing in their natural environment, and if I'd been a journalist I probably could have made a year's salary just by scribbling down five minutes of the gossip.

Tanya fitted in instantly, like she'd been born to this. "*Hi!*" she told an elderly couple, sounding thrilled. "So good to see you again!" The couple beamed back at her, far too polite to admit that they didn't remember her. Tanya grabbed the elbow of a guy who looked like he might be a retired general. "We must talk later!" she told him. "I have a friend who's *very* interested in your expertise." She slipped effortlessly through the crowd, leaving smiling faces in her wake. Everyone wanted to know her. No one would have dreamed she was an interloper.

Meanwhile, I felt hulking and awkward. The shirt was too tight on my chest and the jacket got all caught up under the arms. I wished for one of my t-shirts with the sleeves ripped off. What was weird, though, was that the women at the party didn't seem to think I looked ridiculous. They kept looking my way and smiling. I frowned and rubbed my beard, then frowned harder when my fingers hit smooth skin.

We emerged from the hallway into a huge room with a marble floor. A guy was playing a grand piano and in the center of the room, some couples were dancing. Tanya nodded ahead of us. "There's Steward," she said out of the side of her mouth.

As we watched, Steward sidled up to a guy standing on the edge of the dance floor and put his hand on his shoulder. "It's 2 p.m.," said Tanya. "That must be who he's meeting."

The two men stood with their backs towards us, facing the dance floor. "We need to see his face," said Tanya. She pulled on my hand. "Come on, dance with me."

"He'll see us!"

She gently brushed her fingers down my cheek. "You forget, you don't look like *you* anymore. But even more important, his own expectation bias won't *let* him see you. He thinks you're busy running from the team, somewhere in New York. In his mind, you *can't* be here."

She dragged me towards the dance floor. "I can't dance 'less it's a mosh pit!" I hissed.

"Don't worry," she told me. "I can."

Of course she could dance. "They teach you that in spy school too?"

"Yes," she deadpanned, "between poisoning and BDSM." As we reached the dance floor, she turned to face me and slipped my arm around her waist. "Hold me."

I held her, cursing and looking around self-consciously.

"Like you mean it."

I pulled her closer. Her hips pressed against mine and I inhaled the scent of her, that tang of orchids and sharp berries like a drug. My anger dissolved.

"Now step like me, and move that way," she whispered, nodding towards the center of the dance floor. I stared at her feet and shuffled towards where she said. I didn't know what the hell I was doing but it didn't matter because if anyone was watching us, their eyes were on her. I fell into the rhythm of it and relaxed.

"There they are," muttered Tanya. For the first time, I saw the faces of Steward and the guy he was talking to. They were deep in conversation and weren't paying any attention to the couples dancing. I probably could have stood right in front of them and they wouldn't have noticed.

"He doesn't look like a Chinese ambassador," muttered Tanya.

She was right. He was a white guy, dark haired, American or maybe European. And... I narrowed my eyes. "I know him," I said.

"You *know* him?"

"Give me a minute." I kept staring at him, catching a glimpse every few seconds as we slowly spun around the dance floor. I have a thing for faces. I need to: sometimes when I'm bounty hunting, all I have to go on is an out-of-date photo and I need to be able to scan a crowded bar and pick out the person in seconds, before they run. I knew I'd seen this guy before. Not in a tuxedo, but maybe in a suit. Not on his own but with other people. An image crystallized in my mind. A photo. A group shot. "Oh crap," I whispered.

"What? Who is it?" Her voice grew scared. "*Russia?*"

I shook my head in wonder and looked at her. "It's not a foreign state at all. It's the family. The fucking family."

"*Who?*"

I sighed. "They're called the Bainbridges. European old money. They stay out of the limelight but they've got more money than God and they've got a hand in everything. I saw them all on the cover of *Time* magazine. One of them's in pharmaceuticals, one's in defense... we ran into Hugo, the one who was in oil, in Ecuador. And *that* guy, Lucas Bainbridge, guess which industry he's in?"

"Finance," said Tanya.

"They're not going to crash the dollar to wreck the country," I growled. "They're going to crash the dollar to *make money*. I bet they've been planning this for months, betting against the dollar because they *know* it's going to crash. The day after tomorrow, Maravić carries out a terrorist attack and the market panics. Then the stockbroker's algorithm kicks in and makes the panic worse and worse, until the dollar's worth nothing. Jesus, they'll become trillionaires."

Steward and Bainbridge finished talking and split up. Steward pulled a phone from his pocket. "Maravić said Steward was going to call him," said Tanya. "See if you can overhear anything. I'll follow Bainbridge."

And suddenly she was gone and I was standing alone in the middle of the dance floor, gaping. I looked at Steward's retreating back. I didn't know anything about skulking around! *I wish Bradan was here.*

Cursing, I hurried after Steward. I could see him looking around for a quiet place to make his phone call. He found a stairwell leading down to the basement and was about to head down there when a security guy stopped him. "Sorry, sir. Basement's off limits."

"Do you have any idea who I am?" Steward snapped. He flashed his CIA identity card. "This is a national security matter, I need to make a private phone call!"

The security guy stepped back, chastened. "Sorry, sir."

Steward hurried down the steps and out of sight. *Shit!* I had to get down there and listen in. *What would Tanya do?* I took a deep breath and marched brazenly up to the guy. "Hey, I'm with Mr. Steward. Got to be on this phone call with him. We got a national security situation in, uh...Sweden." It was the first place that popped into my head.

"Sweden?" asked the security guy.

I pushed past him into the stairwell, thinking frantically. "Yeah, my boss is talking to *their* boss in Oslo."

The security guy followed me, frowning. "Oslo's in Norway."

Shit. I looked down the stairs. Steward was making that phone call *right now,* I had to get down there.

The security guy put a hand on my shoulder. "How about you show me some ID?"

I looked around. We were out of sight of anyone in the hallway. *Fuck it.* I turned around and laid him out with a punch, catching him as he fell. "Sorry," I muttered. I dragged him down to the next landing and hid him in a janitor's closet where hopefully no one would find him for a while, then crept on down the stairs.

The stairwell opened into an underground parking garage full of gleaming cars. Steward was pacing back and forth, already on the phone. I flattened myself against a pillar and listened. "...from the Middle East is in a shipping container," he said. "It's down a back road that isn't on most maps, so I'm going to give you the coordinates. Got a pen?"

Maybe Maravić, on the other end of the line, had a pen, but *I* didn't. I looked around for something to write with and found nothing.

"Thirty-five point eight six nine north," Steward reeled off from memory. "Eighty-three point eight three six west."

Shit! I closed my eyes and started repeating the numbers in my head.

"Call me when you have it," Steward told Maravić, then hurried off up the stairs.

I waited a few seconds to make sure he was gone, then raced up the stairs. I could feel the numbers fading in my head. *How do spies remember this stuff?! Thirty-five point eight six nine...* I grabbed hold of the first person I saw. "Got a pen?" He looked at me blankly. I grabbed another man's arm. "A pen! Got a pen?" He recoiled from my Missouri twang. *Thirty-five point eight six nine...*

I saw Tanya across the room and ran to her. "Thirty-five point eight six nine north," I panted, "eighty-three point eight three six west." Even as I said them, the numbers faded and jumbled into garbage in my head. "Tell me you got that!"

She blinked at me. "Thirty-five point eight six nine north, eighty-three point eight three six west," she repeated as if it was nothing. I groaned in relief, lifted her right off the ground and bear-hugged her. She was so amazing and—

Goddamnit. I felt the resolve harden in my chest, becoming iron. I wasn't going to let her go. I was going to find a way to reach her.

"What's there?" she asked, her voice muffled.

I gently put her down and forced my voice to be level. "The package from the Middle East that Steward wants Maravić to pick up," I told her. "My guess would be explosives."

She thought for a second. "Those coordinates are within the US. Somewhere in the Midwest."

I shook my head in wonder. "You just *know* by heart where GPS— Yeah, of course you do." I took hold of her shoulders. "If we get there first and get the explosives, that stops this thing dead. *And* we'll have the hard evidence we need. You can clear your name. I can go back to the team!"

Together, we ran for the door.

43

TANYA

WE LOOKED up the coordinates and they led to a spot just outside Columbus, Ohio. About a seven hour drive from DC, thanks to traffic. Maravić could make it from New York in about eight. It was going to be tight. We rushed back to the hotel to change and grab our stuff and then we drove like hell.

Colton was almost silent for the first three hours. Then, somewhere in Pennsylvania, we turned off the interstate to miss some construction. I was driving and Colton was reading me directions as we blasted down a deserted backroad, our wheels kicking up clouds of dust behind. And suddenly, it happened.

"Let me tell you a story," said Colton.

I glanced across at him, surprised, then frowned. There was a weird look on his face. I turned back to the road.

"There's this girl. And I don't know what happened to her, but at some point in her life, she feels this calling—"—he tapped his chest —"like a lot of us get. She wants to serve her country. Protect it."

I shook my head. "I don't want to have this conversation."

"Not a conversation, a story." His eyes gleamed and I recognized that stubbornly determined look.

"I don't want to listen to this story," I told him.

"Well, we still got four hours to go and we're stuck in this car and you can't drive with your hands over your ears so you ain't got much of a choice."

"*Chyort!*" I said out loud, and gripped the wheel harder.

"So this girl, she's smart, and she's resourceful and she's pretty as hell, so her country trains her to be a spy. They teach her how to lie, and cheat, and double-cross, how to manipulate people, how to use her body to seduce men."

Where is all this coming from? Then I thought back to how quiet he'd been. This wasn't coming out of the blue, he'd been planning it ever since we left the party, choosing his words.

"And this girl, a woman, now, she gets so used to lying and betraying people that she convinces herself she's evil. She starts pushing people away because she thinks no one should like her, let alone love her. But she's wrong. Her heart's in the right place. The bad shit she does, she does it to protect her country."

Stupid, big, lumbering idiot, I thought desperately. *He doesn't know anything.*

"And what's real cruel is: her bosses, they *like* their spies like this, all solitary and twisted up inside with guilt, because if they don't have friends or lovers, that makes 'em harder to compromise. They *let her* tear herself apart inside."

"You're meant to be reading me directions!" I snapped.

"We're on this road for another twenty miles so hush and listen." His voice wasn't cruel but it was firm. He wasn't going to be denied. "The story's only just getting to the sad part. See, this woman, she's lonely but she's okay. But then something happens. She meets somebody."

My knuckles went white on the steering wheel.

"He's a spy, like her," Colton said. "And he falls for her. Probably from the very first moment he sees her." His voice was strained, now. "Because she's that kind of woman. And she knows, she knows straight away that he's in love with her, because she's so good at reading people. But she believes she's too fucked up and too evil, she thinks she doesn't deserve to be happy, so she pushes him away, too.

And it takes years of working together before she allows herself to fall for him, too. And then at last she does and finally, *finally,* she isn't alone anymore."

I tried to speak but nothing would come out.

"But then some fucking bastard comes along, and he kills this guy right in front of her. And the woman doesn't just lose the only person she loves, she loses *herself.* She focuses on just one thing, on killing the guy who killed her man, because she doesn't want to stop and think about how much she misses him, or the fact she's still alive, because when she does that, she starts feeling guilty."

The air vents must have sucked in the dust from the road because my eyes were tearing and I had to swipe at them furiously.

"And this woman, she believes—I mean now it's like fucking *gospel* in her mind—that no one's ever going to love her, and that no one *should,* and that she can't love anyone back."

"*Ona beznadezhnyy sluchay!*" I snapped bitterly. He waited in silence for me to translate. "She sounds like a hopeless fucking case."

"Well, see, that's where you're wrong." I refused to look at him but I heard him shift in his seat, turning his hulking body to face me. "See, even if *she* can't see that she's a good person, someone else can." His voice became rough with emotion. "There's this guy, and to *him*... well, she's his fucking princess. And he's going to save her, no matter what."

"And who is he," I said savagely. "Her handsome prince?"

"More like a monster," said Colton. "But sometimes, you need a monster. 'Cause he's big enough not to be scared of her, and dumb enough not to leave her alone however hard she pushes him away, and strong enough to just throw her over his shoulder when she won't listen."

"It's a stupid fucking story!" I snapped. "Real life isn't like that!"

"Real life is what we make it," he said in that deep, country growl. "And if I want to rescue my princess, you'd better believe *I will rescue my princess.* Whether she likes it or not."

I was silent for a while. I could feel something rising in me, timid as a beaten animal. Hope.

For the first time, I dared to glance at him. Just for a split second, but when I saw his eyes, so solemn and full of love, I gulped and had to blink back fresh tears. The hope rose a little higher.

A sob broke from my chest, turning into words as it came out. "*I miss him!*" Even now, there was an instant, inward explosion of fury and self-hate. *Weakness!* But the words *had* come out.

"It's okay to miss him," said Colton quietly. "You just don't have to do it on your own."

My chest trembled and then quaked and there was another sob, and then another, and I *tried* to keep it in and couldn't, and then realized I didn't need to anymore, and something inside me gave way.

My foot relaxed on the gas, Colton took the wheel and steered us and we drifted to a stop at the side of the road. Colton held out his arms and I threw myself at his chest, burying my face between his pecs. He wrapped me up in his arms and squeezed me tight and I began crying it all out: the loss and the guilt and the fear of being alone and the shame of being weak. And for the first time, I knew how incredibly, unspeakably wonderful it was to have someone to cry it all out *to*.

He held me like that for a long time. When my tears stopped, the pain hadn't gone. But it was easier, somehow. *Feeling* was easier. And for Colton, I felt...

I pulled back, wiped my wet and very unglamorous face, and said, in a voice that didn't sound like mine, "It isn't a stupid story."

Colton nodded.

"And I think I'd q—quite like to be rescued—"—I hiccoughed and sniffed. "Please."

He hugged me close and I pressed myself tight against the warmth of him, the way a child hugs a teddy bear. Then I suddenly pushed back because I needed to tell him, "You aren't stupid. You're smart, smarter than you give yourself credit for. You can remember faces and you're great at tracking people down and you're brave and I really really like you."

He wiped my tears away with his thumb. "I really really like you, too," he rumbled.

He leaned forward and we touched foreheads, and I gave a little laugh that wasn't like me at all. Then I used my sleeve to wipe my eyes and said, "We need to go."

He gently released me and I put the car into gear and pulled away. I accelerated down the dirt road, shaking my head at the strange wonderfulness of it all, but with a new, secret thrill inside. As we rounded the next corner, I glanced across at him and smiled, and he smiled back.

There was a sharp crack I recognized as a rifle shot and then a bang as a tire blew out. The steering wheel jerked under my hands and suddenly we were spinning off the road.

44

COLTON

I WAS GRINNING like an idiot and, inside, I was air-guitaring and fist pumping while the words *I really really like you* lit up in a stadium rock light show complete with sprays of sparks. Then suddenly the car was slewing around, turning a full three-sixty as we skidded off the road and into the dirt. Someone stepped out of the bushes and I registered his face as we flashed past.

JD.

I waited for the car to hit something and flip but Tanya wrestled the skid under control and brought us to a stop about ten feet off the road and side-on to it. We sat there panting as the car rocked on its suspension. Then I was hitting the release on Tanya's seatbelt and pushing her out of the car. "Go! Go!" I told her. "It's them!"

She didn't have to ask who. She scrambled out and I grabbed her hand, trying to figure out which way to run.

"Stop," said JD. "Just *stop*."

I looked round, still a little disoriented. There was open country on both sides of us, softly-swaying grass turning gold as the sun started to sink below the horizon. JD was walking towards me from a patch of scrubby bushes where I guess he'd been hiding. Gabriel,

Danny and Bradan emerged from the fields further back. I guessed Cal was up high somewhere...*there,* stretched out on the roof of that barn. He must have shot out our tire.

There was nowhere to run: in fact, no cover at all. The only thing around was a rail crossing about fifty feet up ahead. There were no people, either. Probably why they'd picked this place for their ambush. Clever.

"Colton?" JD didn't have his gun out, but he had one hand on it. "Take it easy, buddy."

I became aware of a noise in the background, a metal-on-metal scrape and rattle that shook the ground.

"How'd you find us?" I asked.

"Traffic camera, back on the interstate," JD told us. "Facial recognition." He stared in shock. "You shaved off your *beard?*"

I touched my bare cheek and grunted: I'd forgotten. "Listen," I said. "I know she's Russian but we're on the same side. Steward's playing you guys."

"Put your gun down and come in," JD told me, "And we can talk about all this stuff." His eyes were pleading with me, big and blue and soulful, and I felt a tug deep in my chest, strong as an ocean current. All I wanted was to be back with him and the team. I knew he was just trying to look out for me. But he was wrong, this time.

The sound was getting louder, now. It came from somewhere behind me, vibrating up my body and shaking my teeth as something approached.

"JD," I said, my voice fracturing. "The CIA get their hands on her, she's dead. Steward's working with the Bainbridges, they're going to blow some shit up, crash the economy—"

"Colton, we're not asking!" JD shook his head tiredly. "If we don't take you in, they're coming after you with a shoot-to-kill order and the two of you will be dead by tonight. Now put your gun down! It's over!" He glared at Tanya. "Let her go!"

I looked down at Tanya's hand in mine. Then I looked across at her. At those frozen-sky eyes and the lips that were a fantasy all on their own. I thought of her naked by the firelight and her saving me from Maravić and helping me on the balcony and her asleep in pink pajamas.

I turned back to JD. "*No.*"

The sound behind me became a deafening, clattering rattle. Then there were two sharp blasts on an air horn. I checked over my shoulder and saw the freight train thundering towards the crossing.

"*Don't!*" JD's voice went tight with worry. "Colton, *please!* You run, we gotta take you down!"

"Sorry, JD," I muttered. And then I turned and bolted, pulling Tanya along with me. We ran towards the rail crossing and the train that was hurtling towards it at fifty miles an hour.

I heard JD's voice behind me as he spoke into his earpiece. "Cal! Take the shot!"

I was full-on sprinting, now, arms pumping. We were ten feet from the crossing and I could see the driver of the train staring at us through his windshield, terrified. He gave another long blast on his air horn. If we pushed ourselves, we could make it across.

But I knew in my gut that it was pointless. Any second, Cal's shot was going to hit me in the calf or the thigh and I'd go down. I gritted my teeth, trying to brace myself.

A shot rang out and—-

Concrete chips and dirt sprayed my leg as the bullet hit the ground a foot to my right.

I ran on, unable to believe my luck. We sprinted onto the crossing, passing so close in front of the locomotive I could feel the heat from its engine. Then we were across, the slipstream tugging at our clothes as the train blasted past.

We staggered to a stop and looked back. We could see glimpses of JD's furious face between the boxcars. The train looked to be a mile long. It would be minutes before the team could come after us and by then, we'd be gone.

Tanya looked at me, worried. *A shoot-to-kill order.* Things were different, now. I felt her hand loosen on mine and she looked towards

JD. I got her meaning: she could run and I could stay here, rejoin the team and be safe.

I squeezed her hand hard. *No fucking way.* We were in this together. "C'mon," I said.

And we ran.

45

JD

I MARCHED over to the barn and stood there waiting, chest rising and falling in anger, while Cal climbed down into the hayloft, then down to the floor. His nearly seven foot frame made him an intimidating sight: back in the Marines, they'd called him Bigfoot. But right now, he was hanging his head like a child. "Sorry, JD. I missed."

I growled and planted my finger in the middle of his chest. "You never missed a goddamn shot in your life!" I yelled. "You *let him go!*"

Cal stared at his feet for another few seconds. Then he lifted his head and looked me sullenly in the eye. I could feel the rest of the team staring at me, too. I didn't often yell and I didn't like doing it. But I was worried about Colton and it was making me crazy.

Bradan spoke up from behind me. "This doesn't feel right."

I turned to him, sighed and rubbed the bridge of my nose. "Look, I get it. I really do. I know you and Cal have bad history with the CIA—"

"What if their story's true?" asked Cal. "What if there *is* something going on?"

"Then we can figure it out when they're safely in custody." I turned back to Cal. "But that was our *one chance* to bring him in alive! Now they're going to be going after him with everything they've got!"

I stormed away from him. But the person I was really mad with was myself. I couldn't blame Cal or Bradan for not wanting to go against their buddy. It was my job to make the shitty calls, no one else's. And it was my fault we were in this mess. I should never have let an evil, manipulative liar like Yeshevskaya anywhere near a sweet guy like Colton. Thanks to my mistake, there was a good chance that the next time we saw him, he'd be lying in a ditch with his throat cut, or gunned down by our own side. I kicked a pebble and it dinged off the side of one of the freight cars that were still trundling past. *Fuck!*

A hand gently patted my back. I turned, expecting to see Danny. But it was Gabriel. "This is a fucking mess," I muttered. "I'm just trying to get him back alive!"

"I know," said Gabriel.

Something in his tone made me frown. Since this thing started, he'd been firmly on my side along with Danny. But now...I raised a questioning eyebrow.

Gabriel looked at the ground, his hands in his pockets. Then he lifted his gaze and looked me in the eye. "Thing is, I know about manipulating people. *Seducing* people. But when I looked at Tanya and Colton: the way they held hands, the looks she gave him, their body language..."—he chewed his lip then shook his head—"it didn't feel fake to me."

I studied him carefully, saying nothing. When we first met, I hadn't trusted the guy. But he'd come to be a loyal member of the team and a good friend. And as a mostly-redeemed thief, he *did* know a lot about con artists. "She could have started off seducing him and then fallen for him for real," I countered. "It happens. Her story could still be bullshit."

Gabriel nodded. "It could. But she knows she's putting his life in danger. If she really cares about him—and I think she does—and her story's just a hoax, why wouldn't she tell him the truth and send him back to us to keep him safe?"

I stared at him and, for the first time, a thread of doubt began to twist in my stomach.

No. That was crazy. Yeshevskaya was lying. We were on the right side.

The doubt twisted again. *We're on the right side...aren't we?*

46

COLTON

WE RACED DOWN THE ROAD, then down a track that led to an old industrial area. Hidden among the buildings, we finally stopped for a moment to catch our breath. I leaned against a wall, panting, then turned to face it and rested my overheated forehead against the deliciously cool concrete.

"We're going to need transport," said Tanya. "We're losing time."

She was right: we'd been due to arrive at the location of the weapons cache, or whatever the hell it was, about an hour before Maravić could get there. Every minute we were on foot, he caught up.

I looked around. Beyond the industrial area, the ground sloped down towards a town. "Come on."

We hurried down the slope but it still took us a half hour to get into the outskirts of the town. "We need to find something to steal," said Tanya.

The problem was, it was an upmarket commercial area and the cars were all modern ones with electronic locks and immobilizers. There weren't many old beaters we could easily hotwire. Plus, it was broad daylight and it was all big, open parking lots with people strolling around: there were no quiet back alleys. And we were running out of time. I suddenly felt tired of always being the ones struggling and stealing and scraping along while our enemies had billions. "Fuck this," I muttered, and marched towards a Ford dealership.

"Where are you going?" asked Tanya, chasing after me.

"To get us some transport." The team paid well, and I'd been letting the money just pile up in my bank account. I let the others think I was frugal, claimed that I just didn't want to replace my old, rusty wreck of a truck. But the truth was, I was scared of spending money. I was raised poor and it felt like, if I dared to use the money, someone was going to come and take it away. But I wasn't going to let people die just because I was superstitious.

I pushed open the door of the dealership. "I want an F150 Raptor," I told the salesman before he could even open his mouth. "I want all the extras and I'll pay an extra five percent if I can drive out of here in ten minutes."

The salesman gaped at me, then *ran* to his computer to start looking at what he had in stock. Tanya grabbed my arm. "They'll want ID! Bank details! They'll know where we are!" We'd been paying cash for things this whole time because we knew they'd be watching our cards.

I shrugged. "They already know where we are. For once, it doesn't matter."

"But they'll know our license plate!"

I nodded towards the parking lot. "We'll swap it with someone else's before we leave. The cops will be looking for the wrong truck."

She stared at me, then slid her arm around my waist and snugged herself into my side. "Smart," she acknowledged, and my chest filled with pride.

The clerk had enlisted a couple of friends and they were frantically racing through the paperwork. Once I'd called my bank to confirm that, yes, it really was me and I really did want to buy a car, I scribbled a signature on some forms and the salesman was walking me out to a brand new, cherry red F150 pick-up. Less than ten minutes had passed: it's amazing how fast things can move when there's money on the line.

I climbed behind the wheel, slammed the door and looked around in amazement. I was used to glimpsing the road through rust holes in the floor. Now I was sitting in a leather seat that felt like a favorite armchair, behind a console that looked like a spaceship, with enough power under the hood to spin the earth when I hit the gas. I inhaled reverently. I understood now what people meant by *that new car smell.*

Then I glanced at the woman sitting next to me and I couldn't help grinning like an idiot. It was the first time I'd been able to stop and take in the fact that we were *together,* now. We were fugitives, we were hopelessly outnumbered and the whole country was about to go to hell...but right at that moment, I didn't care. I was *happy.*

I started the engine and it came to life with a grunting, throaty roar. I revved it and heads turned all around us: it sounded like a T-Rex in a bad mood. Tanya rolled her eyes, but she was smiling. "It's very American," she told me. "Very *you.*" And she leaned over and kissed my cheek.

"Alright," I said, and threw the truck into gear. "Let's go find out what Steward left for Maravić."

We hauled ass out of there, stopping only once to quickly swap the license plates with those of another red F150 that was sitting in a different dealership. We made good time all the way to Ohio, but then a storm rolled in and the traffic slowed right down. We kept looking around at the other lanes of traffic: was Maravić on the same road, stuck in the same traffic, a few cars ahead or behind? Or had he taken a different route and was blasting past us? We had no way of knowing.

Finally, a little over eight hours since we left DC, we found the backroad Steward had talked about and turned onto it. By now, it was night and we could only see the narrow slice of the world that the headlights lit up. The backroad narrowed and turned to dirt, with thick foliage on either side.

Tanya had been watching the GPS coordinates on her phone. "Should be somewhere along here," she muttered. The truck started to bounce and then squelch as the rain turned the road to mud. Then, Tanya pointed to something on our right. "There!"

I stopped the truck and looked. Just visible through the bushes was a patch of orange-red, painted metal. A shipping container.

We jumped out. There was no sign of any other vehicles. Was that good or bad?

Both of us pulled out our guns and we circled around through the bushes. We looked at the shipping container indecisively. It seemed quiet but with the rain hissing down, it was hard to hear anything. If Maravić was in there, we didn't want to race in and get gunned down. But if Maravić was still behind us, he could be there any minute and we needed to hurry.

We cautiously approached. There was a chain and padlock hanging from the container's doors and the chain had been sliced through with bolt cutters. *Oh no...*

I inched the door open and Tanya shone a flashlight inside. There was a big wooden crate in the middle of the container and the side nearest us had been pried open. Tanya swept the flashlight beam over it and—

It was empty. Maravić must have beaten us there, probably by minutes. Tanya cursed in Russian and I slumped, defeated. *There goes our hard evidence.* And now we had no leads at all.

"We should check inside," said Tanya. There wasn't a whole lot of hope in her voice. "Just in case."

We pulled the doors all the way open and walked inside. The sound of the rain pounding on the metal box was overwhelming, like someone was pouring out a bag of marbles next to my ear.

There was a smell that made my nostrils burn, and it got worse the closer we got to the wooden crate. Both of us wrinkled our noses. "Chemicals," I said. "Maybe they shipped them the raw ingredients to make explosives?"

Tanya shrugged and moved closer to the crate, crouching to look. There was a wet stain on the wood near the front corner, as if something had leaked, and smaller stains on the metal floor of the container.

I left her to it and searched the rest of the container, which didn't take long. There wasn't a damn thing in there except the crate.

Wait: what was *that*, right in the corner? I shuffled forward, squinting. It was hard to see anything because the only light was Tanya's flashlight behind me and it was throwing my shadow ahead of me. I squatted and peered down at the thing. I thought I recognized the shape, but I had to reach down and touch its fur before I was sure. *Yep. Rat. Good thing Tanya didn't come over here.* The poor thing probably got locked inside the container at some point and starved to death.

I shuffled sideways to let some of the light from Tanya's flashlight come past me and—

There was something wrong with the rat. I leaned closer.

Its front and hind paws faced almost in different directions. It had twisted and thrashed so hard, in dying, that it had virtually snapped its spine.

There's one thing that strikes fear into the heart of all soldiers, around the world. We train for it, but we hope to God we never see it. I turned and ran towards Tanya. "*Get out!*" She was just leaning towards the wet stain on the crate. "*Don't touch it! Don't touch it, get out!*"

She started to get to her feet but that wasn't fast enough for me. I hooked my arm around her waist and hauled her to the door.

Suddenly, my foot shot out behind me. I'd forgotten that the bare metal in here gave no grip and my boots were slick with mud. I shoved Tanya out of the door just as I went down. I caught myself on my hands, narrowly avoiding cracking my teeth on the metal floor, and scrambled up—

Fuck. My right palm was stickily wet. I must have put it down right in one of the stains.

I headed for the door but, already, I was starting to stumble. One step and my legs felt like rubber. Two and my muscles started to tense and lock. I went down in the mud just outside the door, the rain hammering my face.

"*Colton?!*" screamed Tanya.

The pain exploded as my muscles spasmed and every tendon stretched to breaking point. I tried to warn her that it was nerve gas but, by now, I couldn't speak. My lungs were barely moving any air. I knew that soon the blood would start to clot in my brain.

I was dying.

47

TANYA

He passed out, probably from the pain. He was thrashing and twitching, his body rocking as his muscles knotted and twisted, tighter and tighter.

Please no. For the first time since Lev, I knew true fear. An icy grip closed around my heart as it sunk in that I might lose what I cared about most. *Not now. Not when we just finally told each other we—*

I knew what was happening to him. Given that my country was one of the few to actually deploy nerve agents, the GRU took great care in teaching its officers to recognize the symptoms. They'd taught us what to do if one of us was accidentally contaminated: inject atropine straight into the heart. Except I didn't have any atropine.

They'd given us advice for that situation, too. *If one of your team is accidentally contaminated and you do not have suitable first aid on hand, leave them. Do not touch them. Do not try to help. You risk endangering yourself and the rest of your team.*

Fuck that. I grabbed Colton by the shoulders and dragged him over to the truck. I knew I couldn't put him in the cab with me or whatever was on him would contaminate me, too. I thought for a few seconds, then opened the tailgate. It took all my strength to heave him up into the back of the pickup. "Hold on, Colton," I whispered, then ran around to the driver's seat.

I fired up the truck. I had to get atropine into him in the next few minutes or he was dead. Colton's new truck had voice-activated navigation and I mashed the button on the steering wheel. "Find me the nearest hospital!" I yelled.

"The nearest hospital is Mount Carmel East, eighteen point three miles away," said the navigation voice calmly. *"Estimated drive time is nineteen minutes. Do you want to start navigation?"*

I unleashed a long string of Russian curses. Then I had a sudden thought. "Find me the nearest *veterinarian!*"

"The nearest veterinarian is Paws and Claws, two point six miles away. Estimated drive time is three minutes. Do you want to start navigation?"

"Yes!" I yelled, and hit the gas. The wheels spun in the mud for a second and then found grip and we shot away.

Ignoring the speed limits, I blasted down the back roads and, a few minutes later, arrived in a small town. I slammed on the brakes when I saw a sign with a cartoon cat.

The vet's was closed. I looked up and down the street: it was dark and the pounding rain was keeping everyone inside, which was lucky because I didn't have time to be subtle. I kicked the front door until the lock gave way, then staggered into a tiled waiting room with posters for flea treatments on the wall. *Where do they keep the drugs?* I saw a door marked *Treatment Room* and ran towards it—

"Hold it."

The voice was elderly, female, and made of flint, like an American version of one of my teachers at the academy. And the order was followed by a metallic double click: the sound of someone working the slide on a pump-action shotgun. I froze.

"Touch the ceiling," the voice said. I quickly put my hands in the air. "Now keep 'em there while I call the cops." She sighed. "Goddamn junkies. I just got that door replaced."

"I'm not a junkie," I said quickly. "I'm sorry about your door. I need atropine. My friend is contaminated with a nerve agent, he's dying."

Taking small, careful steps, the woman circled around the room until she could see my face. She was in her late sixties, her silver hair pinned in an updo. "Russian?" she asked.

I nodded.

She backed away to the door, keeping me covered with the shotgun, then glanced through it to where Colton lay in the back of the pickup. "Big fella, ain't he? He Russian too?"

"No. He's American. Army. He got this stuff on him because he was saving me and—" Suddenly, tears were prickling hotly at the corners of my eyes. *Stupid, weak girl!* I'd made it years without crying at all and now I was like a child's crying doll, just squeeze me and tears sprung to my eyes. *This is what happens when you let yourself care about someone.* "Please, he's going to die and he's a good man and I—" I wanted to say it but I'd spent so long thinking that I'd never say those words again, that I had no right to ever say them, that they stuck in my throat. "I—"

My face must have said what my voice couldn't because the woman sighed. "Aw, hell," she muttered, and laid the shotgun on the reception counter. "Alright, grab that flashlight." She pointed to one mounted on the wall. While I grabbed it, she disappeared into the treatment room. She returned holding a large syringe and led the way outside.

I shone the flashlight on Colton and my stomach lurched. His muscles had gone rock solid, his arms and legs twisted into agonizing, unnatural shapes. He'd gone deathly pale and his chest was barely moving.

"Where's this nerve agent shit?" asked the woman, holding back. "On his clothes? His face? We don't want to get it on us."

"His hand." I told her. "He fell down and put his hand in it."

She climbed up into the back of the pick-up, giving Colton's hand a wide berth. Then she ripped his shirt open. "Alright, big guy, here we go."

Holding the syringe in both hands, she slammed it down into his heart. There was no response for a second. Then his body gradually began to soften, like a guitar string being slowly loosened.

"Let's get him to the emergency room," said the woman.

I shook my head. "The police are looking for him. For both of us."

The woman frowned at me. "Your guy needs a hospital! I'm a *vet*, not a specialist on chemical fucking weapons. I had to guess the dosage on the atropine and God knows what other treatment he needs!"

"I know what he needs," I said quickly. "Oxygen. Blood thinners." The woman started shaking her head. "Please, I can pay!"

She opened her mouth and I could tell she was going to say *no.* Then she saw my face crumple and she huffed and scowled and finally pushed me back inside the vet's. She began collecting things from the treatment room and stuffing them into a bag. "I'm only doing this," she snapped, "because you've got the same fucking puppy dog look *I* had when I met my first husband. You know how to start an IV?"

I nodded quickly, speechless.

"Make sure you clean that shit off him real well before you do anything else. And if anyone asks, you broke in and stole this stuff." She pushed the bag into my arms. "Now go!"

I stared at her, overcome. I'd faked this so many times, turned on the tears to manipulate someone into helping me. I wasn't used to this weird, parallel world where you showed actual vulnerability and, sometimes, people recognized it and were kind to you. "Thank you," I croaked. I dropped a thousand dollars on the counter, then ran.

I drove to the next town, found a motel and paid cash for a room. Again, I was glad of the rain and the dark as I heaved Colton out of the back of the truck and onto the bed.

The first thing I did was put on the latex gloves the vet had put in the bag and scrub Colton's hands to make sure I'd got rid of every trace of the nerve agent. Then I hooked up the little oxygen tank she'd provided and strapped a nose tube to his face so that he could breathe more easily. I did some quick internet searching to figure out the dosage of blood thinner and then got an IV going, zip-tying the bag to the air conditioning grill so it was up high.

After that, there was nothing to do but wait. We'd gotten the atropine into him fast but he wasn't out of the woods: a clot could form in his heart or lungs at any time. And he hadn't yet regained consciousness so I had no idea if there was damage to his brain. It all came down to how big a dose of the nerve agent he'd absorbed through his hand and I had no way of knowing. He groaned in his sleep and I put a hand on his forehead. "*Bud' sil'nym, moy plyushevyy mishka.*" *Be strong, my teddy bear. Be strong.*

48

TANYA

I WATCHED over him all night, until his color improved and his breathing eased. As dawn broke, he seemed to be sleeping peacefully but he still hadn't woken. My eyes kept closing and I kept jerking awake with the same sickening lurch of fear: *has he stopped breathing?* Would he ever wake up and, if he did, would he be okay? I couldn't even remember the last time I'd slept. I had to lie down or I was going to collapse.

With Colton stretched out on his back, there wasn't a lot of room left on the bed. But I found a space just big enough for me between him and the wall and cuddled into his side. Warm, dark sleep tugged me down and I was out as soon as I closed my eyes.

I woke from a dream of an earthquake: the ground was shifting and rising under me. I blinked awake: my head was resting on Colton's pec and he was trying to sit up like a sleepy, grumpy giant. I grabbed his shoulders. *Is there brain damage?* "Are you okay?" I demanded. "How do you feel?"

He pulled off his oxygen tube and scowled. "Like I fell down in the mosh pit at a thrash metal festival and got danced on for three days." He rubbed at his cheek, which was now dark with stubble. "I could use some coffee." His face became hopeful. "And a box of donuts."

A cry of pure joy bubbled up from inside me. I threw my arms around his neck and crushed myself to him like a child. "*Dvah!* All the donuts you want!"

It was already nearly noon. I went out to fetch coffee and donuts, wearing Colton's sweatshirt with the hood up. It was ridiculously big on me but it smelled comfortingly of him. I fed him donuts and took out his IV. Then, around three, I went out again and found a small deli and got us soup and bread, and sticky, flaky pastries topped with white frosting and nuts, together with some fresh clothes. "You need to get your strength back," I told Colton seriously. "You've been through a lot." Given how fast he was recovering, he must have only absorbed a little of the nerve agent, but I wasn't taking any chances.

Colton didn't argue and allowed himself to be nursemaided. When we'd eaten, we sat on the bed with my back against his chest, the solid warmth of him comforting. We talked about all the stuff we'd skipped right past in our weird relationship: what sort of music we liked, places we wanted to go. Colton's voice grew dreamy as he talked me through his favorite bands, which seemed to lean towards thrashy guitars, long drum solos and face paint. "I'll take you to a gig," he promised. "Something light to start out, some heavy rock, maybe ease you into metal." He looked me up and down and his voice went growly with lust. "Get you a little denim skirt—black, of course—that comes down to here." He touched a point a few inches above my knee.

A hot thrill went through me at his touch, but I acted shocked. "*There?*"

He slid his hand indecently high up my thigh. "Fine, *here* then." And I gaped as if even more shocked. "And a bra top," he continued.

"Won't I be cold?"

"No," he said seriously. "'Cause if you are, I'll put my arms around you and keep you warm." And I just melted.

"What about you?" he asked. "What are you gonna introduce *me* to?"

I had to think about it. I'd spent so long thinking of only my mission, I'd almost forgotten what it was like to do things for fun. "Rachmaninov," I said at last. "When the cellos come in, in the second symphony. It's the musical version of an orgasm. You ever listened to classical music?"

He shook his head.

"When all this is over, I will play it for you," I told him. My words hung in the air, unexpectedly heavy. We'd been avoiding the topic of *what do we do now* because there was no answer. We had no hard evidence, no way of clearing my name. I glanced towards the window: we'd talked all afternoon and it was getting dark outside. Tomorrow, when Maravić carried out his terrorist attack and the markets crashed, maybe Colton's team would finally believe us. But by then, it would be too late.

Colton reached down and took my chin in his hand, then tilted my face to look at him. "You know what I need?"

I shook my head glumly.

"A shower. Care to join me?"

A long, hot shower actually sounded *fantastic* and a shower with *him*... "Best idea I've heard all day," I said seriously. "But are you sure you're up to..." I thought of what was likely to happen with both of us naked in the shower, and felt myself flush.

"Get your mind out of the gutter!" he told me. "Just a shower." But his eyes flicked over my body in a way that sent a rush of heat to my core.

"You can control yourself?" I asked.

"*I* can control myself, can *you* control yourself?"

I stuck my tongue out at him.

He took my hand and led me to the bathroom. We stripped out of our clothes while the spray heated and then climbed into the tub. God, it was glorious, the hot water blasting all the dirt and worry from my body and the heat soaking into my bones and banishing the chill of last night's rain. He pushed me in front of him so that I got most of the water, but after a few minutes I shuffled us around so that he could have a turn. At first it was a little chilly, out of the spray.

Then he turned around, picked up the soap and used those big, powerful hands to soap my shoulders and back, and suddenly I wasn't cold at all.

He washed me slowly and lovingly, his hands gentle as they ran up and down my sides and then over my ass. I felt the heat start to build in my core, like a sleeping animal waking and uncurling, but his touch wasn't sexual...yet. His hands ran down my legs, then up between them, the edges of his hands skimming the juncture of my thighs and making me gasp. Then his palms slid up over my stomach, up to my breasts. He only allowed himself to cradle them for a second as he soaped them but the sudden change in his breathing told me how much he wanted to keep squeezing them.

As the spray rinsed the suds from my body, I heard him pick something up. Then there was a sudden coldness on the top of my head. It was only when his fingers started to massage my scalp that I realized he was washing my hair. No one had ever done that for me before and it was strangely intimate...and very, very relaxing. With his immensely strong fingers methodically circling, it doubled as a head massage and I could feel all the stress my body had been holding, breaking free, drifting upwards and evaporating as it reached the top of my head. My shoulders dropped and my knees softened, like a puppet with its strings loosened. *Chyort, he should set up a stall and wash women's hair for $20 a time, he'd have a line a mile long.* Except...I didn't want him doing this for anyone else. Just me. As often as possible.

When he'd finished and the spray had rinsed away the shampoo, I maneuvered *him* beneath the spray and started washing *him.* Reaching up to soap his neck reminded me how small I was, without my heels. Reaching around to run the soap over the muscles of his back was like trying to hug a tree and I had to press myself tight to him. That made my breasts smoosh against his chest and he looked down at me and growled. The warning was clear: this wasn't going to stay *not sexual* very long if I kept doing *that.*

I stepped back, grinning, and started on his chest. As I ran my soapy hands over the huge, hard slabs of his pecs, I could feel the heat pooling and tightening in my groin: the sheer brute strength of him, the thought of what he could—*would*—do to me any moment... I kept going dreamy and had to focus hard to keep my hands moving. Down over his stomach, the valleys of his abs guiding my fingers and directing them down and inwards towards...

I swallowed. The only way I could wash him properly, below the waist, was to get down on my knees. I tried to do it casually and matter-of-factly but just the thought of it, just the words *get down on my knees* unleashed that familiar tremor deep inside me. And when I looked up at him and saw him gazing down at me from so far above, his eyes hooded with lust, I went weak inside.

I started at his feet and spiraled slowly up his legs as if my hands were vines climbing a statue. I traced the bulges of his quads and reached up to soap the hard cheeks of his ass and then I was face to face with...

I stared at his cock as it rose and hardened. I'd never just knelt and watched a man getting hard before, watched the shaft engorge and lengthen, watched the head turn satiny-smooth as it thickened and swelled. And knowing that he was getting hard looking at me, gazing down at my naked breasts and my upturned face as I knelt there watching *him*... Ripples of heat soaked down through my body and made my groin tighten and throb. The power I had over him. The power *he* had over *me*. His cock reached its full, imposing size, the tip barely an inch from my lips. I looked up at him and when I saw him glowering down at me, huge and menacing, I couldn't resist: I smirked and blew lightly on him, letting him feel the heat of my breath.

He cocked his head and narrowed his eyes. *Don't*. Not if I wanted this to stay *just a shower*.

I felt that familiar tremor inside me. That thrilling, silver thread of danger. I was a rabbit, playing with a wolf.

I darted forward and licked the straining head of his cock.

He growled low in his throat and lunged down with one huge hand, capturing my wrist. He hauled me up to standing and then higher, until I was up on tiptoes. I stood there wide-eyed and panting.

The silver thread had drawn guitar-string tight and it was singing with raw excitement, the vibrations washing through me and leaving me weak. I'd teased him beyond control and now I was going to face the consequences.

He ducked his head and licked at one of my bobbing breasts and I yelped in shock and delight. Then he pulled me in front of him, under the spray, and I gasped as the hot water sluiced over my body. He used one of his hands to pin my wrists to the tiles high above my head and the tremor ran through me again, stronger than ever. I tried lifting my wrists but his grip was like steel. I wasn't getting free unless I said *Cincinnati* and I had no intention of doing that.

He wrapped his arm around my waist and tugged my ass back a little so that I was leaning forward, unbalanced and completely at his mercy. I felt his body press against my ass. His cock slapped my inner thigh and I went heady at the hot weight of it. Then I heard tearing foil and a rubber stretch: he must have grabbed a condom from my purse when I wasn't looking.

The blunt head of him spread my slickened folds and he surged up into me. I groaned as, in one long thrust, he went deep, so deep I was lifted almost off my toes. His free hand slid up my soaking body and found my breast, squeezing it and rolling my nipple against his palm, and I cried out in pleasure as a scalding, silvery whip of pleasure lashed down through my body to my groin.

He began to thrust and I opened my mouth wide in a silent 'O' as the silken friction began. Each slow push into me sent silver stars showering from the sensitive flesh he touched. Each slow withdrawal pulled those stars down into the glowing furnace in my core, making the fire burn hotter and me pant with need. He leaned forward and bit my neck, nipping just hard enough to let me know that I was his.

His hand began to squeeze and knead my breast, his fingers strong and just a bit rough, flooding my body with rhythmic pulses of pleasure that made me writhe and buck against him. He shuffled closer, his feet between mine, and I gasped as he moved deeper still. Already, the heat in my core was starting to twist and tighten, building with every powerful thrust. It didn't hurt, he was just so...*big.* "*Fuck,*" I moaned.

He put his lips close to my ear and, in that rough, moonshine accent, he growled, "You asked for this, princess. Now you can take it."

"*Yebat!*" I panted, cursing in Russian. He was so big and brutal and I felt so small, so helpless. His cock inside me was an iron bar wrapped in silk and every thrust sent a new rush of wicked pleasure racing through my body, joining with the heat in my core and tightening it more. I pulled at my wrists again, and tried to move away from him, not because I wanted it to stop but because I needed to feel helpless. His grip on my wrists didn't loosen at all, and, held up on my tiptoes, I found I had no way of shuffling forward. I *was* helpless, and the revelation made the heat turn dense and hot as the core of a star. "*Yes!*" I hissed. "*God, yes!*"

The hand that had been squeezing my breast snaked down my body to my groin. The heel of his hand pressed there, pushing me back firmly against him while also rocking against my clit. His fingertips started to gently caress my ultra-sensitive lips, right where they were stretched tight around his cock. My eyes widened. No one had ever done *that* to me. It was like the entire world narrowed down to just that one part of me, my whole body trembling as his fingers glided back and forth.

"God, you're beautiful." Each word was a red-hot, rough-edged slab of granite that burned down through all my layers of ice. "That body, those eyes, that fucking red hair." He thrust hard, almost lifting me off my toes, and we both groaned as my inner walls twitched around him.

"I don't know what I did right," Colton growled in my ear, "to get to be with someone like you. You really *are* like a princess, so classy. And always in control, always looking perfect, with your fancy clothes and your double crosses and your sweet little lies. But I know what you really need." His hips pumped at me slowly. "What you need is to *not* be in control. To have it all stripped away from you and feel *absolutely. Fucking. Powerless."* He nudged my hair away from my ear and whispered. "Isn't it?"

A flutter of nerves went through my chest. I thought of that need as a weakness. I *did* love being overpowered but I couldn't admit it out loud.

He withdrew and then rooted himself inside me, grinding his hips so that I could feel him throbbing hotly at the very core of me. The intimacy of it burned away any attempt to lie to him.

I sealed my lips shut instead. But his fingers stroked faster and the heel of his hand ground more insistently at my clit, setting up a rhythmic wave that my hips couldn't help but follow. And with every shift of my body, his buried cock caressed me. The hot, dense ball of energy at my core began to spin faster and faster until I couldn't contain it. I couldn't lie but I couldn't stay silent, either...

"*Dvah!"* I hissed. "*Dvah, dvah! Yes!"*

I braced myself for the shame and the stab of fear that would come from admitting something that made me so vulnerable, especially to a man. But they didn't arrive. Instead, I felt like something had been lifted from me. I felt...*free.*

Colton gave a low growl of approval and that made me feel even better. I felt his cock twitch and it seemed to swell inside me: he *liked* that I liked this. His hand on my pussy paused for just a second and he used his palm to press me tighter against him. He was proud of me, and proud that I trusted him, and I wasn't ready for the rush of emotion that set off inside me.

And then he gave me my reward. He began to fuck me again with hard, deep strokes and I writhed and struggled in ecstasy. The water was still hammering down on my back and shoulders and I twisted in his grip like a mermaid captured by a sailor. Every thrust sent the climax spinning deliriously faster until my toes were playing piano scales on the wet tiles.

He pushed even closer in between my legs, pounding me, his hips slapping against my upraised ass. *Chyort,* he was a beast behind me, my body so small and soft and helpless against the press of his massive, muscled form. The fucking became rough, brutal, and I loved it. The pleasure spun faster and faster, until my walls went trembly around his pistoning cock and—

The climax ripped through me, taking hold of my body and making me writhe and shake. I cried out in Russian, my words echoing off the tiles as my pussy clenched and spasmed around him. He kept fucking me, helping me ride the orgasm on and on, and only then did he slow and stop. I wilted, weak-kneed and spacey.

He used his grip on my wrists to stop me falling, then gently drew himself from me and turned me to face him. Floaty and wrung-out, aching in a good way, I just about managed to lift my face to look at him. Then I felt his cock, still hard, pressing against my stomach. He hadn't come yet. His grin said, *I'm not done with you.*

He shut off the shower, lifted me and carried me out of the tub. I panicked for a second: he'd been through a lot in the last twenty-four hours and really shouldn't be picking anyone up. But I wasn't capable of speech yet and, besides, the look in his eyes said that he was damn well going to carry me and I better not argue, so I let myself be carried.

He brought me into the bedroom and dropped me naked on my back on the bed, sending up a shower of glittering water droplets. He climbed onto the bed and hunkered down atop me, grabbing my forearms with his hands and using his legs to pin my ankles. "I want both hands free," he muttered to himself, and the way his eyes dipped to my breasts sent a throb of heat through me. "So let's do this differently, this time."

He lunged forward and grabbed something from the floor behind my head. Then he grabbed my right wrist and I felt something cool and flat loop around it and pull tight. And then my *left* wrist got the same treatment and my arms were pulled out wide, making me into a Y. I craned my head back to see. *How did he...?*

My purse. Its long leather shoulder strap was looped around my wrists and threaded through the iron bars that formed the head of the bed. I tugged, but I was firmly held.

"Now..." he said with great satisfaction, and moved down the bed to my breasts. He took one in each hand and started to stroke and squeeze the soft flesh. I gasped and pulled at my wrists again, that tremor rolling through my core: I was his captive and there was nothing I could do but lie there and be pleasured. I'd only just drifted back down to earth again after the shower and I thought I'd need a while to recover. But he started off gentle and slow and, like blossom wafted by the breeze, I gradually started to spiral upwards again. He heard my breathing change and grinned that wicked smile, and my chest tightened with a roller coaster thrill of fear: *I'm at his mercy. Whatever he wants to do to me...*

He lashed his tongue across my nipples and my breathing went trembly as they rose to aching hardness. He moved from *gentle* to *firm,* his lips and tongue and those huge, strong hands insistent, and my whole body started to follow his rhythm, my back arching and my lower body twisting as I ground my thighs together to try to get the friction I needed.

That's when he used his knees to open my legs, turning me from a Y into an X. I sucked in a huge lungful of air, my fingers and toes dancing in delicious panic. God, I'd never felt so vulnerable...or so free.

He laid his hands on my inner thighs, his thumbs tracing up and down along the super-sensitive skin just shy of my pussy. I could feel how wet I'd gotten and, as he gazed down at me, the amber in his eyes molten with lust, I knew he could see. He brought his cock to my pussy and nestled the tip between my lips. I jerked at the leather strap that held my wrists, squeezed my thighs together hard, trying to close my legs. I did everything I could to escape my fate, because every time I tried and failed, the excitement ratcheted higher in my chest.

Then he hilted himself inside me. Before I'd even recovered from the shock of being filled, he was pounding me and *God,* this was totally different to the shower, where I'd flexed and moved. His weight pinned me to the bed and his hands on my shoulders stopped me moving even an inch. He sank low atop me and my nipples began to drag along the hard slabs of his pecs as he fucked me. The pleasure sparked inwards from my breasts and groin, sending me higher and higher.

My soft little pants and his deep, animal grunts filled the room. He cupped my cheeks in his hands and stared down at me, giving tiny little shakes of his head. "Can't believe you're real," he muttered, and under that deep Missouri growl, under all the lust and roughness, there was a note of vulnerability. Something in me connected with something in him in a way that disarmed him completely.

I knew because I felt the same way.

He leaned down and kissed me, his lips spreading me savagely and mine flowering open under him, welcoming him. The kiss was hot and frantic, our teeth clacking together in our urgency as his thrusts became harder, almost brutal. I panted against his mouth. There was so much I wanted to say, but I wasn't going to get the chance. I was spiraling higher and higher, every satiny thrust of his cock pushing me towards my peak. I was going to come again, while he kissed me, and I couldn't think of anything better. His body slammed against mine, the base of him grinding against my clit on each stroke. I strained at my bound wrists, my hands grabbing at the air, but I was powerless. *Captured.*

The climax rolled through me, making my hips jerk and roll, and he groaned, driving deep one final time and then shuddering and pulsing inside me. We kept kissing, our lips muffling each other's cries as our bodies thrashed together, as close and trusting as two people can be.

49

TANYA

Afterwards, we lay on our sides in the darkness with Colton spooning me from behind. I was naked, and the air conditioning made the room chilly, but his arms and the press of his chest kept me as cozy as if I'd been wrapped in a heated blanket. It wasn't like our first time at the hotel. Then, I'd had a sickening lurch in my stomach afterwards: *what have I done?* This time, the lurch only came when I thought of someone taking him away from me. It was only a matter of time until the CIA caught up with us. Then we'd be quietly arrested, spirited off to some far-off country for interrogation and buried in shallow graves.

I put my hand on Colton's, where it covered my breast, and squeezed his arm around me tighter. *Fuck that.* "We have to figure a way out of this," I said out loud. "And warn your people about the terrorist attack. It's happening *tomorrow!*"

"No one'll believe us," said Colton, his breath hot on the back of my neck. "Even if we go to someone we trust, like Calahan in the FBI, word'll be sent up the chain and the CIA will arrive, screaming national security, and pick us up."

"What about the government? Could we go straight to a senator?"

Colton gave a bitter laugh. "Normally, yeah. Kian, the guy who runs our team, is dating the President's daughter. But I already tried him, his phone's off because he's off on a trip *with the President:* how's that for irony?"

I bit my lip and lay there staring at the dark motel room for a while. Then my spine went rigid. "I can call Moscow!" I spun to look at Colton. "I can call my old boss, in the GRU. He can get a message from our foreign ambassador directly to your government!"

Colton frowned at me. "I thought the GRU gave you up to the CIA?"

"They didn't have a choice, then." I said, shrugging. "They thought I'd killed an American. They had to disavow me to protect Russia. This is different. If they can help stop a terrorist attack on America, think of the political leverage that will give them! Spies are pragmatists, they'll do it."

Colton stared at me, horrified at my casualness. I wondered what it must be like, to have such unswerving loyalty to your country, and to expect it to be loyal in return.

I called Moscow and, after some cursing and a few threats, was finally put through to my old boss, Rurik Bobrinsky. I laid everything out for him while he listened silently. When I was done, I heard a bottle cap unscrewing and him knocking back a shot. "You have done well," he told me in Russian. "I'm leaving now. I'll be there in the morning."

"You're coming *here?!*"

Rurik's voice was like iron. "If I'm there, it might help to keep you safe. We'll brief the foreign ambassador together. It's going to be alright, Tanya."

I felt myself relax. For the first time since this whole thing started, I felt like we weren't alone. "Thank you."

At just after six the next morning, Colton and I were waiting at a remote airfield in northern Ohio. The sun was still coming up and the early morning mist still curled around our ankles. I was pressed up against Colton as we watched the sky: it's funny, I'd spent plenty of time waiting in places like this but I'd never realized how lonely it was, doing it on my own. I pressed against him a little tighter.

"There," said Colton, pointing. A dot had appeared in the sky and we watched as it grew into a plane and came in to land. Rurik must have really pulled some strings to get here so fast. It was an indication of how seriously he was taking this thing.

A few moments later, a private jet was taxiing to a stop in front of us. I let out a sigh of relief as Rurik opened the door and climbed out. It had been two years since I'd seen him, but his camel overcoat and the way he walked with his shoulders up high hadn't changed. Even at sixty-four, there was still some black in his silver hair. "Hang back while I talk to him," I told Colton over the sound of the engines, which were still spinning down.

Colton moved back. Rurik embraced me warmly and then led me a little way from the plane so we could talk more easily. "We have looked into your story," he told me as we walked. "Maravić. The Bainbridge family. It all checks out."

I went shaky with relief. It was so good to be believed!

"Who else knows?" asked Rurik.

"Just the three of us," I told him, nodding towards Colton. "How soon can we brief the foreign ambassador?"

Rurik stopped and turned to face me. "Our government has decided to take...a different course."

I felt ice slowly spread across my chest as I realized what he meant. "No," I said, my voice tiny. "No, Rurik, we have to tell them!"

"The thinking is, if someone wants to cripple the American economy, let them. We can bet against the dollar, too. We'll make *trillions.*" I started to argue, but he put a hand on my shoulder. "Tanya, you can come back to Russia, back to the GRU, your absence forgiven. There'll even be a promotion. A medal, if you want one."

I stared at him. He'd been kind to me, during my training and I'd always thought of him like an uncle. He wasn't a bad man. But he was still going to do what was better for his country, even if it meant Americans dying. I thought of my own words to Colton, the night before. *Spies are pragmatists.*

That's when I realized that, sometime in the last few days, I'd stopped being a spy.

"No," I said, my voice brittle.

Rurik looked at me like I was a child refusing to drink her medicine. "It was not a request, Tanya. We can't have you running around with the knowledge that Russia knew about a terrorist attack on the United States and didn't stop it. That's as good as an act of war!" His hand tightened on my shoulder and I saw the concern in his eyes. He *did* care. "The others wanted you dead, said you were too much of a risk. I had to fight for you, persuade them I could bring you home."

That's when I realized things were even worse than I'd thought. He'd said *bring you home*. He hadn't mentioned Colton. I looked over my shoulder to where Colton waited, then back to Rurik, unable to speak.

Rurik gave me a somber nod, confirming my fears. "The American dies. You know we can't leave a loose end like that. They want *you* to do it. As a show of loyalty, before you come home."

I stared at him, speechless.

"If you won't do it," he said slowly, "My orders are to shoot you both." His firm expression crumpled. "Please, *Tany'echk'a*, don't make me do that."

It felt like a black hole had opened up in the center of my chest and everything was slowly being sucked in, leaving only cold darkness. I turned away from Rurik and walked slowly towards Colton.

I knew what I had to do. It was the only thing I could do.

Colton scowled protectively when he saw the expression on my face. "What happened?"

I took a deep breath and tried to speak, but a tremor shook my chest and I nearly sobbed again. I pressed my lips together and tried again. And then again. *Chyort!* I couldn't afford to cry. Not now. I put my hand on Colton's chest. "I love you," I blurted.

So many emotions played out on his face. Shock. Elation. All abruptly swept away by the realization that something was very, very wrong. "I love you, too," he said, his voice ragged. "What's—"

"I'm sorry." I pulled out my gun and shot him in the chest.

50

COLTON

THE PAIN HIT ME FIRST, white-hot agony that erupted in my heart and spread across my whole chest. It was so intense it pulled the colors from my vision, leaving everything in hazy black and white. I saw Tanya lower her gun, saw the tears in her eyes. Then the sky, where I knew the clouds should still be pink and orange from the dawn but suddenly they were just funeral gray. I was dimly aware I was falling backwards. Then my back hit the runway and jolted everything, and the pain I thought couldn't get any worse, did.

The shock started to hit me. The reality of what had happened. And all of the fear and doubt from the early days came back, crushing me. *You fucking idiot.* Of course a woman like her didn't love me. JD had been right, she'd made the whole thing up, it had all just been an elaborate plan to let her escape back to Russia.

But then my brain kicked in, even though my thoughts were hazy, through the pain. I'd seen Maravić and his men with my own eyes. I'd seen the effects of the nerve agent. The conspiracy *was* real. Tanya had just had a better offer. Maybe she'd even known it would go this way, when she'd called Rurik. *Spies are pragmatic.*

I should have hated her but I couldn't. I craned my head up, even though it made the pain worse.

I wanted to see her one last time. That's how much I loved her.

She'd just reached Rurik. He patted her on the arm: *well done.* Then they climbed the steps of the plane together. She didn't look back at me.

The plane's door closed. My head fell back to the ground and I closed my eyes and lay there, utterly defeated, waiting for death to claim me.

But it didn't. I felt around on the ground next to me. I should be lying in a lake of blood. *Where's all the blood?*

I opened my eyes. Lifting my hand and bringing it to my chest made the pain balloon to the point I nearly passed out, but when I touched my shirt, I couldn't find any blood there, either. *What the fuck?* But the bullet had hit me right—

My fingers found the textured steel of my granddaddy's cigarette case. The bullet had hit it dead-center, bending it from a flat shape into something that looked like a bowl. It had punched straight through the front and come within a hair of making it through the back. I figured I'd cracked a rib or two and I was going to have one hell of a bruise, but I was alive. It had saved me.

Except...it wasn't the case that had saved me. It wasn't dumb luck that she'd shot me there. I remembered her touching my chest, just before she did it. She'd been feeling for the case, checking it was in my breast pocket.

She mustn't have had a choice. She'd *had* to shoot me and she'd found a way to leave me alive.

She hadn't been lying. She *did* love me. She was on that plane against her will and they were taking her back to Russia.

I scowled at the sky. *No they're fucking not.*

51

TANYA

RURIK SAT OPPOSITE ME, leaning back in his soft leather seat. As we taxied towards the runway, he said, "I know you've had a difficult time, Tanya. But it's all over, now. The next few years are going to be a time of great opportunity. America will have no money for war. The Middle East can be ours. And as America rebuilds, we can be there to lend a hand...and make sure the right people are in positions of power." He shook his head in wonder. "We can define the next century, you and me."

I gazed at him, my expression neutral. Inside, my world was in pieces. Rurik didn't know what he'd made me do. If he'd suspected my feelings for Colton, he would have just killed us both. But as far as he was concerned, Colton was just another man I'd used. Disposable, just as I was disposable to him. He wouldn't believe I could fall in love. Even *I* hadn't believed it was possible.

Did it work? I was sure I'd hit the case and it had been a handgun round, not a rifle, but I didn't know if the bullet would make it through. Rurik had been watching so I hadn't dared look back to check. *What if I killed him?* In normal times, I'd be able to check on him from Russia but by the time we got home, America would be in chaos. What if I never found out if he was alive?

The engines roared and the plane trembled as it girded its loins for takeoff. I closed my eyes.

"There's somebody on the runway behind us!" yelled the pilot over the intercom.

Rurik cursed and looked out of the window, trying to see. "Could his team have found us?" he snapped. But before I could answer, I heard a familiar noise. Even in the insulated cabin, even over the roar of the aircraft engines, the low, T-Rex roar shook my chest. I clutched the armrests, not daring to hope.

"Take off!" yelled Rurik.

We started our take-off run. But a second later, a cherry-red pickup truck blasted past us. Rurik and I scrambled out of our seatbelts and crowded in behind the pilot to see.

The pickup truck raced ahead of us. As we started to catch up to it, it did a handbrake turn and skidded to a stop in the center of the runway, rocking on its suspension. Then it accelerated, driving straight towards us.

"Take off!" ordered Rurik. ""Go over him!"

"There isn't enough room," snapped the pilot, his face pale. Both the plane and pickup truck were still accelerating, on a collision course.

"Keep going!" Rurik told him. "He'll swerve."

No he won't. I stepped back from the cockpit and grabbed hold of a seat. The pickup truck roared towards us, bellowing like an angry bull. The pilot gritted his teeth, hunkered down in his seat...and then cursed and sent the plane slewing off to the left. We bounced across grass and then a wire fence was rushing up to meet us. The plane jolted so hard my feet left the ground and then we *dropped*—

I must have blacked out because I woke up on the floor, wedged between two seats. The floor sloped down towards the front of the plane—I was guessing the front landing gear had broken off, and that's why I'd felt us drop. In the cockpit, the pilot and Rurik were still slumped, dazed.

I heard a banging on the door. I scrambled over to it, wrenched on the lever and—

Colton was stumbling towards me, hunched over and wincing in pain. But his face lit up when he saw me. He held out his arms and I ran to him. "Are you okay?" I asked, feeling his chest.

"*Ow!* Yeah, don't touch it!"

"What can I do?"

He grinned through the pain. "Kiss me, princess."

And I pressed myself close and did exactly that, and he kissed me back as if my lips were a healing salve.

Then I heard sirens wailing towards us. The airfield's fire crew were approaching...and behind them, the red and blue flashes of police cars. *Chyort!* Someone in the control tower had called the cops. Colton and I looked frantically around but the airfield was empty, open space. There was nowhere to run.

As the first cop car pulled up, Colton and I exchanged looks...and then we tossed our guns on the ground and raised our hands.

52

TANYA

I'D HOPED that the local police would take us off to some tiny, rural police station where we'd be guarded by a couple of sleepy cops munching on donuts. Then I could fake some tears, show a little cleavage and distract them long enough to hit one over the head and get us both out of there.

But the Ohio cops turned out to be no-nonsense and professional. They'd already seen the APB Steward had put out for us and they took no chances, leaving us handcuffed and sitting on the runway, watched over by three eagle-eyed officers, until Steward showed up in a helicopter. Colton's team must have been monitoring the police bands because they showed up in their own helicopter at almost the same time. They all walked over, led by the big Texan, the one Colton called JD. All except the female pilot, who strolled over to the pilot of Steward's chopper and started chatting.

"Your team is *done!*" yelled Steward, stabbing JD in the chest with a finger. "You had one job, capture her and bring her to me, and your man winds up in league with her! You're never working with the agency again!"

JD just soaked up the abuse, as if that wasn't what was important. "What about our guy?"

Steward scowled at Colton. "I'm taking both of them to a CIA facility for interrogation."

"It's not his fault!" JD told him. "She fooled him. Seduced him!"

"Your man aided an enemy of the state," Steward told him. "That's treason, JD. That's punishable by *death*. So get out of my way and maybe, *maybe* your guy only gets a jail cell."

Steward stalked off to talk to Rurik, who immediately started claiming diplomatic immunity. He'd walk free: Steward wouldn't want to start an international incident.

JD came closer and gazed down at Colton. It broke my heart to see the looks on their faces. They obviously cared so much about each other and I hated that I'd come between them. "Sorry, boss," said Colton, sounding sincere.

JD squatted down beside us. He gave me a long glare. Then his eyes softened and he just looked tired.

"It's real, boss," Colton said sadly. "I swear it is. Steward's got *nerve gas*." He saw Steward turn and head back towards us and spoke quickly. "Look, just check him out."

"I can't go digging into a member of the *CIA!*" growled JD.

"There'll be a link, somewhere, between him and the Bainbridges," said Colton firmly.

Steward and his men grabbed us and hoisted us to our feet, then started marching us towards their chopper. Colton twisted so he could speak to JD one last time. "Boss, I never asked you for shit. But I'm asking you to do this one thing. *Please.*"

The last thing I saw, as the chopper door slid shut, was JD's face, frowning and conflicted.

53

COLTON

As soon as we were airborne, one of Steward's CIA goons leaned over with a couple of cloth bags. I threw Tanya a quick glance, trying to reassure her. *It's gonna be okay.* She nodded back.

Then the bag came down over my head and everything went black. They were trying to intimidate us, soften us up for interrogation and I didn't want to give them the satisfaction of letting it get to me. But my breathing went tight when I realized that might be the last time I ever saw her.

The flight was long and just bumpy enough that my cracked ribs hurt like hell. When we eventually landed and I was hauled out, I had no idea where we were. I guessed we'd landed on a rooftop helipad because we went down several flights of stairs. I knew Tanya was walking beside me for a little while because I could smell her perfume. Then suddenly she was gone. They pushed me into a chair, uncuffed me and strapped my wrists and ankles down. Then the bag finally came off.

I was in a small room with no windows. I was in a big, vinyl-covered chair, like a dentist's chair, and my wrists and ankles were secured with thick, fabric restraints. Tanya was nowhere to be seen but Steward was standing in front of me. He went over to a video camera that sat in the corner and made a big show of turning it off.

"Colton Stockburn," he said with great satisfaction, perching himself on the edge of a metal table. He ran his eyes from the top of my head all the way down to my battered boots while I huffed and glowered and tested the handcuffs. "Jesus, look at you. Trailer trash with a shotgun. Why did JD even let you on the team?" He shook his head. "You must have thought it was Christmas when a woman like Yeshevskaya showed an interest in you. You know, I'm curious. What *is* she like on her back? Or was she on top?" He tried to make the last part sound like just another cruel jibe but there was an urgency in his voice I didn't like at all.

I said nothing.

Steward stood, grinning. "You think this is an interrogation? You think...what, that you can sit there all stoic and strong and not give me anything?" He leaned down to me. "There's nothing I need from you. See, I told your buddies you'd be going to a deep, dark cell for the rest of your life. But I don't like loose ends."

He opened a drawer and took out a floppy, transparent IV bag. My stomach shrunk down to a cold, hard knot.

"Amazing stuff," he told me, weighing the bag in his hand. "Comes out of a lab in Europe. Very expensive." He crouched so he could look right into my eyes. "What it does is, it triggers all of the body's pain receptors. It causes no actual damage, so it's perfect for interrogations: no bruises, no broken bones, no evidence. It's how we get answers in a hurry, when there's no time to take someone off to a black site."

He took an alcohol wipe and began cleaning a spot on my forearm with exaggerated care. "Of course, we have to be careful." He took out an IV needle and slowly, painfully, inserted it into my vein, taping it in place. "Your body isn't designed to experience that level of pain for any length of time. The heart just gives out. So we normally only run the IV a little way open, and only for a little while. We don't want someone dying before we get our answers."

He hung the IV bag on a stand, then connected it to the needle in my arm. "Of course," he said, mock-thoughtfully, "in *your* case, we don't need any information. So we can just run it full open." He twisted the knob on the IV bag, opening the flow all the way. "And we'll just go until your heart gives up. It'll look like you died of a heart attack."

He smiled, then sat down on the edge of the table to watch.

I glowered at him, trying not to show any fear. But my eyes kept going to the clear liquid working its way down the tube towards my arm. I took quick little breaths, trying to brace myself. The liquid reached the needle and I dug my fingernails into my palms—

And then I could feel the liquid flowering inside me and spreading through my body. Everything it touched erupted in blinding, white-hot agony. I screwed my eyes closed and gave a guttural grunt. First, it was my arm. Then my shoulder and chest. It kept spreading and the pain kept building.

Steward leaned closer. "I want you to know that this is nothing, *nothing*, compared to what we'll do to Yeshevskaya. I'm going to fly her out of here to one of our black sites in the Middle East, somewhere there are no rules at all. And in between making her scream in pain, guess what I'm going to be doing to her?"

No. I tried to believe that he was just trying to psych me out. But I could hear that urgency, that lust in his voice again. This was real.

"Not just me," he said. "My men, too. All of us. But I'll make sure that the last thing she ever sees, just before I put a gun to her head, is my face, grinning down at her."

Fear and anger ballooned inside me, pushing back the pain, and I managed to open my eyes to glare at him.

He grinned. "Attaboy." He settled back again to watch. The pain was still building and I began to sweat and pant: it felt like insects were gnawing on every nerve ending. But worse was the sick dread in my stomach, the thought of what they were going to do to her.

The agony increased and I couldn't hold it back: I started to scream. And as I screamed again and again, there was a coldness in my bones like nothing I'd ever felt. Loneliness. Even in my darkest times, even on an icy rooftop in Berlin or stranded in the jungle in Ecuador, I'd been with my friends. Now I knew what it was like for Tanya, being on her own.

No one was coming to save me because I didn't have a friend in the world.

54

JD

We were all sitting in the chopper, ready to go. But Gina hadn't started the engines and I didn't have the heart to give the order. We all just sat there, brooding.

We needed to fly back to New York, drop off the helicopter we'd rented and swap back to the plane. Then we could fly home to Colorado. Our mission was complete.

Except...no one had planned for it to end like this.

Cal wasn't whittling, for once, he just stared at the floor. Gabriel, who would normally be figuring out a way to sweet-talk the rental staff into a discount, just sat there morosely. Bradan, normally so silent and still, shifted in his seat uneasily and even Danny, who I could always rely on for a smile, didn't look glad to be going home.

I could hear the silence where Colton's voice should have been. That broad Missouri accent echoing around the chopper as he asked, *what are we doing for lunch?*

I did the right thing, didn't I?

I looked up and saw Cal was staring at me. I quickly looked away, out the window.

Of course I'd done the right thing. Yeshevskaya's story was bullshit. *Of course* she'd say there was some world-ending disaster about to happen and only she could stop it. *Of course* it would involve Steward, our boss, so that she could turn us against him. It was spycraft 101, sow the seeds of doubt and dissent, divide and conquer. And it had worked, it felt like the team was split in two.

I felt more eyes on me. Bradan was staring at me, now. And Gabriel.

I sighed. I understood why they hadn't wanted to chase down one of our own. Neither had I. It sucked. But it had been our best shot at bringing him in alive and, thank God, we had. But now Colton was going to have to answer for his actions. It wasn't his fault, he'd had no chance against someone like Yeshevskaya with all her tricks and once she seduced him, it was game over. At his trial, I'd make damn sure the jury knew that. But he was still going to jail.

I felt another pair of eyes on me. Danny was looking at me reproachfully. *Danny,* my best friend. The team was in two halves, but my half was shrinking by the second. Then Gina, who'd stayed carefully neutral this whole time, turned around in her seat and looked at me, too.

Goddamnit! I threw open my door and climbed out, stalking away across the airfield.

I did the right thing...right? I didn't like it any more than they did, but I hadn't had any choice. Maybe they were all pissed at me, but better that than if I'd let Colton and Yeshevskaya take us *all* for a ride and we'd all wound up in jail or dead.

I did the right thing.

...unless.

And there it was, that microscopic crack that felt like it could split wide open. *Unless* Yeshevskaya's story *wasn't* bullshit. Unless, for once in her life, she'd been telling the truth.

A million-to-one chance. But could I ignore it?

I thought for a long time. No, I couldn't. But checking came with its own risks. I could get *all* of us sent to jail.

I took a deep breath and dialed Gabriella, one of the Sisters of Invidia, and the best of the three when it came to bank accounts. "I need a favor," I said.

"Name it!" she said lightly.

"I need you to look into someone, but I've got to warn you: he's CIA. This isn't like hacking some Russian mafia guy. There'll be alerts and alarms wired to all his bank accounts. If you get caught..."

Gabriella went quiet. "I'll be careful," she said, more seriously.

"Something else, before you do it," I said. "I want to make this clear: this is *me* asking for this. Just me. The team know nothing about this." I wasn't really talking to her. I was talking to the jury, if this phone call got recorded by the NSA and came out at my trial. I wanted to make sure only I would take the fall.

"Understood," said Gabriella, sounding a little scared, now. "Who's the target?"

"Casey Steward, CIA. I want to know if anyone's been paying him. Go *deep*. This guy's no rookie, if there is something, he'll have hidden it well." I needed to be sure.

"On it. I'm routing it through a back door I have at the Justice department so it looks like the inquiries are coming from them." There was a flurry of typing and then soft, musical chimes as page after page of information popped up. Casey Steward's whole life was being laid out in a glittering map. Every strip club he'd ever been to, every alimony payment he'd ever paid, every medical bill he'd ever had. I knew this was normal, for the Sisters, but they were normally doing it on lowlifes. This guy was CIA, one of *us,* and I felt dirty. I paced back and forth outside a hanger, waiting, while maintenance workers and other airfield staff frowned at me curiously.

"No suspicious payments into his bank account," said Gabriella at last. "No off-shore accounts I can link to him, no shell companies. No cryptocurrency I can trace to him. No property in his name other than his house. No inheritances that seem suspicious." She sighed. "Steward's clean."

I stopped and leaned back against the metal wall of the hanger, closing my eyes. *Thank God.* Now I just had to hope I hadn't landed Gabriella and me and maybe the rest of us in jail—

"Wait," said Gabriella.

My eyes opened. My stomach flipped. *"What?"*

"There *is* something. *God,* he's paranoid!" More typing. "Okay, you know how you said he's not a rookie? I thought about how he'd hide it from someone like me. I figured maybe he has a completely separate cell phone and laptop, a second identity that's not connected to him in any way. So I checked the phone companies and there is an unregistered burner phone, bought for cash, that's been used five times in the last two years, and always at his house. It's been used to access an account in the Caymans and that account has received five separate payments totaling...a little north of twenty million."

It felt like all the air was being sucked out of my lungs. Every conversation I'd had with Colton since this thing started replayed in my head. He'd been right. And I'd been so, so wrong. "Let me guess. The payments trace back, through a whole bunch of shell companies, to one owned by Lucas Bainbridge."

"Checking, checking...*yeah,* how did you know?"

I thanked her and ended the call. The self-hate, shame and anger started at my feet and bubbled up through my body like acid and I let it, let it fill me and burn me because I deserved it. Only when I couldn't take anymore did I finally let it out. "*FUCK!*" I bellowed. The maintenance workers all jumped and stared at me. "*FUCK! FUCK! FUCK!*"

Colton hadn't been led astray by an expert, devious spy. *I* had.

I marched back to the chopper. Everyone looked up as I climbed in. "Steward's dirty," I said simply. "Colton and Yeshevskaya were right. I was wrong."

There was silence. Cal and Bradan stared at me. They'd tried to warn me from the beginning and I'd ignored them. But to their credit, neither of them said *I told you so.* Maybe they could see how much I was tearing myself apart.

"*Fucking* CIA," muttered Cal. And that was enough.

"What do we do?" asked Danny. "Can we have Steward arrested?"

I shook my head. "What evidence I've got was illegally obtained. Plus, we don't have time. Colton said Steward was planning some terrorist attack. And that he was going to kill Yeshevskaya once he had her. We've got to go get them back...but that's going to mean raiding a CIA facility." I looked around at the team. "Even if we can pull it off, we'll be fugitives."

They all nodded. No one was abandoning Colton.

"You're forgetting something," said Gabriel. "We have no idea where Steward's holding them. The CIA has hundreds of safehouses and other facilities."

"I might be able to help with that." Gina's voice made us all look up in surprise. "Remember back at the airfield, when I was chatting to Steward's pilot about their chopper? I might have maybe kinda accidentally on purpose left my phone under a seat."

So Gina hadn't been neutral. I wanted to hug her. "I'll call the Sisters again, get them to track the signal," I said. "Alright. Let's go get our boy."

55

COLTON

I SCREAMED but there was no sound. The pain had short-circuited something in my brain and all sound had stopped, save for a ringing in my ears. The room seemed to be far away, like I was looking out of my eyes from down a long tunnel. Time had lost all meaning. I wasn't even sure if what I was seeing was real, anymore, or whether my mind had broken completely and I was hallucinating.

The pain...that was real. It felt like my bones were on fire and I was burning from the inside out. I knew now why they used this stuff in interrogations. I was ready to do *anything* to make it stop. But there was nothing I could do, because this wasn't an interrogation.

The only thing that kept me going was her. I focused on the frozen sky blue of her eyes, on the way her hair felt against my fingers and the sounds she made as she came.

Steward kept looking at me curiously. I guess I'd lasted longer than I was supposed to. I knew the end was close. I'd never felt my heart hammer so fast and I could feel the blood thundering through my veins. Something was about to give.

The door crashed open and sagged, half of its hinges, but there was no sound. And then I knew I was hallucinating because JD was there, picking Steward up by the front of his shirt and hurling him

against the wall, and Gabriel was there, examining the IV and then—
ow—pulling it from my arm.

Gabriel leaned over me, saying something, but I still couldn't
hear. He started unstrapping my wrists and ankles from the chair.
Behind him, Steward scrambled out of the door and ran.

And then I felt it. Only very faintly, so faintly that I worried I
might just be kidding myself. But...had the pain eased, just a little?

I saw Bradan in the hallway, shouting and JD was shouting back
but there was no sound. *What are they saying?*

The pain reduced again and, this time, I was sure of it. Then again
and suddenly it plunged and was gone altogether. My body wasn't
ready for the shock. My muscles went limp, I fell forwards out of the
chair and Gabriel had to catch me. My heart, which had been racing
from the agony, was suddenly pounding in my chest for no reason
and that made my brain go into a sweat-drenched panic. My senses
suddenly weren't overwhelmed and the room, the people and the
noise rubber-banded from far away to right in my face.

"Easy," Gabriel said as he eased me back into the chair. "Easy, big
guy."

For a few moments, I couldn't do anything other than pant. JD
marched over to me. He put a hand on my shoulder and looked at me
with the most guilt-ridden expression I'd ever seen.

"Later," I managed. "Tanya." My jaw was cramping and I realized I
must have been grinding my teeth the whole time Steward was giving
me the drug. "He's going to take her to a black site."

JD put a hand to his ear, listening to his earpiece. "Cal says there's
a chopper spinning up, upstairs." He grabbed my guns from a box in
the corner and offered them to me. "Can you walk?"

I nodded. All my pain receptors must have been in rebound
because I felt like someone had shot me full of morphine: even my
cracked ribs didn't hurt. I knew that was dangerous but for now, it
was useful. I stood up, a little shakily, and we ran out into the
hallway. I was completely disoriented. I'd had a bag over my head
when I was brought here so I had no idea where to go. It didn't help
that an alarm was blaring and a smoke grenade had filled the

hallway with roiling white smoke, lit up red by the flashing emergency lights.

But the team moved like a slick machine. Someone put an earpiece in my ear and I was hustled up flight after flight of stairs.

We stumbled out into a brutal wind that stole our breath. The helicopter that brought me here was on the helipad, the wash from its rotors blasting us and—

I looked around and stopped, stunned. *Wait, what?*

We'd run up at least five flights of stairs. I was expecting us to be on the roof, but we were on the *ground.* There was only a tiny, one-story building and a helipad, and all around us were golden fields of wheat. It sank in that the whole facility had been underground.

I shook my head and focused on the helicopter. It was about to take off and I could see Tanya strapped in the back, a bag over her head. Steward was just climbing in. When he saw us, he gestured frantically to the pilot: *go, go!* And to my horror, the helicopter started to rise. We stumbled forward through the downwash, but we weren't going to make it in time. "They're taking off!" I yelled helplessly.

"No they're not," came Cal's voice, calm in my ear. A rifle shot echoed and the hub of the helicopter's rotor blades sparked and smoked. The whole thing started to vibrate and twitch, and the terrified pilot quickly landed it again before he lost control.

I wrenched the door open almost before the thing was down and hit the release on Tanya's harness buckle. She started to thrash and panic but I put my mouth next to where I thought her ear was under the bag and yelled over the rotor noise, *"It's me!"* and she calmed and let herself be gathered into my arms. I staggered backwards with her as Bradan and JD fought with Steward's two goons.

Steward himself jumped out of the far side of the helicopter and ran. Gabriel raced after him but he made it back inside the building and slammed the door. Gabriel wrenched on the handle, then kicked the door in frustration. *Locked.*

There'd be time for Steward later. I pulled the bag off Tanya's head and brushed her hair back from her face. Then I brought my lips down on hers and just kissed the hell out of her.

When I came up for air, Bradan and JD were standing panting over the unconscious bodies of Steward's two CIA goons. Gabriel ran over to us. "We need to hustle." He pointed: guys with guns were running across the field towards us. There must be another exit from the underground facility.

We ran down a driveway to a dirt road. The sign on the rusted metal fence said the place I'd been held was supposedly a *Department of the Interior Groundwater Monitoring Station.* There was nothing else for miles: the land was flat all the way to the horizon. "Where the hell are we?" I asked.

"Kansas," said Bradan sadly. From the way he stared out across the wheat fields, the place held memories for him, and not good ones.

A white pick-up bounced down the dirt road and skidded to a stop in front of us, with Danny at the wheel. We piled into the crew cab and Bradan jumped into the cargo bed. The pickup shot forward and we blasted down the dirt road for a few hundred feet before slowing again. Cal stood up from where he'd been lying, hidden in the middle of a wheat field. He bounded towards us with that long, loping run of his, jumped in the cargo bed with Bradan and we accelerated away. I grunted as the rough ride threw us around, my cracked ribs throbbing.

JD twisted around from the passenger seat to look at me. "I owe you an apology." He looked at Tanya. "You, too. I'm sorry."

I could hear in his voice how much he was hurting. I reached out and squeezed his shoulder, nodding and Tanya gave him a nod, too. I looked around at all of them and suddenly it felt like I could breathe properly for the first time since we'd run from them at the motel. We were back as a team.

Gabriel leaned forward. "You said something about a terrorist attack?" he prompted.

JD's face turned grim. "How do we stop this thing?"

56

TANYA

COLTON TOLD the team the whole story, in detail, and this time they listened. I looked around at them. I'd managed to pick up all of their names, now. JD, Danny, Cal, Bradan, Gabriel...a weird, mismatched bunch of guys but, from the way they'd got me out of that CIA facility, very good at what they did. From the time they'd first kicked down my door in New York, they'd been the enemy. Working together was an abrupt shift, even for me. I wasn't sure I trusted them. Wasn't sure I *wanted* to trust them. It had taken me this long to get used to being a duo instead of being out there on my own. I wasn't ready for a whole...*family.*

Then my gaze returned to Colton and I felt myself unknot inside. *He* trusted them, so I could trust them. As long as the two of us were together, everything would be okay.

I caught myself and scowled inwardly. *I'm getting soft.*

Colton finished his story and I filled the team in on my hunt for Maravić. When I'd finished, everyone went quiet, thinking. The problem was, we still had no idea where the terrorist attack would be, only that it was happening today. And we still couldn't go to the authorities, it was our word against Steward's, and the team had just broken about a billion laws breaking into a CIA facility.

I was at a loss and so was everyone else. The team looked helplessly at each other.

But then something happened. One by one, they all turned to one man: Gabriel, the one with the soft black curls. He had brown eyes, too, but where Colton's burned and made me think of the heat deep beneath the earth, Gabriel's glittered, putting me in mind of some frighteningly quick calculating machine made of whirring, meshing cogs. He stared back at us in silence for a moment, considering it all, and then said, "We're looking at this all wrong." He looked at me. "Maravić isn't an extremist, right? He won't want to die in the attack."

I nodded. "He'll want to walk off with his money."

"Right, but you don't carry out a terrorist attack on US soil and just walk away. Even with the economy gone, you better believe Uncle Sam is going to scour the planet looking for whoever killed its people. They *will* find him..."

He left it hanging for us. I got there first. "Unless he can pin it on someone else," I said.

Colton spoke up. "When we were listening to Maravić at the garage, he said something about picking up their friends from New Jersey. You think they could be the fall guys?"

JD pulled out his phone and called Calahan, putting it on speaker. Calahan answered after just a few rings but just growled, "*Wait!*" We could hear him marching through an office and then the sounds of a street outside. "What the fuck is going on?" he asked. "I just got an APB for your whole team! You broke into some CIA place?!"

"Yeah," said JD, rubbing his stubble. "It's been a busy day."

"JD, I have to put the phone down. If they know I talked to you, I'll lose my job."

"Wait!" said JD quickly. "What's happening in New Jersey?"

There was a pause and I could imagine Calahan's brow furrowing. "How did you know about that? That hasn't gone outside the FBI yet!"

"What's happening?" pressed JD.

Calahan went quiet for a moment, considering. Then he gave a long-suffering sigh. "I'm only telling you this because it sounds like you might know something," he said. "We were keeping an eye on this Islamic group. Four guys, early twenties. They were doing a lot of talking on social media which was why we were watching them, but they had no serious connections and we were pretty sure they weren't going to actually do anything. Then this morning, all four of them suddenly dropped off the radar and now we can't find them. My office is going crazy."

"They're the patsies," I said. "Maravić is going to pin it on them."

"Remember the van Maravić had?" asked Colton. "I thought it was too old and beat up for a slick operation like theirs. But it's just the sort of piece of crap four poor kids from New Jersey would use."

"Calahan, you're looking for a brown Chevy van," I said urgently. "It drove from New York to near Columbus, Ohio the day before yesterday. New York plates, GT7 15D" Colton stared at me in wonder and I blushed.

"Alright..." said Calahan gratefully. "Alright, I'm on it. I'll call you back."

The pickup turned off the dirt road and bounced across a plowed field. We pulled up alongside a helicopter and piled in. Gina turned to us. "Don't suppose anyone thought to bring my phone back?"

The team all looked at each other guiltily.

Gina rolled her eyes, grumbled and took off.

57

COLTON

WE WERE BARELY in the air when JD's phone rang. "We got a hit on that license plate!" said Calahan. "A traffic camera caught it yesterday morning heading west on I-30 near Arkansas."

We thanked him, hung up and looked at a map. "So we know the target's somewhere west of Little Rock," said JD, "and we know it's south, or they'd have taken a different route." He yelled to Gina. "Start flying south!"

"That's still a bloody big list of places," said Danny. "Could be L.A., San Diego, Vegas..."

"You're assuming they're going to hit a city," said Gabriel. "For all we know, it could be a town. *Any* town."

"What do we *know?*" I asked desperately. "They're going to use a nerve agent. It's a gas, right?"

Tanya nodded. "It's stored as liquid, under pressure, but it comes out as gas. They'd want a confined space."

"Okay," said Gabriel. "So anything outdoors is out. No football stadiums, no parades."

"Where do a lot of people gather, indoors?" asked JD. "A shopping mall? A basketball court?"

"What about a movie theater?" I asked. "One of those big ones with like ten screens?"

"Oh Jesus," said Danny, going pale. "A school?"

All of them were good ideas but now we had tens of thousands of possible targets. For nearly three hours, as Gina flew south, we all wracked our brains but we couldn't figure out any way to narrow it down. I stared into Tanya's eyes but she looked as helpless as me. Even Gabriel looked stumped.

I wanted to rage and punch something but this wasn't a problem I could solve with brute force. A lot of people were going to die if I didn't figure this out. I looked at Tanya. She'd claimed I was smarter than I thought. *So think! What am I missing?*

I thought back to Steward and Lucas Bainbridge. To Maravić. To the guy we'd met at Butcher's, the mercenary bar...

"The guy who Maravić hired," I said suddenly. "He was boasting to his buddy that Maravić had a big screen TV with the full NFL package. Does Maravić strike you as a guy who cares about his guys enough to give them perks?"

Tanya immediately shook her head. "No."

"So what if there was another reason they were watching NFL games?"

Gabriel shook his head. "We already ruled out a football stadium. It's outdoors, the gas would just dissipate."

Danny sat bolt upright in his seat. "There are stadiums with roofs that close. Arlington, in Texas, they have one. Erin was telling me about it before we left because..." His jaw went slack. "Shit. Because that's the game Kian's going to...with the President."

58

TANYA

WE ALL STARED at each other in horror.

"It makes sense," said Gabriel coldly. "They want to make sure. They need to be *certain* the dollar will *absolutely tank*. If there's a massive terrorist attack *and* it kills the President...and then the algorithm kicks in and amplifies the panic..." He shook his head. "It'll be like nothing anyone's ever seen. Worst financial crash in history." He looked as if he might throw up. "The Bainbridges are going to be trillionaires. And they're going to kill a whole stadium full of people to do it."

The chopper banked and turned. "Heading to Arlington," Gina told us. "We're about thirty minutes out. When does the game start?"

"Forty minutes," said Danny, his voice strained. He looked at JD. "Let's call the Secret Service, They can evacuate the place."

JD pulled out his phone...but then stopped, looking ill.

"*What?*" asked Danny. "Call them!"

JD pressed his lips tight together. "What if they don't believe us?" He looked around at all of us. "We've got no evidence. It's our word against Steward's. And we just broke into a CIA facility, we're fugitives." He glanced over at Colton and me and now I knew why he looked sick. He was realizing how we'd felt, when *he* didn't believe *us*.

"It's got to be worth a try!" begged Danny. "Just call them!"

"It ain't that simple," said JD. "If they don't believe us, they won't evacuate the stadium. But they'll also trace the call, scramble a jet and force us to land. We'll be sitting in handcuffs when this thing goes down. We won't be able to help."

Gabriel nodded slowly. "We have to do this ourselves. Get into the stadium, get the President out of there, stop Maravić." He looked at me, rubbed at his bandaged ear...and then passed me a spare radio. I nodded and put the radio on.

A half hour later, we flew over the stadium, a vast oval with a white, domed roof. And the roof was firmly closed, sealing everyone inside. *Chyort!* Gina touched down in the parking lot and we jogged towards the rear of the stadium. It loomed bigger and bigger as we approached, until it filled our entire vision. "How the hell are we going to find Maravić in *there?*" growled Colton.

With the game about to start, everyone was already inside and the entrances were quiet. But they all had Secret Service agents standing guard. Gabriel led us around the back and down a ramp that led to the underground employee parking lot. It had been locked and then padlocked for good measure, but Gabriel pulled out a set of lockpicks and opened both as fast as if he'd had the keys. "What did he do before he joined the team?" I whispered to Colton.

"Professional thief," rumbled Colton. I checked but...no, he wasn't joking.

Inside, it was dark and eerily quiet, a maze of trucks and vans belonging to cleaners and TV crews. As we moved through it, I suddenly drew in my breath and tapped Colton on the arm, pointing. I'd spotted the crappy brown van we'd seen in New York.

We crept over to it, guns drawn. Danny reached for the driver's door handle but I grabbed his arm just in time. "*Wait!*"

I'd glimpsed something inside. I shone a flashlight through the windshield for a better look. Two men of Arab descent sat up front, both dead, their bodies contorted in agony. "There's gas in there," I warned.

I played with the flashlight behind them. I could see two pairs of feet on the floor in the back of the van. "After the attack, when the police comb the place, they'll find these four," I said, my voice choked. "They'll think they were about to escape, but their van had been contaminated and they were killed by their own gas. Case closed. No one will ever look for Maravić and his men."

Colton was peering at their clothes. "They're all in the same overalls and baseball caps. Maintenance workers."

"Maravić and his men will be dressed the same way," said Gabriel. "Clever. They keep the caps pulled down to hide their faces and if they get caught on the security cameras, everyone will think they're these four."

We hurried deeper into the stadium. At first, the hallways were deserted. We were down in the bowels of the place, where colored tape on the floor directed all the backstage workers: turf crews *this* way, uniform laundry *that* way. But as we started climbing stairs towards the seating, we began to see Secret Service patrols. Bradan, who was unnaturally good at sneaking, took the lead and helped us dodge past them. But when we reached the final set of double doors that led to the main seating area, we found three agents standing guard, and they weren't moving.

"There's no other way through," said JD. "And we're out of time." he looked at Colton and me. "The rest of us will clear the way. You two get to Kian and the President."

I blinked at him. He'd distrusted me for so long. Now he was relying on me to get the job done. I felt something I couldn't describe, something I hadn't felt since I was a naive young thing at the academy, eager to serve my country. I looked at Colton, flustered, then back at JD. "Sure," I muttered.

"You got it, boss," said Colton.

"Leave your guns with us," said Danny. "If you run up to the President with them, they'll shoot you."

We handed over our weapons. Then JD, Danny, Gabriel and Bradan ran at the three Secret Service agents, tackling them and grabbing their radios before they could warn anyone. As soon as they

were down, Colton and I picked our way through the sea of fighting
bodies on the floor, hauled open the double doors and—

Chyort!

I knew we had to move, before one of the Secret Service agents
behind us raised the alarm. But my legs wouldn't function. The space
in front of me was just so unthinkably vast. I was looking across the
field at a towering wall of screaming, cheering people ten stories
high, the figures so tiny they were just blobs of color. And the wall
extended out to the left and right, all the way around me.

I'd had no idea what eighty thousand people looked like.

I saw men and women of every race. *Families.* Oh God, so many
children. All cheering together.

Except they weren't cheering. As my ears adjusted to the
deafening noise, I realized they were singing.

"...*and the home of the brave.*"

The game was about to begin.

59

COLTON

I'D BEEN FROZEN, along with Tanya, by the sheer scale of the place. By how many people were going to die if we didn't stop this thing. But as the national anthem faded and the crowd whooped and applauded, I finally got my ass in gear. *Where is he? Where is he?* I didn't have a hope of spotting the President in the crowd, so I looked for the biggest concentration of Secret Service agents. And there they were, a dark-suited protective ring around one particular block of seating. In the center was a man with silver hair. And next to him was a dark-haired, stubble-jawed figure I recognized. *Kian!*

The problem was, there were three stories below me, and there were about six Secret Service agents on the stairs between us and him. Already, they were eying us with suspicion.

I squeezed Tanya's hand. *"Run."*

And I took off, head down, charging like a bull straight towards them. I knew we were going to be stopped. We just had to get close enough before we were.

Agents started yelling for me to stop. If I'd been wearing a big, bulky jacket or anything else that might have concealed a suicide vest, they probably would have pulled their guns and shot. But I was in a heavy metal t-shirt with the sleeves torn off and there really weren't a lot of hiding places. They hesitated, figuring me for some beered-up football fan, and that let me reach the first rank and shove two agents out of the way.

Now they got serious. The next line of protection ran up the stairs towards me, desperate to keep me away from the President. But I kept my weight low and battered my way through them, scattering them like skittles. My cracked ribs hurt like hell, but I was running on adrenaline, now. I could hear Tanya racing down the stairs behind me: if I couldn't get there, at least I was clearing a path for her.

There was still a full block of seating between the President and me. And now the Secret Service had gotten their act together and were completely blocking the stairs below me. I swerved, climbed up onto the back row of the next block of seats and went *through* the block, using the backs of seats as stepping stones and putting my hands on shoulders and heads to steady myself. I was getting close, now. *I'm going to make it!*

But then the fans woke up to the fact that some crazy guy was making a beeline for the President. *"Stop him!" "Grab him!"* Hands closed around my legs. I shook them off but more took their place. Behind me, I could hear grunts of frustration from Tanya as people tried to grab her and sharp cries of pain as she kicked herself free. Our progress slowed to a crawl and then stopped altogether and the President was still twenty rows ahead, still oblivious. *"Mr. President!"* I yelled, but *everyone* was yelling. He didn't turn around. And now the Secret Service were pushing their way between the seats to arrest us.

I filled my lungs and *hollered. "Kian! Kian O'Harra!"*

A Secret Service agent grabbed my arms and wrenched them behind my back. *No!*

And then I saw Kian turn around, frowning. He saw my face and his jaw dropped. Then he was waving to the Secret Service agents: *bring him here.*

Tanya and I were patted down and frog-marched down the stairs and over to the President's seating block. The agents kept a firm grip on us and didn't let us get within ten feet of Kian or the President, but it was enough.

"Colton, what the *fuck?*" Kian's Northern Irish accent came out more when he was worried.

I was panting. "Get the President out of here. Everybody, get everybody out."

The President, Jake Matthews, stepped forward. The Secret Service tried to hustle him back but he waved them out of the way. "You better tell us what's going on, son."

I swallowed, a little in awe. "Uh, Mr. President, Sir, there's a plot to kill you. And everyone else in this stadium, they're going to release a nerve agent."

One of the Secret Service agents, a woman with blonde hair pulled back in a ponytail, said, "Sir, we haven't heard anything. No word from the CIA about an increase in chatter."

Tanya spoke up. "The CIA are *involved.* Casey Steward, the acting chief of the Special Activities Division, he's behind this. He's paid a Serbian mercenary to release nerve gas."

The Secret Service agent showed the President her phone and I glimpsed a photo of Tanya there. *Shit.* "Sir, this is Tanya Yeshevskaya, she's a former Russian agent wanted for murder. This could be a ploy: we rush you out of here and then they attack the motorcade."

The President looked questioningly at Kian. Kian looked me in the eye, then nodded. "You can trust what he says, Sir."

The President nodded curtly. "Alright then. Sound the alarm, let's get everyone out of here."

The female Secret Service agent shook her head. "No sir, protocol is to get you out first."

"Goddamn it, there are women and children here!" snapped the President. "I'm not running and leaving them here!"

I spoke up. "Sir, she's right. Right now, everyone who knows that Steward's behind this is *in this building!* We need to get you out safe so you can catch the fucker."

The President scowled but nodded. He turned to the female agent. "Sierra, stay here and help." She nodded.

Kian turned to the woman sitting next to him. "Emily, go with your dad. I'm staying too." Emily, the President's daughter, hugged him tight and kissed him, then allowed herself to be hustled away by the Secret Service. Kian caught one of the agents as they hurried past him and said something, and the guy gave Kian his gun.

"What do you need from me?" asked the blonde-haired Secret Service agent, Sierra.

"Your guys have our friends in custody up there," I said, pointing. "Can you set 'em loose?"

Sierra spoke into her radio and, a few moments later, JD and the rest of the team hurried down the stairs to join us. Gabriel gave Kian a radio and passed us our weapons.

Sierra listened to her earpiece. "The President's out," she said. "We'll start evacuating people, but—" She looked around the stadium to indicate the scale of the problem. It would take time to get this many people out. "We've gotta stop them releasing the gas. Who are we looking for?"

"Four guys in maintenance uniforms," Tanya told her. "Led by a big guy, late fifties, white hair."

We all looked around the stadium. The place was *vast.* How the hell were we going to find them? They could release the gas any minute. The President was safe but they'd still kill tens of thousands of people.

"This gas," said Sierra. "Heavier than air or lighter than air?"

"Heavier," said Tanya immediately.

"So they'd have to release it high up so it sank down," said Gabriel.

We all looked up at the roof, searching frantically.

"Got 'em!" called Cal, pointing. He had his rifle's scope up to his eye.

I followed his finger but I couldn't see anything. He passed me his rifle for a second and...*yes,* there they were. They were in maintenance uniforms and baseball caps, but I recognized Maravić's hulking build. They were climbing around on a catwalk which was—

I took the rifle away from my eye and the catwalk seemed to shoot away from me, becoming tiny in the distance. My head swam and my skin went sweaty with vertigo. The catwalk was right up in the roof, hundreds of feet above the football field. *Shit.*

"We've gotta get up there," said JD. "Bradan, you stay with Kian in case any of them are down here. The rest of you, with me."

60

TANYA

WE POUNDED UP A STAIRWELL, corkscrewing up and up, then up narrower stairways, each one marked with more and more warning signs. We barreled through the final door and—

Chyort!

We were at the edge of a network of flimsy-looking white metal catwalks. Most of them ran around the edge of the huge, oval stadium, with a few leading in towards the center like the spokes of a wheel. They didn't join in the middle, they just ended, hanging out over space like diving boards.

The catwalks were only a few feet wide and the walls only came up to knee height. Worse, they were made in ten-foot sections and there were gaps between each one we'd have to step over. It was designed for workers with climbing harnesses and safety lines, neither of which we had. And the catwalk sections hung from the stadium roof on steel cables so the slightest movement made them swing and sway. They really weren't designed for running around on.

Worst of all, the floors were metal mesh, to reduce the weight. We could look down and see the drop beneath us and that's when it sank in that we were three hundred feet up. The football field looked like a child's game, the people dots. I gulped, feeling my stomach knot.

Then I looked at Colton. He was just behind me, standing in the doorway with his face sheet white, staring at the tiny rectangle of green far below. My chest ached for him: this was his idea of hell.

He swallowed. Looked up and met my eyes. And then he stepped bravely onto the catwalk.

We moved slowly forward, shuffling carefully, arms outstretched for balance. Then, a hundred feet ahead of us, we saw one of Maravić's mercenaries walk across our view, a gas mask on his face. He was carrying a metal cylinder. Danny snapped his gun up to shoot—

I grabbed the barrel and pushed it down just in time. *"No!"* I hissed. "The cylinders are pressurized! If you hit one and it explodes, everybody dies!"

Everyone cursed and put their guns away. We'd have to do this hand-to-hand.

Creeping forward, we counted three men, plus Maravić. *Good.* All four were up here. Each was carrying a cylinder and they were spreading out, one moving to each of the four corners of the stadium. They wanted to make sure their gas reached every person in the crowd below.

I frowned. *Four* cylinders? The crate we'd found in Ohio had been big enough to hold much more than that.

JD used hand signals to point each of us to a different target: Danny, Cal and Gabriel got a man each, JD was backup for whoever needed it and Colton and I got Maravić.

I started forward with Colton right behind me. Maravić and his men hadn't seen us yet. Walking along the catwalks took a lot of concentration and doing it carrying the cylinders meant they couldn't use their hands for balance. Plus, their gas masks blocked all of their peripheral vision. I could see that Cal had already almost reached his man. *Maybe we can pull this off.*

As we crept closer to Maravić, he turned a little. I glimpsed his profile and, suddenly, the memories all rushed back. I could feel Lev jerking in my arms. Hear him pleading with me to save him as he drowned in his own blood.

I stopped dead.

This mission had become about so much more than revenge. But now, looking at Maravić, all the anger came back. My muscles tensed and the blood thundered in my ears. *He has to die.* There was a flutter of fear in my chest, too. If I got close to him, he'd kill me. My only chance had ever been to shoot him from a distance and now that option had been taken away.

My breathing went tight. Ever since I first went after Maravić, I'd known, deep down, that I'd most likely die trying to kill him. Maybe I'd even wanted it. But something had changed. I didn't want it anymore.

Then a hand found mine and squeezed it, and Colton's chest pressed gently against my back. I felt my breathing ease.

Something else had changed. I wasn't on my own anymore.

I squeezed Colton's hand. Then, together, we moved forward along the catwalk.

We were less than six feet from Maravić when he heard us and whirled around, the cylinder clutched to his chest. He glanced around, taking in the scene. The fight was going our way: Cal and Danny were tussling with their men and JD was helping Gabriel with the final one. Maravić was trapped: the catwalk to his right led to Cal, we were moving in from his left and the only other catwalk was one of the ones that led out into space.

Colton and I tensed, ready to tackle him if he ran at us. But instead, he pulled out a radio.

And that's when I realized how badly we'd underestimated him.

"Release it into the air conditioning now," Maravić said.

My stomach dropped. *Who's he talking to?* We'd assumed there were only four mercenaries, to match the four dead men in the van who'd be the scapegoats. But of course someone like Maravić would have a backup team waiting in reserve, when so much was at stake. And because the gas was heavier than air, we'd assumed they'd have to release it from up in the roof. But there was another way to make sure it got everywhere in the stadium: release it into the air conditioning system. I groaned as I remembered the network of pipes

I'd seen on the laptop screen at the garage. *That's* what they were! Maravić had planned to release the gas both from the roof and into the A/C simultaneously, just to be sure. But either one would kill everyone in the stadium.

I yelled into my radio, "Kian, where's the air conditioning plant in this place?"

He repeated the question to someone. Then, "Ground level, west end of the stadium."

I looked at Colton in horror. The team was up here: there was no one down there to stop them!

I looked down. The evacuation was well underway but, just as we'd feared, it was slow going. Every stairway was packed solid with people and the stadium was still half full. Then three blobs of color caught my eye because they weren't moving towards the exits. I recognized the blue maintenance uniforms with their bright red baseball caps: Maravić's men. Curved metal glinted in their arms: they each had a canister. I'd been right, there'd been more than four in the crate.

As I watched, they jumped over the barriers and onto the east end of the field. The crowd had blocked all the normal paths, so they were going to take a shortcut straight down the football field. If even one of them reached the far end and got to the air conditioning plant, it was all over.

61

KIAN

I PICKED up a howling three year-old who'd gotten lost in the crowd and held him up above my head. Then, as soon as I heard his mother shout in relief, I pushed through the sea of bodies and handed him to her. The evacuation was going as well as could be expected. People were scared but they weren't shoving and crushing each other and in another ten minutes we could maybe have the stadium clear.

That's when Colton yelled in my earpiece. "You've got guys in maintenance uniforms running down the field with gas! Don't let 'em get to the air conditioning!"

I looked, and saw three guys running onto the field. *Shit.* "Bradan!" I yelled. "Sierra!"

I raced down to the barrier and vaulted it, the other two close behind. We spread out in the middle of the field, arms spread to tackle them.

That's when three *more* guys ran onto the field, making six in total.

"Feck," said Bradan. "We're a little outmanned."

"No we're not," I said. "I brought the family." And I turned towards where we'd been sitting and shouted. It was loud, in the stadium, but this shout had been honed on a Belfast housing estate to cut through a playground or a busy street when a brother was in trouble. *"Oi!"*

Heads turned. Three in particular.

Then my brother Aedan came racing down the stairs. Already, he was stretching his shoulders and neck, getting ready to hit something. He pulled off his hooded top as he ran and tossed it over his shoulder. Sylvie, his wife, plucked it out of the air.

Behind him, Sean, looking almost respectable in a white shirt. "Take Grace," I saw him say as he pushed a red-haired little girl to Louise, *his* wife. Then he was running towards the football field.

And finally Carrick, who could never look respectable, in his *Hell's Princes* biker kutte. He kissed his wife, Annabelle, then ran for the field.

As they vaulted the barrier onto the field, I yelled and pointed. "Don't let any of those fuckers in blue get to the other end!"

Maravić's men were focused entirely on Bradan, Sierra and me as they thundered down the field towards us. They weren't expecting three big and very determined Irishmen to slam into them from the side. Aedan, Sean and Carrick tackled three of them and took them down to the ground, then started punching them into submission. Bradan grabbed the fourth and did something to his neck, so fast I couldn't see it, and the man dropped, limp. Sierra spun and kicked the fifth man in the face and he crashed to the ground. And the final man was running right at me.

I lunged at him but he shoved me aside, sending me stumbling back. I sprinted and threw myself at him, managing to grab him around the legs. But he was a big guy and he just kept going, dragging me along with him—

I heard the sound of an almighty punch landing and the guy who was dragging me crashed to the ground.

I rolled over onto my back and looked up, squinting against the stadium lights. Carrick was standing over me. "You've gone soft," he told me.

"Fuck you," I took the hand he offered and hauled myself upright, panting. All six of Maravić's men were down and Sierra was carefully gathering the canisters they'd been carrying.

"The rest of us all tackled *our* guys," said Carrick. "That's all I'm saying."

I made as if to punch him, then hugged him instead. Then I looked up at the catwalks high in the roof. Things were under control down here. But what was happening up there?

62

TANYA

ALL OF US, Maravić included, watched, breathless as the tiny blobs of blue and red far below were intercepted by other blobs. I felt my heart start beating again when the last one fell. And up here on the catwalks, Colton's team had subdued the rest of Maravić's men. We'd nearly done it.

But not quite. Maravić was still free, still facing off against Colton and me. And he still held the last cylinder. Through the circular eyeholes of his gas mask, I could see him glancing around as he weighed his options. Then I saw him reach for the cylinder's valve. He'd kill me and Colton, the team...and then the gas would drift down into the panicked crowd below, invisible and deadly. Even one canister would still kill thousands.

There was only one thing I could do. I took two running steps and leapt at him. If his hands had been free, he could have easily batted me aside, but he was clutching the cylinder and I managed to climb his body and cling on with my legs like a monkey while I clawed at his face. He reached up with one arm, grabbed my wrist and brutally ripped me off him, flipping me over his shoulder. I cried out as the force of the throw wrenched my shoulder. Then I slammed into the metal catwalk behind him. I lay there limply, bruised and aching, panting in pain. But I'd done it.

Maravić touched his bare cheek, gaping in shock. Then he saw his gas mask dangling from my hand. He lunged towards me.

My training made me hesitate for a second. The gas mask was the only way to ensure my safety. Thinking only of self-preservation, thinking like a *spy*, I should hold onto it.

But as long as I had it, Maravić might get it back. I opened my fingers and the mask tumbled to the ground far below. Then I glared up at Maravić defiantly. If he released the gas now, he'd die too.

Maravić looked at me. At Colton. At Colton's team, who'd ziptied most of Maravić's men and were moving towards us to help. Then he dropped his canister on the catwalk and ran down the walkway that led inwards towards the center of the stadium, the one that just finished in mid-air. He sprinted, accelerating, and then as he reached the end....he jumped.

I scrambled up onto my elbows, wide-eyed. He *jumped?!* Why would he—

Then I spotted him. Ten feet below the walkways, in the center of the stadium, was the colossal TV screen that showed replays and highlights. Really, it was four TV screens, each twenty feet long, facing outwards to form a square. The whole thing hung from steel cables and at one corner was a ladder that led all the way up to the roof. Maravić had landed on one corner of the square and, as I watched, he started shuffling carefully along the top of a screen towards the ladder.

He hadn't been jumping to his death. He was going to escape.

My stomach dropped. He'd disappear again. How many more people would he kill before I caught up with him again? What if I never did?

I clambered to my feet: even that small act set the catwalk swinging. I hurried to the end of the catwalk Maravić had jumped from and looked down. My stomach sank. The TV was four feet away and ten feet below me. Worse, the top of the TV, where I'd have to land, was only a few feet wide. But if I didn't do this, Maravić was going to get away. We didn't have anyone up on the roof of the stadium and there were too many routes down for us to cover them all. I ran back along the catwalk to get a run up, took a deep breath and started to run—

Colton crashed into me from behind and tackled me. We fell to the floor of the catwalk together, his arms wrapped around me. *"Are you insane?!"* he yelled. "It's over! *We won!*"

"He'll get away!" I panted, struggling.

His arms tightened protectively around me. "He can be someone else's fucking problem!"

"I might never find him again!"

"The whole world's going to be looking for him after this! *Let him go!*"

I lost it. "*I can't!*" I screamed in his face. "*I can't,* Colton! *Ty, chert voz'mi, ne ponimayesh,* don't you get it, *I can't!*" There were tears in my eyes. "I have to know he's gone, I have to get him out of my head!"

He stared into my eyes. And then he reluctantly released me. He'd realized I was right: I had to do this.

We clambered to our feet. Colton looked at the jump to the TV and all the blood drained from his face. The jump was next to impossible. It was terrifying even for me. For *him...*

I saw his expression fall as he realized what I already knew.

He couldn't come with me.

"It's okay," I told him. I found that I was smiling. "It was always meant to be this way. I love you, *plyushevyy mishka.*"

I kissed him, turned and ran...and jumped off into space.

63

COLTON

SHE JUMPED and I couldn't breathe. Her body sailed through the air, so tiny in the huge void. *Please make it, please please please—*

Her feet landed on the top of one of the TV screens. But her momentum tipped her forward and she teetered on the edge. My heart jumped into my mouth. *No!*

She grabbed one of the TV's support cables and managed to steady herself. I could see her chest heaving with fear, but she was okay.

I'd had to let her go. I knew that. She didn't deserve the guilt she was carrying, but it was still tearing her apart. If she was ever going to find peace, she had to do this.

But she didn't have to do it alone. That's what I'd told her.

I marched down the catwalk. It rocked and swayed under me, making my stomach flip. *Of course* I had to go after her.

But as I got to the end and looked down at the jump, I just froze. My head went swimmy at the sight of the tiny rectangle of green far below. My feet went light and I could feel myself falling, could see the football field rushing up to meet me as I tumbled down and down. I took a breath but I couldn't seem to get any air. *Aw shit—*

My knees buckled and I fell on my ass, clinging onto the catwalk rails, chest heaving in panic. The fear was the worst it had ever been. This wasn't like jumping between the balconies, back in DC. I was jumping *down* so I couldn't not look at the ground. And the ground was *three hundred feet* below. The top of the giant TV, where I'd have to land, was insanely narrow. I wasn't graceful, like Tanya. I wasn't sure I could make that jump even on the ground.

I *wanted* to go. I just couldn't. The shame and guilt clawed at me. I'd never felt so helpless.

Tanya had got her balance, now, and she was starting to make her way along the top of the TV screens towards the ladder. *Oh, God,* she meant to get there first and block him from going up it. The ladder was on the opposite corner of the square, so she'd have to go along two sides. Meanwhile, Maravić was moving along the other two sides. He had a big head start but he was big and bulky like me, and he had to shuffle along inch by inch. Tanya was doing quick little steps, graceful as a gymnast on a balance beam, trying to catch up. *Not too fast,* I willed her, *don't go too fast—*

She slipped, her foot stabbing out sideways into thin air. She fell forward and my throat closed up. But she caught herself on her hands and clung there for a second, straddling the edge of the TV. Then she climbed back up and carried on. She reached the corner and turned it. She'd caught up, now, she was going to get to the ladder first. But *then* what? He'd kill her, if they fought.

I have to go. I heaved myself up again, cursing at myself for being such a fucking coward. I staggered to the edge and—

The scene swam in front of me. My head went spacey and my vision went dark at the edges. I could hear myself hyper-ventilating and my body locked up: my feet might as well have been welded to the catwalk. I was screaming at myself, the anger and self-hate burning me up inside. *You big fucking pussy, do it! Just do it!* I wanted to go, I was fucking *desperate* to go, but the fear was just too big to overcome.

Something clicked in my brain. *He's not holding a canister anymore. We can shoot him!* But my shotgun was useless for anything except close range. "Shoot him!" I yelled into my earpiece. "Shoot him! Somebody shoot him!"

I glanced around. JD, Danny, Cal and Gabriel had finished securing Maravić's men and I saw them raise their rifles. But three of them were blocked by the dangling catwalks. Only Danny could even see Maravić.

Maravić was only six feet from Tanya, now, and shuffling closer. He took out his knife.

"*Shoot him!*" I screamed.

"He's too close to her!" Danny snapped in frustration. "And this catwalk's swinging around all over the place, I could hit her!"

Maravić's arm snapped out and his knife flashed. Tanya had to dodge back and almost lost her footing. Both of them were having to work hard to keep their balance on the narrow platform, but I'd seen how deadly Maravić was with his knife. I knew how this would end.

Maravić twisted and lunged, slashing. Tanya's scream carried even over the noise from below, and I saw blood drip from her forearm. She shuffled backwards, panting in pain.

And suddenly, I was backing up along the catwalk. As soon as I had enough room, I started forward: a jog and then a sprint and then a full on *charge.* My feet pounded the metal, the weight of my big body sending the whole thing tilting and swaying, but I didn't care anymore.

I wasn't being brave. I was *more* scared than before. But *this* fear filled my lungs with oxygen and made my heart pump harder. It made my muscles swell with blood as my body dumped all its adrenaline into my system at once.

As the edge of the catwalk came up, I gave a death cry and launched myself out into space, arms and legs flailing.

It turns out, there *is* something that can overcome fear: an even bigger fear.

I didn't *land,* as such. I didn't have time. My feet touched down on the top edge of the TV and I just staggered forward, letting my momentum carry me towards Maravić. He'd heard my yell and turned around. I saw his expression change to total shock—

I punched him in the face as hard as I could.

He swayed sideways and fell. But I was out of control and off balance and on my next step, I slipped. I went full-length and the top of the TV smacked me in the face. Dazed, I started to slither off—

Hands grabbed my wrists, stopping my slide just long enough for me to wake up and grab on. I found I was dangling from my arms, the rest of me hanging in space. I looked up and saw Tanya stretched out along the top of the TV, her hands on my wrists. *"Don't look down!"* she told me.

But I did. I looked down on a green football field and a blue-and-red figure getting smaller and smaller below me. I closed my eyes as he hit the ground. Maravić was finally gone.

I heaved myself up onto the top of the TV screen and lay there panting, my face inches from Tanya's.

She looked behind me, at the crazy jump I'd made. Her eyes were shining, even though she was smiling. "I thought—" she croaked, "I thought you were too scared?"

"I was," I panted. "I was just more scared of losing you."

And then I kissed her.

EPILOGUE

Colton

WE LAY there for a long time while, far below us, thousands of tiny dots scurried around. First the stadium got quieter and quieter as the last of the audience evacuated. Then it started to fill up with people: dark blue dots who must be police officers, black dots who must be FBI and Secret Service agents and then bright yellow dots pushing everyone else out: hazmat personnel telling everyone else to stay the hell away until they were sure the nerve gas was safe.

I looked for too long and suddenly remembered *why* the people looked like dots. My head started to swim and I put my head down on the top of the TV. The bad news was, I was very high up. The worse news was, there was no way down except up the ladder Maravić had been heading for. I breathed slow and deep and finally worked up enough courage to go for it. "You go first," I told Tanya.

Tanya shook her head. "You should go first. What if you freeze and I need to encourage you? I can poke you in the ass if I'm behind you."

"Trust me," I groaned. "I've thought this through."

She looked at me doubtfully, but got up and moved carefully

towards the ladder, graceful and sure-footed as ever. When she'd got herself onto the ladder and started up, I gingerly crawled forward, eyes locked on the narrow top of the TV, pretending nothing else existed. I reached the ladder and slithered up it like a snake. And there, right in front of me, was Tanya's gorgeous, heart-shaped ass. I couldn't think of anything that would distract me better and I didn't take my eyes off it for a second as we climbed. When we finally pushed through the hatch and emerged onto the roof of the stadium, I pulled Tanya hard against me and kissed her like I'd just stumbled over the finish line of a marathon. It was funny: we were still standing on a rooftop, hundreds of feet above the ground, but after what we'd been through, it seemed like nothing.

Back on the ground, we met up with JD and the others and there were relieved hugs all round. A paramedic dressed the cut on Tanya's arm. She'd also strained her shoulder when Maravić threw her, but both would heal in time.

The police, local FBI and Secret Service all had questions and we started trying to answer them. But then a convoy of black SUVs rolled up and Steward jumped out, demanding we all be arrested. "These people conspired with a known Russian agent to orchestrate this whole thing," he told anyone who'd listen. "They were working *with* Maravić. Get cuffs on them, I'm taking all of them to a secure site for interrogation."

The head of the Texas FBI office opened his mouth to argue—

"It's a national security matter!" Steward snapped.

The FBI guy chewed his lip and looked at us apologetically. Then he brought out a pair of handcuffs.

JD and I exchanged worried glances. Steward was still CIA and all he had to do was say the magic words *national security* and even the FBI had to fall into line. With Maravić dead, it was mostly Steward's word against ours. *Shit.* He was going to spirit us off somewhere and then kill us and say we were shot while trying to escape.

Then another black SUV rolled up behind him, and a familiar figure in a suit climbed out. She marched up behind Steward and tapped him on the shoulder, and he turned to look.

It's hard to describe the look of pure thunder on Roberta's face. The chief of the CIA's Special Activities Division has always struck me as a calm person. I've never seen her lose her temper. But when she wakes up from a coma to discover that her underling put her there? That he did it so that he could murder the President? That he was going to kill tens of thousands of Americans, people her agency is sworn to protect?

That'll do it.

Roberta grabbed Steward's shoulders and brought her knee up between his legs as hard as she possibly could. The *crunch* was the single most satisfying sound I'd ever heard. As Steward curled himself into a fetal ball on the ground, Roberta touched the bandage wrapped around her head, winced, and crouched down beside him, "I'm going to put you in the deepest, darkest hole you can imagine," she told him. "Your sentence is going to be so long there'll be commas between the digits."

She stood and turned to the FBI agent who'd been about to handcuff us. "Use them on *him,*" she said.

"Yes *ma'am!*" the guy said with feeling, and started cuffing Steward.

It was almost midnight before we were allowed to leave. By then, Agent Calahan had showed up from New York with his boss, Carrie, and the van we'd found in the parking garage with the dead guys from New Jersey had been secured. The APBs on all of us had been lifted and the President had called to say there were going to be medals for all of us. There'd no doubt be more debriefings over the next few months and Kian and JD would probably have to put on suits and go and get grilled by senators in an enquiry again but for now, it was over.

My phone rang. Yolanda. "Have you seen what happened to the markets?" she asked, her voice awed.

I cursed. I'd completely forgotten about the algorithm. Had the markets crashed after all?

Yolanda sent through a graph. There was a sharp dip from when the first news stories had appeared screaming about terrorists, nerve gas and the President. But moments later, when the story had been updated to say the situation was under control, things had started to climb. And then the President had gone on TV to calm the nation and now things were almost back to normal. "What happened?" I asked.

"Without the big disaster to make the dollar drop, things never got bad enough for the algorithm to kick in." I could hear the grin in her voice. "You know what that means?"

"No. What?"

"The Bainbridges will have spent billions betting against the dollar because they were *sure* it was going to drop...but it didn't. They've lost all that money!"

I imagined Lucas Bainbridge and the rest of his family watching the news in slack-jawed horror, seeing their fortune dissolve. I started to laugh and, even though it hurt my ribs, I couldn't stop.

Tanya

We said goodbye to Sierra, the Secret Service agent who'd helped us, and Kian hugged his brothers. Then the team all trooped out into the darkened parking lot, towards where Gina waited with the helicopter.

For the first time, it hit me that the mission was over. I'd cleared my name and—

Maravić was dead. It slowly sank in. *Maravić is dead!* I felt something lift from me, a cold, crushing weight that had been there since Lev died.

I felt like a helium balloon some kid had let go of: light and free but also completely untethered, in danger of being whipped away by the wind. I didn't have a job. I didn't have any friends in America. I didn't have a *mission*.

I'd never planned a future after Maravić. I'd never thought I'd have one.

Then a huge, heavy hand landed on my shoulder and someone was gently turning me around. I looked up into Colton's face. "I don't know what happens now." I asked in a lost voice.

"That's okay," Colton told me. "'Cause I do. You get yourself in that chopper and you come back to Mount Mercy with me. Then I'm gonna throw you down on the bed and—" he leaned in close and told me exactly what he was going to do to me and each filthy word he growled soaked into my brain and rippled down through my body, leaving me trembly. "—and then we'll get some sleep, and *then* we'll get some food." He drew back a little and those brown and amber eyes burned down into mine. "And whatever happens after that, we'll figure it out together. That okay?"

I threw myself against him and he wrapped me up in a bear hug. "*Yes!*" I told him, my voice muffled. "*Yes,* that's very okay."

It was dawn before we neared our destination. I pressed my nose against the window, transfixed. We were flying over a carpet of rolling mist, lit up gold by the rising sun. The peaks of mountains stabbed up through it, islands in a golden sea. And there, emerging from the mist, was the little town of Mount Mercy. I saw beautiful wooden storefronts that looked like something out of an old movie and quiet streets lined with quaint, brick townhouses. Rising above it, a huge mountain draped in pine forests and capped with snow. And part way up, the outcropping that gave the mountain and the town their name, millions of tons of rock that hung over the town but never fell.

It was beautiful. But could I really fit in somewhere so quiet and wholesome?

We landed at the team's base and Gina yawned and stretched. The team tumbled sleepily out into the chilly morning air. There was talk of a party to welcome us home, but that could wait until we'd all had some rest.

Colton took my hand and I felt myself *fill* and lift. "My place is down there," he said, pointing off into the distance. "Kinda a walk, sorry."

I had to just nod that it was fine because I was suddenly speechless. As we started walking into the forest, I kept looking down at our joined hands. I hadn't walked holding hands with someone— for real, not with a target—since I was a teenager. Even Lev hadn't done that. I hadn't expected something so light and romantic from Colton and I wasn't ready for how it made me feel. Every time I felt his strong hand gripping mine, I got this heady surge of...what *was* that?

I realized that, just maybe, it was happiness. I bit my lip, feeling flighty and delirious and not too far from tearful. Happiness was going to be an adjustment.

Colton led me into the forest and down a slight hill. I began to glimpse water through the trees, just a hint at first but then, as the sun rose, more and more. And then the trees thinned out and—

Suddenly, I was looking into a mirror world. I could see the forest, the town, the mountain rising behind it. And right at the water's edge, a red-haired woman and a huge, silent man gazing out across a wide, calm river.

I saw a cream, boxy trailer in the reflection and turned to look at the real one. Colton showed me up the steps and opened the door.

It was cozy and perfect. There was a double bed that folded away to make space, a tiny kitchenette with gas burners and a soft red couch that looked perfect for cuddling up on to watch TV. There were posters on the wall from heavy metal concerts and...was that a wrestling mask, pinned to the wall?

Colton looked around and rubbed at his stubble. "Sorry."

I turned to him, confused. "What's wrong with it? It's great!"

"It ain't what you're used to."

"What am I used to?"

"Your place in New York. And, y'know, all those fancy parties and embassies and hotels, and folk like Konstantin..."

There was a tiny catch in his voice when he said *Konstantin*. He was still jealous in a wonderful, possessive way, and I loved that. "Well, firstly," I told him, "I've also spent a lot of time sleeping on the floors of bombed-out buildings in Syria, or lying on a mountaintop for three days with bugs crawling into my underwear while I gathered surveillance. And secondly, none of the places I've lived have been real. The safehouses were temporary. Disposable." My voice trembled a little. "Like me."

He put his hands on my waist and tugged me to him, letting me know that I most certainly was *not* disposable. Not anymore. "But when you..." His mouth tightened—"*lived with* your targets..." That possessiveness again, the amber in his eyes burning hot. "They were rich guys in mansions."

I nodded. "But that wasn't real either. I was on a mission. Playing a role." I looked around at the trailer. "It wasn't my..."—my voice unexpectedly cracked—"home."

He blinked at me as if amazed and I blinked back because I wasn't used to breaking like that in front of someone. He visibly relaxed and grinned at me. Then he picked me up by the waist and kissed me, a full-on romantic kiss, spinning us around so that my feet skittered across the linoleum, literally sweeping me off my feet. He pinned me up against the kitchen counter and the kiss became fiercer, deeper, that possessiveness coming out. His lips said *you're mine* and mine answered *yes I am.*

And I realized that maybe showing weakness in front of someone wasn't so bad after all.

There was a soft *thump* from somewhere deeper in the trailer and then, out of the corner of my eye, I saw something brown and furry gamboling towards us, still blinking and heavy-lidded from sleep. Before I could really accept what my brain was seeing, it had reached us and was climbing us like a tree, swarming up Colton's legs and back and then wrapping a furry arm around me and peering curiously at my face. I blinked at shiny black eyes and a wet, black snout. *He really does have a bear.* A young bear, playful as a cub but not much smaller than a refrigerator.

"Atlas," said Colton with deep affection. "Tanya. Tanya, Atlas."

Atlas leaned towards me and snuffled at my cheek, his fur incredibly soft. Then I was being licked by a rough, wet tongue. And then Atlas tried to shift his weight over to me and—*Chyort,* I realized just how much he weighed. It was like being climbed on by a linebacker.

"No, Atlas," said Colton quickly. "No—"

Atlas jumped onto me for cuddles and I shrieked and went down, flat on my back with the bear on top of me. The shriek turned into a giggle and then I couldn't stop. As Colton tried to wrestle Atlas off me, I just lay there on the linoleum, being thoroughly licked and laughing like I hadn't done in a long, long time.

The next afternoon, I stood in front of the mirror in Colton's trailer, my hair gathered up in my hands. I let it fall down onto my shoulders, then huffed and gathered it up again. I turned to Colton. "Up or down?" I asked urgently.

"Hmm?" He was staring at my chest. I'd arrived in Mount Mercy with literally the clothes on my back, so that morning I'd had to buy something to wear for this afternoon's party. The town only had one small boutique and the only thing I'd found in my size was a deep green, stretchy dress that wasn't really right for a barbecue. It hugged my curves in a *va-va-voom* way and featured a scoop neck that Colton couldn't stop looking at.

"Eyes up here," I told him, mock-sternly. "Hair up or down?"

"Down," he told me. I nodded and let it fall again, then started second-guessing my make-up. *What's wrong with me?* I'd met the Italian prime minister and the king of Lakovia and I hadn't spent as much time getting ready for them as I had for this.

But deep down, I knew what the problem was. I wanted them to like me.

Colton showed me to his rusting wreck of a truck. I saw now why he'd replaced it but the new one was in an impound somewhere in Ohio and it would take time to arrange for it to be shipped to

Colorado. The truck started on the fourteenth attempt and he drove us up a winding track to the base.

My eyes widened when we pulled into the parking lot. Colton's grill was already up and running, with JD keeping a watchful eye on some pork steaks that were sizzling and spitting as they dripped fat onto the coals below, The smell was amazing and the table next to the grill was loaded up with enough food to keep the grill busy all night long: beef steaks and chicken legs, sausages, home-made burgers with melting cheese centers. And not just meat but tuna steaks, corn, vegetable kebabs...

Colton put his hand on my arm. "I know what you're thinking, but don't panic. We didn't want to have all the food out in the sun, so that's just the first batch. We've got most of it in coolers, in the base."

"Oh. That's okay, then," I said in a small voice. *How many people are coming to this thing?*

Further along the parking lot was a table set up for burger and hot dog assembly: buns, onions, lettuce, ketchup, four types of slaw and three types of mustard. Then a table loaded with bowls of salad: avocado, chicken and mango; eggplant and halloumi with harissa; and a roast potato salad with chimichurri dressing that looked amazing. There was a table of homemade cakes, cookies and traybakes, which had the same effect on Colton's attention as the neckline of my dress. Next to it was a bar, with cans of beer and soda packed in ice, a keg and tap for draft beer and an area for making cocktails, with olives, fruit slices and a wall of bottles.

Finally, there was an inflatable castle complete with pointed towers. Atlas, who was riding in the back of the pickup, sat up, excited, which made the whole truck rock on its suspension.

"*No*, Atlas," warned Colton. "Not for you, buddy." He patted the bear's paw. "*Claws*. Remember the beach ball?" Atlas looked chastened.

Danny, Gabriel, Bradan and Kian had been put to work carrying tables and chairs and yet *more* coolers of food, but the women were all standing in a tight knot, discussing something. *Why do they all have to be together?*

I'd been dreading this. I'd shot Gabriel in the ear, left Danny with a red welt across his cheek that hadn't completely faded and stabbed Cal. Not to mention being the cause of all the division in the team and the reason their men had been away from home for so long. If I was going to stay here, I needed them to accept me. But they had every reason to hate me.

I knew that my nerves were only going to get worse if I stalled for time. So, leaving Colton to take over the grill, I walked over there. As I approached, the knot spread out, becoming a defensive wall. *Chyort*, they were all in jeans and casual summer dresses and I was in this ridiculous, *look at me* thing.

I only recognized one of the women: Emily, Kian's girlfriend. I'd been hoping Gina would be there, too, but I couldn't see her anywhere. There were five women I didn't know and I had no idea who was connected to whom. *Whose boyfriend did I stab?*

Emily and another woman, with dark hair cut in a sleek bob, was pushed to the front by the others. "Hi," she said energetically. "I'm Stacey, Bradan's girlfriend." She lifted her hand just as I went in for a hug. Then I tried to correct to an air-kiss just as she tried to correct to a cheek kiss and I wound up mushing my lips against hers.

"Is that how they do it, in Russia?" I heard one of the women at the back whisper.

I jumped back, red faced, my hand to my mouth "*Chyort!* I'm so sorry!"

Stacey blinked for a moment, then shook her head: *it's fine and* pulled me in for a quick, firm embrace. "Let me introduce everyone," she said. "Emily you know. This is Lorna, who's with JD. Bethany, who's with Cal. Erin, who's with Danny—oh, and she's also JD's little sister, *that's* a whole story. And Olivia, Gabriel's fiancée."

She was down-to-earth and open and I liked her immediately. I turned to Bethany. "I'm sorry about Cal," I said. "It wasn't personal." I winced. *That's terrible.* "I was careful not to stab him too deep," I tried. *That's even worse? What's the matter with me?* "I hope he's okay," I managed.

Bethany nodded, but she was pale and silent. Lorna was sipping on a cocktail, not making eye contact. Olivia was examining her toes and Erin was hiding behind her so she didn't have to talk to me.

They hate me! My first attempt at making friends and it had all gone horribly wrong.

Stacey put her hand on my shoulder and sighed. "Don't mind them," she told me. "They're just a little intimidated."

What? "Why would *they* be intimidated?" I asked.

"Are you kidding?" asked Erin, peeking out from behind Olivia.

"We're not really..." mumbled Olivia, and gestured at me.

"We're a bunch of shy nerds," blurted Lorna.

"And then they heard you were coming, this super-sexy femme fatale who can seduce any man," said Stacey.

"All exotic and Russian and glamorous," said Bethany. "And you're like—" She indicated the *va-va-voom* dress.

"Believe me, I feel ridiculous," I said, plucking at the fabric. "Like I should be draping myself on a piano."

Lorna spluttered on her cocktail and turned scarlet. "That's nothing to do with you," Emily whispered conspiratorially. "Just something she and JD got up to in New York."

I felt the tension ease. "You were really intimidated?" I asked, amazed.

"You can *kill people,*" said Erin, awed.

"Emily knows how to use a gun," countered Stacey. "And Bethany can shoot a rifle. They can kill people."

"Yeah, but not with their *thighs,*" said Erin. They all cracked up, and I did, too. Maybe this was going to be okay.

I heard the sound of a car behind me and turned to see an SUV with an airport rental sticker pulling into the parking lot. I hadn't seen the woman behind the wheel or her husband before, at least not up close, but the man's features were familiar enough that I figured it out before Kian ran over to them. "Everyone," he announced, "this is Aedan. My brother." I could hear the emotion in his voice, and the Northern Irish in his voice came out a little more than normal. Bradan raced over and all three of them hugged.

The woman, small and slender but with enviably toned arms,

introduced herself as Sylvie, Aedan's wife. There were two kids, too, who spilled out of the backseat and hurled themselves into the inflatable castle.

The low thump of a two-stroke echoed off the hills and a moment later a Harley pulled in beside the rental car. *This* dark-haired Irishman was in a biker kutte and his jeans were held up by a chain belt. A beautiful red-haired woman had her arms wrapped lovingly around him from behind. "I *almost* beat him here," the man told Kian as he was pulled into the growing O'Harra hug. "But a cop pulled us over."

"Carrick," Kian told us. "And Annabelle."

At that moment, the ground shook. My stomach lurched and I spun to look up at the mountain, thinking it was a landslide. But it was just the throaty roar of a V8. A beautiful vintage Ford Mustang was pulling into the parking lot. The driver wore a white tank top and I could see the dark ink of tattoos through the thin fabric. He joined the now five-strong hug and then introduced himself to us. "Sean. And my wife, Louise." A curvy beauty with tumbling red locks climbed from the passenger seat and then helped a little girl out of her car seat. "Our daughter, Grace..." Grace, who had her mother's red hair, sprinted off and hurled herself into the inflatable castle. Louise lifted out a boy of two or three. "...and our youngest, Martin," Sean finished.

Everyone went quiet as a woman began to climb out of the back seat of the Mustang. She was maybe twenty-two and gorgeous, with blonde curls that spilled down over her shoulders. Kian frowned and then leaned close to Sean. "Who's that?" he asked.

Sean sighed theatrically. "And *that,*" he said loudly, for everyone to hear, "is what happens when you're too busy with Washington, and running a security team, and dating the President's daughter, to ever visit!"

The blonde woman rolled her eyes. "Oh, *Kian!*"

Kian's jaw dropped. "*Kayley?!* Little *Kayley?!*"

∼

The party got underway. Erin had wired up speakers around the parking lot and people began to mingle to the sound of pop and smooth R&B. Cal, who'd run back to his house to fetch more plates, showed up with a huge black and gold long-haired German Shepherd called Rufus. Rufus immediately bounded up to me, put his paws on my shoulders and woofed, then started licking my ear, which tickled enough to reduce me to helpless giggles. As he ran off to meet the O'Harras, Colton slipped his arm around my waist. "I'm letting JD work the grill for a little while," he told me. "He's from Texas, so I figure he can handle some steaks. And in other news, JD told me that about an hour ago, the FBI arrested Lucas Bainbridge. He's trying to hide behind his fancy lawyers but the FBI ain't messing around. Looks like he might be the second Bainbridge to wind up in jail."

Colton led me off to where Stacey had taken up position behind the bar—apparently, her cocktails were becoming a staple of these parties and when I tried one of her Manhattans, I saw why. Colton grabbed a beer and we circulated, his arm still around my waist. I'd been to a million parties, from lavish balls thrown by billionaires to knocking back bootleg vodka in dark cellars with a bunch of freedom fighters. But I'd always been there to manipulate someone, or get information from them, or plant a bug, never just to enjoy myself. I'd always been there as someone else, never as *me*. And I'd never felt so secure. Or so happy.

We passed by Annabelle and Erin, who were sitting cross-legged beside the Harley. Annabelle was talking Erin through the complexities of the bike's systems, from the clutch cable to the circuit breakers, while Erin listened in rapt attention. Meanwhile, Danny and Sean had the hood of the Mustang up and were deep, *deep* in conversation about the benefits of different types of air intakes.

We had to dodge back out of the way as Rufus tore past us, woofing. Right behind him was Atlas, making a Chewbacca warble of excitement. We bumped into Lorna, who was looking a little misty-eyed as she watched her nine year-old son, Cody, turn somersaults with the younger kids on the inflatable castle. "Another couple of years and he'll be too old for that kind of thing," she muttered. I nodded as if I understood, but in truth it was a whole area I'd never even thought about. As a spy, the idea of having kids was ludicrous. I was away overseas all the time, I never knew when or if I'd come home and family was just another thing my enemies could use against me. But suddenly, that feeling hit me again, like I was a balloon without a tether. For the first time in many years, I was...*free.* I could have a family.

If I want one. I blinked and looked at Martin, who was sitting on Sean's knee, being told a story. *Do* I want one? I stared at the child and tried to figure out if I felt broody. And this presumed that Colton would even want children. And *Chyort,* I couldn't believe I was even wondering things like that. Being free was *hard.* I grabbed Colton with both hands and pulled him back against me, smooshing myself to his broad back and resting my chin on his shoulder. Immediately, I felt better and I sighed softly in relief. Colton twisted around to look at me, curious.

"I just wanted to feel you," I told him simply.

He grinned and his eyes burned bright. He'd looked great clean-shaven but I was glad his beard was growing back: it was more *him,* somehow. "You should have said. I'd have turned around."

"*Hush!* There are children present!"

We dodged back again as Atlas raced past, this time chased by Rufus. Atlas stopped and Rufus crashed into him. Then the two friends looked at each other: *what now?* Rufus threw back his head and woofed. Atlas attempted to do the same, and gave a half-woof, half roar: *rrrralph.* Rufus woofed again and it became a contest, getting louder and louder, until Colton and I distracted them with a piece of rope they could play tug with.

Kian was catching up with his brothers and I swore his accent had intensified by about four hundred percent, and was increasing with each beer they sank.

"I've got news," Carrick said, shuffling his feet but grinning at the same time. "Looks like I'm gonna be a dad. Annabelle told me last night."

They all slapped him on the back. Kian smirked. "That's going to be a rough transition for you."

Carrick shrugged. "I'm not afraid of changing a diaper."

"Not *that,*" said Kian. "You're going to have to start driving a *car!*"

Carrick's face fell. *"Aw, feck!"* He glared at the ground for a moment and swigged his beer. Then he looked across at Annabelle, shook his head and straightened up. "She's worth it," he said firmly. He turned to Aedan. "How are *you* doing?"

"Busy," said Aedan. "The little ones are a handful. I've only been doing one or two fights on the boxing circuit a month, these days, and the rest of it's classes and personal training at the gym, but..." He looked sheepish, but excited.

"Tell them!" said Sylvie, rubbing his back.

Aedan put his arm around his wife and snuggled her close. "I was going to wait a while but since you're all here..." He took a deep breath. "Sylvie and I are opening a gym," he blurted. "It feels like a crazy time, with the kids still young, but I had some prize money from fights saved up, and we saw a deal on a place that we just couldn't turn down, so..."

"It's just a little place," said Sylvie, her eyes gleaming. "For boxers, or anyone who wants to train like one. Like the place Aedan used to train me in, in New York, but right in the heart of LA. And a little more female friendly." She looked at Kian. "You and Emily should come to LA for the opening party. Bradan, you and Stacey, too." It wasn't a suggestion. Sylvie was small but formidable.

Sean and Carrick crossed their arms and gave Kian and Bradan a look. Kian hung his head and put up his hands. "Point taken. I've been too wrapped up in Stormfinch stuff." He looked across the parking lot towards Kayley, Louise's younger sister, who he hadn't recognized. She was chatting to Gabriel and Olivia. "I'll make time. I'll come to LA." He met his brothers' eyes. "Nothing's more important than family."

"Damn straight," growled Carrick, and pulled all his brothers and Sylvie into a fierce, five-way hug.

Bradan looked over towards Emily, making sure she was out of earshot. "And what about you?" he asked Kian. "Did you finally ask the President for Emily's hand?"

Kian sighed. "Yeah."

"And what did he say?" asked Carrick.

"He said..." Kian took a deep breath. "He said," *What took you so long?*"

They all clinked beer bottles. Then Kian turned, caught my eye and nodded off to the side: *we need to talk.* He called to JD and made the same gesture, and JD handed the mantle of Grill Chief over to Gabriel and came over.

At that moment, Gina, the team's pilot, finally showed up. "Where have *you* been?" asked Kian.

"I had an *epic* sleep," Gina told him, yawning and stretching. "That was a long flight. I'm gonna sink a few cocktails and then I might sleep some more."

Kian and JD exchanged looks. "You probably broke all sorts of rules, flying all that distance solo. If we—"

"Ohhh, no!" Gina interrupted. "Don't start with that *we'll get you a co-pilot* talk again—"

"It'd be safer, you wouldn't get so tired—"

Gina opened her eyes comedy-wide. "You know what? I'm wide awake! Wow! I've never *felt* so alive! I might go do an Ironman or something." She leaned close to JD. "I'm not sharing my cockpit with anyone."

Kian sighed and shook his head, then nodded for JD, Colton and me to follow him around the side of the building. The sun was going down, painting the houses of the town with liquid bronze and making the clouds glow orange and pink.

Kian and JD turned to face me. "Seems like as good a time as any to ask you," said Kian. "How would you feel about coming to work for Stormfinch?"

I stared at him, dumbstruck. "I'm a *spy*, not a soldier."

"We've got soldiers. We could use someone who's a little more..." —Kian rubbed his stubble—"subtle."

Colton nodded firmly. "Subtle, we're not."

I looked across at him. "Did you know they were going to do this? And what do *you* think?"

Colton took my hand. "I didn't know but I kinda guessed they might. And it's up to you. Whatever you want to do with your life. As long as I get to be part of it." He squeezed my hand and I squeezed back even harder, my chest going tight.

I thought hard. If I shopped my skills around, there'd probably be some sort of job for me, working for some country's intelligence agency. My old life, working on my own, was still there and however dangerous it was, it was...*safe.* This new life, feeling and crying and trusting other people with my life...that was confusing and scary.

But it was also wonderful. I'd seen the way the team looked out for each other, even breaking the law to rescue us when we'd been captured. In Stormfinch, no one was *disposable.* "I'm in," I told them, and Colton whooped and spun me around and kissed me long and deep.

The party continued long into the night. The sun went down, the stars came out and the strings of lights that Erin had hung over the parking lot began to glow. The children gradually tired and were carried into the base, where a room had been set up with air mattresses and sleeping bags for a sleepover.

I mingled with the women again and now that the ice was broken, I started to make friends. Bethany turned out to be gentle and kind, with the most soothing voice I'd ever heard. Erin was charmingly awkward and Olivia was earnest and adorably naive whenever the conversation turned to sex. Stacey was busy planning Olivia's bachelorette party and was determined to outdo Danny, who was planning Gabriel's bachelor party. "Where do you think they'll go?" she thought aloud, stirring her drink. "Vegas? That's what the O'Harras did for Aedan and Sean's joint bachelor party. But I know they got banned from at least a few places..."

"There are plans afoot for a girls' vacation, too," Gina told me. "Somewhere hot. You in?"

I looked around at their expectant faces, delighted. A few hours ago, I'd been worried they hated me. "*Yes*," I said with feeling. "Absolutely." I glanced behind her, to where the houses of Mount Mercy formed a carpet of warm, snug lights at the base of the mountain. Maybe I could fit in here after all.

Sometime past two in the morning, after we'd helped box up the leftovers and waved goodbye to everyone, we realized we were the last ones left. Erin had switched off the lights and when I looked up, I found that the sky was full of stars. It really was beautiful, up here in the mountains. I walked through the darkened parking lot with Colton, swinging our joined hands.

"Got something to say to you" he growled.

I stopped and turned expectantly.

He cleared his throat. "*I catch you*," he told me in Russian.

I looked at him blankly. *Catch* like *catch you when you fall?* Did he mean he wanted to support me?

"*I catch you*," he said again.

Did he mean in a kinky way? He wanted to catch me and tear my clothes off? The thought made me crush my thighs together. But it wasn't lust, in his eyes...

"*I catch you*," he repeated, more urgently.

I mouthed the words. And then I went through all the Russian words that could be mispronounced as *catch* and...oh. *Oh!* I flung my arms around him and kissed him, "*I catch you, too!*" I told him in Russian.

He beamed. "Danny taught me. He knows how to say *I love you* in like thirty languages. I've been practicing in my head all night. I'm pretty good, right?"

"Flawless," I said with a straight face. *God bless my training.* I squeezed him tight, overcome that he'd do something like this for me.

And, I decided, *I catch you* was an oddly appropriate way of saying it, for us two.

We started walking through the deserted parking lot again. "Been thinking," he said. "I'm glad you like the trailer, but it *is* kinda small. At some point, we're gonna need a bigger place."

I nodded and turned to look at the town. "An apartment, maybe."

"You know what I'd really like?" asked Colton. Then he shook his head. "Nah."

"What?"

"Nah, it's dumb."

"Tell me!"

"Forget it, it's a dumb idea."

I put my hands on his shoulders. "I will put my thighs around your neck and scissor hold you," I warned.

He mock-frowned. "If I *don't* tell you or I *do* tell you?"

I flushed and punched him in the arm.

"Okay, okay." He sighed. "A houseboat. I want a houseboat. I used to live on a lake, back in Missouri. Best sleep I ever had, like being rocked all night."

"Then we will get a houseboat," I said firmly, and hugged myself to his chest, burying my nose in that warm, safe place between his pecs. He stroked my back and we stood like that for a long time.

As we finally unwound, he saw something behind me and nodded for me to look. I looked over my shoulder and saw the inflatable castle. Then I looked back at him and saw the look on his face. "We can't!" I told him, shocked.

"There's no one else here. And it's soft. Like a waterbed." His hands closed on my waist and I felt the heat of them throbbing through the thin material of my dress. "I could throw you around," he said. "Throw you *down*."

The mood changed. I looked up at him, my breathing starting to get faster. He looked down at me, the amber in his eyes blazing.

And suddenly, I'd ducked and slipped out of his grip. "You've got to catch me first," I told him. Then I was off and running, kicking off my heels as I went, sprinting down the darkened parking lot. I heard him curse and then his huge, heavy footsteps getting faster and faster as he pounded after me. I dodged around a table, feinted left and went right, darted past him—

He grabbed my wrist, hauled me back to him and then I yelped as I was heaved up and over his shoulder. His hand came down once on my rump in a spank that promised more to come, and then he was marching towards the inflatable castle and bounding onto it, setting the whole thing wobbling crazily. He flung me down on my back, as promised, and I bounced a foot in the air before I flopped, giggling.

He grabbed my wrists and pinned them above my head, then hunkered down on top of me. He looked down at my dress. "Now do I tug this thing all the way up?" he mused. "Or just rip it off?"

He didn't get a chance to do either. Because at that moment, there was a growl from Atlas, who'd woken up and was feeling left out of the fun, and then *he* was bounding onto the castle, his warm, furry body butting up against us. There was a ripping, hissing sound, and the battlements started to collapse around us. "Aw, *Atlas!*" sighed Colton. And then he leaned down and kissed me, and I kissed him back, and Atlas licked both our ears, and I decided there was no better place to be in the world.

The End

Thank you for reading! If you enjoyed *Capture Me,* please consider leaving a review. Every one helps!

This is the fourth of my *Stormfinch Security* books.

Gabriel and Olivia's story is told in *No Angel.*

Danny and Erin's story is told in *Off Limits.*

JD and Lorna's story is told in *Guarded.*

Kian and Cal have their own books, too. Kian becomes the bodyguard for Emily, the President's daughter, but winds up falling for her in *Saving Liberty.*

Bethany saves Rufus...and in turn is ferociously protected by both him and Cal in *Deep Woods.*

The other O'Harra brothers have their own books as well.

Sylvie will die unless she learns how to fight, and goes to brooding Irish boxer Aedan for help in *Punching and Kissing*.

Good girl Louise teams up with gang enforcer Sean to save her little sister Kayley's life in *Bad For Me*.

When she's a child, Annabelle saves the life of a young biker by the side of the road. A decade later, her life is on the line...and Carrick returns to save her in *Outlaw's Promise*.

Finally, Kian and the rest of the O'Harra brothers rescue Bradan from the cult in *Brothers* (the ebook of which is free when you join my newsletter, a paperback is also available).

The story of how geeky girl Hailey had plastic surgery and swapped places with the glamorous girlfriend of Russian mob boss Konstantin is told in *The Double* (Agent Calahan is in it, too).

Calahan meets Yolanda when they team up to catch a serial killer in *Hold Me in the Dark*.

All my books are available in paperback and can be ordered from any bookshop or requested from your library: there's a list of ISBNs on my website.

Printed in Great Britain
by Amazon

37671145R00202